PRAISE FOR

"Action and danger bring coastal Florida to life as compelling characters seek to unravel long-held secrets before time runs out. In *Tangled Lies*, Mann does it again . . . A surefire must-read."

—Lisa Carter, award-winning romantic-suspense author

"Connie Mann has penned a romantic suspense that captures the reader on the first page with a deadly secret and refuses to let go until the last word—masterful pacing."

—DiAnn Mills, bestselling author and Christy Award winner

"Connie Mann has crafted a unique suspense with the sea as a backdrop for hidden danger and exciting romantic interludes. Prepare to be swept away!"

—Katy Lee, RITA Award–nominated author

PRAISE FOR *ANGEL FALLS*

"This heart-pounding novel doesn't stint on its characters . . . masterful."

—*RT Book Reviews*, four stars

"If you're looking for nonstop action and heart-pounding excitement, then *Angel Falls* is just the read you've been looking to find. Connie Mann deftly weaves danger and suspense into a story that left me sitting on the edge of my seat, flipping the pages."

—Debbie Macomber, #1 *New York Times* bestselling author

"A perfect blend of fast-paced thriller, inspiration, and romance."

—Fresh Fiction

"In *Angel Falls*, Connie Mann has penned an edgy, gritty book that pushes the boundaries of Christian romance fiction while giving readers a hero and heroine to root for."

—Irene Hannon, bestselling author of the Guardians of Justice series

"A riveting read starting with the first page all the way through the book."

—The Suspense Zone

"Dark, intense, and breathlessly paced, Connie Mann's edgy novel, *Angel Falls*, is exciting, romantic suspense that kept me guessing. With tight writing and fast-paced action, Connie does a fantastic job of grabbing the reader from the first page and never turning loose until the last. *Angel Falls* is not your usual Christian suspense. Filled with intrigue, murder, and sensuality, and set in Brazil's steamy underbelly, Connie's debut is riveting."

—Linda Goodnight, author of *A Snowglobe Christmas* and *Rancher's Refuge* and contributing author of the Prairie Romance Collection

"*Angel Falls* is a powerful read from the beginning with a hero and heroine who emotionally grip you and won't let go. The chemistry between Regina and Brooks along with the suspense keeps you riveted to the story."

—Margaret Daley, author of the Men of the Texas Rangers series

"Connie Mann takes her readers on the heart-stopping journey of a woman who puts her life on the line for an orphaned baby boy and her heart in the hands of the man who came to save them. It was a remarkable story I won't soon forget."

—Sharon Sala, author of the Rebel Ridge trilogy

HIDDEN
THREAT

HIDDEN THREAT

CONNIE MANN

Waterfall
PRESS

Published by Waterfall Press, Grand Haven, MI
www.brilliancepublishing.com

Amazon, the Amazon logo, and Waterfall Press are trademarks of Amazon.com, Inc., or its affiliates.

ISBN-13: 9781477809020
ISBN-10: 1477809023

Cover design by Faceout Studio

Printed in the United States of America

For Harry—thank you for being my hero, greatest cheerleader, and best friend.
And for all those who defend and protect our water resources, in big and small ways. Thank you.

Chapter 1

March—Rural Virginia

Eve Jackson crouched in the mud outside the chain-link fence and wished she'd worn different shoes. Wet sludge oozed into her new ankle boots and her fingers were numb, but a niggle of excitement bubbled up just the same. If her informant's tip panned out, she'd finally have the proof she needed to nail this company for contaminating the nearby stream. She'd been after them for almost a year but had never been able to come up with hard evidence. If she got it this morning, every shivering minute would be worth it. Nobody messed with the water supply and made children sick, doggone it. Not if she was around to stop it.

She lowered the viewfinder on her brand-new digital camera and rubbed her arms in the predawn light. She'd grabbed her peacoat on the way out the door, but the heavy wool was no match for a cold, damp stakeout, never mind that it was already March. She hadn't expected the sudden downpour as she'd driven to this sleepy little town in the Virginia countryside, either.

She'd been staked out behind the aging warehouse for almost three hours. Her cramped muscles were beyond stiff, and she would have traded her left arm for a cup of coffee and a hot bath. Nothing and no one had moved since she'd arrived.

She shifted position and wobbled. She flailed her arms and grabbed the fence just before she landed backward in the mud. The camera strap yanked her neck as the camera smacked her chest, but at least it stayed out of the mud. By the time she steadied herself, she was breathing hard, wondering if this would prove to be yet another wasted night.

Several minutes later, her head snapped up when she heard the distinctive rumble of a diesel engine firing up nearby.

Here we go.

Her heart rate quickened as she raised her camera and zoomed in on the activity near the warehouse. Several more trucks rumbled down the dirt road from the main highway. All of them tankers.

Oh yeah. We've got you now. She clicked the shutter and gasped when the flash went off. She ducked, panicked. What if someone had seen it? She curled around the camera and leaned against the fence post for support, fumbling with the menu, desperate to fix the settings. When she was sure she had it set properly, she poked her head up and took another picture.

The flash went off again.

What was wrong with her? She fumbled around, afraid to use her phone's flashlight and draw yet more attention. She popped her head up again. A quick peek confirmed that no one seemed to have noticed her.

Her hands trembled as she raised the viewfinder and took another picture. No flash this time. *Thank you, Jesus.* She peeked again, anger and excitement building at what she saw. This was why she'd come. The slimeballs had pulled their trucks over to the stream behind the warehouse, attached hoses, and casually started pouring the nasty contents directly into the stream. As though this weren't a problem. But it was and they knew it. They'd deliberately positioned themselves behind the building, where they couldn't be seen from the main road.

Your secret won't stay secret for long, Eve thought as she snapped dozens of pictures. She couldn't wait to tell her boss. Mr. Braddock would thump his desk in triumph and be as excited as she was to see them brought to justice.

Her phone buzzed with an incoming text, and panic spiked when she saw Sasha's number. With Mama Rosa fighting cancer, early-morning messages from her sister were never good news.

Mama dehydrated from chemo side effects. We're headed to hospital. Call me later in a.m.

Dear God, no. Eve stared at the phone, trying to think past the knot of fear that paralyzed her whenever she let what-if scenarios take hold. She had to stay focused, think.

Her phone buzzed again with an incoming call. Thinking it was Sasha, she grabbed it and said, "How bad is it? Just tell me."

But it wasn't Sasha. It was her boss at Braddock Environmental.

"Just what in the Sam Hill were you thinking, Jackson?" Mr. Braddock shouted.

Eve pulled the phone away from her ear and stared at it a moment, confused, not only by the question, but by the fact he'd called her in the early-morning hours. "Sir? I'm not sure what you're talking about." And then, with a sudden, sinking feeling, she knew. This had to be about Woodward.

"Don't play dumb, Jackson. It doesn't become you." Pages rustled and then, "The front-page story in *USA Today* leads with, 'Congressman Woodward denies illegal dumping. Threatens lawsuit against Braddock Environmental.'" Each word came out clipped.

"Sir, I can explain."

"You'd better. And fast."

"I have proof of the dumping. We had Mark out at the congressman's industrial park watching and taking pictures at night. Woodward had heavy equipment out there and a bunch of men working to bury half a truckload of rusted fifty-gallon drums in a field in the back of the property."

"And did Mark follow up, verify the contents of those drums?"

"He wasn't able to get that close. But my sources told me that Woodward was burying oil and grease from his restaurants all over the city. And the condition those drums were in, they'd start leaking in no time."

"And if I told you every single one of those drums is empty? Then what would you have to say for yourself?"

"I'd say he's lying. Mark saw them working."

"But we have no actual proof, one way or the other. And now, since he's on alert, there is no way we'll get back on the property for another look. What were you thinking, talking to a reporter about this? Especially before you talked to me."

"I'm sorry, sir. I didn't want Congressman Woodward appointed to that task force. He could destroy years of progress. I was trying to apply pressure so they would appoint Congressman Milton instead. He's much more conscious of environmental concerns."

Eve heard a thwack, as though he'd smacked the paper onto his desk.

"My phone has been ringing all night, mainly the congressman screaming in my ear. He wants a formal apology from you, in person, and he wants a written retraction in the paper. I've already sent our statement to the paper. You are due at the congressman's office at ten this morning."

"But, I don't—"

"Not another word, Jackson. If you weren't so good at your job and your instincts weren't generally so right on, I would fire you this minute. But as it is, I want you to avoid reporters and work from home until this blows over."

She'd been so busy biting back her anger—she knew that sneaky congressman was guilty—she almost missed the last thing he said. "You want me to work from home?"

"Yes. Stay out of the public eye until a war breaks out somewhere or something else takes center stage in the news cycle."

She wasn't going to hide. "He's guilty, Mr. Braddock, and I'm going to prove it. He won't get away with this."

He sighed. "Not this time, Eve. I've already assigned someone else to this case. You'll hand over your notes, and they'll take it from there."

Eve thought she might break a tooth from clenching her teeth. He couldn't take this away from her. "Sir, with all due respect, I'm not sure—"

"Do you want to continue working here or not, Jackson?"

Shock and a frisson of panic shivered through her. "I love my job, sir." Which was absolutely true. Ten years ago, she'd interned for the crusty old gent while studying at the University of Florida, and he'd hired her right after graduation. She'd never looked back.

"Then go home. I'll email you several press releases I need written, and I have a lead on another violation I want you to pursue. Carefully. And out of the limelight."

Her chin came up, and before she'd thought it through, she said, "Actually, if it's all right with you, I'm going to take some time off and go to Safe Harbor instead."

"Time off? You never take time off, Jackson." He paused. "That's in Florida, where your family is."

"Yes, sir. Mama Rosa is back in the hospital."

"Tough thing, cancer. Go on, then. Take all the time you need. But stay in touch."

"Yes, sir. And thank you, sir."

The last words were drowned out by the sound of sirens, getting closer with every second. Eve slid the phone into her pocket and looked toward the warehouse.

Two things registered at once. The tankers were gone, and someone near the warehouse was shining a flashlight toward the woods.

Right where she was hiding.

She'd been made.

Slipping and sliding, Eve scrambled back to her car and raced off down the dirt road that led away from the warehouse. Her heart pounded as she drove, one eye on her rearview mirror. She hadn't been trespassing—but she didn't want to chat with the cops tonight, either. Not until she had all her proof tied up with a nice, neat, no-wiggle-room bow.

She didn't take a deep breath until she was back on the highway, headed to her small apartment in DC, no sign of flashing lights in her rearview mirror.

Tampa, Florida

After her meeting with Congressman Woodward, Eve staggered off the jetway in Tampa, and the humidity smacked her in the face like a soggy washcloth. She hadn't slept on the noon flight, too consumed with worries about Mama Rosa to shut down her brain.

She climbed into her rental car and headed north, hands trembling slightly from too much caffeine and too little sleep. She forced herself to take deep breaths as she headed away from the noise and traffic of Tampa and eventually entered the small-town atmosphere of Safe Harbor.

Her first stop would be Mama Rosa, though the little girl inside her wanted to hide, pretend that if she didn't actually see Mama, she wasn't really sick. But Eve didn't hide, so she parked her hybrid Prius outside the community hospital and steeled herself. She spotted Mama's aging-but-immaculate Buick and Jesse's pickup. Jesse and Sasha. She grinned. Eve still couldn't believe Jesse had convinced her commitment-phobic foster sister to marry him.

She hurried inside to the room number Sasha's text had indicated and eased inside. "Hey, everyone," she said quietly.

She thought she'd prepared herself, but Mama's sickly gray skin color scared Eve to the marrow of her bones. Mama's eyes fluttered open and she smiled, so Eve hurried over to place a gentle kiss on her forehead.

"I'm not dying yet, my girl. No need to rush down here."

Even her voice didn't sound right, but Eve smiled, as she knew Mama wanted her to. "Glad to hear it. I mostly wanted to see if Jesse was handling Sasha all right."

She winced when Sasha smacked her on the arm before tugging her into a bone-crushing hug.

"You're still a pain in the neck, Eve. You know that, right?"

"And you're still so easy to tease." She pulled back. "You good?"

Sasha met her gaze with eyes that shone and then patted her belly. "Actually, I'm better than good."

Eve glanced down at the small mound, then back up to Sasha's beaming face, and as the words registered, she let out a squeal, then clapped a hand over her mouth and hugged her again, hard. "Oh, my goodness. You're pregnant?"

"We are."

"Oh. That's so awesome." They all laughed as tears ran down her cheeks, typical Eve, but at that moment, she didn't care. This was too cool.

She hugged Jesse next, then exchanged an awkward hug with Pop. Eve still hadn't worked through her conflicted feelings about some of his past decisions and wasn't sure how to act. She stepped away and gave Blaze, the newest foster sister, a one-armed hug before the teen shrugged away. The blue in her hair had been replaced with fuchsia. "Nice color, kiddo."

"Thanks. I saw the article in the paper about you accusing that congressman of burying grease from his restaurant. So did you get fired, or what?"

All eyes turned to Eve. Leave it to Blaze to cut to the heart of the matter. She wasn't ready to talk about this just yet, so she tried a bit of deflection. "Since when do you read *USA Today*?"

Blaze huffed out a breath. "A girl's gotta stay informed. Isn't that what you've been preaching? So why are you here?"

Despite herself Eve grinned and hugged Blaze again before she could escape. "Right. But, no, I didn't get fired. I'm taking a short leave of absence. I figured I'd come home."

"What congressman?" Sasha wanted to know.

Eve waved that away. She wasn't ready to deal with Sasha's questions yet, either. "I'll fill you all in later." She pulled up a chair. "Right now I want to hear how Mama is doing."

Mama opened one eye and glared at all of them. "Mama is doing fine, and I want you all to go home so I can rest. I can't sleep with you staring at me." She looked over at Eve. "But I want a word with Eve, first."

The family trooped out of the room after another round of kisses on Mama's cheeks while anxiety slid under Eve's skin. The last time Mama wanted something from her daughters, it turned out to be far more than any of them had bargained for.

Mama waited until the door shut, then took one of Eve's hands in her thin one. Eve bit her lip, hard. No matter how much she tried to resist, those dratted tears leaked out at the worst times.

"Do you remember my friend Althea Daughtry?"

Eve smiled at the memory. "I do. Miss Althea was our Sunday school teacher." The tiny, gray-haired woman with dusky skin and a will of iron had used the same no-nonsense approach to Sunday school as she had during the week as a public-school teacher.

"She was also my friend. The Lord called her home last year. Bladder cancer." When Eve opened her mouth to say she didn't want to hear about friends dying, Mama held up her other hand. "Let me finish.

Her great-grandbaby, little Glory, is very sick. They think it might be from the water."

Eve's every sense went on alert. "Where did you hear this?"

"I heard the nurses talking about it, but it was also in the *Gazette*."

Eve whipped out her phone and punched in the *Gazette*'s website. The headline slammed into her like an unexpected fist.

LOCAL INFANT HOSPITALIZED, NEAR DEATH. DOCTOR SUSPECTS BLUE BABY SYNDROME.

Eve's heart pounded as she scanned the article. Most people had never heard of blue baby syndrome, and medical professionals often attributed the blue lips, fingers, and skin tone to a heart issue. Which it might well be, but Eve knew there could be another cause, one often overlooked, that could be deadly. If four-month-old Glory Daughtry had consumed water contaminated with high levels of nitrates, often from nearby agriculture, she could become mentally impaired or die if she wasn't treated right away. Eve had seen it too many times. The results could be tragic.

Did this doctor know to check for that? The article seemed to hint at it, saying Dr. Stern was "exploring all possibilities." He'd also done some work in third-world countries for Doctors Without Borders, where blue baby was much more common.

Either way, baby Glory didn't have much time.

"You will look after Althea's granddaughter, Celia, and make sure the doctors are doing all they can. I'll not have her going through this alone." Mama narrowed her eyes. "Is there more to this than the paper said?"

"I don't know yet."

"You will find out. For me. And for that baby's sake."

Since that was exactly what Eve planned, she nodded and kissed Mama's forehead. "I'll keep you posted." She would talk to Dr. Stern, make sure he checked beyond a simple heart issue. He should also check where the Daughtrys lived and whether there was agriculture nearby.

Eve thought of her boss's earlier tirade and winced. Mr. Braddock would no doubt have some choice words when—if—he found out what she was doing. So for now, she wouldn't tell him. She'd always been able to talk her way around his anger, but a small part of her worried she was going too far this time. Still, a baby's life was in danger. That had to come first.

"Go see them right now," Mama commanded. "They need you." And with that she closed her eyes and pretended to go to sleep.

Eve joined her family in the hallway. "I'll meet you all back at the marina. I need to make a quick stop on the way home."

"Where are you going?" Blaze crossed her arms over her chest in a fair imitation of Mama's expression and narrowed her eyes.

"No big deal. I just want to check on something I read about in the *Gazette*."

Blaze clearly wasn't fooled by her nonchalant tone. "You're talking about the blue baby, aren't you? The article said the doctors think it's her heart."

"It could be."

"You think it might be something else."

"I read about that," Jesse added from where he stood propped against the wall. "Poor kid. You going to check it out?"

Sasha marched over and poked Eve in the shoulder, backing her against the wall. "That's why you're really here, isn't it? Not for Mama. But because you found another 'cause' to fight for."

Eve shook her off and stepped away. "That's not fair, Sash, and you know it. I'm here for Mama."

"And to investigate." Sasha's chin came up as she dared Eve to deny it.

Jesse laid a calming hand on his wife's arm. "You're making assumptions, Sasha. Besides, none of us can sit by Mama's bedside 24-7. She wouldn't stand for it."

Eve stared her sister down. "Yes, I'm going to investigate. Mama asked me to—and little Glory's mother needs an advocate. It's what I do."

Sasha brushed Jesse off and glared at Eve. "You can't save everyone, Eve."

Eve's chin came up, too, just as it did whenever they had this particular argument. "Maybe not. But I can try. I have to try."

Blaze furrowed her brow. "What's going on?"

Jesse leaned close to Blaze, but Eve heard every word. Even after all this time, the pain dug deep.

"Eve's mother died from drinking contaminated water when Eve was about thirteen, back in Chicago, so she's pretty passionate about preventing that sort of thing."

Blaze locked eyes with Eve. "You think this blue baby drank poisoned water?"

Eve thought of her mother and rubbed over the ache in her heart. "Maybe. That's what I want to know."

"Then I'm coming with you." Blaze stepped beside her and silently dared her to say no.

"OK, but let me do the talking. We'll catch up with the rest of you at the marina."

She'd deal with Sasha later. Right now she had questions for Glory's mother. Blaze, in her usual army boots, clumped down the hall by her side as they headed for the intensive care unit, where a nurse directed them to a small waiting room off to one side. Curled up on a plastic sofa with a sweatshirt for a blanket, a young twentysomething woman with curly dark hair blinked her eyes open when Eve and Blaze approached.

"Celia Daughtry?"

The young woman nodded and slowly sat up, pushing her hair off her face. The dark circles under her eyes attested to her worry, and indicated she'd been sick, too. "Who are you?"

"I'm Eve Jackson, and this is my sister, Blaze. How is little Glory doing?"

Celia blinked and looked from one to the other. "Why are you here? Do I know you?"

Eve studied the young woman, searching her memory. "I grew up in Safe Harbor, and Miss Althea was my Sunday school teacher."

Pain filled the young mother's eyes. "Grandmama Althea passed last year."

"That's what I heard. I'm so sorry for your loss." Eve paused, tried to figure out the best approach. "I live and work in DC, now. I read about your baby in the *Gazette*. Is she getting any better?"

Celia came to her feet, suspicion in her eyes. "Are you a reporter? I don't know what you're doing here, but you need to leave."

Eve edged closer, palms out, desperate to appear warm and friendly. She needed Celia's cooperation, and she wouldn't get it if she scared her away. "I'm not a reporter. My mama and your grandmother were friends. I work for an environmental agency, and I'd like to help you figure out what caused your daughter to get sick."

The young mother's eyes filled with tears, and Eve felt her own heart clench.

"How can you know more than the doctors do? I just want them to make her better." Celia lowered her face to her hands and cried. "But so far, they don't know what's wrong, and my baby keeps getting sicker."

Celia's helplessness washed over Eve, tugging her mind back to the night her mother died. The helplessness, the terror, the overwhelming guilt that this was her fault. If she hadn't given her mother that water, she wouldn't have died. If she'd come back sooner, no matter what her mother had said, she might have been able to save her.

Eve swallowed hard and forced her mind back to the present. She couldn't go there mentally, or she wouldn't be able to think. "Dr. Stern has officially diagnosed her with blue baby syndrome, right?" At Celia's nod, Eve continued. "But she wasn't born with any kind of heart defect?"

"No. Not that we know of, but they checked, just to be sure. She'd been fine until a few days ago. But then she got real quiet and listless, and started having trouble breathing. It kept getting worse, and when she started turning blue, I brought her here."

Celia sagged back down on the couch as though she didn't have the strength to stand. Eve sat beside her and gently took the young mother's hand in hers. "I'm sure Dr. Stern is running all kinds of tests and doing everything he can. Do you nurse Glory? Have you had the flu?"

"I couldn't nurse her. But I've had a stomach bug for a couple of days." Celia shrugged. "But it's nothing like what Glory has."

Eve's brain ran through possibilities. "I'd like to go out to your property and look around, see if I can find any clues that would help pinpoint what caused this in the first place. If that's all right with you."

Celia shrugged. "I don't care. I just need my baby to get well. Glory is all I have." She broke down into sobs, and Eve gathered her close, rubbing her back and making soothing noises. She blinked back her own tears and looked over at Blaze, whose eyes held their own suspicious sheen.

After Celia's sobs subsided and she'd dried her eyes, Eve pulled out a business card and handed it to her. "Could you give us the address and a way to contact you?" When Celia rattled off the information, Blaze entered it into the smartphone she had pulled from her back pocket. Eve patted Celia's hand as she stood. "Try to get some rest. Glory will need you to be strong. If you don't mind, we'll peek in on her on our way out."

On the other side of the ICU, she and Blaze peered through the window at the tiny baby girl in a huge crib. She had blue lips and fingers and was connected to far too many tubes and wires.

Eve straightened and clenched her hands at her sides. Every instinct screamed this was nitrate poisoning, and she planned to prove it. She had to find Dr. Stern.

Before she could, a woman marched up to the ICU window and placed both hands on the glass. "Sweet Jesus, heal our precious little girl." She bowed her head and her voice faded away, but her lips kept moving in prayer. The man beside her shifted uncomfortably.

For a moment Eve thought she was seeing Miss Althea, but then she realized this must be her daughter, though she was much broader in the beam than her mother had been. The tall, well-built man beside her looked about her age, but carried himself like a former football player.

When the woman raised her head, she eyed Eve. "How do you know my grandbaby? You one of them reporters?"

"No, ma'am. I've Eve Jackson. Miss Althea used to be my Sunday school teacher."

"I'm Althea's daughter, IdaMae. This here is my brother, Leon." She studied Eve. "Don't have no Jacksons here in Safe Harbor."

"No, ma'am. I'm one of the Martinelli daughters. This is Blaze, another of their daughters. Mama Rosa was a friend of Miss Althea's. She asked me to stop by and check on little Glory."

"That's right kind of you. Tell Mama Rosa we hope she gets to feeling better soon."

"You don't live around here," Leon said.

"No, sir. I live in DC. I came to check in with Mama Rosa."

"You and your sisters stirred up a boatload of trouble last time you were in town." He narrowed his eyes like he was searching for some memory, then jabbed a finger in her direction. "You've always been one of them tree huggers, stirring up trouble since you were in high school. We don't want your kind around our little Glory."

Eve kept her smile firmly in place, tone polite. "Like I said, Mama asked me to stop by. You all have a nice day."

As soon as they were out of earshot, Blaze said, "You didn't tell them you were looking for the cause."

"Nope. I want to gather as much information as I can before people get suspicious of me and shut down."

Blaze glanced back over her shoulder. "I hope that baby makes it."

"Me, too. We'll do everything we can from our end." Eve raised her voice. "Excuse me, Dr. Stern?"

The gray-haired doctor stopped long enough for them to reach him. "How may I help you?"

"Are you thinking nitrates caused Glory Daughtry's illness?"

He seemed surprised by the question, then narrowed his eyes. "Who are you?"

"I'm a friend of the family. Are you going to treat her for nitrate poisoning?"

"That's confidential information." His cell phone buzzed, and he took it out of the holder at his hip. "Now, if you'll excuse me, I have patients to attend."

"If you don't act fast, that baby could die."

He puffed up, and Eve wanted to call back her impulsive words.

"I am well aware of my patient's needs, young lady. Good day."

As he marched away, Blaze muttered, "That went well."

Eve sighed. Too often her desperation to get answers got in the way. Drat her unruly tongue. "I need to go out to Celia's house. I'll drop you off at the marina."

They walked out to the parking lot. As Blaze climbed into the passenger seat, Eve scanned the hospital, and that twitchy feeling of being watched skittered between her shoulder blades. It caught her off guard, but she shouldn't really be surprised, since she'd given the townspeople plenty of reasons to distrust her and her "reckless crusading" years ago. Maybe this time, she could not only help little Glory, but she could help set the past to rights, too.

Chapter 2

Cole Sutton shoved his black Stetson back on his head and squinted up into the blazing sun, wondering what in blue blazes he was doing back in Florida. If not for his promise to Ma, he would still be in Montana, working the run-down ranch he'd recently sunk every penny into buying. But then his father had died, Ma had called, and now here he was, fighting to save the ranch his father had kicked him off of seventeen years ago.

Cole shook his head and rubbed a hand on the back of his neck as he scanned the area. Another cow had given birth to a deformed calf early this morning, which made the third this month. The vet was trying to help him find the cause, but so far nothing.

He sighed. This was not the way to get the ranch out of the red. Ma had seriously hedged when she said things were a "little lean." If he didn't figure out a way to turn things around, fast, the situation was going to get a lot worse than lean. They were headed straight for foreclosure.

He placed a booted foot on the paddock rail as he watched one of the dirt roads that came onto the ranch, still soggy after an early-morning rain shower. A girly little blue hybrid slipped and slid through the mud as the driver fought to make forward progress. He squinted.

Nobody came in the back way, through the mud, in a car like that on purpose. Which meant they were either selling vacuum cleaners or religion, or they were lost.

As the car sank down in the mud on the other side of the paddock, the driver's side opened and a beautiful woman with a cloud of curly black hair gingerly stepped out and immediately sank ankle deep in the mud. Cole grinned as the woman flailed and tugged, trying to pull her feet from the quagmire.

He figured he should lend a hand.

He crossed the paddock and ducked under the fence to hear the woman muttering about ruining her favorite shoes as she tried to extricate herself from the mire. "Can I help you?"

She hadn't heard him approach and yelped in surprise. She tried to spin around, but with her feet stuck, she wobbled and would have fallen. He reached out a hand to steady her just as she lunged backward to free herself. He managed to scoop her into his arms and brace his feet so they didn't both end up in the mud. Before he could get a secure grip on her, she started squirming.

"Let me go. Put me down!" she demanded.

Cole grinned as he shifted his hold. She was cute, issuing orders while in his arms. And her snug curves felt really nice tucked against his chest, but he wouldn't think about that right now. "Easy there, darling, or we're both going to end up in the mud."

"Put me down! Who are you?"

Cole headed over to the fence and carefully set her on the top rail, caging her with his arms so she wouldn't topple over. He grinned at her disgruntled expression. "I'm the guy whose family owns this property. Who are you?"

"Oh. I'm—wait." She pushed the hair out of her face, and her eyes widened as she studied him. "Cole? Cole Sutton?"

Cole looked closer at the chocolate-brown eyes, the rich mocha-colored skin, the big puff of hair, and recognition dawned. When her eyes darted to his right arm and she bit her lip as she looked away, a twinge of pain shot through his once-shattered elbow. Along with a sharp prick of remembered anger. Who knew what his relationship with his father would have been if she hadn't singlehandedly ruined his chances for a football scholarship with her crazy, do-gooder ways? He deliberately thickened his drawl. "Well, I'll be. If it isn't little Evie the Crusader. What are you doing back in town? Last I heard you were off in DC saving the world."

Eve shook her head, and for an insane moment he was tempted to see if that cloud of hair was as soft as it looked. "Maybe not saving the world, but trying to keep the drinking water safe." Her glance skimmed his arm. "How are things with you?"

He shrugged, kept his eyes focused on her face as he straightened his arm, then bent it again. "I'm fine, thanks."

She winced. "How long have you, um, been back in Safe Harbor?"

He did not want to get into a discussion of that long-ago day his father kicked him out, so he said, "Since just after my father passed away two months ago."

"I'm sorry. Truly." She looked past his shoulder, the silence stretching uncomfortably. Finally she said, "My shoes are still in the mud."

Cole turned to look, breathing in her scent as he did, annoyed with himself for noticing. "Yep. Looks like."

She huffed out a breath and tried to cross her arms, but almost lost her balance, so she scowled instead. "Could you get them for me?"

He raised a brow. She'd always been so passionate and serious about her causes, he'd never been able to resist teasing her. "Oh, so the most militant feminist from Safe Harbor High wants me to fetch for her? Isn't that against some code or something?"

She narrowed her eyes. "Those are Kate Spade." At his blank look, she clarified. "Shoes. Designer. Expensive."

He waited, enjoying the simmer in her dark eyes.

"Please. Could you get them for me?" She practically spit the words from between clenched teeth.

He laughed and tipped his hat. "But of course. Since you asked so nicely."

For some insane reason, he'd always been drawn to Eve, to the fire inside her that fueled all her environmental passion, even though he knew it could burn him, badly—as it already had. No matter how much he wanted to, he couldn't blame her for all that had gone wrong between him and his father, though her crazy stunt certainly hadn't helped. But that didn't mean he would let her get close enough to hurt him again.

He walked over, pulled the flimsy sandals out of the mud, and gave them a shake to get rid of the worst of the sludge. He held them out by the straps, and she snatched them from his grasp. "So what brings you out this way, Eve? Didn't know you were back in Safe Harbor."

"I came home because Mama is in the hospital again. Dehydration." She wouldn't meet his eyes as she shook more mud off the sandals, so he figured there was a truckload she wasn't saying.

"I heard she's fighting cancer. I'm sorry."

"Thanks. She's tough, though. If anyone can beat this thing, she can."

"That's why you're in Safe Harbor. Why are you at Sutton Ranch, Eve?"

"Oh, ah, that. Well, I got lost." A flush crept up her cheeks. "I was on my way to Celia Daughtry's place. I'm terrible with directions, and my phone's GPS got a little confused, and well . . ." She shrugged and fiddled with her shoes.

He turned and pointed to a patch of woods off in the distance, wondering about her behavior. "You missed the turnoff to her road by about a quarter mile. When Miss Althea passed last year, she left the property to IdaMae and Leon, her two kids, but she left the little cottage over yonder to Celia." He turned back. "I didn't know you knew Celia.

She's quite a bit younger than we are. She came back home a couple of months ago. Has a little girl, Glory. Cute as a bug, but I heard she's sick."

Eve nodded, and he could almost feel the fury radiating under her skin and out her clenched fists. He just didn't know where it came from.

"I just came from the hospital. Glory is in the ICU. Critical. They're thinking blue baby syndrome."

"I'm very sorry to hear that." He'd have to go by the hospital, see if Celia needed anything. He tried to remember what he knew about blue baby, but came up empty.

Eve leaned forward and poked him in the chest, the air crackling around her. "You should be. That baby got sick drinking contaminated water."

A warning shimmered down his back, but he kept his voice calm. "What does that have to do with me?"

She narrowed her eyes, and Cole thought flames would shoot out of them at any moment. She scanned the ranch, then brought her eyes back to his. "I don't know yet. But I will. Blue baby usually comes from nitrates in the water, especially near agricultural operations."

Cole studied the determined tilt of her chin. He'd seen that look before. When he suddenly realized what she was thinking, he ground out, "Wait just a minute. Don't you go making unfounded accusations, Eve. That kind of thing can hurt folks."

She stiffened as though he'd slapped her. "When I need you to tell me what to do, Cole Sutton, I'll be sure and let you know."

She made to slide off the rail, but he caught her just in time and swung her back into his arms as he strode toward the barn. He clamped his jaw shut, knowing anything he said right now would just make her more determined.

"Will you stop carting me around? I need to get back to my car."

"And until I get my truck to pull your little car out of the mud, you won't be going anywhere."

She harrumphed, but stopped squirming. Every step brought her closer against his chest and reminded him uncomfortably just how long it had been since he'd been this close to a woman. He couldn't remember his last date, and he hadn't had anything resembling a relationship in too many years to count. It was pathetic, really. And having Evie the Crusader with her perfectly curved little body reminding him of it just irritated him more.

He walked over to his truck and plopped her in the passenger side without fanfare. Then he walked around, climbed in, and headed back to her car.

Eve didn't say a word while he attached a chain to her car and used his truck to pull it free. Once it was clear, he scooped her up once more—dang she smelled good—and deposited her back in her car. He handed her ruined shoes through the open window.

She frowned at him. "I suppose I should thank you."

He grinned despite himself and tipped his hat. "I suppose you should."

But she didn't. She drove until she hit the main road, without once looking back. Cole shook his head. Every instinct he possessed wanted to grab her and force her to abandon whatever plan she was hatching in that clever, misguided brain of hers. But he knew Eve, remembered more than he wanted to. He would bet the ranch that when she was pushed, she pushed back harder, just like before.

Back in high school, when he'd tried to convince her the football team was perfectly fine drinking from a garden hose out by the practice field, not only had she ignored him, but her campaign to get them "clean" water had intensified.

Never mind that fateful night she'd set their calves free to make sure they weren't sold for veal. And inadvertently ended his chances for a football scholarship.

He sighed and rubbed his elbow. Whatever she was up to, he had no doubt he hadn't seen the last of her. While his body really liked the idea, his brain warned she would cause him no end of trouble. And that he couldn't afford. Not now, while he was doing everything in his power to keep the ranch afloat and a roof over his mama's head.

Especially since he still wasn't sure how many corners his father had cut over the years, and how many regulations he'd bent, environmentally speaking.

While he tried to figure out what was going on with his calves, he'd also have to keep an eye on Eve.

And make sure there wasn't a nitrate problem on Sutton land.

———

Ruined shoes in hand and Cole's smug sarcasm ringing in her ears, Eve drove back to the two-lane road. She tried to focus on that stand of trees in the distance, she really did, but all she could see was Cole, with those piercing gray eyes that saw too much, the chiseled jaw that begged to be touched, and that lean, hard body that somehow had always made her feel safe.

She felt a flush steal over her skin that made every nerve ending tingle. If he ever found out what a crush she'd had on him in high school, his good-ole-boy act would get even worse, just to irritate her. He'd always liked teasing her, while she'd never been able to manage more than a stammer and some inane comments. But her attraction ran much deeper, back to that terrifying night when she'd snuck onto Sutton Ranch and let all the calves out so they wouldn't get shipped off to become veal. When she almost got trampled by the terrified animals, Cole slid off his horse and rescued her without hesitation—and got his elbow shattered in the process. She'd never be able to make up for costing him that football scholarship.

She hadn't known he'd come back to Safe Harbor. When his father kicked him out years ago, she'd heard he joined the Marine Corps and then had gone somewhere out west. Colorado, maybe. Everyone thought he'd never come back. Yet here he was, looking better than ever. She sighed, then brought her thoughts sharply back to little Glory. Focused, she had to stay focused. Because of the proximity of their properties, Cole's ranch might very well be the cause of that baby's illness.

Had she taken another wrong turn? Eve kept inching along, worried Cole had deliberately sent her in the wrong direction, when the trees suddenly opened up and the cottage appeared in a small clearing. Grass in need of mowing and weed-choked flower beds gave the place an abandoned air. Like many local homes, the little house had a tin roof and covered porch across the front. The white clapboard siding could use a coat of paint, and the whole 1930s-era cottage listed slightly to the left. Off in the trees, a single-wide mobile home that had seen better days stood in the shade.

Eve climbed out of her car and carefully made her way to the porch steps, avoiding the grass. She didn't want an encounter with a snake if she could help it. She stood on the sagging porch and looked around, trying to find the well. There had to be one. The only section of Safe Harbor with town water was the downtown area, and that had been converted in only the last ten years. Everyone else had their own well. And Eve was betting that was the cause of baby Glory's illness: contaminated well water.

From her vantage point she saw the aging mobile home nearby and could make out the roofs of the barns on Cole Sutton's ranch. A quick turn in the other direction and the buildings of Blackwell Farms, an agribusiness, were also visible. From what the paper said, Richard Blackwell had started buying up neighboring properties after he took over the farm when his father passed away ten years ago. Richard Blackwell's daughter, Candy, a popular cheerleader, had died in a car accident when Eve was in high school. She'd wondered how you recovered from something like that. Or maybe you didn't. The paper said Candy's mother died two years after her daughter. Very sad.

Eve gauged the distance. She'd have to check out his operation. Big agribusinesses were logical suspects for contamination.

Right now, though, she had to find Celia's well. Eve couldn't see it from her spot on the porch, so it must be out back. But before she headed there, she tried the front door, surprised when it opened. Then she grinned. What would be the height of stupidity in DC was commonplace in Safe Harbor. People rarely locked their doors here.

Even though Celia had given her permission, Eve felt like a criminal as she eased the door open and stepped into the tidy living room. The aging sofa sagged in the middle, but the wood floor gleamed and family photos dotted every available surface. Eve picked one up and smiled at Miss Althea with her arm around a then-teenage Celia. They were obviously happy to be together.

Eve walked into the kitchen and looked around. Though the cupboards were almost bare, every square inch gleamed. Which told Eve the contamination hadn't been caused by carelessness. There was no rotting food sitting around, and the ancient curved-front refrigerator was plenty cold.

She reached over and turned on the kitchen faucet. No nasty, stinky water spewed out. Eve grimaced. *You didn't think it would be that easy, did you?*

A peek out the kitchen window showed nothing but more weedy grass. She looked for a doghouse-shaped structure, which locals often used to protect their wells and well pumps, but found nothing. She ventured out the back door but didn't see a well house there, either. Of course, even if she found it, it wouldn't really tell her anything. The proof of contamination had to come from a lab, after the water was tested.

She pulled out her smartphone and did a search for local water-testing companies. Not surprisingly, there was only one.

"Pure Water, Incorporated, how may I help you?" a cheerful female voice chirped.

"Good afternoon, this is Eve Jackson, and I'd like to schedule a water test."

A long silence followed, and Eve wished she'd never said her name. "Eve Jackson? The same Eve Jackson who cost the Safe Harbor Panthers the 1999 district championship?"

Eve fought the urge to bang her head on the counter. "Unfortunately, that would be me. But it was a long time ago."

"Not that long," the woman muttered; then she cleared her throat. "Unfortunately, Ms. Jackson, it's going to be a couple of weeks before we can send someone out. But if you give me the address, and a phone number where we can reach you, we'll call you the minute we have an opening in our schedule."

Eve narrowed her eyes. "You're not going to ask why I need a water test? No curiosity about water safety?"

"Clean, safe drinking water is always our primary concern. Now, if you'd give me your phone number, we can get your request into the system."

Eve rattled off the information, irritated with herself as much as with the woman on the phone. People had long memories in Safe Harbor. The fact that the Panthers hadn't won a championship since losing Cole as their star quarterback didn't help, either.

"Thank you for choosing Pure Water, Inc., Ms. Jackson, where clean water is always our first priority. We'll be in touch." Click.

Eve smacked the table in frustration, then pocketed her phone, thinking through her next move. Suddenly a car door slammed, and a man's raised voice caught her attention. She turned and saw a white pickup parked sideways in front of the nearby mobile home, as though the driver had slid to a stop. A big black man stood below the tiny porch, shouting.

"Are you crazy, IdaMae? You can't just sell the place! You don't own it! Mama left it to both of us!"

Eve recognized Leon, Celia's uncle, and eased into the shadows of the porch so they wouldn't see her.

IdaMae opened the door of the mobile home and fisted her hands on her ample hips. "I didn't say I sold it. I said I got another offer. And it's a good one."

Leon stormed up onto the porch and got right in her face. "Over my dead body." He shoved past IdaMae and disappeared inside.

"Don't you come barging into my house, Leon Daughtry." IdaMae followed him inside and slammed the door.

They kept shouting, but Eve couldn't make out what they were saying. A few minutes later, Leon burst out the door.

"This isn't over, IdaMae. Not by a long shot," he shouted over his shoulder. He stood for a moment, fists clenched, then climbed back in his truck and roared away.

As Eve stood on Celia's back porch, an uneasy chill slid down her spine, despite the heat and humidity. Could the water contamination be about a fight for the property? She could easily see a big company involved in some kind of underhanded corporate maneuver, but what about IdaMae or Leon? Would they do such a thing, especially since it had affected little Glory? Or was this an unfortunate accident?

She dialed her private investigator.

"Mark, I need your help," she said.

"Of course you do, but I'm not sure I can get what you need."

"What are you talking about? You always do. Listen, I need you to find me a lab I can get a water sample to quick—"

He interrupted before she could finish. "Your boss called a little while ago, said if I wanted any more work from Braddock, I need to go through him only. Not you."

Eve pulled the phone from her ear and looked at it a moment, not sure she'd heard correctly. "Seriously?"

"Seriously. And I need my paycheck, love, so I can't help you. Sorry."

It took a moment for Eve to realize he'd hung up on her. She knew Mr. Braddock was angry, but she hadn't realized it was quite that bad. She'd have to smooth things over with him later.

She folded her arms, eyes narrowed as she looked around. That twitchy feeling of being watched slithered down her spine again, but she didn't care. She had a sick baby in trouble, and she wouldn't rest until she found out what was going on.

———

Eve's little car hadn't been gone five minutes when another vehicle turned down the dirt road leading to the ranch. Cole pulled his hat brim lower and squinted into the sun to see who it was. When he recognized his uncle Duane's dusty black pickup, he stifled a groan. He did not have the energy for another round with him today.

Still, family demanded respect, so he walked over and greeted his mother's brother with an outstretched hand, glad when his uncle climbed out of the truck and shook it. "Howdy, Duane. If you came to see Ma, she's inside, just back from some meeting or other at church."

A whiff of alcohol floated on the breeze. "I didn't come to talk to her. I came to talk to you."

Cole braced himself for another round of a conversation he hadn't wanted to have the last six times, either. "How can I help you?"

"You know how. Get your mother to sell me the ranch. It's what your father wanted."

Cole thumbed his hat back on his head. "You know, you keep saying that, but all I have is your word on it." The minute the words left his mouth, Cole wanted to call them back. Apparently, his encounter with Evie had rattled him more than he realized.

Thin and wiry, his uncle stiffened and puffed up like a bantam rooster. "And since when is my word not good enough, boy?"

Cole held both palms up. "Easy now. All I'm saying is that I wasn't here when Hank was . . . sick, so I don't exactly know what he said or didn't say."

"Well, whose fault is it you done run off and left him to run the place alone?"

Cole refused to get into a debate about ancient history. If his father hadn't told the whole story while he was alive, Cole surely wasn't explaining it after the man's death. He owed him that much, at least. "Look, Uncle Duane. I don't want to fight with you or anyone else. But the bottom line is that Sutton Ranch isn't for sale."

"And when the bank comes to take it away, and it gets sold for nothing to that big Blackwell outfit? Then what?"

Before he realized he'd moved, he stood toe to toe with his uncle. "First off, the bank is not taking the ranch. And even if it did, that would be my problem, not yours."

"This ranch should stay in the family."

Cole smiled grimly. On that they agreed. He'd move heaven and earth to make sure his ma had a place to live. "It will. Don't you worry about that. Now, why don't you head on up to the house to see Ma? I have work to do." He tipped his hat and turned to go back to the barn before he decked the man. He loved his family. But his mother's brother he could do without. Especially since his drinking had gotten worse.

"You keep on with that stubborn attitude, boy, and you may not have a choice."

Cole stopped, turned back, and studied the mulish tilt of his uncle's chin. "You care to explain yourself, Uncle Duane?"

Cole stared at the other man, but he wouldn't answer. Fists clenched, Duane turned away and marched up to the house, while the threat lingered like a bad smell.

Cole slapped his Stetson against his thigh, then settled it back on his head. Why couldn't everyone just leave him alone to save the ranch, for crying out loud?

As he went back to the barn, Cole replayed their conversation. First Evie and now this. He wasn't sure what either one of them was up to, but he intended to find out.

And make them quit. He did not have the time—or patience—to deal with anyone's hidden agenda.

———

Eve walked back through Celia's house and onto the front porch, trying to sort through what she'd just heard. She pulled the door shut behind her and debated locking it, but decided it was best to leave things exactly as she'd found them.

Once on the main road, her GPS had no trouble directing her to the fancy electronic gate just off the main highway that guarded the entrance to the biggest commercial farm in the county. As she pulled up, a disembodied female voice asked, "Blackwell Farms. How can we help you?"

Might as well take the bull by the horns and start at the top. "I'm Eve Jackson, here to see Mr. Blackwell."

"Is he expecting you?"

Eve thought about that for a moment. Not too far fetched, given the Safe Harbor grapevine. She put all her confidence behind the words. "Yes, he is." The worst they could say was no, right?

"Just a moment."

While she waited, Eve scanned the hay fields on either side of the road. The less feed a rancher had to buy, the more profitable his cattle operation. Did Blackwell run cattle, too? Or did he merely sell the hay? And what kind of fertilizer was he using on his fields? Nitrogen was cheap, and too much could cause contamination. But if that happened, Blackwell surely wouldn't leave any evidence lying out in the open. Still, she'd like to take a look, just to be sure.

The intercom came back to life. "You are not on Mr. Blackwell's calendar, Miss Jackson."

Eve put a smile into her voice. "Whoops. I thought I was. Could I just have a quick minute with him anyway?"

"Mr. Blackwell is not available. Have a good day."

Eve tapped the steering wheel. It had been worth a try. As she turned her car around, she glanced in the rearview mirror. A large ATV drove up on the other side of the gate and stopped, two cowboys in the front seat, watching her. Both wore cowboy hats and cradled shotguns in their laps.

She got the message. She waved out the window as she turned back toward town.

But as she drove, she scanned the fence line, searching for another way onto the property.

Chapter 3

Cole spent the hour before supper in his father's office on the main floor of the ranch house, working and reworking the numbers, trying to figure out a way to repay the loan to Richard Blackwell that was due in a couple of weeks. Considering the bad blood between the two families, why had Hank asked Blackwell, of all people, for money?

Pride and necessity, near as he could tell. From what his mother grudgingly divulged, they hadn't had insurance because the premiums had been too high, so his father had paid for the heart surgeries himself. By borrowing money and using the ranch as collateral. Cole ran his hands through his hair. Even if Hank had lived, how on earth had he planned to pay the money back? Now Cole had several deformed calves he couldn't sell and Eve Jackson making noise about contamination. He wanted to believe the two weren't connected, but the more he uncovered about his father's lax environmental practices, the more his worry grew. Cole rubbed the space between his eyes and drew a deep breath as he glanced at the clock. He would not take his frustration out on Ma at the dinner table. This was hard enough on her.

He stood and headed for the kitchen, where Ma had just pulled a roast out of the oven. He leaned over and kissed her cheek, alarmed all over again at how much weight she'd lost recently. "Smells good, Ma, thanks."

At that moment, the two farmhands, Hector Ramirez and Buzz Casey, walked through the back door and stopped to wash up at the sink in the mudroom. Hector had never talked about his life in Mexico before he showed up at Sutton Ranch thirty years ago looking for work, and no one had ever pressed. Buzz had been his father's best friend since well before that. Ten years ago, after Buzz's wife died and he retired from the air force, Ma said he moved into the bunk house with Hector one day and took over as ranch foreman. According to Ma, Buzz had expected to take over after Hank's death, so to say he wasn't happy that Cole was back would be a serious understatement.

"Don't y'all dawdle and let my food get cold," his mother said.

Both men answered, "Yes, ma'am."

Cole smiled at the ritual that had been repeated every night for as long as he could remember. Something about the familiarity of it all soothed him tonight.

After the food had been blessed and passed, Buzz said, "Lots of people coming and going today. Who was the cute little number in the flashy car?"

Cole felt a flush spread over his cheeks as he remembered the feel of Eve in his arms. "Eve Jackson. She got lost trying to get to the Daughtry place." He grinned. "And then she got stuck in the mud here."

"We were just talking about Althea's granddaughter at Bible study today." At Cole's raised eyebrows, Ma narrowed her eyes and aimed her fork in his direction. "Not gossiping. Praying. And talking about ways to help. Celia has not had an easy road, and now she's raising that baby on her own. From what I heard, the doctors still aren't sure how to help that precious little girl of hers. Dr. Stern is a good man, but baby Glory is still in critical condition."

"This Eve Jackson a friend of Celia's?" Buzz asked.

Cole shrugged. "I don't know. Eve grew up in Safe Harbor, and now she works for some kind of environmental group in Washington, DC." He'd looked her up online after she left.

"Wait a minute. Is that the same girl who drove everyone crazy trying to get the high school to put filtered water out on the football field so you boys wouldn't have to drink from the hose?" His eyes narrowed. "And the dang fool who let the calves out and cost you your throwing arm?"

"The very same."

Hector hadn't said anything until now. "People gave her a hard time because of the color of her skin, too."

"No," Buzz retorted. "They gave her a hard time because she's an environmental wacko."

Something inside Cole shifted. Eve's ideas might be a little extreme—OK, a lot extreme—but he hated knowing she had been harassed and he hadn't seen it, hadn't known about it. He should have defended her, even during his most idiotic stage. Though he wondered if he would have had the guts to take action back then. He shook his head. So many things he would have done differently.

Hector kept his eyes on his plate as he shoveled food into his mouth. "I think people tried to use that as a way to get her to be quiet." His head came up. "But she never backed down."

No, she sure hadn't. It had been impressive, the way she fought for what she thought was right. Completely misguided, fighting the town over a garden hose and then trying to free all their calves, but he had to admire her principles.

"Is Eve here because she's trying to help Celia?" his mother asked, and all eyes turned to him.

"That was the impression I got. And since Celia's cottage is close to here, I imagine we haven't seen the last of Miss Jackson."

He chose his next words carefully. He'd done some research this afternoon. "According to the *Gazette*, Dr. Stern thinks it's blue baby syndrome. Little Glory might have a heart defect. But if not, it's probably from contaminated water. From what I read, the number-one culprit is nitrates."

Silence descended, and Cole knew they were all thinking the same thing. Nitrates were common as flies in the fertilizer everyone used because it was cheap and worked great. If contamination was suspected, there would be tests and investigations of every outfit in the area, because high nitrate levels were always a concern with agriculture and livestock. Now he knew they could cause blue baby, too, if the levels were too high.

This was just the kind of scrutiny Sutton Ranch didn't need right now, not right before he tried to sell his calves.

Buzz pushed back his chair and stood. "We'll just keep her off the property."

Cole stood and met him stare for stare. "No, we won't. If there's an investigation, we'll cooperate fully. We have nothing to hide."

Buzz opened his mouth, closed it, then muttered, "Your father wasn't a coward." Ma gasped, and he left without another word.

Hector stood, took his plate to the sink. "Thank you for supper, Miss Alice," he said, just as he had since the night he arrived. He headed out, but Cole noticed him moving slower, like he hurt.

Cole helped his mother clear the table, his mind on the implications of an investigation. The timing couldn't be worse. But what if he'd somehow caused that baby's illness? He had to know.

"I'm worried about Duane," Ma said quietly.

Cole brought his mind back to the present.

"He smelled like a distillery when he came by today. It concerns me."

He gave her a quick hug. "Losing your wife isn't easy."

She snorted. "He didn't lose her. She walked out on the ornery old coot, and I can't say as I blame her." She thumped the fridge door closed. "But that doesn't mean I don't worry about him. I don't know what's going on between you two, but try to be nice, OK? For me."

Cole kissed her cheek before heading for the back door. "I'll do my best." Hand on the doorknob, he paused, looked back over his shoulder. "He wants to buy the ranch."

She sighed. "I thought that might be it. You told him no?"

"I did. And not for the first time."

She nodded and turned back to the sink.

Cole headed outside, but as he stood by the paddock, he remembered Duane's veiled threat and wondered if his best would amount to more than spitting into the wind.

———

Eve drove down the paved road for several minutes, then turned down a dirt track, following the fence line that surrounded Blackwell Farms. She drove along the grassy edge to avoid the worst of the ruts, leaning over the steering wheel, searching for a way onto the property.

Her efforts were rewarded when she drove under a canopy of huge live oak trees. Their low-hanging branches would provide a way up and over the fence. But even more important, they backed up to a whole row of what looked like small storage sheds. The perfect place to keep fertilizer. She winced as she realized she'd have to do this barefoot, but there was no help for it.

Her heart pounded as she climbed out of the car and looked around on both sides of the fence, but she didn't see anyone. Slowly she walked along the fence until she found a nice sturdy branch and climbed up on it, muffling a gasp when her bare foot connected with something sharp. She inched her way up and grasped the next branch. A quick shimmy and shuffle and she got a good grip. She hoisted herself over the branch, then scooted over the fence before she carefully picked her way to the ground on the other side.

She turned and came face-to-face with one of the men who'd been on the ATV. She didn't see the other, but figured he was nearby.

Eve eyed the shotgun he casually cradled in the crook of his arm and widened her smile. "Guess I took a wrong turn."

She'd hoped for at least a little half smile, but the guy's expression didn't change.

"You're trespassing, Ms. Jackson. Mr. Blackwell says that unless you skedaddle on back over the fence, quick-like, I'm to call Chief Monroe to come pick you up."

"Right." She waved a hand behind her. "I'll just go on back to my car now."

He pushed the hat farther back on his head. "I'll wait."

"Of course you will," Eve muttered as she turned toward the fence. She stopped. From this side, the branch wasn't low enough for her to reach. She jumped up, but missed. She tried again. Still too short to reach.

She looked over her shoulder at the man. "Um, a little help?"

He heaved out a long-suffering breath, and instead of offering a hand up as she expected, he grabbed her waist and lifted her straight up. He held her as though she weighed nothing until she got herself onto the branch. Then he stepped back and retrieved his shotgun.

Eve scrambled back over the fence and hurried to her car, wincing with every step. She'd snagged her slacks and figured the soles of her feet were probably bloody and filthy, but she made it.

The man watched her as she drove away, but she wasn't giving up. She'd find the source of the contamination, whatever it took.

———

After a quick stop at the hospital to check on Mama, Eve planned to head straight to the marina so she could grab her camera and find some glass jars to take water samples. But as she drove through downtown, she noticed all the on-street parking spaces were full, and people milled around the open doors of the community church one block off Main. Right, Pop had told her the high school band concert was tonight.

Eve drove another block west before she found a spot at the curb, parked, and walked over to the church. The spring concert had been held in the hundred-year-old building for generations, since the first band director declared the acoustics better than those in the school gymnasium. Mama Rosa and Pop had dragged Eve, Sasha, and their other foster sister, Cat, every year, though Cat was the only one who had actually enjoyed it.

The band never made it further than the district competition, but what they lacked in skill they always made up in enthusiasm. The town turned out in force on concert night. What better place to get a feel for what was happening in town and see who was talking about Glory Daughtry?

As she threaded her way inside, Eve tried to ignore the frowns aimed her way. She scanned the crowd for her family and finally spotted Jesse and the rest of the family about halfway up the aisle. She maneuvered her way forward until she could slide into the pew beside Blaze. Pop, Sasha, and Jesse shuffled to the left to make room just as the conductor tapped his baton, signaling the band to finish tuning up.

"I thought you were with Mama," the teen muttered by way of greeting.

"Hi, Blaze. Good to see you, too. I'm well—thanks for asking."

Blaze narrowed her eyes. "Pop came because Mama Rosa said you were going to be with her."

"And I was, until she said she was tired and kicked me out."

Pop leaned over from down the row, on the other side of Sasha and Jesse. "Mama was all right when you left?"

Eve smiled, though she knew it was a little thin around the edges. "I read Psalms to her. She got sleepy and told me to leave."

Pop nodded and sat back just as someone nudged her leg.

"Got room for two more?"

Eve recognized Cole's voice a split second before the clean scent of his aftershave hit her. She looked up and swallowed hard. Freshly shaved and hair still wet from his shower, he looked better than any guy she suspected of contamination should ever look. When she simply stared, one corner of his mouth kicked up.

Beside her, Blaze poked her thigh as she hissed, "Scoot over and stop drooling."

Eve jerked to attention. "Oh. Ah. Of course. Sure. Plenty of room." She slid closer to Blaze, leaving a respectable gap in the pew between herself and Cole.

Cole raised a brow as he stepped into the pew and scooched over until nothing but a whisper separated his thigh from hers. He introduced his mother, Alice, whom Eve had met years ago at the hospital after the calf incident, but Eve had no idea what she said in response. All she saw was Cole, and those teasing gray eyes that always looked straight into her soul—even when he was poking fun at her. To make matters worse, that hard, muscled body wrapped in soft denim and a Western shirt made her want to climb onto his lap and snuggle close.

For one insane instant, she had an urge to yank on his shirt and see if it really did have snaps instead of buttons. She tucked her hands firmly under her legs and breathed an audible sigh of relief when the band launched full tilt into their first number.

Beside her, Blaze fidgeted and glanced over her shoulder until Eve swiveled her head around to see who had the teen squirming. She locked eyes with a lanky, long-haired teen with beautiful blue eyes sitting three rows behind them. She turned back and whispered, "What's his name?"

A blush crept up Blaze's cheeks, but she said nothing.

Eve still felt she was being watched, so she casually looked behind her again and was shocked to see several people glaring at her. Along the back wall of the packed church, Safe Harbor's longtime mayor stood nose to nose with Leon Daughtry in some kind of whispered confrontation. Interesting. Too bad she couldn't hear what they were arguing about.

She looked along the wall to her right and saw several of the hands from Blackwell's farm scowling in her direction. They shifted slightly, and Eve saw a man standing in their midst, eyes on her. He looked vaguely familiar and rather threatening with that lord-of-the-manor air. Richard Blackwell. Of course. He definitely fit the image of ruthless commercial farmer. She stared back. He wouldn't intimidate her.

Finally turning away, Eve recognized the new owner of the *Gazette* along the other wall, who frowned as she focused on Eve and scribbled in her notebook.

The music went into a crescendo at the end of a particularly long piece, and Cole leaned over. His breath tickled her ear. "If you're trying to figure out what's going on around here, glaring at everyone may not be the best approach."

Eve stiffened at his words, but he was right, drat the man. She eased back in her seat and fixed a pleasant expression on her face.

"Better, but you still look like you just bit into a frog."

Eve applauded along with everyone else and tried to ignore him, but it proved impossible. After the concert ended, finally, and Eve made her way back to her car, she realized he had so distracted her, she hadn't learned a single thing tonight that would help Celia's daughter.

She didn't understand him. She'd expected him to hate her after what happened years ago. Yet it seemed like he'd sought her out tonight. Why? Just to keep an eye on her and her investigation? That didn't seem right. Even as a cocky jock in high school when he'd teased her mercilessly, it had never been mean spirited, not like with the others.

The man intrigued her, but she had to stop thinking about him.

Naturally she dreamed about him all night, which annoyed her no end and made her cranky and disoriented the next morning. In a desperate bid to regain her equilibrium, she headed downstairs for great quantities of coffee. She would not let him throw her off.

Blaze sat at the table, reading the *Gazette* and drinking coffee, dressed in her usual black.

She glanced up when she saw Eve, then went back to the paper. "Heard you got caught trying to sneak onto Blackwell Farms yesterday. Why didn't you say anything last night?"

Eve almost spewed out her coffee. "Where did you hear that?"

Blaze shrugged. "I have my sources."

Eve raised a brow. "Long hair, blue eyes?"

Blaze scowled, but didn't respond.

Eve took another sip of her coffee before she answered. "Not much to tell, except Mr. Blackwell obviously didn't want me there." She smiled, but Blaze's frown didn't change.

"You should watch your back. People are griping about how you destroyed Cole's life—and the football team's winning streak—back in the day, and that they don't want you causing more trouble."

Eve's radar twitched at the teen's sudden concern. And the fact that she wouldn't meet her eyes. "Tell me more about these sources. Did they have anything else to say?"

Blaze stood, rinsed her cup, and headed for the door. "Just be careful, OK?"

"Wait. Do you need a ride to school?"

"Nah. A friend picks me up." She walked out, slammed the door behind her, and clumped down the steps in her black combat boots.

Eve wandered down to the marina, trying to figure out how to get the prickly teen to tell her what else she knew. She found Pop behind the cash register, ringing up coffee and bait in equal measure. She exchanged greetings with several of the local captains, then leaned over the counter and kissed Pop's clean-shaven cheek, just as she always had. Her conflicted feelings didn't mean she didn't love him.

"Morning, Pop. Did you get some sleep?" As soon as she asked, Eve wanted to smack her forehead. His bloodshot eyes answered the question. "Sorry. I'm sure you didn't. Me either. But Mama will be home soon. This is just a minor setback. She's tough."

Pop didn't respond, and Eve stopped talking. She sounded like a cheerleader at a losing game, all false merriment and extreme optimism. But it beat the alternative: voicing the fear that Mama was slowly losing the battle. Not an outcome she was willing to consider.

"I'll stop by the hospital this morning to visit Mama. Do you need anything while I'm out?" She tried to ignore the dark circles under his eyes, the way his clothes hung on him. He looked like a man who didn't have much fight left, and that made her heart hurt.

"No thank you. Sasha and Jesse will be here later to take over the marina so I can go by the hospital. I am hoping Rosa will be released today."

Eve didn't know how to respond, so she gave him a hug and went back up to the house, swallowing her tears while she tidied up the kitchen.

A few minutes later, she grabbed several empty canning jars to take water samples and headed for her rental car, praying baby Glory was finally responding to the treatment.

As she walked up to her car, she saw a white square on her windshield. She scooped it up—damp from the humidity, so it must have been there a while. She opened the envelope and found a note, written in black marker by a bold, probably masculine hand.

Curiosity killed the cat.

Eve reread the note three times. Someone was threatening her? Seriously? In Safe Harbor? Sure, things had gotten ugly when Sasha and Jesse got in the way of drug dealers—which still blew her mind—but this was crazy. She shook her head, determined to dismiss the whole thing, when she noticed something on the ground by the driver's side door.

She crouched down and picked it up for a closer look. Despite the humidity, a chill slid down her spine when she saw what it was.

Someone had left her a children's toy, a stuffed cat to be exact, with a noose tight around its neck.

Anger flashed, quick and hot. Nobody was going to scare her away. If someone felt threatened enough to leave a note and this creepy warning, then the odds of Glory's blue baby syndrome being caused by deliberate contamination just went way, way up. Which only served to make her more determined than ever to ferret out whoever was responsible.

But first things first. She pulled out her cell phone and called the Safe Harbor police.

———

Nick Stanton stepped out of his official SUV and headed her way. Eve stopped pacing long enough to give him a bear hug. "Thanks for coming, Nick. How're things going?"

Nick glanced uneasily toward the marina and shrugged. She couldn't blame him. It was taking some time for all of them to get used to the idea that Nick was really Tony, Mama Rosa and Pop's biological son, something they'd all found out just before Sasha and Jesse got married. The fact that the people he'd loved and grown up with had actually stolen him had to be a tough pill to swallow. It couldn't have been easy to find out everything you'd ever known or believed about your life was a lie.

She handed him the note she'd found on her windshield, which he placed in a clear plastic evidence bag. Then she showed him the cat, which she'd dropped right where she found it. He put that into a larger bag, then pulled out his little pocket notebook, taking notes. "What time did you go to bed last night, Eve?"

"I'm not sure. I fell asleep on top of the covers. But the last time I checked, it was after one."

"And what time did you get up this morning?"

"Not until after seven. But Pop and the local fishermen were up long before then. If they'd seen anyone, I'm sure somebody would have said."

He speared her with a gaze. "Unless one of them did it."

Eve swallowed. "Or that."

When Sasha and Jesse had been in danger, Eve had been safely in DC, getting updates from Sasha by phone. She hadn't been in town to feel the disbelief, the uncomfortable sensation that she didn't really know the people she'd been around for years. Would one of them have done this? Why?

She shook her head. In this case, the why was patently obvious.

"Can you think of anyone who wants you to leave town?"

"You heard about little Glory Daughtry in the hospital? Blue baby syndrome?"

Understanding, then annoyance, lit his eyes. "You're investigating."

She shrugged, careful not to say too much. "Let's just say Celia Daughtry asked me to see what I could find out."

"You should stay out of this. Let the health department handle it, if there's a problem."

Eve planted her hands on her hips. "Is the health department investigating? Because so far, I've not heard a thing about it."

He shook his head. "Not that I know of. But if there's cause for concern, they will."

"Not good enough. That baby is fighting for her life. Someone has to find the source of contamination and stop it, if that's what is causing the problem. If this is deliberate, someone has to make sure those responsible are found and punished."

"Which is exactly what the Florida Department of Environmental Protection will do—if the health department finds a problem." He speared her with a look. "Right now I'm more concerned about someone leaving threats on your car."

She waved that away. "I'll be fine. Little Glory is the priority."

Nick stepped forward until they were nose to nose. "My priority is someone threatening you. Stand down, Eve, and stop stirring up trouble while I do my job."

"Fighting for justice is not stirring up trouble." She stared him down. "I won't let anyone scare me off."

"And I don't want to see you hurt. Lie low while I figure out what's going on. I mean it."

Eve opened her mouth, closed it, narrowed her eyes at him. He wasn't bluffing.

Well, neither was she.

She watched Nick stride back to his SUV. Pop hurried over from the bait shop to intercept him, and she saw Nick's whole demeanor change. Where he'd been tough and firm with her, now he seemed tentative, unsure. She couldn't hear what they said, but after a few minutes, she saw Sal stick out his hand. Nick nodded once, shook it, and then climbed into the cruiser and drove away.

Eve pulled out her cell phone and dialed the county health department. "Hello, I'd like to order a water test on a private well." She rattled off Celia's address.

"Is there a problem with the well, ma'am?"

"I believe so, yes."

"Your name, please? Are you the homeowner?"

"Eve Jackson. And, ah, no. I'm a friend of the family."

"I'm sorry, Ms. Jackson, but you'll need to have the homeowner call us directly."

"She's at the hospital. Her baby is sick."

"If the illness is somehow related to the well, ma'am, I'm sure the doctor will order all the appropriate tests. Thank you for calling."

Eve stood for a moment, thinking, before she pocketed her phone. She'd head to the hospital and get Dr. Stern to do exactly that.

But first, she had another stop to make.

Chapter 4

Cole wasn't surprised to see Eve's rental car bump down the main drive to the ranch. His only question was why it had taken her so long to get here. He'd expected her to show up pointing her finger in his face at the crack of dawn. He pushed his Stetson back on his head and leaned on the split-rail fence as he watched her little car approach, kicking up dust as she went.

He wandered over, opened her door, and watched her head snap up in surprise. "Morning, Ms. Jackson. What brings you out this way?"

He could almost see the wheels turning in her head as she tried to decide how to respond.

She stepped out of the car, wobbling a bit in a pair of ridiculous high-heeled boots before she yanked off her sunglasses and aimed those gorgeous brown eyes his way. "You know why I'm here. I'm trying to figure out what caused Celia's baby to get sick."

"I heard they've ruled out a heart condition."

She looked surprised. "Where did you hear that?"

"I have my sources."

"Therefore, there has to be another cause."

Though he already knew the answer, he asked anyway. "Agreed, but what does that have to do with me?"

She huffed out an annoyed breath and swept a hand to indicate the piles of manure peeking out from behind the barn. "Manure is one of the most common sources of contamination."

He crossed his arms. "It can be, if it's not treated properly. I have mine bagged and sold for fertilizer, which, when spread in small quantities, won't cause any harm."

She leaned closer, though from her height, she still had to crank her neck way back to glare at him. "I'm not worried about the little bags sold to consumers. I'm worried about what that manure mountain is leaching into the ground right here."

He tried to hide his grin at her word choice. "Manure mountain?" At her scowl, he sobered. "I'm not laughing at you. I know this is serious. I take it seriously. But your contamination is not coming from my manure mountain."

"How can you say that?"

He turned. "Come with me, Ms. Jackson, and I'll show you you're barking up the wrong tree."

Ten steps into it, Cole looked over his shoulder and realized she couldn't keep up in her high-heeled boots. He waited for her to catch up, then slowed his steps to match hers as he led her around behind the barn.

As they rounded the corner, Buzz marched up to them. "What's she doing here again?" he demanded.

Cole ignored the man's tone. "Eve, this is Buzz Casey, a good friend of my father's. Buzz, this is Eve Jackson. She's trying to figure out why Celia's little one is sick, so she's checking out our manure mountain."

Buzz's jaw dropped open, and he snorted. "Whatever has made that little dumpling sick, it sure as sugar ain't from our manure. Crazy Cole here done poured enough concrete to build three houses, and piled the manure on top of it, just so's he could keep 'contaminants,' as he calls 'em, outta the aquifer."

Cole watched Eve look from one to the other. He raised a brow. "That answer your question, Ms. Jackson?"

"Show me," she demanded, and turned toward the steaming pile.

Cole led the way as Buzz muttered behind him. "Craziest dang fool idea I've ever heard of."

She stayed safely out of range as Cole went to the edge of the pile, grabbed a shovel, and cleared enough to show her the concrete slab beneath.

When she nodded, he led the way back toward her car, away from the stench. Here in Florida, with the heat, there was no way to hide from it. You learned to ignore it.

"Glass of lemonade, Ms. Jackson?" he asked when they neared the ranch house.

"No thank you." She paused, then added, "Though I appreciate the offer." She slipped on her sunglasses and took a moment to scan his property, then looked over toward the Daughtry property in the distance. "Maybe it isn't your manure, but something made that baby sick, and I'm betting it's coming from here, since your land is the closest to the Daughtry place. You need to have your wells tested."

Cole said nothing, just watched her climb into her little rental and bump back down the driveway. He intended to have his wells tested right away, but not on Eve's say-so. If the problem was coming from Sutton Ranch as a result of something his father had—or hadn't—done, he needed to find out immediately. And then take care of it before Eve found out and caused an even bigger problem than when she'd set all the Sutton Ranch calves free years ago.

———

As Eve drove back to Safe Harbor, she tried to figure out how to get Cole's wells tested.

She pulled out her phone to see if she could change Mark's mind about helping her, but before she could dial his number, it rang. She saw her boss's name and debated letting it go to voice mail, but at the last second, she answered. "Hello, Mr. Braddock."

"It's a fine kettle of fish you've stirred up, Jackson. Woodward is not letting this go. He says he didn't buy your namby-pamby apology. Now he's threatening a defamation-of-character lawsuit against the company and against you personally. He also somehow managed to get himself appointed to that task force instead of Milton, so Milton isn't happy with us, either."

Eve didn't know what to say. "I'm sorry, sir."

"Don't tell me, Jackson. Tell Woodward. Call him and convince him you mean it. Make this go away, or you'll be looking for another job."

Eve gritted her teeth. The congressman was dirty and trying to deflect attention by throwing the spotlight on her. "Yes, sir. I'll call him."

"Today, Jackson."

She swallowed hard. "Yes, sir." She didn't think he'd actually fire her, but just in case, she dialed Woodward's number. The man's secretary put her call right through.

"If you're calling to apologize again, Ms. Jackson, you'd better make it good. I have no patience for meddlers who spread lies about upstanding leaders like myself."

Eve wanted to gag at his pompousness, but instead she said, "I was mistaken, sir, and I apologize most sincerely. Again."

"That's all you have to say for yourself?"

"The paper has already printed our formal apology, and I wanted to reiterate mine, again. I'm not sure what else to say, sir."

The silence lengthened. "See that you stay out of my business from now on."

Click.

All things considered, that had gone better than she'd hoped. While Eve debated her next move, her cell buzzed with a text from Blaze. *Mama Rosa is having a hard time. Go by the hospital.*

Part of her didn't want to go, which made her feel like pond scum. As long as she didn't see Mama, she could pretend Mama was getting stronger and would beat this thing. But when Eve came face-to-face with her frailty, the terror of not being able to save her tore at her heart. Still, she pasted on a smile as she entered Mama's room, determined to keep her feelings hidden.

"Good morning, Mama," she chirped, bending to kiss Mama's forehead.

Mama blinked awake and sent her a weak smile. "It's good to see you, my Eve. But stop scowling."

So much for hiding her feelings. "I'm worried, Mama. How are you?"

Mama gripped her hand. "Do not worry, Eve. I am in good hands."

"I'm sure the doctors are doing everything they can—"

"I'm not talking about doctors, though they are doing their best. My healing will come from God. Our job is to trust."

The calm words ignited Eve's frustration, and she spun away and stormed around the room. "If He's going to heal you, He should get on with it already." She clenched her fists, fueled by helplessness.

"Always the impatient one, my Eve. But God's timing is not ours. And sometimes, healing comes when we reach heaven's shores."

Eve stopped, spun around. "No! That's not how this is going to go. You're going to be fine, and you're going to rock your grandbabies and see them married and—"

Mama reached for her hand as she stomped past. "Look at me, Eve."

Eve stopped moving, but couldn't quite meet Mama's eyes. Her own emotions were too close to the surface.

"Your passion and need to fight are admirable, but you didn't cause this, and you can't fix it. Just like you didn't cause your mother's death so long ago, either."

The stark words ripped the bandage off the wound that never healed. She shook her head. "If I hadn't left when she told me to—"

"Then that awful man you were hiding from would have found you, and who knows where you would have ended up." She squeezed Eve's hand. "My sweet Eve. Stop carrying burdens God never intended you to carry. Fight for justice. Speak for those with no voice. But remember that the power of life and death has always been in God's hands."

A soft tap sounded on the door, and Nick Stanton poked his head in. "Hi. I, ah, just wanted to—"

Mama waved him in. "Please, come in. Thank you for stopping by."

Nick looked from one to the other. "I can come back if this isn't a good time."

Eve swiped at the tears on her cheeks and tried to smile. "It's fine. I have to go anyway. I love you, Mama." She kissed her thin cheek and walked out, her heart a tangled mess.

Out in the hallway, she paced some more as she tried to walk off her frustration and anger. Nothing was worse than this helplessness churning inside her. Maybe Mama was right about letting God handle it—maybe—but Eve didn't wait for others to save the day. She took action. And that meant that right now she had a baby to save.

She straightened her shoulders and marched over to the ICU to find Dr. Stern. She saw him in the room with Glory and waited until he came back out to step up beside him.

"Dr. Stern."

When his eyes narrowed as he recognized her, Eve knew she didn't have much time. "I wanted to thank you for all you're doing for little Glory. I also wanted to apologize for the way I spoke to you. I was worried, but that's no excuse to be rude."

He seemed to soften slightly at her words, so she rushed on. "I understand you've ruled out a heart condition. Are you treating Glory with methylene blue?"

He cocked his head. "You seem to know quite a bit about blue baby syndrome. Who are you again?"

"I'm Eve Jackson, and Celia Daughtry asked for my help. I'm also Rosa Martinelli's daughter. Since you've spent time overseas with Doctors Without Borders, I figured you were familiar with blue baby."

When he raised his eyebrows, she shrugged. "I looked you up online."

He crossed his arms. "And I've been told you're a troublemaker."

Eve had no doubt he'd gotten an earful from more than one person. Still, she kept her smile in place. "I'd rather be called persistent."

"Fair enough. You know I can't share patient information with you unless Celia expressly authorizes it, and so far, she hasn't. But I will say your guess is correct, and little Glory seems to be responding."

"That's wonderful news. I'm trying to determine where the nitrates came from. Have you ordered the well tested?"

"No, I haven't. I've been too busy trying to save my patient."

Eve put up her hand. "No offense, Doctor. She's the top priority. But now that you are getting her stabilized, would you order the well tested—and the surrounding wells, too?"

"I would have thought you would have already done that, Ms. Jackson."

"I would have done it immediately, but the local water-testing company has not been what you'd call eager to help. Especially after they, uh, learned my name."

He raised a brow. "I can't imagine why."

Eve shrugged. "Fair enough. Would you call the health department, Doctor? Get them to test the water?"

His phone chirped, and she knew her time was up. He checked the number, said, "I'll try," and hurried away.

Eve climbed into her car and headed for downtown Safe Harbor. She parked in front of the *Safe Harbor Gazette* office, hoping to find an ally in Walter Ames's niece, who took over after he passed away at his desk, bow tie firmly in place and a stogie clamped between his teeth.

She rather thought Mr. Ames wouldn't have minded going out like that, since he'd spent most of his life at the newspaper office.

As she stepped out of her car, that same whisper of unease slid over her skin as it had at Celia's cottage. Someone was watching her again. She locked her car and casually scanned the neighboring shops and businesses, but no one seemed to be paying her any attention whatsoever.

A little shiver of excitement tiptoed in beside the unease. Sasha would call her crazy—and she might be right—but Eve knew that when she started asking questions and people got nervous, it meant she was on the right track. She just had to keep digging.

Buoyed by that thought, she walked into the newspaper office, smiling as the old-fashioned bell above the door jingled and the smell of paper and ink assaulted her senses. The small office looked like a movie set from the 1960s, with two massive wooden desks and the bookcases along every wall groaning under the combined weight of books, newspapers, and stacks of files.

Eve waited several minutes, taking it all in, before she walked to the door that led to the big printing press in the back. Just as she reached for the handle, the door opened, and she hopped back to avoid getting smacked in the face.

"Can I help you?"

Eve studied the woman she'd seen at the band concert last night. She looked every inch a gracious southern lady, with her church-suitable dress and requisite pearls, big hair, and sensible pumps. Well, except for the narrowed eyes and decided edge to her voice.

Eve stuck out a hand. "I'm Eve Jackson, and I'm guessing you're the new owner of the *Gazette*."

The woman shook her hand, grip firm. "That's correct. I'm Avery Ames. I own the *Gazette*."

"I'm very sorry for your loss. I understand Mr. Ames was your uncle." Eve scrambled for the best way to win this intimidating woman over to her way of thinking.

"Again, can I help you, Ms. Jackson?" She didn't actually tap her foot, but the sense of irritation came through loud and clear.

"You've heard about Celia Daughtry's baby who's in the hospital, with blue baby syndrome?"

"I've heard blue baby is the diagnosis, but the cause is still being explored."

Ah. She was one of those old-fashioned news people who dealt strictly in facts. Which Eve appreciated, absolutely, but right now she was trying to ferret out wrongdoing, and a little speculation could often go a long way. "Did you know that the Daughtry place is bordered on one side by Sutton Ranch, which runs cattle, and Blackwell Farms, a big agribusiness, on the other? Both of which could be the source of the nitrates in the water that poisoned little Glory Daughtry."

Avery Ames crossed her arms over her chest and eyed Eve like an unwanted fly at a picnic. "Provided nitrates have been confirmed as the cause of the baby's illness, which seems to be quite a leap. Has anyone run tests on the water supply at either Sutton Ranch or Blackwell Farms?"

"Not that I know of. But I'm working on it." She paused, kept her eyes on Ms. Ames to gauge her reaction. "Someone left a threat on my windshield yesterday. Not proof of wrongdoing, but certainly an indication that I'm on the right track."

"What do the police say?"

Eve barely kept her irritation in check. "To let them handle it."

"That's good advice, Ms. Jackson. I suggest you take it. Now, if you'll excuse me—"

"You should write a story," Eve blurted.

"This is not a scandal sheet, Ms. Jackson. And I won't toss out speculation as fact, no matter how you might do things in Washington, DC. When you have a single shred of proof, you come back and see me, and we'll talk. Until then, I have a deadline to meet. Good day."

Before she realized what happened, Eve found herself standing on the sidewalk, the door firmly shut behind her.

Ms. Avery Ames might not be ready to do a story yet, but she'd be thinking about it. Eve hadn't missed the curiosity in her eyes, the same desire to ferret out the truth that drove her. In that, they were very much the same. The seed had been planted. Now all she had to do was wait for it to grow.

Eve got back in her car and drove to Sutton Ranch. She hadn't figured out how to get back on Blackwell's land—yet—but her gut was screaming that the two properties' proximity to Celia's place meant the answers were on one of them. She just had to figure out which one.

When she arrived, she didn't see anyone about, which could work to her advantage. She wasn't sneaking, exactly, just taking a look around. She wandered over to the barn, careful of where she stepped—she loved these boots—and followed the sound of voices toward one of the stalls in the back.

"It's a bit overdue, but I'm sorry for your father's loss, Cole." The voice paused. "To be honest, I'm glad you've taken over the ranch. This place needs your touch."

Before Eve could find a place to hide, a man stepped out of the stall and spotted her. He tipped his Stetson. "Ma'am," as he walked past, an old-fashioned medical bag at his side. This must be the vet.

She turned and found Cole leaning against the stall, hat pulled low over his eyes, arms folded over his hard chest. Eve's eyes locked on the tattoo around his bicep, a rope with *Sutton Ranch* spelled out. *Oh, be still my foolish heart.*

"Something you need, Ms. Jackson?" he drawled, and Eve heard the frustration beneath the sultry tone.

"I, ah, just came out to . . ." She swallowed, unsure suddenly what to say.

"Sneak around? Poke your nose into my business? Make more unfounded accusations?"

The best defense was always a good offense, in Eve's experience. She walked over, peered into the stall. "What's wrong with your calf?"

Cole worked his jaw, and Eve wondered if he'd answer. "Not sure yet. Something's not right with one of his legs."

The calf lost his balance and collapsed into the hay. "Will he be able to walk right?"

Cole took off his hat, ran his fingers through his hair. "Don't know that yet, either."

The calf looked up at Eve with his big brown eyes, and her heart clenched, just as it had all those years ago. "You'll try to sell him young, won't you? For veal?"

He sighed. "Why are you here, Eve?"

The way her name rolled off his tongue made a little shiver tingle over her skin, but she wouldn't let it show. "Still checking, trying to find the source of the contamination." She hitched a thumb over her shoulder at the calf struggling to his feet. "Looks like I may have found the source."

"You're trespassing, Ms. Jackson. Get off my land." His voice sounded tired, defeated.

"Do you use chicken manure on your hay fields?" She wasn't sure if he'd answer, but she had to ask. That could cause high nitrate levels, too.

"Not anymore, no. Not for a while." He took off his Stetson and ran a hand through his hair before he settled it back on his head. "Stop fishing."

She met his eyes, caught off guard by the mix of sadness and frustration swimming in their gray depths. Her tone was quiet. "Will you have your wells tested?"

"They've already been ordered. I'm not heartless, Eve." He turned and walked away.

Chapter 5

Cole sat astride Morgan, an easygoing quarter horse, as they rode the ranch perimeter checking fences, Hector riding alongside him. The ranch Cole had worked on in Montana used more ATVs than horses now, but there was something elemental about riding fence on horseback.

Despite that and the beautiful day, he couldn't quell his frustration. There had to be something out here, somewhere, that was making his cows birth deformed calves. He just couldn't pin down what it was.

"What are you looking for, boss?" Hector asked.

"My father was the boss, Hector. Not me. I'm just Cole."

Hector shrugged. "You are the boss now, amigo."

Cole chaffed against the title like it was a new shirt, stiff and uncomfortable. Sutton Ranch wasn't his, though growing up he'd thought it would be, someday. Hank had always said so. But then his father kicked him out, and he hadn't been back since. "Just for a while. Hank left it to Ma, remember?"

Hector shrugged. "She put you in charge."

Cole spotted a low bush and swung down from Morgan's back. He crouched low and examined the plant.

Hector crouched down beside him. "This is Queen Anne's lace. You are trying to find something poisonous, no?"

The man didn't have a fancy education, but his instincts were always spot on. Cole nodded. "There has to be something out here that the cows are eating. It's the only thing that makes sense. But I can't find a single leaf that would cause what we're seeing."

Hector stood alongside Cole and scanned the area. "Perhaps we are looking in the wrong place."

"I've been all over this ranch, several times. I don't know where else to look."

Hector removed his Stetson and ran his fingers through his dark hair. "Perhaps the plant didn't grow here, but was given to the cows."

Cole studied the other man's somber expression. He'd been thinking the same thing, but figured he was just being paranoid. "That's what I'm afraid of. But I've been hoping I'm wrong."

"There are many people who would like to buy the ranch."

The silence lengthened as Cole considered Hector's words. "You think this is sabotage of some kind."

Hector shrugged and wouldn't meet his eyes. "The troubles started after your father's health got very bad. I do not think that is a coincidence." He paused, looked Cole in the eye. "I do not believe you think so, either."

It was one thing to think such thoughts in the dead of night, where paranoia and crazy ideas flourished. But here, in the harsh light of day? He didn't want to believe it. But only a fool wouldn't treat it as a serious threat. Cole was many things; stupid wasn't one of them.

"You have any suspects in mind?"

Again uncertainty flared in Hector's dark eyes before he looked away, and an alarm tripped in Cole's mind.

"You know Blackwell wants to buy the ranch," Hector said. "He's been coming around for years."

"Bet Hank loved that."

Hector chuckled. "He would listen politely—and then point his shotgun and ask the slimy weasel, as he called him, to leave."

Yet his father had borrowed money from Blackwell. Cole still couldn't figure that one out. "Any others I should be looking at?"

"Leon Daughtry has said he wants to buy the ranch, too." He raised a brow. "You are aware of that."

"Yeah, he mentioned it last time he came out to fix the John Deere. But I can't figure why he'd want it. Or how he can afford it. I've heard one of the big-box stores wants his and IdaMae's property. He thinking to buy it from me and then sell it all to them, hoping to make a profit?"

"Don't know, boss. But I heard that his sister wasn't happy about any of it. IdaMae wants them to sell to the property to Blackwell so she can take care of Celia and the baby."

"I heard that, too, but I can't see either one of them feeding our cows a poisonous plant. Which leaves Blackwell or one of his men. He's gotten a reputation for being ruthless in getting what he wants. And he's decided Sutton Ranch is next on his list." Cole didn't mention the outstanding loan.

"You could sell to him, go back to Montana."

"And what happens to my mama, then? I put her out on the street? She's lived here most of her life."

"If you don't get a good price for the herd, Blackwell may get the ranch anyway."

Cole clenched his jaw and nodded. So Hector did know about the loan.

"I heard your uncle Duane wants the ranch, too, though I don't think he could run it. Seems like a lot of people with reason to ruin you."

Cole flinched at the blunt truth, but Hector was right. But that still didn't provide any answers. Just more suspects.

They remounted and kept moving. Hector glanced over his shoulder. "I didn't find hemlock or anything that shouldn't be here when I checked last week, but I think we should check again, just in case."

Cole nodded, and they kept looking.

It was past time he got to the bottom of this.

———

Eve was too restless to sleep. Had Dr. Stern gotten the health department to go out and get a sample from Celia's well? She itched to see the results, but she knew that even if someone had gone there today—which was unlikely, given how slow government entities generally worked—the samples would need to be overnighted to the state lab in Jacksonville, so there wouldn't be results yet. Tomorrow, at the earliest.

But that didn't stop the nagging feeling that she was missing something, something important. Otherwise, why would someone have left her that threatening stuffed cat the night she arrived? Who would have known she was investigating?

She snorted. Please, this was Safe Harbor. One did not question how news traveled, only appreciated the speed at which it did. Which meant someone was worried. Maybe the contamination had been deliberate. Or, maybe, it had been an accident and now someone felt guilty.

She glanced at the clock. After midnight. She slipped into a pair of jeans, a dark T-shirt, and black shoes, grabbed her camera, and tiptoed downstairs, carefully avoiding the creaky steps. She eased out onto the porch and carefully closed the screen door behind her. She started the car, grateful for the hybrid's battery start, because you couldn't hear it running. The last thing she wanted was to wake anyone or cause them a moment's worry.

When no lights flicked on in the house, she slowly rolled up the long gravel driveway and out to the road. First stop, Blackwell Farms. She headed down the quiet streets until she came to Sutton Ranch. There were security lights around the house and barn, but she couldn't make out lights in any of the windows in the house. The barn was too far away to get a good look.

She passed the driveway to Celia's cottage and didn't see any signs of life there, either. Confidence building, she drove on until she got near the entrance to Blackwell Farms. This whole stretch of road was beautiful, with giant live oak trees lining both sides of the road and creating a canopy. The Spanish moss that draped the stately trees gave the area a ghostly, otherworldly feel. For her purposes, it was perfect, as it made her harder to spot.

She pulled off into the shadows of one of the huge trees and cut the engine. No stranger to covert surveillance, she turned off the dome light in the car before she opened the door, stepped out, and eased it shut behind her. Camera in hand, she walked along the high fence that lined the perimeter. Farther in the distance, she could make out the shapes of the outbuildings, silhouetted by the security lights on and around them. She thought she heard voices, and she paused, straining to hear. Just snatches flitted by on the night breeze. Enough to know people were talking, probably male, but not nearly enough to get a sense of what they were saying. Right now she wished she'd brought the sound amplifier she'd ordered online a few months ago. It allowed her to pick up voices from far away. But she hadn't thought to throw it into her bag when she left home.

She stopped at a fence post and braced her shoulder against it. She zoomed in as close as she could get and saw a group of men clustered in front of a long, low building. She slowly panned the group, searching the faces, not surprised to recognize two of them from the welcoming committee when she'd tried to see Blackwell. So what were they doing outside this late at night?

She heard laughter, but then the group went silent. She strained to hear, but she couldn't tell who, if anyone, was still speaking. Suddenly there were raised voices and arms waving, men shoving each other as though a disagreement had broken out about something.

Eve crouched behind the camera and started snapping pictures, zooming farther here, trying to capture a face there.

In the blink of an eye, things escalated, and it looked like a bar fight you might see on television: guys throwing punches, people flying through the air. She'd never seen anything like it.

Then she heard a shout, and just as quickly as the violence had erupted, it ceased. No one said a word; no one even seemed to move. Next, everyone simply turned and left.

All but one, who remained lying on the ground. Unmoving.

Eve gasped. How badly was he hurt? She held her breath to keep from moving as she tried to zoom farther in and get a good look at the man's face. He was turned away from her, so she couldn't see him clearly.

Wait a minute. Were they just going to leave him there? What if he needed medical help? She should call an ambulance. Or the police. She pulled her cell phone from the back pocket of her jeans, finger poised to dial, then stopped.

What if the men heard her? But she couldn't do nothing, either. What if he died?

While she wrestled with her conscience, a flicker of movement caught her eye. She turned back and saw two of the cowhands grab the other man under the arms and drag him off toward another building, which now had lights on in most of the windows. Bunkhouse, she guessed.

The man woke up and struggled to free himself, but they didn't let go—simply marched him between them and out of sight. Then Eve spotted another man, off to the side, holding a long-handled shovel. He followed the others. Were they going to bury him?

Her heart pounded and fear coated her tongue, but more than that, fury burned through her. She wouldn't let them get away with it.

Wait. Calm down. Her imagination had run amok again. The man was conscious. Someone holding a shovel did not mean they were going to kill anybody. *Sheesh.* She had to get a grip.

She ducked down and used her body to shield the light as she scrolled through her photos. None of the faces showed up well, but she'd know more once she got home and enhanced them on the computer. For now, she had to get out of here.

Eve eased back into her car and dialed Nick's number. It went right to voice mail. "Hi, Nick, it's Eve. I was out at Blackwell Farms and saw a fight, a bunch of guys beating up another guy. It was bad. Then they hauled him toward the bunkhouse and a guy with a shovel went with them and . . . well, I'm worried about the guy. Could you swing by and check on things? Thanks."

Eve hung up and pulled onto the road. Nick might call and lecture her, question what she was doing out here, but he wouldn't blow her off. He'd go by and check it out. She'd rather be wrong than have something terrible happen while she'd done nothing to try to stop it. She didn't need more guilt in her life. She already had plenty.

Still worried about the guy, she drove back toward Cole's ranch. Once she got within a quarter mile, she pulled behind another giant live oak and slid out of the car.

She walked toward his property, unsure where to start looking. Everything seemed still and quiet. And very dark.

A jagged fork of lightning lit up the sky, followed by a crack of thunder that made her jump. She glanced up, surprised to see a storm rolling in. The wind picked up speed, and the feeling in the air changed, filled with the smell of rain.

She didn't have much time to investigate. She'd spent enough years in Florida to know you didn't want to be under a tree during a thunderstorm. She'd just take a quick peek into a few of his storage sheds, see what kind of fertilizer he kept on hand.

She crossed the road, though the trees were farther apart along this stretch and afforded less cover. Still, unless she got closer, she'd never be able to see a thing.

Technology to the rescue. Eve propped her camera on a fence post to steady it and zoomed in on each of the ranch buildings. It was like the night before Christmas at Cole's place—not a creature was stirring.

Another bright flash of lightning had her scanning the sky. The storm was moving fast. Thunder rumbled through the ground under her feet. She looked back at the silent ranch and lowered her camera. She'd have to look in his sheds another time, though even if he had barrels of nitrate fertilizer, she knew it didn't prove a thing. It was too much of it that made it a problem. She sighed. The water tests would be the best indicator.

Time to go home and get a better look at her photos. She'd call Nick again, too—see what he found out.

She turned to go, but stopped short at the sound of someone chambering a round in a shotgun.

"Hands in the air and state your business."

Chapter 6

Eve let out a shaky breath when she recognized Cole's voice. She raised her hands and slowly turned to face him, her best smile in place. A good bluff worked in most situations. "Hi, Cole. Crazy storm that's blowing in, huh?"

Cole stepped closer and lowered the gun. "What are you doing out here with a camera in the middle of the night, Eve?"

Shoot. The man didn't miss a thing. "Ah, taking pictures of the lightning?" Her voice shook, and she knew she sounded ridiculous.

"Nice try. Why are you really out here spying? What are you hoping to accomplish?"

She kept her smile in place. "I wouldn't call it spying, exactly." She folded her arms over her camera as the first drops of rain began to fall. "Look, we'd both better get going before the sky opens up."

"I want to see those pictures first."

More rain spit from the sky, and Eve seized the opportunity. "It'll have to wait. I need to get this camera inside." Without waiting for a reply, she turned and dashed back across the road to her car and hopped in, locked the doors. She didn't really expect Cole to climb in and force her to show him the pictures, but she wasn't taking any chances with this evidence.

She shoved the key into the ignition, turned it, and got nothing. Not a click. No lights on the dashboard. Nothing.

She tried again. Still nothing. Outside, the rain came down harder.

Cole tapped on her window, so she hit the switch to lower it, but nothing happened. He leaned closer and shouted, "What's wrong?"

"I don't know. It won't start. I'm thinking battery because there are no dash lights and the engine won't even turn over."

"I'll take a look. Pull the hood release."

He disappeared, and Eve fumbled under the dash until she found the right lever. Seconds later he had the hood up and produced a flashlight to look around. "Try again."

Still nothing. Less than a minute later, he tapped on the passenger door and slipped inside after she unlocked it, water dripping off his hat brim. Outside, the rain drummed on the roof.

"Somebody cut the battery cables."

"That doesn't make sense. I drove over here." Eve hoped he would let the why-are-you-here part slide for now.

"How long have you been here?"

She shrugged. "Not long."

"Did you stop anywhere else first?"

She chewed the inside of her lip. "I made one stop before I got here."

"Celia's place or Blackwell Farms?"

Her eyes flew to his. "Blackwell Farms."

"What kind of trouble did you cause there?"

"Who says I caused any kind of trouble?" Now, that was just irritating.

"Eve, you've done nothing but cause trouble since the minute we met when we were teenagers."

"How can you say that? You didn't know I was alive!" The minute the words slipped out, Eve clamped her jaw shut. Where had that come from?

She sneaked a peek at his face and saw him shaking his head. "Oh, I knew all right. And I vowed to stay far, far away from whatever crusade you were on." He flexed his right arm. "Especially after, what was it the *Gazette* called it? The calf caper." The little half smile that flashed over his face gave her hope. And made her admire him even more. He had every right to be bitter.

Eve looked away and bit her lip as she searched for words. Realizing there weren't any that could fix the past, she met his gaze head-on and went with gut honesty. "I'm truly sorry, you know. I never, ever wanted to hurt you. I just couldn't stand the thought of all those calves being butchered." She shuddered at the memory. "I couldn't stand by and do nothing."

"I think I always knew that, even back then when I was furious." He rubbed a hand over his stubbled jaw. "What are you trying to accomplish tonight, Eve?"

"I just wanted to look around. See if anything was going on."

"And was it? See anyone dumping toxic waste? Burying radioactive materials?"

"Stop making fun of me. This is what I do. Keep people from destroying our water supply. Believe me, people do stuff like that all the time."

He sighed. "I know. But I'm not one of them. So somebody must have seen you tonight, followed you, and when you stopped here, they cut the battery cables."

She wrapped her arms tighter around her middle, not sure if it was because of the chill of her wet clothes or the thought that someone had snuck up on her. "No. I would have heard them."

He eyed her steadily. "With the storm, probably not."

She narrowed her eyes, looking for a reaction. "How do I know you didn't do it?"

He had the nerve to laugh. "What? So I could play the hero? You've been watching too many sappy movies. Stay put and I'll go get my truck, take you home."

Before she could protest, he stepped out and slammed the door behind him, rocking the little car. She hated, absolutely hated, being at his mercy. With just a few words, he could rob her of years of hard-won confidence. The man treated her like she was a complete idiot. Or too dumb to find her way out of a paper sack. She wasn't chasing unicorns here.

She shivered as she glanced around. As much as it creeped her out to know someone had followed her, it was yet more confirmation that she was on the right track. Someone had something to hide. All she had to do was figure out what it was.

———

The woman grated like a burr under his saddle. One minute the absolute honesty and vulnerability in those big brown eyes made him want to kiss her senseless. And the next she was spouting some wacky environmental nonsense and he wanted to shake her until her teeth rattled. And sometimes, he wanted to do both. He sighed. Yeah, that would help things.

It struck him as funny that in her mind, he'd never noticed her in high school. What she didn't know was that it had taken every ounce of his former cockiness to make sure she'd never known the effect she had on him. Eve was passionate and gutsy and rushed in to defend those she cared about without hesitation. Even when he didn't agree with her, a part of him wanted to let the fire that burned so brightly inside her warm the cold places in his heart.

Right. He jammed the key into his truck's ignition. Even thinking in those ridiculous, touchy-feely terms made his skin itch. This was what the woman did to him. The faster he could get her back home—and ultimately, back to DC—the easier he would sleep nights. Not that he slept much now, but it surely couldn't hurt.

He pulled up behind her car and raced through the downpour to yank open her door. She gasped in surprise and almost fell out of the car. "Come on." He took hold of her arm, but she jerked out of his grasp. But then she must have tripped on something because he barely caught her before they both ended up in the mud.

Without thinking he scooped her into his arms, strode around the truck, and dumped her on the passenger seat. By the time he sprinted back to his side and hopped in, he was soaked to the skin.

He took a minute to catch his breath and remove his dripping Stetson. Beside him, she'd pulled off one muddy shoe and was trying to figure out how to get the mud off it. He reached behind the bench seat and handed her a rag. She took it with two fingers and started wiping away the mud.

"I can't believe you came out here to spy on me in those shoes." He shook his head as he adjusted the temperature. The last thing he needed was for her to catch a chill and blame it on him.

"I didn't come out here to spy on you." He expected the instant protest, but he could tell even she didn't believe what she was saying.

He simply raised one eyebrow and started the engine.

He watched as she checked her cell phone, then slid it back into her pocket, looking near tears. "That baby could die. I have to find out who caused this."

"Maybe you're not looking for a who, but a what?"

She pierced him with those amazing eyes. "Contamination always, always has a source."

"I'm not arguing that, Eve. I'm saying sometimes the source is accidental, or intentional, or sometimes, it happens and people don't even know it's happening. You know enough to have already considered all that. Why are you so quick to blame it on someone? Calling it deliberate?"

She turned back to look out the window, and for a while, he didn't think she'd answer. Then she speared him with another one of those accusatory looks. "Someone also left a threatening note on my windshield and a stuffed kitty with a noose around its neck. That tells me someone has something to hide."

"Wait. Back up. When was this? Did you call the police?"

"Yes, I called the police, filled out a report."

"What did the chief say?"

"Officer Stanton said he'd look into it." She raised her chin and crossed her arms over her chest.

"Bet he told you to stay out of his way, too, didn't he?" He could practically see the steam billowing out of her ears, but he couldn't resist.

"I told him to stay out of my way, too."

He grinned at the typical Eve response, then sobered. "I'm sure getting used to the fact that he's Tony Martinelli is an adjustment for everyone." Cole, along with everyone in Safe Harbor, was still reeling from the news that Nick Stanton was really the Martinellis' long-lost son. Even harder to swallow was that one of the local captains had set up the boy's kidnapping when he was three, and his cousin or somebody had taken him and raised him as their own. For all the craziness in Cole's own family, he couldn't imagine waking up one day to find out his whole life had been a lie. It boggled the mind.

Eve shrugged, but he saw through the nonchalance. "We're getting used to each other. It'll take some time."

They fell into silence the rest of the ride home. When they pulled into the driveway, Eve gasped. Every light in the house was on.

"Mama Rosa!" She hopped out of the truck and raced onto the porch.

Chapter 7

"Where have you been?" Blaze was demanding as Cole walked in behind Eve.

Bella, Sasha's golden Labrador retriever, pranced up and rubbed against Eve, licking her hand, tail waving with joy, then came up to Cole and gave a cursory sniff.

"What's happened to Mama?" Eve demanded, panic in her voice.

Sasha stepped out of the shadows, Jesse beside her. "Mama's still in the hospital. What happened, Eve?"

"What? I thought something was wrong with Mama. Why are you all here in the middle of the night?"

Blaze stalked over and poked Eve hard enough to move her back a step. "You snuck out of the house, and then the storm came and you didn't come back."

"How do you know I snuck out?" Eve demanded; then her eyes widened. "You were worried about me."

Blaze just scowled. "After somebody threatened you, I figured we should be worried."

"Who threatened her? When?" This from Jesse, before he turned and shot Cole a look. "What are you doing here this time of night?"

Cole took a step in the other man's direction, then stopped. In his place, he'd be asking the same questions. He held up his hands. "Eve had a bit of car trouble, so I gave her a ride home."

Sasha looked from him to Eve and back again. "What was she doing at your place to begin with?"

Eve glanced his way, and he took a step back. This wasn't his story to tell.

Jesse glanced at Sasha, then back at Eve. "The threat, Eve. What happened?"

She shrugged and said, "I found a note on my windshield that said, 'Curiosity killed the cat,' along with a stuffed kitty with a noose around its neck." At Sasha's indrawn breath she added, "And before you ask, yes, I called the police. Nick said he's looking into it."

"Has he figured out who did it?" Sasha's eyes were wide as she eased closer to Jesse. If Cole remembered correctly, there'd been several threats when Sasha and Jesse had first come back to Safe Harbor.

"Not yet. But I'm sure he will."

Blaze narrowed her eyes. "So where did you go tonight?"

"Out! I don't answer to any of you."

An instant of stunned silence descended after her outburst. Sasha spoke up first. "Generally, that's true. But after what happened when Jesse came back and now this, yeah, actually, you kind of do answer to us. We all need to look out for each other. Besides, how many times did you call to check on me while you were in DC? Six times a day? More?"

Eve waved that away. "That was different. Someone was trying to kill you."

"It's not different. You've stirred up another hornet's nest, and somebody is already buzzing or they wouldn't have threatened you."

Jesse grinned. "Give it up, Eve. You won't win this one." But then he turned to Cole, eyes hard. "Meanwhile, I still haven't gotten a clear answer as to what he's doing here."

"He drove me home when my car wouldn't start."

Jesse glanced from Eve to Cole and back. "And why wouldn't your brand-new rental start?"

Cole met Jesse's eyes head-on. He didn't really know the other man well, but he'd heard enough to know he protected those he cared about. "Someone cut the battery cables."

"Where was Eve when all this was happening?"

Eve made a frustrated sound. "Oh, for heaven's sake, I was watching Blackwell Farms, taking a few photos. With the sound of the storm, I must not have heard whoever it was." She glanced around the room, seeming to finally notice Sasha's yoga pants and T-shirt. She turned to Blaze. "You called them?"

Up went Blaze's chin again, and Cole decided they might not be blood relatives, but all the sisters were cut from the same stubborn cloth. "I was worried. Family looks out for each other."

Eve stepped over and wrapped the teen in a hug that appeared to surprise them both. "Thanks, kiddo. But as you can all see, I'm fine, so let's all get some sleep." She turned to Cole. "Thanks again for the ride. I'll try to get out there tomorrow to pick up my car."

"If you give me your keys, I'll get it back to you in the morning." He spotted a notepad clipped to the fridge and jotted down his cell number. "Just in case." After she handed him the keys with a muttered thank-you, Cole settled his soggy Stetson back on his head, gave the brim a little tug as he scanned the silent room. He knew when he was being dismissed. "Good night, then, all."

———

Cole's truck had barely cleared the driveway when the bombardment of questions started. Eve let them talk for a few minutes and waited until they all wound down. Finally she said, "I'm fine, OK? I will not be foolish or careless. But I am trying to figure out what is going on here."

"How does Cole enter into it, besides him being the guy you had a major crush on in high school?" Sasha asked.

"She did?" Blaze grinned. "He is pretty hot, for an old guy."

"Hey," Jesse protested. "We're the same age."

"Yeah, well, you're pretty hot for an old married guy." At Sasha's arch look, she grinned. "Just sayin'."

Sasha planted a kiss on Jesse's cheek. "Can't say I disagree with you, Blaze." She turned to Eve. "So, what gives with Cole? I heard he finally came back after his father died. If I remember right, his father kicked him out in high school after he got Candy Blackwell pregnant."

"He got a girl pregnant?" Blaze's eyes were round.

"No, he didn't get a girl pregnant." Anger flooded Eve with a force she hadn't expected. "He would never have done that."

"So then why'd his father kick him out?" Blaze wanted to know.

"I don't know all the details," Sasha put in, "but from what I heard, his father wanted him to marry Candy right away, and Cole said he wanted proof first."

"That's seems fair. Why would he want to get married if it wasn't his kid?"

"Apparently, Cole's father didn't see it that way. And then Candy died in a car wreck."

"Wow. That bites."

Eve looked at Blaze and remembered the guilt etched in Cole's face after Candy died. "Yeah, it was very sad." She glanced at Sasha. "How do you know so much about it, anyway?"

Sasha shrugged. "I overheard people talking about it at school right after it happened."

"He's been gone all this time? What's he been doing?" Blaze petted Bella, who'd come back for another round of loving.

"Guys at the marina said he's been out west in Montana or somewhere, running somebody else's ranch," Jesse said. "From what I've heard, he came back after his father passed to run the ranch, which is in big trouble, financially. Local speculation is that's due to medical bills his father racked up."

Sasha eyed Eve. "Isn't Cole's ranch near Miss Althea's property? Are you thinking Cole had something to do with little Glory getting sick?"

Eve sighed inwardly. Sasha might get distracted easily, but she was sharp. "I'm trying to explore all the possibilities."

"You think the water got contaminated from too many nitrates, from the manure on Cole's ranch." Blaze phrased it as statement, not question.

Eve didn't try to hide her shock. "You've been doing research."

Blaze shrugged like it was no big deal, but Eve knew better.

"That was my first thought, but he's had big concrete slabs poured that he stores the manure on before it gets bagged and sold. So that isn't it. But since Cole's is the nearest property to the Daughtrys, he's still the most likely suspect."

"Isn't *suspect* a bit harsh?" Jesse asked. "Maybe nobody realized what was going on."

Eve crossed her arms. "Ignorance is no excuse. You know that. Whether you intend to cause harm or not, when there is harm done, someone must be held accountable."

Eve's phone buzzed with a text from an unknown number. When she read it, she gasped. "It's from Cat."

"What does it say?" Sasha's tone was cautious, and Eve couldn't blame her. Cat hadn't exactly been warm and welcoming when she came home for Mama's sixtieth birthday party.

"She says, 'Will call when I can. Things crazy. How's Mama?'"

They all looked at each other.

"Sounds like she's still in some kind of trouble," Jesse said.

"Or maybe she's just really busy," Eve said, but she saw the same doubt on their faces that she felt. Something was wrong in Cat's world. But she wouldn't tell them what.

Sasha hid a yawn behind her hand. "Sorry, this pregnancy thing is wearing me out. Let Cat know we're, ah, thinking of her, OK?"

Jesse put a hand on Sasha's back. "You need to get some sleep. We can talk more tomorrow."

After a round of hugs, Sasha and Jesse headed home.

Eve texted Cat. *Mama holding her own. Call me when you can. Worried. Love you.*

With a sigh, she locked the front door and turned, surprised to see Blaze still there watching her. "You should get some sleep, too," Eve said.

"I'm sorry your mother died."

Blaze tossed the words out and disappeared down the hall, leaving a shocked Eve to turn off the last of the lights and climb into bed, the words echoing in her heart.

Chapter 8

Cole stood in the ranch kitchen after another near-sleepless night, leaning on the counter and gulping down coffee. Every time he'd drifted
off to sleep, visions of deformed cows and his father's angry face galloped through his mind. But the thing that woke him every time was
an image of Eve, mouth wide open in a scream of terror, water closing
over her head.

After the dream had jerked him from sleep for the third time, he'd
given up and gone to his office, where he went over the ranch accounts
again, which was a different kind of nightmare. He scrubbed a hand
over his cheeks, surprised at the stubble. He couldn't remember when
he'd last shaved. Between the ranch's finances and Eve's meddling, he felt
like he was slogging through the days, going from crisis to crisis, solving
nothing, just getting further mired in debt and uncertainty.

The screen door slammed behind Buzz, who stalked over to the
table and slammed down a copy of the *Safe Harbor Gazette*. "That crazy
nut job needs a muzzle put on her."

There was only one "nut job" Cole could think of, so that had to
be who Buzz meant. What had Eve done now? He walked over and
scooped up the paper, scanning the headline.

DC ENVIRONMENTALIST ACCUSES LOCAL RANCHERS OF CONTAMINATION

Safe Harbor, Florida—DC environmentalist and former local resident Eve Jackson was quoted as saying she suspects several local agricultural operations (including Sutton Ranch and Blackwell Farms) may be contaminating the water supply, and she is pushing for area wells to be tested to locate the source of the contamination, which she believes made a local child deathly ill. Infant Glory Daughtry, whose home is near both properties listed above, is in intensive care. Her primary physician, Dr. Stern, has diagnosed blue baby syndrome, whereby an infant can't process oxygen in the blood, so the lips, fingernails and skin tone turn blue. Dr. Stern has ruled out a heart condition, often the cause of blue baby, and says the child is responding well to treatment of methylene blue. The other cause of blue baby syndrome is nitrates, often found in agricultural operations, which Ms. Jackson claims caused the infant's illness. Richard Blackwell has vehemently denied Jackson's allegations, saying, "Ms. Jackson needs to be careful about tossing out unsubstantiated speculation as fact. She'll be hearing from my lawyer."

To date, Jackson has provided no proof of wrongdoing by any local operation, though her tendency to make premature accusations is not new to the residents of Safe Harbor. Most recently, her accusations against a congressman forced her employer, Braddock Environmental, to put her on administrative leave in hope of avoiding defamation-of-character charges.

Ms. Jackson's passion for environmental causes began when she was a student at Safe Harbor High and started a petition to replace the water hose the football team drank from after practice with a filtered water system. But she is best known for sneaking onto Sutton Ranch one night and releasing all their calves before they were shipped off to become veal. She was in danger of being trampled by the scared livestock when high school senior Cole Sutton plucked her from danger. In the process, a calf kicked his elbow, shattering it, thereby costing Sutton his chance for a football scholarship—and costing Safe Harbor High the district championship. The school has not won a championship since. One of the calves jumped into a nearby pond and was attacked by an alligator. The calf didn't survive, and Jackson spent several months working for the local veterinarian to pay off the cost of the calf.

Cole finished the article and shook his head. Avery Ames, who owned the paper, had included photos of the concrete slabs under the manure at Blackwell's operation, though none from his. Though if she'd shown up, he doubted he'd have given her permission to take photos anyway.

As much as it galled him to be accused without a shred of proof, he knew the part of the article detailing all the times Eve had made premature accusations that had later been proven false would get her hopping mad. He was almost disappointed he wasn't there to see her reaction.

But the end of the article was what set him in motion. He poured more coffee into his to-go cup and turned, almost tripping over Buzz, who stood behind him, arms crossed, a scowl on his face.

"What do you plan to do about that meddlesome woman?"

Besides give her a piece of my mind when I return her car? He wouldn't tell Buzz that, though, so he said, "At the moment, nothing. I have more important things to do. She's gone off half-cocked before, as you read, so I'm sure this will all settle down soon enough."

Buzz narrowed his eyes, and Cole was surprised at the animosity shining in them. "You were a coward back then, and you still haven't grown a spine. If you don't take care of that woman, I will."

He turned to go but stopped short when Cole's hand shot out and gripped his arm. Cole spun Buzz back around with enough force that the other man's hat flew off. "You will do nothing of the kind. I will deal with Eve. And if I find out you've done different, you're done here."

"Your father would have—"

"My father is dead. I call the shots now. Deal with it or pack."

Cole didn't so much as blink while Buzz worked his jaw, weighing his sincerity.

He waited until Buzz looked away before he released his grip.

The other man scooped up his hat, jammed it on his head, and stomped to the door. Hand on the doorframe, he glared over his shoulder. "You'll regret this."

Cole let out a sigh as the door slammed shut behind the other man. He already did.

———

Eve walked out onto the porch when Cole rapped on the door.

"We brought your car back."

Eve looked over at Hector, who stood next to the ranch pickup. She waved, and he tipped his hat and climbed back into the truck.

"Thank you so much. I appreciate it. I could have gotten—"

"No problem." By his expression, she knew he'd seen the article in the *Gazette*. Which told Eve she'd get the same warm welcome from all of Safe Harbor today. She'd wanted Avery to do an article, but this wasn't quite how it was supposed to go.

"Don't you ever get tired of causing trouble for people?"

"I wasn't trying to cause—"

"If people think there's a problem at Sutton Ranch, how do you think that will affect buyers for my livestock? Or the sale of the crops we're growing?"

Eve thought of the calves they sold for veal and didn't think a lack of buyers was a bad thing. But she wasn't naive. Selling calves was part of the business, an income ranchers like Cole depended on—no matter how much it horrified her. "I was just trying to—"

Cole planted both hands on his hips. "For once, Eve, I wish you would think about the collateral damage your crusading leaves behind."

Without another word, he climbed behind the wheel of the pickup, and he and Hector disappeared.

Eve paced the porch for several minutes, then headed for the hospital before she exploded with frustration. She never wanted to hurt people, but she couldn't just stop fighting for justice. Without people like her, who fought for the Glory Daughtrys of this world?

Time crawled by in Mama's hospital room. After a while, Eve popped up and started pacing. She couldn't sit still for another minute. It felt like she'd spent days at Mama Rosa's bedside, but when she checked her phone again, it had actually only been two hours. It wasn't so much the hospital itself she hated as the waiting. She had never been good at that. She took action. Did things. Made things happen.

Here, alone with Mama and her cancer, there was nothing in Eve's arsenal she could use to fight with. And that made her feel helpless, which always made her angry.

So she'd hopped up from the uncomfortable plastic chair and started pacing. She used her phone to google various medical sites, looking for the newest advances in the fight against cancer. But she'd already read them all—and Mama Rosa had tried most of them, to no avail.

"You are going to wear a trench in the floor, Eve," Mama rasped.

Eve spun around and went to her, tucking one frail hand in hers as she leaned over the bed to kiss Mama's cheek. "Did you get a bit of rest?"

"Some." Mama eased her hand away so she could pat Eve's hand. "It's OK, Eve. Go. See what you can do to help little Glory. Things with me will be exactly as God wills. Your concern and pacing will not change anything."

Eve wanted to argue, but when she saw the effort it took for Mama to console her, shame washed over her. She should be the strong one, the one offering comfort. But right then, she had none to give, and that made her feel awful. She leaned over and gave Mama another kiss, then eased away. "I love you, Mama. Get some rest. I'll be back tomorrow."

She sent Sasha a quick text that she was leaving Mama before she headed to Glory's room in the ICU.

Her steps slowed as she approached the room and heard a male voice. Once she got close enough, she saw that Cole was sitting with Celia in the nearby waiting room. Without thinking, she ducked out of sight, not wanting to interrupt.

From there, his voice carried clearly.

"It will all work out, Celia. Your job is to take care of that sweet baby girl."

Eve heard rustling and Celia's sharp intake of breath. "No, I can't take that. You've done too much for me already."

Cole must have given her money.

"You need to eat, keep your strength up so you can take care of Glory."

Eve's admiration of Cole shot up several more notches. She heard more rustling and straightened, prepared to walk into the room as though she'd just arrived.

Before she'd gone two steps, Cole stepped in front of her, Stetson in hand. "Hear anything interesting?"

"How did you know I—"

He grinned and settled the hat on his head. "I didn't, but I do now." Then he sobered. "Be careful about making accusations without facts, Eve. They can hurt people."

Eve stared after him, wondering if he was still talking about the newspaper article, or about the accusations leveled against him in high school. Which everyone in Safe Harbor was no doubt talking about again—and which she'd never believed for a moment. If Cole had gotten Candy Blackwell pregnant—which she doubted—he never would have denied it. He wasn't that kind of man.

She walked into the waiting room and chatted with Celia for a few minutes, relieved beyond measure that little Glory seemed to be responding well to the treatment. "Celia, now that you've had a bit of time to catch your breath, do you know of any reason why someone would deliberately contaminate your well?"

Celia looked up from Glory's crib. "I saw the article in the paper, and I've been thinking about it. I don't think Cole had anything to do with it. He's a good guy." She frowned. "Not like Mr. Blackwell. Even though Mama has worked for him for years, and Grandmama Althea did, too, I don't trust him at all."

"Why do you say that?"

"He's been by here twice this week, wanting me to convince Mama and Uncle Leon to sell him Grandmama Althea's property. No matter how many times I tell him it's not mine to sell, he doesn't seem to hear me."

Trying to bully a young mother with a sick child moved Richard Blackwell higher on her suspect list, on general principle. "Anyone else you can think of who might do something like this?"

Celia shrugged. "I really don't know. Mama wants to sell to Mr. Blackwell. But she says the big-box store is offering a lot of money so they can build a distribution center here. Uncle Leon is against selling, says the property should stay in the family."

Eve tried to phrase the question carefully. "Does your uncle have the money to buy the property from his sister, do you think?"

Celia scoffed at that. "Not that I can tell. But that hasn't kept the two of them from shouting at each other about it."

Eve gave her a hug. "Thanks for telling me. And I'm delighted that Glory is making progress. Call me if you think of anything I should know."

Eve went in search of Dr. Stern and found him at the nurses' station, filling out charts.

"Hello, Dr. Stern. I'm so glad Glory Daughtry is responding well to the methylene blue."

"As am I, Ms. Jackson. As am I."

"Have you ordered the well tested at Celia's cottage?" When he stiffened, Eve wished she had phrased the question a bit more smoothly.

He put the chart away and glanced at the two nurses who were following the conversation closely. "I was unaware I needed to report my actions to you, Ms. Jackson."

She held her hands up, palms out. "I'm sorry, Doctor. Like you, I just want to make sure little Glory doesn't get sick again once she's released from here. Those test results will help with that."

"Which is why they were ordered yesterday. I asked them to put a rush on it. The health department said the samples were shipped to the state lab in Jacksonville. They should have results today or tomorrow."

He handed the chart to a nurse and walked away without another word.

Eve wanted to pump a fist in the air, but instead she merely smiled at the gawking nurses and left the hospital.

Outside, she stopped beside her car and scanned the parking lot as she unlocked the door. Just because she didn't see anyone watching her didn't mean they weren't.

A police SUV pulled up beside her, and Eve sighed as Chief Monroe rolled down his window.

"How's your mama today, Eve?"

"She's holding her own, Chief. Thanks for asking."

"Well, you give her my best."

"I'll do that, thanks." Eve had one foot in the car when the chief continued.

"I warned you a while back about making unfounded accusations, Eve. It doesn't appear you were listening."

Eve tried to read his expression, but it was hard to tell under the hat brim. "I heard you, Chief. I am doing my best to figure out what caused Glory's illness."

"This is not some crazy witch hunt, Ms. Jackson, and we don't cotton to people throwing stones until something sticks."

"I agree with you, Chief. This is very serious. That little girl almost died. I know Cole Sutton is having his wells tested. Is Richard Blackwell doing the same on his property?"

"The Safe Harbor Police Department does not answer to you, Ms. Jackson. But if you continue to make unfounded accusations, you'll find yourself in a jail cell."

Before Eve could respond, he rolled up his window and drove away. She'd never liked his pompous, self-important attitude, but she couldn't dismiss it, either. He could do what he wanted in this town, and she didn't doubt he'd enjoy every minute of it.

———

Later, the sun had finally set, the supper dishes were done, and Pop had gone back to the hospital to sit with Mama for a while, but Eve still couldn't settle. She wandered down to the marina and walked out to the end of the dock, pacing back and forth, hoping the sound of the waves lapping the pilings would help her think.

Something was nagging at the back of her mind. She pulled out her cell phone and looked up Miss Althea's obituary. The words *bladder cancer* hit her right between the eyes, as that could be caused by exposure to high nitrate levels over a period of time. She put the name Daughtry in the search engine, and after some more digging, found several other obituaries with the same cause of death. But was that heredity or contamination? She'd have to find out.

She did another search, looking for cases of blue baby, but didn't find anything that would help there, either. A search of several environmental sites confirmed what she already knew. Blue baby wasn't a reported illness, so she didn't find any real records of incidence. In third-world countries? Yes, but not here in the USA.

She chewed the inside of her cheek, thinking. Other kinds of contamination were much easier to investigate. But for something like this, it would come down to the results of the ion chromatography tests done by the state lab.

So whether the contamination was deliberate or accidental, the threat on her car said her investigation was making someone nervous.

She heard footsteps clomping down the dock and looked up to see Blaze headed her way. The sixteen-year-old had come a long way in the past few months, but still wore her defenses like a shiny metal shield.

"Hey, Blaze, what's up?"

When she spoke, her words came out clipped. "So, I have this stupid project due for my history class, and I need some supplies. Can you drive me to Stuff Mart to get what I need?"

"Sure. When did you want to go?"

This earned her an eye roll. "Like, now?"

"Gotcha. Let me get my keys and purse. Due tomorrow?"

"Yeah. It's totally lame."

Eve smiled. "I remember. Lame projects mean good grades, which mean getting scholarships, right?"

Blaze stopped and blinked at her, as though it hadn't occurred to her that Eve had experienced the same struggles in high school. Finally she shrugged. "I want to go to college."

"Good for you. If you want to go, you'll figure out a way to get there. Let's not let a lame project stand in your way."

It didn't take long to get to the store, get what Blaze needed, and head to the checkout line.

When Eve pulled out her wallet, Blaze shook her head. "I don't need your money."

Eve stopped, open wallet in hand, and glanced at the teen's set expression. "Tell me something, Blaze. If Mama Rosa weren't sick, would you have a part-time job somewhere? Be saving for school or a car?"

Blaze looked away and shrugged, and Eve had her answer. "Then let me get this, OK?"

Another shrug, but it started Eve thinking. Somewhere in all the worry and doctors' appointments for Mama, Blaze and her needs were getting lost. She'd make sure that ended, tonight.

Once back in the car, they had to take a detour in the middle of town, since the road crew was restriping the yellow lines on the pavement. They ended up on some streets Eve hadn't been down in a long time.

At a stop sign, Eve looked across the street and saw two figures standing in a small parking lot, nose to nose in what appeared to be a heated discussion. Since all the businesses were now closed and there wasn't another soul around this late at night, that struck her as odd. The two men looked her way, and Eve reared back in surprise.

What were Richard Blackwell, owner of Blackwell Farms, and Hector, the older man who worked at Sutton Ranch, doing out here arguing so late at night? Did Cole know about this?

Eve rolled down her window, turned off the air conditioner, and reached behind her seat for her camera bag.

"What are you doing? It's hot!" Blaze protested, reaching for the controls.

Eve kept patting the area behind her seat. "Shh, I want to hear what they're saying." Where was her camera? Why couldn't she reach it?

She finally sank back in her seat and gave up. She didn't want to raise suspicion by turning on the interior light to look for it, so she eased through the intersection at a crawl while she strained to make out what they were saying.

Both men scowled as she went past and hurried to their cars.

"What's going on? I know one of them is that Blackwell guy, who owns the big agribusiness. I've seen him at school for career day. But who's the other guy?"

"He works at Sutton Ranch."

"Seems a weird place to meet."

"It does."

"If looks could kill, you'd have been dead right there."

Eve nodded. Neither man had looked especially happy to see her.

"What are you going to do now?"

"For tonight, not a thing." But once they got back to the marina, Eve got down on her hands and knees and searched her car. Her camera wasn't there. Someone had broken into her car and stolen it, the dirty rotten scoundrel.

She stopped pacing and smacked her forehead. The last place she'd had it was at Cole's. He'd demanded to see the pictures, but then they got sidetracked by the whole battery-cable incident.

She stomped around some more, furious. She had given him her keys so he could bring her car back.

She whipped out her cell phone and stabbed in his number. The minute he answered, she said, "I can't believe you took my camera."

He sighed. "Still making unfounded accusations, Eve? When are you going to start asking questions before you assume you know the answer? For the record, I didn't take your camera."

Click.

Eve stood there, a bit shocked that he'd hung up on her, but then she replayed her end of the conversation and realized she hadn't handled that in quite the best possible way. But someone had stolen her new camera. And it hadn't come cheap.

She thought back and tried to remember if she'd locked her car, but came up empty. She shook her head. So anyone could have come by, seen her car, and taken the camera.

She owed Cole an apology, even though eating crow had never been her favorite activity. She dialed his number, and the minute he answered she said, "I'm sorry for making accusations and jumping to conclusions without all the facts."

"Wait. Is this Eve Jackson? You must have the wrong number."

Eve smothered her laugh. "I deserved that. You're right. And I'm sorry."

"I'm going to jot this down on my calendar." She could hear the smile in his voice. "Good night, Eve. Put your crusader cape down and get some sleep."

She was still grinning as she dialed Nick's number, but reality rushed back in as she told him about her stolen camera.

"I'll file a report, but you know that's not much to go on, right?"

She sighed. "I know. And I appreciate it. Did you find out anything at Blackwell Farms? Is the guy OK?"

"I went by. All the hands were accounted for, and the guy who'd been beaten up said it was just a drunken fight and refused to press charges. So you can stop worrying they buried someone out by the horse trough."

Eve chuckled as he'd meant her to, but after they hung up, her mind still ran through possibilities. Was there something else on her camera someone didn't want coming to light?

And did that something else have anything to do with Richard Blackwell and Hector's late-night meeting?

Chapter 9

"Do you need a ride to school?" Eve asked the next morning as she walked into the kitchen.

Blaze, sitting at the table dressed all in black, drinking coffee, and scanning yesterday's *Gazette*, looked up. "Are you going to ask me that every single day?"

Eve poured a cup of coffee and sat down opposite her, grinning at her over the rim. "I guess not. But will you let me know if you do need a ride?"

"I've got it covered." She stood and rinsed her mug, slung her backpack over her shoulder. "I don't think I'd go near Blackwell Farms today. That article made you sound like a complete nut job."

Eve saluted her with her coffee cup. "Thanks for that. Hope the lame project turned out OK."

Blaze didn't respond, just clomped out the door. Three minutes later, Sasha wandered in and headed for the coffeepot.

Eve popped bread into the toaster. "You and Jesse manning the bait shop this morning?"

Sasha leaned against the counter. "I am. He's working on *The Painted Lady*. But he's covering while I take a break." Sasha nodded toward the twice-weekly *Gazette*. "You saw that, I take it?"

Eve nodded, not wanting to explain this yet again to a well-meaning relative. "Look, Sasha—"

Sasha held up a hand. "I get it, Eve. I really do. You have to find out what happened. So go, investigate. Just be careful. And let me—or Jesse—know if you need help."

From outside came a shout, then raised voices. Eve hurried outside and across the porch and headed toward the marina, Sasha right behind her.

As they rushed down the dock, Eve looked past the cluster of fishermen and onlookers and realized Cole's uncle Duane and Buzz, Cole's ranch hand, were throwing punches, despite Jesse's attempts to separate the two men.

"You won't get away with this, Casey," Duane yelled, and socked the other man in the jaw.

Sasha tried to dive into the mix, but Eve grabbed her around the waist and held her back. "Let Jesse handle this, Sasha. You've got a baby to protect."

Sasha instantly stilled, but Eve kept ahold of her as Buzz stumbled back until he found his footing. "I won't take this from you," he shouted, and stepped around Jesse and launched himself at Duane. He hit hard enough that the other man flew backward into the water.

When Buzz moved to dive in after the other man, Jesse held him back. "Enough. Get on out of here and calm down."

Buzz rubbed a hand over his jaw, opened his mouth as if he had more to say, then stormed off the dock and climbed into a BMW convertible. Just to be safe, Eve didn't let go of Sasha until his car spun out of the parking lot in a hail of gravel.

After Jesse helped Duane out of the water and sent him on his way, too, Eve walked back toward the house, her mind spinning with possibilities.

She wondered if Cole knew about the animosity between the two men.

She stopped by her car and looked around, tapping her fingers on the roof. Not being able to wrap her hands around whatever was going on in this town was starting to drive her completely crazy.

———

Cole walked into the ranch kitchen the morning after Eve's apology and found his mother sitting at the table drinking coffee with none other than Richard Blackwell. The moment he walked in, the other man stood, and Cole was surprised again at how short he was. Must be his attitude that made him seem taller.

"What brings you here so early in the morning, Mr. Blackwell?"

"Please, call me Richard." He sat back down and picked up his coffee cup as though he was perfectly at ease in Cole's mother's kitchen, which irritated Cole no end.

Cole slanted a glance at his mother, but she wouldn't meet his eyes. What in the world?

"Have a seat, Cole," Richard said, indicating the chair opposite him.

"I'll stand, thanks." Cole sipped his coffee and waited. Seventeen years ago, Richard Blackwell had made no bones about the fact that he blamed Cole for the car wreck that killed his daughter, Candy. So it made no sense that Hank had borrowed money from the man, and even less sense that Richard now appeared to be friends with Cole's mother.

"You know the loan deadline is rapidly approaching."

Apparently, Blackwell also still thought Cole a complete dimwit. "I am well aware of that."

"I'm sure your mother also told you I'd like to buy the ranch. If you sell it to me, I'll simply deduct the loan amount from the selling price."

"That's generous of you, but Sutton Ranch isn't for sale."

"Maybe it should be. With what I'm offering, your mother would have the freedom to start over someplace else—and so would you."

"We're content right here, but we appreciate the offer."

Blackwell frowned as though Cole's response surprised him. "The offer comes with a time limit. If proof comes out that the contamination that made that little baby sick came from here, your spread could end up worthless."

And wouldn't Blackwell love to scoop it up for almost nothing during foreclosure? "That won't happen, because we haven't done anything wrong. In fact, we've done everything right."

"That may be, but Ms. Jackson seems a determined sort, doesn't she, with what appears to be an uncanny knack for shining a light on things folks would rather keep dark."

"I appreciate the concern, but Sutton Ranch is not for sale," Cole repeated. He strode to the door and held it open, waited for the other man to walk through. "Have a nice day."

"Don't be too quick to dismiss my offer, Sutton. It may be the best one you're going to get."

Cole shut the door behind Blackwell and turned to his mother. "What gives, Ma? Why was he sitting here like this wasn't his first visit?"

His mother still wouldn't meet his eyes. "We've run into each other in town a time or two. He's not the monster people make him out to be."

"He's buying up all the ranches in the area, and he threatened me with his shotgun years ago." Though given the circumstances, he didn't hold the shotgun incident against the man. He tried to lighten the mood. "And he looks like a smarmy used-car salesman."

That last got a chuckle out of his mother, as he'd hoped it would. He leaned over, kissed her cheek. "I'll see you later. Quit fraternizing with the enemy."

She waved him away, though she still looked troubled. Cole decided he'd push for answers later. Right now he had a ranch to save.

Chapter 10

Eve drove down the dirt road to Cole's ranch, a plate of homemade cookies riding shotgun. She'd apologized last night, but she felt something more was needed after the way she'd behaved. At least that's what she told herself on the way over.

As she drove down the long ranch driveway, she searched for signs of Cole, but didn't see him. She opened her door, stepped out, and there he stood, looking like a magazine ad for well-worn jeans. Or boots. Or . . . something.

Today he wore a straw cowboy hat and white T-shirt, and she caught sight of his rope tattoo where it wrapped around his bicep. *Oh my.* She would have fanned herself, but she didn't want to look like any more of an idiot than she already did. She clicked her mouth shut, afraid her tongue was hanging out.

"Eve. What brings you out here again? Doing more research?"

The sarcasm stung, but she figured she deserved that. She extended the plate of chocolate chip cookies. "I came by to apologize in person." His rigid stance softened a bit, so she added, "And to thank you for the help with my car."

"My pleasure. But you didn't have to make cookies." He took one, ate it in one bite. "But thanks. These are really good."

Eve felt the compliment all the way to her toes. But then she shook her head, determined to stay focused. She took a deep breath, met his eyes so she could gauge his reaction. "So last night about ten thirty, Blaze and I were coming back from Stuff Mart and saw Richard Blackwell and Hector having a heated discussion in town."

Cole didn't say anything, just turned and scanned the area. "Did you hear what they were saying?"

"No. But they seemed surprised to see anyone. Workers were striping the main road, so we'd been routed a back way."

"I appreciate the information. Now, if you'll excuse me—"

"I'm really not trying to cause you trouble, Cole. I'm trying to find the truth."

He studied her long enough that she wanted to squirm. Then his gaze slowly ran down her torso to her sandaled feet and back up. He shook his head. "Stay here. I'll be right back."

Before she could respond, he disappeared back inside the house. Eve looked around at the tidy yard around the ranch, the aging but well-kept buildings, and the feeling of hostility that hovered in the air. A quick turn toward the barn and she spotted Buzz watching her from the open door. He spit tobacco juice, sent her another glare, and disappeared inside the building.

Seconds later, Cole returned and shoved a pair of cowboy boots in her direction. "These are my sister's, but they should fit you well enough. If you're going to be snooping around out here, you need the proper footwear."

Eve looked from the well-worn boots to her flimsy sandals and back up to Cole's unreadable expression. "Um, thank you. I, ah, appreciate it."

He reached into one of the boots and pulled out a pair of socks. "You'll want these, or you'll have blisters."

"Thank you." The silence lengthened, and she wasn't sure if she should put them on, or leave, or . . .

He nodded. "Put 'em on. I've got a few things to show you."

Right. Eve leaned against the car and quickly pulled on the socks and boots, which fit almost perfectly. She felt a tad ridiculous in her linen shorts and silk top, but she didn't have time to worry about any of that. Cole started off toward the barn at a fast clip, so she tossed her sandals into the car and hurried to catch up.

Inside the barn, Cole stopped in front of one of the stalls and showed her a very pregnant cow. "She should be ready any day now."

Eve watched as he spoke softly to the cow, who gazed at him with adoring brown eyes. He rubbed her between the eyes, and you could feel the cow relaxing under his gentle touch. Eve couldn't look away from those strong hands, couldn't avoid the pull of that deep baritone.

She had taken a step forward before she realized what she was doing and stopped herself. The man had a pull all his own. What would it be like to have that smooth voice whispering in her ear, feel those strong arms stroking her skin? She shook off the thought and with it the realization it had been a very long time since anyone but family had touched her.

"Right?"

Eve blinked and saw Cole watching her, one side of his mouth crooked up in a grin that sent a thrilling little zing straight through her. No man had made her nerve endings quiver like that in, well—OK, she had to admit it—years. What a sad commentary on her life. But she'd been busy, sheesh.

"Are you going to tell me what's going on in that pretty head of yours? You look like you're debating something."

Truth be told, she'd spent a precious few seconds debating throwing herself into his arms just to see if that rock-hard chest felt as good as it had when he'd carried her to her car. A flush crept over her cheeks at the thought, and she cleared her throat. "Ah, I was just thinking that your cows are lucky to have you."

He raised a brow and flashed her a quick grin, and *Wow* was all Eve could think. Was there anything better looking than a smiling cowboy?

But just as fast his smile vanished, and Eve wondered where she'd stumbled verbally this time. He turned and strode down the barn's long center aisle as she hurried to keep up. When he stopped at a small office, she followed him in to the battered desk that sat against one wall. It was surrounded by a file cabinet, three saddles, and all kinds of ranchy-looking stuff she couldn't begin to identify.

He plucked a straw cowboy hat from a peg on the wall and plopped it on her head. It slid down and covered her eyes. "Nope. Too big." He took the first away and replaced it with a smaller one. "Try this one." It fit perfectly. When she turned to look at him, he grinned. Time seemed to freeze, and for one suspended instant a look flashed through his eyes Eve couldn't identify. It vanished so fast she was sure she'd imagined it. She must have, because for a second it looked as though he wanted to kiss her.

Which was ridiculous, right?

He grabbed her hand. "Let's go. I want to show you something."

Eve hurried to match his pace, not wanting to risk him releasing her hand. What kind of hermit had she become that this simple gesture had her heart galloping in her chest? She really had to get out more.

He led them back down the center of the barn and out the door on the other side. Eve blinked while her eyes adjusted, surprised to see rows of strawberry plants stretched out in either direction.

"Are you good to walk a ways?" he asked.

———

Cole kept a firm grip on Eve's hand, unwilling, suddenly, to let her go. The woman tied him up in knots. Confident and running full steam ahead for her causes, she stuttered and stammered whenever he smiled at her. He found he liked smiling at her, a lot.

Which, when he thought about it, was crazy, since the woman could cause all kinds of problems. Maybe that was part of why he wanted to show her around, make her understand that they were on the same side, in a way. He was a rancher, sure, and he was expanding the farming side, but he was determined to do it in an environmentally friendly way.

"We've always grown enough for a small farm stand, but this year we expanded it and found a few local restaurants to buy our produce."

"How do you fertilize it all?" Eve asked, as he'd known she would.

"We have what we call a fertigation system, which means it's a way to irrigate and fertilize at the same time, but that way we have all kinds of control over the amount of fertilizer. We use just enough to keep the plants healthy, but not enough to harm the aquifer."

"What about pesticides?"

"We check the plants every day and are trying to avoid using any at all."

"That's risky, isn't it?"

"It can be. But we're hoping the risk will pay off with better crops."

Suddenly Eve stiffened, and her dusky skin paled. She stopped dead in her tracks and wouldn't move, even when he tugged lightly on her hand.

"Eve? What's wrong?"

Her eyes were fixed on a point in the strawberry field, and he followed her gaze but didn't see any cause for alarm.

"Bees," she whispered.

"Are you afraid of them?" He couldn't imagine Eve afraid of much, except maybe her feelings.

"Allergic. Deathly." The words were a mere whisper, and she had started inching backward.

"Do you carry an EpiPen?"

"Always, but it's in my car."

He moved closer and whispered, "I've got you. We'll just ease back until we're safely out of range, OK?"

Her nod was barely perceptible, but he kept her moving slowly in the right direction. Her eyes never left the bees, not until they were too far away to see them anymore. Then she let out a sigh and collapsed against him. He could feel her trembling, so he wrapped an arm around her to steady her, taking in her clean scent and the way her cloud of hair tickled his chin. "It's OK," he murmured, trying to erase the panic that lingered in her eyes.

After several minutes, she eased away and her color returned. "Sorry about that. Bees, ah, make me a little nervous."

"I'm guessing there's a story behind the EpiPen."

"There is. College. Maybe I'll tell you one day."

"Why don't you grab it and we'll keep going?" When she hesitated, he added, "Or not."

"No, that's fine. I'd love to see more. I just, ah—"

They heard voices and saw Buzz, Hector, and Uncle Duane walking toward them with Leon Daughtry, obviously debating something. All four stopped short when they saw him with Eve. Cole was surprised to see a nasty bruise on Buzz's jaw.

"What's she doing here?" Uncle Duane demanded.

Cole shifted so he stood slightly in front of Eve. "I might ask you the same question."

"I'm family. This here is part of my heritage. She's nothing but a reckless do-gooder, meddling in things that don't concern her, stirring up trouble."

Cole waited until he wound down, then ignored everything he'd said. "What brings you out here, Uncle Duane?"

"I came to see you."

"You found me. What can I do for you?" Cole would bet his best cow he knew, but he wouldn't make it easy.

"Your mama said you still ain't selling. I made a decent offer, boy."

"Mama is right. We're not selling. The offer isn't the point."

"You just don't want me to have this property, even though it's what your pa wanted." Duane moved closer, and Cole held his ground. "You owe him this. And me."

"I don't owe either one of you a thing except respect for your place in my life. Which is all that's keeping me from throwing you off our land."

As always, his uncle puffed up, sputtering his outrage. He turned to Buzz. "You gonna let him talk to me that way?"

Buzz flicked his eyes from one to the next. Then he pulled off his hat, ran a hand over his crew cut. "I think he's making a mistake, Duane, about a lot of things, but"—he shrugged—"it's his funeral."

"Not yet, but it might be." Duane spun on his heel and stomped back toward his truck. Cole watched him go, then turned his attention to Buzz, Hector, and Leon. "Did you need me for something?"

"Hector and I are headed out to check fences while Leon takes another look at that stubborn generator. After, Hector and I plan to make a supply run to town."

Cole nodded to the big man, whose expression was hidden under the brim of his ball cap. "I appreciate it, Leon. If anyone can fix that ornery piece of equipment, it's you."

"I'll do what I can."

"Did you need anything, boss?" Hector grinned, because he knew Cole hated when he called him that.

"I'm good, thanks. I'll text you if I think of anything."

Hector grinned again and tipped his hat to Eve. "Ma'am." Then he and Buzz walked back the way they'd come. Cole watched them go, wondering what that was all about. They didn't normally just show up to talk to him. They sent a text or left a note somewhere.

"They were fighting this morning," Eve said.

Cole studied her face. "Who?"

"Duane and Buzz. They got into a shoving match at the marina, and Duane ended up in the water."

"I take it that's where Buzz got the bruised jaw?"

When Eve nodded, his unease grew, but he decided to think about that later. He held out a hand and waited, wondering if she'd refuse, but then she put her hand in his as they walked back to her car. Cole decided he liked the feel of her small hand in his. Maybe too much.

"Leon works for you?" Eve asked.

"He does work for most of the outfits around here. I don't think there's a machine ever made that Leon can't fix, so he's a busy man."

Eve grabbed her EpiPen, and he led her up and down the rows of vegetables; broccoli, cabbage, cucumbers, greens, and peas all marched in nice, neat rows.

Halfway down she stopped, shaded her eyes. "This is really impressive. I had no idea you had all this back here." Eve stood on her tiptoes and pointed to the edge of the field. "So, are those blueberries I'm seeing?"

Cole grinned at the excitement in her voice. "They are. Let's go."

She practically skipped over to the bushes, smiling like a kid on Christmas morning. Cole hurried to keep up with her, enjoying watching her. Once there, he plucked several of the berries and held them out to her.

"Wow, these are huge!" She swallowed, then practically jumped up and down. "Can I have a few more?"

"You can have all you want."

"Better be careful. You haven't seen how many berries I can eat."

He indicated the rows of bushes. "I'm not worried."

Eve flashed him another of those amazing grins of hers and then ducked her head and went back to oohing and aahing over the berries like she'd never seen such bounty in her life.

Cole wandered the rows next to her, soaking in her carefree excitement over such a simple pleasure. Had he ever enjoyed something with such abandon? He stepped closer, and she almost bumped into him when she stood. "Don't they have blueberries near where you live?"

She stuck her tongue out at him. "Of course, but I live in the city, cowboy. So ours come in little boxes at the grocery store." She looked at him. "What?"

"Your tongue is blue. From the berries." Without planning to, his hand cupped her cheek and he moved closer, wanting, suddenly, to taste the berries on her tongue.

The laughter in her eyes turned to surprise as they stared at each other. He moved closer, giving her time to change her mind. At the last second, she turned her face away, and his lips brushed her cheeks.

He eased back, disappointed, and watched her pluck another handful of berries.

When she turned back to him, he raised a brow and she shrugged.

They spent the next hour wandering up and down the rows, and Cole wondered when he'd ever enjoyed a woman's company more.

"I wanted to say I'm sorry about your father's passing, but I haven't known quite how to work that into the conversation."

So much for his sense of peace. He kept his expression neutral.

"Had he been ill?" As soon as she said the words, Eve held up a hand. "Sorry. None of my business."

Cole didn't like to talk about his father, ever, but somehow he knew she would understand complicated family relationships. Hers certainly were. "It's fine. Yeah, he had heart problems. Had several stents put in over the years."

"Were you guys close?"

Cole looked at her and raised an eyebrow. "Come on, Eve. I know you remember what happened in high school."

She shrugged and grabbed another handful of berries. "I do. But I hoped you guys worked that all out years ago."

"My father wasn't a forgive-and-forget kind of guy." He hated the bitterness that coated his tongue as he said the words. He thought he'd finally put the past and his father's ugly words—and actions—behind him. Apparently, not far enough.

She looked at him then, big brown eyes full of sympathy. "I'm sorry to hear that, truly. Family is everything."

He shrugged as though it didn't matter. "Depends on the family, I guess." Eager to return to their earlier camaraderie, he stepped in front of her and bent his knees. "Climb on; I'll give you a ride."

She cocked her head to judge his seriousness, then hopped up. He grabbed her legs and gave her a piggyback ride to another section, stopping to spin around every once in a while because he found he couldn't get enough of the sound of her laughter.

Once they reached the big cluster of gerbera daisies, he stopped so she could slide off his back. He had figured she'd enjoy the flowers and was rewarded with another huge grin.

"Oh, these are so gorgeous."

He plucked a pretty pink one and handed it to her with a bow and a flourish. "My lady."

She grinned and did a curtsy. "Why, thank you, kind sir."

———

Eve couldn't believe the change in Cole. Get him out in the fields and showing her around his operation and the man became someone else entirely. Gone was the anger he showed when his uncle Duane showed up. Out here, he laughed and even showed his playful side, giving her a piggyback ride and spinning her in circles. Who knew the man had a playful side? She was surprised, and found her admiration for him grow. She liked this lighter, younger-seeming Cole.

The almost-kiss had thrown her, just like the different facets of the man himself. Was this the same guy she'd known in high school?

As they neared the ranch house and her car, her cell phone rang. She glanced at the display and reality slammed into her. This was why she was here. Not to roam around a ranch flirting with a sexy rancher. She kept her voice calm as she answered. "Hi, Celia. How are things? How's Glory?"

"Can you come to the hospital?" Celia sounded concerned, but not frantic, so Eve took that as a good sign.

"Sure. What's wrong?"

"I need your help."

"Of course, but it'll help if I know what this is about."

"I'll explain when you get here. Just come. Please."

"Wait. How's Glory?"

"She's the same. This isn't about her. Not really."

"OK. Sit tight. I'll be there in a little while." Eve pocketed the phone and turned to Cole, puzzled. "That was Celia. I need to get to the hospital."

"Is Glory holding her own?"

"She said she was. She wants my help but won't say what for."

As she opened her mouth to thank Cole for his hospitality, her stomach did a sudden lurch and roll followed by a cramp that doubled her over.

"Eve? What's wrong?"

Chapter 11

Eve straightened, breathing through her mouth, trying to keep from tossing her cookies all over his dusty cowboy boots. "I, ah, I'm not sure. I might have eaten too many blue—"

She never finished the sentence as her stomach turned itself inside out, and she heaved until there was nothing left. When she slowly straightened again, Cole handed her his bandana to wipe her mouth.

"Let's get you up to the house. I'll get you some water."

He took her elbow and guided her into the spacious ranch kitchen, but ten steps into the lovely room, Eve turned to him in a panic.

"First door on the right."

She shoved past him and bolted for the room, barely making it in time. Before she could quite grasp what was going on, she was in the midst of the worst stomach upset she'd had in years.

Eventually things appeared to settle down, at least for the moment, and Eve heard a quiet tap on the door.

"You OK in there?" Cole asked. "I brought you a bottle of water."

She splashed water on her face and dried it before she opened the door. "Thank you so much." She took a sip of the water as she stepped into the hall. "That was embarrassing."

"Not sure you had a thing to do with it. But I have to ask, do berries usually affect you that way?"

"No. Never. Generally, I'm the one with the cast-iron stomach. I can eat anything, including various culinary failures I've created when trying new recipes."

"You like to cook?"

Eve managed a grin, though she knew it was a bit strained around the edges. "I do. And I eat lots of fruits and vegetables, so this is surprising."

He led her into the big living room with its thick cypress paneling, heart pine floors, and comfortably worn leather sofas. Eve curled up on one of the sofas, and Cole chose an armchair just to her right. "Did you eat anything you don't usually eat today? Were you feeling bad this morning?"

"No, nothing. That's why this is so weird. It's either one of those twenty-four-hour things, or . . ." She let the thought trail off, gauging his reaction.

Cole nodded and rubbed the back of his neck. "Or it's related to the water contamination. That's what I'm worried about."

Before she could formulate a response, her stomach cramped up again, and Eve raced back to the bathroom.

Two hours later, Eve barely had the strength to stand. She'd done the mad dash several more times, and now her skin was soaked with sweat. Cole helped her to the sofa again and covered her with an afghan when she started shaking.

"I'm sorry. I should go. If this is a flu thing, I don't want to get you sick, too."

Cole looked at her like she was an idiot. "You're not going anywhere like this. You can barely stand."

Eve heard the back door open, and a woman's voice said, "Cole? You home?"

He stood and said, "Ma, you remember Eve Jackson. She's not feeling well."

Eve had been too preoccupied the night of the band concert to do more than glance at Cole's mother. But now she noticed her high cheekbones, striking gray eyes, and thick dark hair. It was obvious she'd given those same features to her son. She leaned over and placed the back of her hand on Eve's forehead in the way of mothers everywhere. "You have a slight fever. What's wrong otherwise?"

Eve opened her mouth to answer but ended up making another dash down the hall. By the time she came back, Cole's mother was waiting for her with a plate of saltine crackers and a glass of ginger ale.

"Thank you. I'm sorry to be such a bother."

Alice held up a hand. "You will stop apologizing, right this minute. You have done nothing wrong. And my blueberries would not have made you sick." She stood, aimed a glance at Cole. "Take care of her while I rustle us up some dinner."

Cole grinned. "Yes, ma'am."

Once she disappeared, Cole took her hand again, and Eve instantly felt better.

"She's a formidable woman, your mother."

Cole's expression darkened, and he looked away. "She wasn't always." He looked back at her. "Things might have been different if she had been."

Eve waited for him to elaborate, but he didn't. But she liked the way he stroked her hand.

"I'll figure out what made you sick, Eve. Count on it."

She nodded, and a few minutes later, she felt her eyes slide closed and heard Cole whisper, "It's OK. Sleep."

———

Eve wasn't sure how long she was out, but when she woke it was dark outside. She had to run down the hall again, but things seemed to be getting slightly better. She sipped her ginger ale and ate a few crackers, then wandered into the kitchen where a light burned over the stove, surprised to see that it was almost ten at night.

She heard music of some kind and stepped onto the porch to see where it was coming from. Off near one of the paddocks, she saw Cole silhouetted against the night sky. Funny how she didn't know him well, but she knew absolutely that it was him.

She found the boots Cole had given her, though she had no memory of taking them off, slid her feet into them, and walked out to the paddock, the afghan wrapped around her shoulders.

As she got closer, she realized what she was hearing and smiled. Cole was playing the harmonica. Several of the horses had wandered over and appeared to be listening.

Eve walked up next to him, and he stopped and smiled at her. She smiled back. "Don't stop on my account. It's beautiful."

"How are you feeling?"

"Like a truck ran over me, but things are hopefully settling down." She patted her stomach, praying it was true.

"I'm sorry you had to go through that."

"It was annoying, but I think the worst is over." She smiled again. "Keep playing. It's beautiful." She laughed as one of the horses nudged him in the shoulder. "I think your audience is getting impatient, too."

He played several folk tunes and then switched to "Amazing Grace." Eve leaned on the fence and fought tears. The sound was haunting and quiet, and she knew she would hear it exactly this way in her memory from now on.

When the last strains drifted away, they stood in silence, listening to the horses shuffle, the rustle of the breeze through the trees that lined the fence.

"How long have you played?"

"Most of my life, I think. Hector taught me. He bought me a harmonica for my seventh birthday, said every cowboy needed one of his own."

"I didn't realize he'd been here that long."

"I can't remember a time he wasn't here on the ranch."

Eve thought about seeing him with Richard Blackwell and wondered if the other man had somehow purchased Hector's loyalty.

"He's a good man, and he's like part of the family." Cole's voice hardened as though he'd read her mind. "No matter what you saw, he wouldn't do anything to hurt us."

Eve said nothing. There was nothing to say. Much as she'd like to place blame, all she had was a meeting between two men. It might have been completely innocent, but she didn't think so. For tonight, though, she would enjoy the music and the man. And she would watch.

And wait.

"Would you like to go for a ride?" Cole's voice whispered near her ear, and she jumped in surprise. She hadn't realized he'd moved closer.

"Ah, thanks for the offer, but, um, no. Not tonight."

"Right. Sorry. What was I thinking? How about tomorrow sometime?"

"Um, no. See, here's the thing. I don't ride."

"As in, you don't ride because you don't know how?"

"As in, I don't ride because I'm terrified of horses."

He reared back in shock. "You? I didn't think Eve Jackson was afraid of anything—well, except bees."

She tried to make light of it. "You'd be surprised."

"Why are you terrified of horses?" He made a clicking sound, and the nearest horse stepped closer and held up its nose for Cole to rub a hand over. Eve took a quick step out of reach.

Cole murmured to the animal, and just like earlier in the barn, the horse seemed to melt under his gentle touch. It whickered softly, and Cole chuckled and rubbed between its ears. "This is Pansy, and she's lived here since I was a boy, haven't you, love," he crooned, and Pansy tossed her head like she was nodding. "Pansy wouldn't hurt a fly. You can pet her if you'd like."

He looked over his shoulder in invitation, but Eve stayed where she was, a shiver in her belly that had nothing to do with her earlier situation. "I'm good. I'll just stay right here."

His eyes grew serious. "Will you tell me what happened to make you afraid?"

Eve debated. She never talked about this. Of course, living just outside DC, it usually didn't come up in conversation. "I grew up in Chicago—housing project."

"I remember."

Eve smiled at that, surprised. "Anyway, downtown, they had carriage rides over near Water Tower Place for the tourists, like in most big cities. I was not far from there one night"—somehow she couldn't bring herself to tell him she'd been panhandling so she'd have enough money for something to eat that day—"when something spooked the horses. I think a kid threw a rock—at least that's what everybody said later—but the horses panicked just as a woman was climbing in. She fell, and somehow the horses and the carriage ran over her. It was terrifying."

"How old were you?"

"I was ten."

"That's a horrible thing to witness. Did the woman survive?"

"I snuck into the hospital the next day and asked one of the nurses. They said she would, but just barely." Eve tried to shrug as though it were no big deal. "So I try to keep my distance."

Cole nodded, then reached a hand back and tugged her forward. "Come here." He stepped out of the horse's reach and tucked Eve safely into the circle of his arms, with her back against his front. They stood that way for a long time, watching the moon peek out from behind the clouds and listening to the crickets.

Eve stood completely still for the first time in a long time and just took in the quiet of the night around her. No meetings to rush to, nowhere to be at this very moment, just the moon and the thud of

Cole's heartbeat behind her, the strength of his arms wrapped around her middle. As she stood there, she thought this might just be the most peaceful place on earth.

It was an illusion, of course, given what was happening, but for tonight, she enjoyed the peace.

Chapter 12

Eve woke to the sound of her cell phone buzzing. Sunlight streamed through the sheer curtains at the window, and she looked around, trying to figure out where she was while she groped for the phone. She jabbed at buttons and caught the call before the other person hung up.

"Hello?"

"I thought you were somebody I could trust. Somebody who would actually do what they said. I guess I was wrong." Click.

In a rush, Eve remembered the phone call from Celia the day before, along with her own promise to come right away. Only moments later the stomach plague had hit like a freight train. "Wait, no, Celia." But the line was dead. *No, no, no.*

Eve hit redial, but Celia didn't answer. She had to get to the hospital, figure out what was going on. She jumped out of bed and swayed as her head spun and her stomach did a slow roll. She gripped the iron headboard for support and took several deep breaths while she waited, hoped her stomach would settle back down.

Not quite yet. She sprinted down the hall, and after a bout of dry heaves, she showered and brushed her teeth, feeling a bit steadier on her feet by the time she entered the kitchen.

"Good morning, Eve. How are you feeling?" Alice looked lovely in a T-shirt and jeans, her hair tied at the nape of her neck in an elegant tail. "Can I offer you toast? Coffee?"

"Normally I'd love a cup of coffee, but I think I'll pass." She looked around, disappointed that Cole wasn't anywhere about.

As though she'd read her mind, Alice said, "He's in the barn. One of his mama cows is acting funny this morning." Alice plucked two slices of toast out of the toaster and set the plate in front of her, along with a glass of water. "Would you like some eggs, too? I'd be happy to cook some up for you."

Eve's stomach made menacing noises, and she shook her head. "I'd better pass, but thank you." She sipped the water. "Is it common for cows to act funny?"

Alice shrugged and looked away. "It happens."

Eve waited, but she didn't offer anything else. "I so appreciate your hospitality. I know you weren't expecting overnight guests last night."

Alice waved that away. "I love company. Besides, I don't think you were expecting to overeat blueberries when you came, either."

Eve didn't think simply eating too many blueberries had caused her distress, but she held her tongue and chewed her toast. As soon as she finished her breakfast and felt reasonably sure it would stay put, she pushed her chair back and stood. "I need to get going. But thank you again."

Alice turned from the sink and folded her hands in front of her. She looked at Eve, then away, then back again. Eve waited while she worked up the courage to say what was on her mind.

Finally she met Eve's eyes, then looked at a spot over her shoulder. "Cole hasn't had an easy life. His father . . . his father was not an easy man."

From what little Eve knew, that was an understatement.

"I respect what you're trying to do, protecting the environment and all, especially the water supply, but whatever went wrong at Althea's place and made little Glory sick, Cole had nothing to do with it."

Eve chose her words carefully. "I follow the facts where they take me, Mrs. Sutton. Sometimes contamination is unintentional, but the results are terrible, just the same."

"He didn't do this. I know he didn't. He has enough people telling him he's not measuring up. He needs you to stand with him."

Eve didn't know what to say to that. She understood a mother's passion to protect her children. Hadn't she seen Mama Rosa go all mama bear more than once when she thought one of her cubs was threatened? Eve tried for a light tone. "I'm not sure support from me would help his cause any, Mrs. Sutton. I'm not exactly a popular person around here."

"Call me Alice. You make him smile, and that matters. And as for the rest, this narrow-minded town can go pound sand and take their racial views with them."

Eve snapped her jaw closed. She hadn't expected this insight from Cole's mother. Which only proved she needed to stop making assumptions about people, just like she wanted them to quit making them about her.

An uncomfortable silence stretched over the room. Eve finished the water and carried her plate to the sink. "Thank you, again. I need to go."

When Eve glanced over her shoulder as she left, Cole's mother was still standing at the sink, wringing her hands. She had to wonder what was behind all that. There was more than what Alice had said, no question, Eve just had no idea what. And that bit about Cole needing her? Eve remembered the feel of his arms around her and found herself wishing, maybe, for one split second, that it might be true.

———

Cole came out of the barn, and a twinge of disappointment hit him when he realized Eve's car was gone. What had he expected? That she'd come find him? Wait around for him to find her? He'd expected neither. But a part of him had wondered if, when he saw her, she'd remember their shared closeness of the night before and whether it would make a difference.

A difference in what, he didn't know, and he shook his head at his own foolishness. Crusader Evie was on a mission, and when she got the bit between her teeth, there was no stopping her.

Buzz came out to stand beside him, spit off to the side. "Surprised your mama let that woman stay the night under her roof."

Why was it that every time the man opened his mouth these days, Cole wanted to punch it closed? "She took ill, was in no condition to drive."

"Her own fault she ate too many berries. Dang fool woman."

And how did Buzz know that, exactly? Cole clenched his teeth. He wasn't convinced it was the berries, but he wasn't getting into that with Buzz, either. "Need you to give Leon Daughtry a hand with the tractor today. It's running rough, and he's coming by to take a look."

Buzz spit again, looked him in the eye. "I have other things to do today."

Cole straightened and sighed inwardly. Buzz had made snide remarks and argued since the day Cole had come home. It had only been a matter of time before the hostility came to a head. Apparently, today was that day. Cole pushed his Stetson farther back on his head and met the other man's look head-on. "I am obviously not my father, a fact you remind me of often enough. But Ma asked me to run the place, like it or not. You can do what I ask, or you can pack your things. Your choice."

Cole kept his gaze steady. Finally Buzz gave a short nod and walked away. "Hank is probably spinning in his grave, the way you're running this place into the ground."

Cole let him go and shook his head. Did Buzz know Hank had mortgaged the place to the hilt and borrowed from Blackwell to pay for his medical procedures—after he'd cancelled his health insurance? No way was he explaining a single word of that to Buzz. His father's best friend might have a heart of gold, at least according to Cole's mother, but right now he was nothing but a huge pain in Cole's backside.

Cole heard the tractor fire up and turned to go. One battle won today. Only ninety-nine more to go.

———

Eve rushed into the ICU waiting area, determined to find Celia and apologize. Given how alone Celia seemed, Eve figured the young woman had been abandoned by enough people in her life. Eve didn't intend to be another. She scanned the room, but it was empty. She walked to the nurses' station and asked about Celia.

"She went with the baby to her room."

"You mean Glory is out of the ICU?"

"They moved her to room 126."

"Oh, thank you so much." Eve hurried down the winding corridors, finally arriving at the right room. She tapped lightly on the door and poked her head in. "Celia?"

The young mother jerked awake from where she'd been sleeping in a chair beside her daughter's crib. "Go away."

Eve tiptoed into the room and took a moment to glance at Glory. She looked so tiny in the big crib, but her skin was definitely less blue. She breathed a quiet prayer of thanks and turned to Glory's angry mother. "Please, Celia, let me explain, OK?"

Celia studied her and finally gave one jerky nod.

"I didn't blow you off, truly. I was standing by my car when you called, and before I could get in, my stomach cramped up like it's never done in my life, and I spent the rest of the night fighting all kinds of intestinal ugliness."

Celia jumped up. "Then why are you bringing your germs here? Go, get out. Now!"

Eve's heart dropped to her stomach. Oh, sweet Jesus, she hadn't even thought about being contagious. "I'm sorry. I'm so sorry. Please, step outside and tell me what you were going to last night."

Instead of answering, Celia made frantic flapping motions with her hands. Eve understood and slipped out of the room. She stood in the hallway, her head against the concrete blocks, and silently berated her own stupidity. How could she have been so focused on explaining herself that she'd not given a single thought to Glory's health and what horror she could inadvertently be bringing her? A silent tear slipped down her cheek, and she angrily swiped it away. *Please God, don't let me have made this sweet baby even more sick.*

Eve wasn't sure how long she stood there, beating herself up, before the door to Glory's room eased open and Celia slipped out.

Her hair was tangled and matted, and her clothes looked like she'd been wearing them for days.

"I'm sorry—" Eve began, but Celia just shook her head.

"You were sick. Fine. Whatever. But if you made Glory worse . . ." Her voice was thick with tears, but she swallowed hard and her expression darkened. "You say you want to help people, but you need to think before you do stupid stuff."

Eve wanted to defend herself, but she couldn't. Celia was absolutely right. "What did you want to tell me yesterday, Celia?"

Desperation filled the young mother's eyes. "Dr. Stern said my well tested just fine. But then they did a test on Glory and found nitrates in her system."

Eve's mind raced with possibilities. If the well water tested in the acceptable range, the nitrates had to come from somewhere else. "Since they ruled out a heart issue as the cause of her blue baby syndrome, I would expect them to find nitrates in little Glory's system. Too many nitrates can cause it, especially since little ones can't process them like adults."

"Yes, but then this lady from the department of children and families showed up and started asking all these questions, like she thought

I somehow made Glory sick on purpose." Her voice rose. "What kind of crazy person would do that? How can they think I hurt my baby?" She burst into tears, and Eve wanted to pull her close, but decided she'd better not, just in case she really was contagious. Instead, she rubbed Celia's back while she cried.

After a few minutes, Celia pulled back and wiped her eyes.

"I don't believe for a second that you tried to hurt your baby, Celia. No way. But it's possible you gave her something contaminated without knowing it. You feed her formula, right? Nothing else?"

"Yes, I tried to nurse her for a while, but then I ran out of milk. But I'd never hurt her."

Eve wrote down the name of the formula Celia had been using, but before she could ask more questions, Celia looked up and down the hallway, as though making sure they were alone. She leaned closer and said, "I don't know if it matters, and maybe he has a really good reason and maybe not, but I've seen Buzz Casey riding a horse from Sutton's Ranch out past our place and over by Blackwell Farms, lots of times. He's always alone, and it's always really late at night when he goes by."

"Do you think he did something to your well? Did you see him do anything?"

"I don't know if he did or not. But one time, I saw him riding up and then he disappeared for a while before I saw him again. He could have easily come onto our property and done something."

"You were up late with Glory?"

"Yeah, babies don't sleep too much at night."

Eve smiled. "Thank you for telling me this. I'll see what I can find out." She paused. "Would you like me to stop by your place and pick up some clothes, or food, or anything for you?"

"No thanks. I'm good."

"I'm glad Glory is out of the ICU."

"Me, too."

Eve's phone buzzed. "Excuse me." She waited until Celia went back inside the room before she answered. "Hey, Sasha, what's up?" As she spoke, she started walking back toward the entrance to the hospital.

"Where did you spend the night?"

The blunt question raised all of Eve's hackles. "I'm sorry. Since when do I answer to you?"

Sasha sighed. "We went over this the other night, Eve. We stick together until we figure out what's going on. So where were you? We were all worried sick. I lost track of the number of times I tried to call you."

Eve grimaced. She hadn't even glanced at her missed calls this morning; all her focus had been trained on Cole. And Celia. "Sorry. I really wasn't trying to worry anyone. I was out at Sutton Ranch and came down with the worst food poisoning I've ever had in my life. I couldn't go anywhere. I ended up sleeping in a guest room."

Sasha hesitated, and Eve knew she was fighting the urge to lecture. Instead, Sasha asked, "Are you feeling better now?"

"Much. I stopped by the hospital, but I'm thinking that was a mistake. If this is somehow the flu and not food poisoning, I don't want to risk anyone getting it, especially Mama. Or baby Glory."

"How is little Glory?"

"She's out of the ICU, and her color is starting to get better, so that's a relief. How is Mama?"

"She's holding her own. Her color is getting better, too, and the infection around the port is starting to clear up. Hopefully, she'll be able to go home soon. Pop is with her."

"Is Blaze OK?"

"As far as I know. Why? What's going on?"

"Do you know this boy who picks her up for school?"

"Boy? What boy?"

Eve sighed. "I'll take that as a no."

"I thought you were taking her to school."

"Nope. She says she has a ride."

"Not liking this. Jesse and I will check on it."

"I'll see what I can find out, too."

"So, do you want to go for a boat ride tomorrow evening? I thought maybe you could invite Cole, too."

"I don't want you playing matchmaker, Sash."

"Who said anything about that? It's just that he's part of this investigation, right, and we don't really know him at all."

"You don't fib any better than I do, sis."

Sasha sighed. "Right. So, truth. Yes, we do want to get to know him, know if he's good people or not. And you could use a man in your life."

"I'm only here for a little while, Sasha. I don't have time for a relationship."

"Who said anything about a relationship? I'm thinking mild flirtation, maybe a few dates, that kind of thing. You need to get out more, Eve."

"I do get out. All the time. My calendar is always booked."

Sasha snorted. "Picketing some poor farmer or business is not what I'm talking about."

"Hey, shared interests and all that. Don't knock it."

"So how about it? Boating tomorrow night? You'll invite Cole?"

Eve thought it over. She didn't have the same love for the water that Sasha and Jesse did, but a ride out in the evening sounded lovely. She hadn't done that in too many years to think about. "You'll invite Blaze, too? We can find out more about her mystery man."

"I'll take care of it. Are you coming home?"

"Heading that way. Be there soon."

The whole way back to the marina, her thoughts drifted to Cole and the way he stroked and murmured to the animals in his care. She shook her head. Obviously Sasha had a point. She clearly needed to get out more.

Chapter 13

When Eve got home, she stopped by the bait shop to say hello to Sasha and Jesse, let them see that she was in fact fine. Bella came up and pranced in greeting, so she spent a few minutes giving her some love, too.

Jesse looked up after ringing up Safe Harbor Marina mugs for a family of tourists. Eve wandered over, picked one up. "These are new. They look great."

"Blaze's idea," Sasha said. "She designed them in one of her classes, too."

Eve looked from Sasha to Jesse. "I'm impressed."

"You don't look too bad," Jesse commented.

"Stop, you'll make my head swell with your compliments."

He grinned and wrapped an arm around Sasha when she slipped in next to him. "Glad you're OK. Any idea what caused it?"

"Either something I ate—which could possibly be too many blueberries—or I had the twenty-four-hour stomach flu." Since she was trying to stop making premature accusations, she didn't mention the possibility of contamination, since Cole was still checking on that.

"Who had blueberries?"

"Cole showed me his vegetable fields, too. They're growing enough to sell to some local restaurants."

Jesse nodded. "Smart to diversify and add some cash crops besides just the cattle."

"What's his mother like? She still lives on the ranch, right?"

"She's lovely, and was very welcoming having a stranger show up on her doorstep and end up staying overnight."

Jesse nodded, and Eve raised an eyebrow. "The captains have anything to say about Alice?"

Jesse rubbed a hand over his face, expression serious. "They say Hank was a harsh man and that she seemed to fade into the background behind him. Whether there was more to it than that, no one has said."

"She said Cole has had a hard life, and he needs me on his side." The words slipped out, and Eve instantly wanted to call them back.

Sasha leaned against the counter, crossed her arms, and grinned. "Interesting. And why did she say that, exactly?"

Eve couldn't meet her eyes. Anything else she said would be taken all wrong. And besides, she wasn't ready to talk about Cole and the strange feelings he stirred up in her. They were too new, too unsettling.

She shrugged and headed back to the house, her mind jumping from Cole to baby Glory and back again. While she tried to think, she fixed sandwiches and brought them back to the bait shop for Sasha and Jesse. She spent the next few hours organizing inventory, her mind still spinning. She was staring off into space when the screen door banged open and made her jump. Blaze clomped inside in her black boots. Bella woofed a greeting and got petted and rubbed behind the ears.

"Heard you spent the night with Cole Sutton."

"Actually, I spent the night at the Sutton ranch. And where did you hear that?"

Blaze looked from Eve to Sasha to Jesse. "Isn't that what I just said? Kids at school were talking about it. Someone saw your car parked there all night."

Eve rolled her eyes. "Gotta love the Safe Harbor grapevine. Actually, I either ate too many blueberries or had the twenty-four-hour flu, and I was too sick to drive home."

"You sure someone didn't poison the berries?"

Eve froze at the blunt question. She had to remember Blaze was frighteningly smart. "Cole's looking into every possibility." She kept her eyes on Blaze and ignored Sasha's start of surprise.

Blaze nodded. "I'd be looking for poison. Just saying." She grabbed a pack of chips off the counter and headed for the door. "I have homework. Are you making supper tonight, Eve?"

"Sure. I'll be up in a little while to figure out our options."

Blaze stopped, one hand on the screen door. "How's Mama Rosa today? Is Pop with her?"

Sasha smiled. "She's getting stronger every day. She's not dehydrated anymore and the infection is clearing up, so things are looking up. She'll be home soon."

Blaze rolled her eyes. "When will you stop treating me like I'm five, already?"

The door banged shut and Sasha grimaced. "I so want her to be able to be a kid, to protect her from the hard stuff."

Jesse put his hands on her shoulders. "I think she's proven over and over that she's one smart cookie. We need to give her credit for that, and for being stronger than she looks."

"She shouldn't have to be; that's what I'm saying."

Eve walked over, gave her sister a hug. "I get it. I want to make it easier for her, too. But she's more like us than we want to admit: tough and independent and with a big chip on her shoulder."

"Right. No more babying. Got it."

"I'll call the hospital. See you guys in the morning."

"Don't forget to ask Cole about tomorrow," Sasha called after her. Right. As though she'd be able to think about much else.

———

After she and Blaze ate a simple spaghetti dinner, Eve left Blaze to clean up while she marched out to the marina. She gathered her courage and dialed Cole's number.

"Sutton Ranch." He sounded tired.

"Hi, it's Eve Jackson."

"How are you feeling, Eve Jackson?"

"Much better, thanks. So, um, I was wondering if you were busy tomorrow night? Sasha and Jesse want to go for a boat ride after supper, and they invited you, too."

The silence went on long enough that Eve wished she'd never said anything. "Never mind, if you're busy or whatever, it doesn't matter—"

"I'd love to go. Thanks for the invite. Just give me details."

She did, and then there was another awkward pause. She had no idea what to say next. When would she stop stammering like an idiot around him?

"I'll see you tomorrow night, Eve. I'm looking forward to it."

After he disconnected, Eve stood there with the phone in her hand, grinning like an idiot for way too long. She finally shook her head and dialed the hospital. "Dr. Stern, please."

"I'm sorry, but Dr. Stern is making rounds. Would you like me to transfer you to his voice mail so you can leave a message?"

After Eve agreed and the call was transferred, she said, "Dr. Stern, this is Eve Jackson. Celia said her well came back with acceptable nitrate levels, but that you found nitrates in Glory's system. Cole Sutton is having his ranch wells tested, but I'm asking if you'd please have the health department test those at Blackwell Farms, too, because of their proximity to Celia's cottage. Thank you so much."

Eve stayed up way too late in her slant-roofed bedroom, hoping Dr. Stern would call her back, but he never did. About ten o'clock, she tried to call Cat, but her sister didn't answer. Eve still wasn't sure what was going on in Cat's life, but all of the possibilities scared her. Had Cat gotten into trouble with drugs? She didn't even want to think it, but that would explain her gaunt features and nervousness. Of course, that could be from something else, too. Still, the fact that Cat didn't *want* anyone to know was the part that really worried her.

She tossed her phone on the bed and used its hot spot to get an Internet signal for her laptop. Maybe she should get Internet installed. Blaze probably needed it for school, and it would be cheaper than a hotspot.

But for tonight, she researched food poisoning and reactions to blueberries, and the latter clearly said that eating too many could result in the runs. So she could rule out a simple blueberry overdose at least.

On her yellow legal pad she wrote: *How did little Glory get sick?*

If Celia's well tested in the normal range, the nitrates didn't come from there. So where had they come from?

An online search of the formula company did not show any recalls. She did a larger search for any kind of formula recall and came up empty there, too. She made a note to call the formula company in the morning, just to be sure.

But if not through the well or the formula, what was left?

People. Someone else who might have given little Glory water or formula that was contaminated with nitrates. Richard Blackwell's name came to mind first, because he'd made no secret of wanting the Daughtry property to expand his own operation, but even if she could picture him being that horrible, she couldn't see him offering a bottle to Glory and Celia being OK with that. It was too much of a stretch. Same with Buzz Casey—though she'd have to see if she could find out more about his late-night riding habit. She dismissed Hector, too, because she didn't think he knew Celia and Glory very well. Though she did make a note to see if she could find out what he and Blackwell had been talking about. She wondered what he'd say if she asked him outright.

Eve gnawed on her pencil. What about Celia's mother, IdaMae, and her uncle, Leon Daughtry? What reason would either of them have for doing such a thing?

She tapped the pencil on the pad. Nothing. They'd have no reason at all, since it seemed IdaMae wanted to sell the property and Leon didn't. Making Glory sick wouldn't help either of them, that she could see. And they both seemed to love little Glory. Eve couldn't picture them deliberately causing her harm.

She hopped up and started pacing, careful of the low-hanging beam. The floor creaked with every pass, and she flopped back down so she wouldn't disturb anyone else in the house.

There had to be something she was missing. Could the nitrates have gotten into little Glory's system through bottled water? She'd ask Celia, though she didn't think she bought water.

Eve pulled the article off the dresser and reread what Avery had written in the *Gazette*.

Maybe the library archives was a good place to get a sense of previous water issues and get a better feel for the local situation. Mrs. Robertson, the librarian, had always been a fount of information—as well as gossip. Eve was betting she still was.

With a plan of sorts in place, Eve crawled into bed, her dreams filled with horses galloping toward her and Cole's strong arms rescuing her at the last second.

———

The next morning, Eve walked into the library and headed straight for the checkout counter and the birdlike older lady behind it. "Good morning, Mrs. Robertson. How are you?"

Mrs. Robertson looked up and put on the half glasses that had been dangling from a rhinestone chain around her neck. "How may I help you?"

"I'm Eve Jackson; I used to live in Safe Harbor."

No spark of recognition lit her eyes, which surprised her. Mrs. Robertson looked over her shoulder as though she was looking for someone, then leaned closer and patted Eve's hand. "That's nice, dear. Safe Harbor is a nice little town. Most of the time," she added in a low voice, before she resumed scanning the room.

When she said nothing more, just plucked at the buttons of her white cardigan, Eve's concern grew. This was not the feisty lady she remembered. "Mrs. Robertson, is everything OK?"

She seemed startled by the question. "Of course, dear. Why wouldn't it be?"

"I was wondering if you happen to have back issues of the *Gazette*?"

"Of course. This is a library. Follow me." She hurried over to a small room in the back and indicated both a computer and a microfiche machine. "The more recent editions are now on the computer. One of our teenagers puts them on there for us; I have no idea how all that works. The older editions are on microfiche. Was there a particular year you were wondering about?"

Out of curiosity, Eve asked for her senior year of high school. Mrs. Robertson expertly loaded the microfiche machine, but she didn't chatter like she used to. As soon as it was loaded, she left without a word.

Eve stared after her and then scrolled through the microfiche until she came to the articles dealing with Candy Blackwell's death. There were quite a few photos of the popular cheerleader, and Eve enlarged them, reminiscing over many familiar faces. She saw Cole's triumphant grin as he stood with his arm around Candy after a winning football game, surrounded by other players and locals. Sasha and Eve were in a few group shots. Even Leon Daughtry showed up in one of the photos, sitting in the stands with the football alumni. She pulled out her cell phone and took pictures of several of the photos.

She scrolled further and cringed as she skimmed the article about what the paper called "The Calf Caper." Seeing Cole's arm in a cast and the pictures of the dead calf brought all the guilt rushing back. She closed down the machine, went to the computer, and scanned the recent editions of the *Gazette*, even though she'd read them online in DC as soon as they were published. There was nothing that gave her any inkling of why someone would want to harm little Glory Daughtry or Celia. She did a search on Celia's name, thinking maybe Glory's father had something to do with it. Celia had never mentioned his name, and neither had anyone else in town. He was a long shot, but she'd have to ask Celia about him, too.

By the time she left the library, she didn't have any more info than when she'd arrived, except a worry that Mrs. Robertson's mental state was becoming fragile.

———

Later in the evening, Sasha barged into their former shared bedroom and surveyed the damage with her hands on her hips. Then she laughed at the piles of clothes on the bed. "It's a boat ride, Eve, not a fancy ball. Just throw something on or we'll miss the sunset."

Eve eyed the silky top she held and tossed it on the pile. It had been one frustrating day. She looked at the pile of discarded clothes. "I give up. What should I wear?"

Sasha dug through the pile and tossed her a pair of linen shorts. Then she went to her old dresser and rooted around until she found a T-shirt and tossed that to Eve, too. "That'll work. Let's go."

Eve eyed the teal-colored Safe Harbor Marina T-shirt, then looked at Sasha, realizing she was equally casually dressed. "Right." She pulled it over her head, slid into the shorts, and reached for a pair of heels.

Sasha yanked them away from her hands. "No. This is not a yacht. It's a boat. I have an extra pair of flip-flops on the porch. Wear those."

Eve hesitated, though she knew Sasha was right. But wearing flats made her feel at a disadvantage, and she didn't want to feel vulnerable next to Cole's impressive height. Sasha poked her head back in the door. "Come on, Eve. Blaze is getting impatient. I invited Nick, too."

As Eve stepped onto the dock, Cole turned from where he'd been talking with Jesse. His eyes swept from the top of her humidity-frizzed hair to the painted toenails in the borrowed flip-flops, and a slow grin spread over his face. That grin did funny things to her insides, and since she couldn't harness even one coherent sentence, she simply stood there and smiled back like an idiot.

Jesse looked from one to the other, winked at her, and said, "All aboard. Let's do this."

In no time they were settled on the *Clipper*, a beautiful speedboat that was Jesse's newest project, and headed out to watch the sunset over the Gulf of Mexico. The warm breeze caressed her skin, and the Gulf shimmered like a mirror. The yellows and reds streaked the sky and tinted the clouds. Eve looked around and sighed. She'd forgotten the simple beauty of watching the sunset from a boat.

"Did you guys pack any snacks? I'm starving," Blaze said.

"Of course you are, never mind that we just ate." Eve rolled her eyes and grinned. "I put some cheese, crackers, and grapes in the cooler for everyone."

"Wow, fancy. Thanks." Blaze rooted around, and before she stuck her hand in the plastic container with the cheese, Eve took it from her, whipped out the melamine plate she'd brought along, and arranged everything prettily: grapes in the middle, cheese and crackers in a circle around them.

Sasha raised an eyebrow. "Feeling like royalty now. Thanks, Eve."

Eve didn't know how to respond, so she simply nodded and sat back down while everyone helped themselves.

Cole fixed some for himself and settled down beside her. "You went to a lot of trouble. It tastes great."

Eve was still trying to stop bobbing her head like an idiot when Cole's cell phone rang.

"Hey, Hector. What's up?"

Eve watched his expression darken.

"You're sure it was deliberate? It couldn't have broken?" He listened a moment, then said, "Thanks, Hector. I appreciate your letting me know."

Cole hung up and turned to her. "Hector says he figured out why you got sick." His glance took in the group. "Like I told Eve, we use a combination irrigation-and-fertilization system, called fertigation. Someone tampered with the valve that controls the flow and flooded the field with nitrates." He paused, took off his Stetson, and rammed a hand through his hair. "He says it had to be deliberate. There's no way it would have happened by accident."

"So someone tried to poison Eve?" Indignation rippled through Blaze's voice.

"No one knew I was coming that day. Even I didn't know."

Blaze looked at Cole. "Did you eat berries, too?"

Cole sent Eve a rueful grin before he answered. "I did. But not quite as many as Eve."

Eve bit the inside of her cheek. She couldn't argue that. She'd eaten far too many.

Jesse looked at Cole. "They were trying to destroy your crops."

Cole heaved out a tired sigh. "Looks like it."

"Besides people who want to buy the ranch, who else has a grudge against you, Cole?" Nick asked. "And why?"

"I don't know who. As for why?" he shrugged. "Like you said, several people want to buy the ranch, and I'm not selling."

"Be careful, Eve." Jesse pierced her with a look. "You have enough on your plate with the whole blue baby situation."

"How is baby Glory?" Sasha asked. "Is she getting better?"

"Definitely, though they found nitrates in her system. Interestingly, Celia's well tested in the normal range for nitrates." Eve scanned her family. She didn't want them to worry, but she could use their opinions. "So, I'm thinking that maybe Glory's nitrates and the sabotage at Cole's are related."

Nick met her eyes, nodded once, as though he'd been thinking the same thing.

"Makes sense," Jesse said. He turned to Nick. "You thinking Blackwell?"

"He seems the most likely suspect, but . . . ," Eve interjected with a shrug. "I don't know what to think right now."

"Let me look into it," Nick said firmly, and changed the subject. "I thought you'd want to know we're still trying to get information out of Captain Demetri about the drug smuggling that was going on here at the marina, but he won't say much."

Eve watched Jesse wrap his arms around Sasha's shoulders and felt a shiver slide over her own skin, too. It would be a long time before any of them recovered from the knowledge that Captain Roy, someone they'd known forever, had tried to kill Sasha.

A while later, as they were heading back in, a small jon boat came racing toward them on the diagonal and cut into the channel right in front of them. Jesse muttered as he expertly maneuvered the *Clipper* to keep from running over the much smaller craft.

"That's Hector and Leon," Cole said, frowning. "You'd think Leon knew how to handle a boat better than that."

They followed the other boat back in, and Jesse slid the *Clipper* neatly into her slip just as the sun slid below the horizon. While Sasha and Jesse secured the boat, Cole hopped onto the dock and marched over to the other men, Nick right behind him.

"What were you doing, Leon? Jesse almost ran into you."

Leon straightened and propped his fists on his hips. "Then he should quit speeding in the channel." He turned back to the boat. "I have things to do." He grabbed a cooler and fishing rod and headed toward his truck. Behind him, Hector turned to Cole and shrugged. Nick followed Leon to his truck, and it looked like he delivered a stern lecture, based on his intensity and Leon's defensiveness.

Cole shook his head, and then he and Eve watched the last rays of sunshine dance on the water as the others drifted away. "It's beautiful out here." He looked over at her and smiled. "Everything is."

Eve felt a flush creep up her cheeks, but she managed to say, "I'm glad you came."

Blaze came bounding down the dock. "Eve. Eve. You gotta see this."

"What is it? What's going on?"

"Hurry up."

Eve exchanged a glanced with Cole and followed Blaze back toward the house. Blaze stopped in front of Eve's car and waved a hand to indicate the windshield.

Eve stared, and a shiver slid down her spine.

This time, someone had left her a dark-skinned Barbie doll with a noose around its neck and a note that read, *You're still not listening.*

Chapter 14

By the time Nick had packed up the evidence and issued stern warnings to be careful and let him handle it, it was late. Eve tossed and turned, trying to get the image of that noose out of her head, but nothing seemed to work. So she was surprised when she rolled over and realized it was morning and she had just enough time to make breakfast for Blaze before she left.

"Guess you didn't sleep much, huh?" Blaze asked. "You look terrible."

Eve grimaced. "Thanks so much."

Blaze shrugged. "Somebody is really ticked off at you. Don't be stupid." She scooped up her backpack. "Thanks for breakfast."

Eve's stomach seemed to have settled down, and her hands had stopped shaking from last night, so after breakfast she checked in with Sasha and headed for the hospital.

She found Mama sitting up in bed, fumbling with a scarf. Mama's bald head made her want to cry, so she pulled up her best smile as she walked into the room. "Good morning, Mama." She leaned over to kiss her forehead, then said, "Let me help with that."

She wrapped the scarf securely and helped Mama ease back afterward.

"I heard you were sick from eating too many blueberries."

Eve grimaced, unsure how much to say. "It appears so. But they were so good."

"Have you figured out yet what made little Glory so sick?"

"Not yet. But I'm working on it."

"I heard you're spending time with that handsome Sutton boy, too. It's good he's finally come home. You could use a good man in your life."

"I'm only here for a short while, Mama. And besides, I'm not looking for a man in my life."

"Well, you should be. I'm not getting any younger. I want to live to see my grandchildren."

"You will, since Sasha seems to have that covered." She stood, kissed her cheek. "I need to go." The door swung open and Pop walked in, carrying a sandwich. She gave him an awkward hug on the way out.

Pop whispered, "Be careful," in her ear.

She found Celia down the hall, looking much better. She had obviously stopped home for a shower and clean clothes.

Eve leaned over the crib and watched as Glory slept, her little arms and hands twitching every so often as though she was dreaming. "She looks good. I'm so relieved."

"The doctors say I might be able to take her home soon." Her voice hardened. "As long as DCF doesn't decide I've been poisoning my baby."

"They have no reason to think that. I'll talk to them, see if I can help." She paused, thought about how to phrase the question she'd been running through her mind. "Celia, do you know of anyone who might try to sabotage your water in order to get the property?"

"That wouldn't make sense. You want good water if you're buying or selling. What are you saying?"

"What if someone was trying to devalue the land, so it was worth less?"

"And they could buy it cheaper," Celia finished. "I hadn't thought of that. But I have no idea. Mama and Uncle Leon are divided on it, but I can't see either of them doing something like this."

"I can't, either. Let me know if anyone else comes to mind, OK?"

"Sure, but . . ."

Eve stopped, turned back into the room. "What is it?"

Celia stood, wrung her hands. "You're going to think I'm crazy."

"No, I won't. Just spit it out."

"I think someone is following me."

Eve saw the worry in Celia's eyes and kept her voice level. "What makes you say that?"

"Every time I go down the hall to the bathroom, or go get a soda, or go to the cafeteria, I get that weird feeling between my shoulder blades, like someone is staring at me. You know what I mean?"

"I do. Have you ever seen anyone behind you when you looked back?"

"No, but a couple of times it seemed like someone ducked around a corner just as I looked."

Eve's nagging sense of unease grew. "Be careful, Celia, OK? And if you do see anyone, let me know. Don't go anywhere alone."

Celia sent her a sad smile. "I live alone, and my mama is too busy at Mr. Blackwell's to do more than stop by once in a while, though I do appreciate it." She sighed. "I will try to be careful."

Eve left the hospital, thinking. Did the fact that IdaMae and Miss Althea both worked for Blackwell Farms matter to the investigation? She wasn't sure, but she carefully scanned the hallways on her way to the parking lot. She didn't spot anyone watching little Glory's room, but she understood exactly what Celia had been saying. She was sure someone was watching her, too.

———

An hour later, Eve pulled up at Celia's cottage and grabbed the groceries she'd purchased in town. She staggered under the weight of the cardboard box she'd filled with food, but managed to get everything inside in one trip. She swallowed hard when she opened the almost-empty pantry. She knew about poverty, had grown up in it in Chicago. She and her mother had lived in the notorious Cabrini-Green housing project, where her mother turned tricks to put food on the table, and Eve had learned to panhandle by the time she was ten. She understood going to bed hungry, but that wouldn't happen to Celia, not if Eve could help it. She knew Celia waited tables at the Blue Dolphin, but she also knew they wouldn't, couldn't hold her job for long. While Celia spent her days at the hospital, she had no money coming in.

Eve heard a vehicle pull up and walked to the sagging front porch to see Cole exit his black pickup truck. "What are you doing here?"

He shrugged and walked up the steps until they were eye to eye. He was still two steps below, but she found she liked looking into his gray eyes.

"I saw your car turn up the drive and wanted to be sure everything was OK with Celia and the baby."

"They were both holding their own when I left there a little while ago. Celia is hoping Glory will be released soon, so that's good."

Eve turned and walked back into the kitchen, with Cole on her heels. He eyed the empty box, the food neatly stacked on the shelves. "That was nice of you."

Embarrassed, Eve turned and closed the cabinet door. "I've been there. I just wanted to help, that's all."

"There's far more to you than meets the eye, Evie the Crusader."

She turned in surprise and saw something that looked very much like admiration in his eyes. Unsure how to react, she shrugged and scooped up the box. "Celia has had it rough. Just giving her a bit of hand up, that's all."

"Yes, but you didn't have to. And you did it when no one else was around to see it."

Why did he keep talking about it? It made her uncomfortable. This was how she'd been raised. Mama Rosa and Pop were always taking food over when there was a birth, or death, or medical emergency in town. Why would he assume she wouldn't follow that example? "Didn't your mama raise you to do the same when you see people in need?"

A slow flush passed over his skin. "She did, though I admit I haven't always been as diligent about it."

"Then you should be. It's part of that whole 'love thy neighbor' thing."

One side of Cole's mouth tipped up. "Yes, ma'am. Now you sound like my mama." He stepped closer. "You're good people Eve, no matter what they say."

Her eyes widened, and she planted her hands on her hips. "Really? And just what are they saying about me now?"

Cole scrubbed a hand over the stubble on his jaw, and Eve forgot her irritation with him long enough to wonder what it would feel like to run her palm over his cheeks, feel that stubble against her skin. Then she remembered what he'd said and pierced him with a look. His discomfort reminded her of a little boy caught with his hand in the cookie jar.

"That didn't come out right at all."

Eve laughed; she couldn't help it. "No, I don't expect it did. But I want to know, what are they saying about me in town this time?"

The tips of his ears reddened, and Eve's smile faded. He didn't even have to say the words. She knew. They were talking about her past and her mixed-race looks, and her meddling ways. Just like they always had. She couldn't say why the small-minded attitude still pierced her heart so deeply, but it did. Some things, it seemed, never changed, no matter how much time went by.

Eve waved a careless hand. "Never mind. I'm pretty sure I know. Same song, second verse."

"It's not true, though. None of it. You're good people."

She met his gaze head-on. "I appreciate the words, but they don't change a thing. Besides, you don't know me at all. For all you know, everything the gossips are spreading around town is absolutely true."

Before she realized he'd moved, he'd taken two steps across the small kitchen and placed both palms on the counter, effectively caging her in. His gray eyes stayed steady on hers, and in them she saw the same pull of attraction she was fighting for all she was worth. She couldn't get involved with anyone. She was only here in Safe Harbor for a little while. She'd promised Mama Rosa she'd figure out what made Glory sick—and then she'd make those responsible pay before she headed home. She couldn't let Cole's killer smile, rock-hard body, or, more importantly, everything that made the man himself so attractive derail her from her path. Her life and work were in DC, where she'd made it her mission to keep what had happened to her mother from happening to anyone else. In the nation's capital, working with Braddock Environmental, she could make a difference on a large scale, bring national attention to issues and lawbreakers, get lawmakers involved in changing things for the better. That kind of change couldn't happen from a little town like Safe Harbor.

She knew, deep in her heart, that if she righted enough wrongs and blew the whistle on the bad guys enough times, the guilt over her mother's death would finally stop gouging her heart like a sharp spike. But she wasn't there yet. She hadn't done nearly enough to make up for letting her die.

"I may not know everything that's happened in your life since you left Safe Harbor, but I know you, deep down where it counts."

"I, uh—" She had no idea how to respond. Back in high school, he'd been the jock who ignored her and had girls flocking around him. She didn't know anything about his life since then, but she knew the way he treated his mama, and the way he treated his animals.

Their eyes met and held, and Eve found herself leaning toward him just the slightest bit, wanting him to wrap her in his arms again as he had that night at the ranch. She'd felt safe there, like she never had before in her life. Which was fanciful and ridiculous, but there it was. His eyes, when they searched hers, touched something deep inside her, an answering loneliness she understood too well.

His look intensified, and she knew he was going to kiss her. She panicked and blurted out the one thing she knew would push him away. "I'm not sure I know you at all. The guy I knew in high school didn't impress me much."

He stepped back, and Eve saw a flash of pain in his eyes that vanished so quickly she was sure she'd imagined it.

"I guess I deserved that. I was a cocky kid for whom everything came too easy." He paused. "Until it didn't. Then I grew up fast."

"I'll never be able to undo what happened to your arm. But I'll always be so sorry it happened."

"I know. It wasn't even losing the scholarship that was the worst."

"You mean when your father kicked you out."

"Yes. I lost his approval along with everything else."

"He kicked you out for getting Candy Blackwell pregnant." She didn't believe it, but watched his reaction.

"No, he kicked me out because I wouldn't marry Candy the day she and Blackwell showed up at the ranch with that story."

Eve heard what he wasn't saying. "Was it true?"

"That Candy was pregnant?" Regret filled his expression. "The autopsy confirmed it."

Eve's instincts went on high alert. "But were you the father?"

"That was the consensus."

"Just answer the question, Sutton. Were you the father of her baby?"

He rubbed a hand over the back of his neck, then met her look head-on. "No."

Eve scrambled to process the implications. "Then who was?"

He sighed. "I tried to get her to tell me. She wouldn't say."

"But your father still didn't let you come home?"

"It never came up. As far as he was concerned, the fact that I didn't immediately agree to do my duty made him ashamed of me. He said I was no son of his."

Eve thought of all the years that had passed since then. All the missed opportunities for father and son. "What made you come back?"

"Ma needed me." He said the words flatly, as though no more information was needed, and apparently, nothing more was forthcoming, either.

"What are you two doing in here?"

Eve spun around, surprised to see IdaMae standing in the doorway, arms folded over her ample chest.

Eve wondered how long she had been there, how much she'd overheard. "IdaMae, I didn't hear you arrive. I was just at the hospital and Celia said they may be releasing Glory soon, so I came by to make sure she had a few essentials."

IdaMae straightened, eyes narrowed. "We don't take no charity. We take care of our own."

"Of course you do. I was thinking this was more on the lines of a welcome-home gesture is all."

IdaMae nodded once. "Then thank you kindly for stopping by. Now, if you'll excuse me."

"Ma'am." Cole tipped his hat and held the door so Eve could precede him back to their vehicles. Eve tried to remember the last time a man had held a door for her. Except for Pop or Mr. Braddock? Never. She'd thought the gesture had ended with their generation. It was nice to know chivalry wasn't entirely dead.

Cole leaned over her car's door frame while she waited for the air conditioner to cool things off a bit. He looked up at the house, where IdaMae leaned against a porch post, watching them.

"Not throwing out the welcome mat, is she?"

Eve shrugged. "I'm not really surprised. If they're trying to sell off this property, contaminated water is not helping their chances. And since she thinks I'm the problem, well . . ." Eve let the thought drift away.

Cole's expression changed, became unreadable. "You certainly do turn things on their head, Evie the Crusader." He paused. "And not always in a bad way, either. Drive safely."

He slammed the door and slid into his truck. Eve spent the whole drive back to town trying to figure out what he meant by that, exactly. And whether it had anything to do with the look in his eyes when he said it.

Chapter 15

Eve headed back toward Safe Harbor, her mind whirling. She had no idea what to do about Cole and the way he made her feel. So she did what she always did when she was unsure: she focused on her work.

She needed answers, and the best place in town to catch up on all the news had always been Beatrice's Hair Affair.

Main Street wasn't busy this time of day, so Eve parked two doors down and walked over. Her always-out-of-control curls could use a quick trim. With a side of information.

When Eve walked through the door of the old-fashioned beauty shop, all conversation stopped. Miss Beatrice, who'd been old when Eve first came to Safe Harbor, looked up from the perm she was rolling. Next to her, two white-haired ladies were getting their hair cut, and at the far end of the shop, another woman was getting shampooed.

"Help you?" Beatrice asked.

Eve fluffed her mop of curls and smiled. "I could use a quick trim, if you can squeeze me in."

Beatrice looked uncomfortable. "We're pretty busy right now."

Undaunted, Eve forged ahead. "I understand. I can wait a bit."

"She can wait until you-know-what freezes over," one of the customers muttered.

Another customer chided the other woman, and Beatrice scowled in the woman's direction. "Sit, then, and I'll get to you when I can."

"I appreciate it," Eve said. She selected an outdated magazine and plopped into one of the uncomfortable plastic chairs, pretending to read.

The other voices carried clearly. "I don't know what she thinks she's doing, stirring up trouble again, right here in our town. Wasn't what she did to Cole Sutton bad enough?"

Eve heard every word as they discussed her in low tones, but she wouldn't give them the satisfaction of letting on that she'd heard them. Instead, she said brightly, "Did you hear that little baby Glory Daughtry has been moved out of the ICU?" Eve figured that was common knowledge, but it might get the old biddies to talk about something that might actually help her.

"My niece's sister-in-law works over at the hospital and said the little one's color is much better."

"Thank you, Jesus," another lady murmured, and Eve wondered how Jesus felt about the way they gossiped, but decided that was between them and God.

"Celia said they may be letting her bring baby Glory home soon," Eve said instead.

"That surely is good news," Miss Beatrice said as she led her customer to the back and sat her under the drier. She came back and motioned Eve to her chair.

Eve let out a little sigh of relief when Beatrice snapped the cape around her shoulders and spun her to face the mirror. Their eyes met in the glass, and Beatrice touched the end of Eve's cloud of hair. "Ah, how much did you want me to take off?"

Beatrice had cut Eve's hair since she first came to Safe Harbor, but she'd always seemed ill at ease, even though she did a great job. Eve hid her frustration. Her hair, like everything else, was a hybrid of her mother's African American genes and the no-doubt Caucasian genes she'd gotten from the man who'd had sex with her mother. She couldn't call him her father, since that gave him a place in her life he'd never held. From what her mother had said, his sperm was his only contribution to her life. Eve had no name, nothing but *Unknown* on her birth certificate where the father's name should be. In her mind, Pop Martinelli was her father, strained though things were between them right now.

Eve took pity on the hairdresser. "How about you just trim half an inch all the way around. Enough to get it a bit more under control." She smiled at the other woman, trying to put her at ease enough to go back to talking.

Beatrice nodded and got to work. "Heard you caused quite a stir at Sutton Ranch, getting all up in Cole Sutton's face," she commented as she started trimming.

This wasn't exactly what Eve wanted to talk about, but she'd go with the flow. "I was trying to get information, that's all."

"Heard you was making accusations is what I heard." This from the station next to them.

Eve met the other woman's eyes in the mirror. "A little baby almost died. I want to know why; don't you?"

The woman shrugged. "Things happen, sad though it is. But we don't need no outsiders stirring up trouble."

"We're talking about a baby's life here, and that should merit more than a shrug from us, I think. Besides, I grew up here. I don't consider myself an outsider," Eve returned, irritation growing with every word the woman uttered. Really? Nothing more than a shrug?

"Shows what you know. We don't need you here. Never did. All you've ever done is stir up trouble."

Now she'd crossed the line. Eve had opened her mouth to put the woman firmly in her place when Beatrice laid a hand on her shoulder and gripped it, hard. A warning that Eve really didn't want to heed.

"I think what Dora is trying to say is that we're all concerned about little Glory," Beatrice said. "Have the doctors figured out what caused her to get sick?"

"I heard it was her heart." This from Dora. With a superior sniff.

Eve exchanged a glance with Beatrice in the mirror. "Actually, they ruled that out. They believe the cause is water contamination." She glanced around the shop. Apparently, word that Celia's well tested clean had not made it here yet. Time to get a reaction. "Does anyone know if somebody in town would have a reason to contaminate the water on Miss Althea's property?"

A collective gasp went up, though whether it was from the question or her audacity in asking such a thing, Eve could only guess.

"Contaminate the water? This is Safe Harbor. Nobody would do such a thing here," Dora exclaimed.

"I wouldn't put it past that Sutton boy," another woman called from the back of the shop, sitting up after her shampoo while the beautician wrapped her wet hair in a towel. "He might have been the quarterback, but the way he treated that poor Blackwell girl . . . well, you just can't trust somebody like that."

Eve wanted to set the record straight so badly her teeth itched, but that wasn't her story to tell.

"Heard his ranch is in trouble, too," said the other customer, fluffing her newly teased do.

"I know Alice's brother has offered to buy the ranch, but his nephew claims he ain't selling," Dora added, looking smug as this news brought raised eyebrows all around. "Alice mentioned it at Bible study the other week. Duane says the land should be his, that Alice's husband should never have been able to get his hands on it, even though her daddy sold it to her and Hank, fair and square, years ago."

Eve digested that news while Beatrice kept snipping. Apparently, IdaMae and Leon weren't the only siblings in town disagreeing about family property.

The woman from the shampoo bowl settled into the only empty chair and kept talking while the hairdresser rolled her hair onto curlers. "I think maybe Leon Daughtry might have done it."

Dora scoffed while the other ladies gasped. "Leon? Why would he do that? I heard he and IdaMae got an offer from a big-box store that wants to build a distribution center on the property. He wouldn't do a thing to jeopardize a deal like that."

Eve focused on the woman getting her hair rolled. "Why do you suspect Leon?"

All eyes turned the woman's way, and she flushed. "I didn't say I suspected him, just that I thought he could have done something like that. I've heard he has a mean streak when he doesn't get what he wants."

Several ladies dismissed that, but it caught Eve's interest. She wanted to question the woman further, but by the time her hair was done, the other woman was long gone.

As she stood at the register to pay, another woman came in, saw Eve, sniffed, and then spun on her heel and walked out. Beatrice grimaced as she handed Eve her change. "They have long memories—and football is like a religion in this town. Just give them time to figure out you've grown up."

Since Eve wasn't sure she'd ever "grow up" enough to stop being passionate about things she believed in, she simply shrugged. "I'll try."

Beatrice nodded. "Let me know if there's some way I can help."

Eve left the shop, stunned to have found such an unlikely ally. Beatrice was the same age as most of the biddies who were talking trash about Eve.

She climbed into her Prius and had barely made it out of Safe Harbor on her way to Cole's when a shiny black pickup truck appeared in her rearview mirror. At first she thought it might be Cole, but this was no work truck. This one gleamed like a showroom special. Eve had turned up the radio, flipping stations, looking for something to soothe her jangled nerves, when the truck rammed into the back of her car.

What in the world? Eve gripped the wheel and hung on, fighting to keep the car on the road.

She glanced in her rearview mirror, trying to see the driver, but he was wearing dark glasses and a ball cap, and she couldn't make out a thing.

She sped up and hugged the shoulder, hoping he'd pass, but he stayed on her bumper. Her heart pounded and fear raced through her. Why was he doing this?

He sped up and rammed the back of her little car again. The taillight shattered, and Eve started praying out loud as she fought to keep the car on the road. Thankfully there was no one coming from either direction on the two-lane highway who might get hurt. "Dear Jesus, help me, please."

He rammed her a third time, and this time, she heard glass shatter as the car went into a slow spin. Eve went with the spin, overriding her body's urge to turn the wheel the other way. She held her breath, praying she'd made the right choice, and the car finally stopped spinning and regained traction on the road.

She risked a glance in her rearview mirror and saw the truck getting closer again. She didn't know how many more times she could do this.

Just then, another car came around the bend from the opposite direction. But not just any car—a Safe Harbor police SUV. Eve flashed her brights at him just as the truck eased back behind her, a nice, normal distance away.

She looked in her rearview mirror, hoping the cop would turn around, but he just kept going. The truck passed her in the opposite lane and she squinted to read the license plate, but there wasn't one. Eve looked in her rearview mirror and saw that the cop had finally done a U-turn, and he pulled up behind her and turned on his lights.

She pulled over and hopped out of her car. "Thank goodness you're here. That man—"

"Get back in your car, ma'am. Now."

"What?" Eve waved off into the distance. "That truck just tried to run me off the road. You have to go after him."

"Ma'am. I won't ask again. Get back in the car."

Eve studied his expression, but it was the gun he'd pulled from his holster that really got her attention.

She raised her hands above her head. "OK, I'm going. But you don't underst—"

Another police SUV swung in behind the first, lights and sirens on. The siren thankfully shut off, but the lights didn't. Eve glanced behind her as she climbed into her car and groaned when she realized who it was. She did not want to deal with Chief Monroe.

But she did want to know what he was saying, so she rolled down the window and strained to listen.

"What's going on here, Buddy?"

She could almost hear the young cop swallow from here. "I'm not sure yet, sir. I pulled her over for a busted taillight, but she came flying out of the car like a crazy woman, so I told her to get back in the car."

Eve rolled her eyes as she looked in her side mirror and watched the chief swagger up to the car, hands on his utility belt. He leaned closer and Eve grinned, just because she knew he'd hate it.

"Eve Jackson, why are you giving my officer a hard time?"

Eve wanted to roll her eyes, but she knew it would only make things worse. The truck was long gone by now, anyway. The best she could hope for was to get him to look into it. "Look, Chief, someone was following me out of town and tried to run me off the road. That's why my taillight is smashed. He smashed it. And the shattered glass in the back is from some canning jars that broke from the impact. I tried to get Officer Friendly to go after him, but he wouldn't listen."

The chief pushed his hat farther back on his head, then turned and walked to the back of her car and took a long look at her taillight. He took his sweet time coming back, glancing at the broken jars in her back seat, and then he pulled a little notebook from his shirt pocket. "What kind of truck did you say it was? Did you get a license plate?"

"It was black. Big. Sounded like maybe it was diesel. It didn't have a plate."

He raised a brow. "I'll do what I can, but you know that's not much to go on."

Eve fought to keep her frustration in check. "Right. If he tries to run me off the road again, I'll be sure to let you know."

Her sarcasm went right over his head. "You do that. Don't go looking for trouble, though. Your sister caused plenty of that recently."

Did he realize how close she was to slapping him upside the head for being a complete idiot? She locked her hands together to fight the impulse. "Sasha did what she had to do. I wouldn't call that trouble—"

"I'm not talking about Sasha, although she's caused her fair share."

"Wait. Who are you talking about, then?"

"The new one. The one with the pink hair."

"Blaze? What kind of trouble is Blaze in? What happened?"

"Seems she picked a fight after school, just outside the Sunrise Café. Early release today."

"Is she OK? Did she say what happened?"

"She wouldn't say, but it looks like it was three to one." He grinned. "She's a scrapper, that one." Then he sobered. "But the others said she started it."

Eve didn't doubt it, but there had to be more to the story. "Thanks for letting me know, Chief. I need to get going."

"Not so fast, young lady; there's still the matter of your taillight. I could write you up for that."

"Oh, for crying out loud, Chief. Seriously? The guy in the truck smashed it. I'll call the rental place right away, OK?"

He scratched his head, then finally nodded. Eve drove away, slowly, and that's when the shakes set in. Someone had tried to run her off the road! The fact that the chief didn't take her seriously could mean several things. Either he didn't believe her, which was her first thought, or he knew something she didn't.

The second possibility made her teeth start chattering, too, and she gripped the steering wheel until her knuckles turned white. She knew people in town thought she'd cried wolf too many times, or made mountains out of molehills, as the clichés went, but when something was wrong—or even if she thought something was wrong—she acted. Simple as that.

Because she'd learned the hard way that if she didn't do anything, bad things could happen to the people she cared about. She didn't need any more guilt in her life.

On that long-ago night in Chicago, if she hadn't left when her mother told her to, or had come back sooner, Eve was convinced she'd have been able to save her mother's life. Maybe called 911, or found one of her mother's friends who would help her. Maybe even found her English teacher and asked her for help. Or better yet, never given her mother that nasty-looking water to begin with. But her mother had been so sick, and so thirsty, begging for water. Eve should never have left her mother alone. But she'd been terrified that the man who'd been there earlier would come back and try to take her away. Her mother had feared the same thing and made Eve promise not to come back until morning.

So Eve had hidden in a dark alley, a cold, terrified thirteen-year-old, huddled in the smelly shadow of a dumpster, until the sun came up. But by the time she crept back to their roach-infested apartment, her mother was gone, her body already cooling. Eve had been too late, and all the recriminations in the world wouldn't bring her back and wouldn't atone for Eve's indecision.

She wouldn't let her own fears hurt anyone else, ever again.

Chapter 16

Eve raced home and slid to a stop beside Jesse's truck. She grabbed her purse and hurried into the house. "Blaze. Where are you?"

"Kitchen," Sasha called, and Eve burst through the kitchen door and stopped short.

"Oh, ouch. That looks bad." Eve tried to hide her shock. Blaze had a cut on her cheek, and when she pulled the ice bag away, it showed one eye was almost swelled shut. The other was half-closed. "Geez, I hope the other guy looks way worse."

Blaze tried to smile but winced. Eve glanced at her swollen lip and understood.

Jesse paced the end of the kitchen. He stopped, jabbed a finger in Blaze's direction. "There were three of them." He shook his head, visibly trying to control his anger. Then he grinned. "But Blaze pounded them into the ground."

Eve slid into the chair opposite Blaze. "Can you tell me what happened?"

Blaze glanced at Sasha. "Hurts to talk."

Sasha nodded, turned to Eve. "So, from what Blaze said, she was walking downtown when she got into an argument with a couple of kids from school. Things got heated, punches were thrown, and one of the shop owners called the police. By the time Nick got there, Blaze was the only one left standing." She grinned, then sobered. "Not that fighting is the way to solve anything," she added, as though she'd just remembered to act parental.

Eve held up her hands in a time-out gesture. "There's a whole boatload of information you're leaving out." She looked steadily at Blaze. "What started the argument?"

Blaze shrugged and wouldn't meet her eyes. "Just some kids being dumb. Staying stupid stuff."

"What kind of stupid stuff?"

Another shrug. "Just stuff." She tried to push back from the table, but Eve reached over and grabbed her hand.

"Tell me. Please."

Blaze looked away, then turned back. "They were saying stuff about you, OK? That you were some kind of environmental nut job, and this town would be better off without a mixed breed like you stirring up trouble."

Eve sat back, shocked. But then, people had been calling her both of those things for a long time. She just hadn't realized they'd passed those terms on to their children, though she shouldn't be surprised. Not in Safe Harbor. No, the surprise was that Blaze had stood up for her. A lump formed in her throat, and she swallowed it back.

"If you start blubbering, I'll punch you, too," Blaze warned, and Eve laughed, breaking loose from the emotional quicksand.

"No blubbering. Promise." But Eve leaned forward and grabbed one of Blaze's hands again, hanging on even when she tried to pull away. "But I do want to thank you. No one's ever gone to bat for me that way. Ever. It means a lot."

"Though fighting is never a good idea," Sasha added quickly, and both Blaze and Eve rolled their eyes.

"Yes, Mother," Eve said. She looked at Blaze. "She's right, but I do appreciate what you were trying to do."

A blush slid over Blaze's bruised face, and she shrugged it off. "Family sticks together. Right?"

"Right." Eve smiled, then looked to Sasha and Jesse. "Did the cops say what happens next?"

"Probably nothing. There was a lot of he-said-she-said about what happened."

"I know what happened," Blaze added. "They were total jerks."

"Will this affect your scholarship applications?" Eve asked. She knew Blaze had already started applying for scholarship money to help pay for college when the time came.

"If I don't get the money, I'll stay here. Take care of Mama. I should probably do that anyway."

"No," all three adults said at once.

Sasha leaned over, touched Blaze's shoulder. "You need to go to school, live your life. Jesse and I will be here to help Pop take care of Mama. That is not your job."

Blaze looked at Eve, who nodded. "She's right. You need to—"

The old-fashioned phone on the wall jangled and interrupted what she'd been about to say.

Jesse stalked over and answered. "Martinellis'." He looked over at Sasha. "She is. Who's calling?"

Sasha raised her eyebrows, but Jesse only shrugged. "Hold on a minute." He covered the receiver with his hand. "It's a woman, asking for Sasha Petrov. Not a voice I recognize, but her accent appears to be Russian."

All the color leached from Sasha's face, and Eve automatically squeezed her hand before she reached for the receiver. Jesse immediately stood behind his wife and put his hands on her shoulders, and Eve's heart melted at the obvious love they shared. A twinge of envy slid over her, a quick stab of longing to be loved like that. Cole Sutton's face burst into her mind, but she shoved all of that aside and focused.

"This is Sasha Petrov." Eve watched Sasha stiffen at whatever the woman was saying, then reach back for Jesse, who immediately wrapped both arms around her middle and pulled her securely against his chest. Sasha's hand on the receiver tightened until the knuckles turned white. Eve watched, shocked, as a single tear slid over her sister's cheek. Sasha, the fearless one who never cried. Eve exchanged worried glances with Blaze, who looked equally shell shocked.

The caller talked for several minutes, but Sasha didn't say a word. Finally she croaked, "I'll have to think about it." She swiped at the tears that were now streaming down her face. "OK. Let me get a piece of paper."

Eve hopped up and grabbed the grocery list from the fridge along with a pencil. Sasha glanced up, her eyes filled with confusion, and wrote down a number, carefully repeating it before she said, "I'll call you in . . . in a few days."

She hung up, and Jesse turned her into his arms, holding her as she sobbed soundlessly on his shoulder.

Eve gripped Blaze's hand as they waited, and for once, the teen didn't pull away. Something was seriously wrong, but what?

Finally Jesse pulled back and wiped the tears from his wife's eyes. "Tell me."

Sasha looked from him to Eve and Blaze, and a tremulous smile slid over her face. "That woman says she's my aunt Sophia, my mother's sister. She saw the picture of me after I won the Tropicana, and she recognized my name, and the mariner's cross I was kissing in the picture. She said . . ." Her voice trailed off, and she had to start over. "She said she's been looking for me for years and had thought she'd never find me again."

"That's fantastic news," Eve said, and hurried over to hug her. When Sasha didn't respond, Eve pulled back. "Isn't it?"

Sasha shrugged and swiped at her tears again. "I think so. I don't know. It's so weird, you know? I'm not sure what to do with it. She said she's in Tampa."

Jesse turned her to face him. "You don't have to do a thing. Not today. Just give it a little time to sink in. Then decide what to do next."

Eve wasn't sure what to say, so she was relieved when Pop walked in. "What happened to your taillight?"

All eyes turned to Eve. She didn't want to add to their worry, so she shrugged and said, "I need to pay closer attention when I back up. I'll call the rental company. How's Mama?"

He smiled, but Eve saw the effort behind it. "She is as stubborn as ever, my Rosa. The doctor says she is improving."

"Of course she is." Eve smiled and patted his arm, then grabbed a plastic trash bag and went outside to her car. After she called the rental company, she carefully scooped the shards of glass into the bag, hauled the shop vacuum from one of the sheds, and cleaned out the inside of the car.

She put the vacuum back and wandered out to the dock. With her back against one of the pilings, out of view of the house, she loosened the grip she'd kept on her emotions. Someone had deliberately tried to run her off the road. She wrapped her arms around herself as the shakes increased.

As the trembling eased, her resolve hardened. It would be tempting to quit, but she knew that was exactly what whoever had done this wanted. She wouldn't stop until she figured out who was behind this. That driver wouldn't scare her away. She owed it to little Glory—and her own mother's memory.

Chapter 17

The next morning, Blaze moved like an old woman, but insisted on going to school. "I'm not hiding out at home," she snapped, and headed out the door, again picked up by the mystery boy she didn't want to talk about.

Eve stopped by the hospital to check in with Mama Rosa and reassure her that Blaze was fine. They all knew the grapevine would deliver the news if they didn't tell her first, so Eve had called her last night and told her a kinder, gentler version of what happened.

"Good morning, Mama. How are you?" Eve kept her smile in place as she leaned over and kissed her cheek, the skin paper thin. She sat in the chair by the bed and gently took Mama's hand.

"Good morning, my Eve. How is Blaze?"

"Like I told you last—"

Mama waved that away. "You didn't want me to worry. But I'm a mother. Worry is part of the job. Now, how is she, really?"

Eve sighed. "She's moving slow this morning, but she insisted on going to school."

"That sounds like Blaze. She reminds me of you at that age."

Eve grinned. "I think you're right." She pointed to the colorful scarf Mama held. "Where did you get that? It's lovely."

"I found it on my bedside table this morning. There was no card."

Eve picked it up and expertly wrapped it around Mama's head, then tied a pretty knot. "There you are. You look ravishing."

They chatted until Mama tired, so she left. She ended up at the local Stuff Mart, trying on jeans and T-shirts. It felt weird to wear the kind of clothes she hadn't worn since she had left for college and decided she would dress for success, always, even if the clothes came from a thrift store. Now here she was, back in the clothing of her childhood, and she wasn't sure what to think. The ladies' fitted T-shirts felt good against her skin, and she couldn't deny she liked how she looked in the jeans, especially with the boots from Cole. She felt like she'd gone back in time and been reborn, all at once.

She made a face at her reflection. She was being ridiculous, and she had far more important things to worry about. She checked her watch and hurried to the checkout. Celia said they were releasing Glory from the hospital soon. But Eve still didn't know the cause of the contamination. She had to get another look at that well, check the water filtration system, too, before the baby came home.

———

Cole dismounted and led his horse to the watering trough. He walked over to the hose beside it, turned it on, and took a long swig, wiping the back of his hand across his mouth. His mother kept trying to talk him into carrying a water bottle around, but he'd been drinking from this hose since he was a kid. Had done it all through sports at school, too, until Evie the Crusader launched a campaign to install a water fountain. He smiled at the memory, then looked up as a cloud of dust caught his eye.

A prickle of awareness warned him a split second before he saw Eve's little rental bump down the road and turn off into Celia's driveway.

She was driving too fast for the dirt road, which wasn't slowing her down a bit.

Something was up. Cole swung back up into the saddle and turned his horse in that direction.

———

Eve pulled to a stop in front of Celia's house and hurried up the porch and into the house, compelled by a sense of urgency she couldn't explain—but had learned not to ignore. Once she stood in the kitchen, she looked around. Was there a chlorination system? She hadn't even checked. She shook her head at her own stupidity and forced her mind to focus.

If the well had tested in the acceptable range for nitrates, but Glory had nitrates in her system, then either someone had fed them to her deliberately—which Eve couldn't fathom—or they came from the formula, which was doubtful. Eve had called the manufacturer of the brand Celia used, and they had confirmed there were no recalls.

But powdered formula was mixed with water, so that left checking the taps in the house and any chlorination system between the well and house for breaks or tampering. And it had to happen today. There was no way Eve would let Celia bring the baby back here until they knew for sure that everything was OK.

She didn't have time to waste. Instead of trying to get the water-testing company to finally get out here, she'd get her own water sample and either overnight it or drive it to the lab in Jacksonville herself.

She opened cupboards, banging doors as she searched for a jar or something to put the sample in. Thanks to whatever idiot tried to run her off the road—and her hands still wanted to shake from that—she didn't have her own jars.

Down in the bottom, at the very back of the last cabinet, she hit pay dirt. A multipack of canning jars with screw-top lids. That would work just fine. Of course, she'd rather have sterile jars to make sure there wasn't anything already there to contaminate the sample, but this would have to do. She didn't have any other options.

Now she needed a cooler. The samples had to be kept on ice. She searched around in the small lean-to off the back porch and found a crumbling Styrofoam cooler that would have to do.

She filled the cooler with ice cubes before she took a sample from the kitchen and another from the bathroom. After what happened yesterday, she knew the threats were escalating. She had to act fast. She labeled both with a piece of paper towel held on by tape she'd found in a drawer.

She went back outside and put the cooler in her car, but she couldn't leave yet. She got one more jar and started looking around the property. Did they have a chlorination system? If so, where was it?

She went back to the lean-to and spotted a small closet she'd missed in her earlier hurry. Sure enough, the chlorination system stood inside.

"What are you doing, Eve?"

Eve spun around so fast she almost dropped the jar, fumbling it before she got a solid grip. Cole sat next to the porch astride a beautiful paint, Stetson on his head, leaning on the saddle horn. Dressed in a snug blue T-shirt and jeans, he looked good enough to eat, looking at her with that wicked twinkle in his eye. Not that she would let herself notice. She had priorities. Things to do. *Yeah, yeah, yeah,* her brain said. *But look at those gray eyes.*

Eve opened her mouth to make some sophisticated remark, or at least something that didn't sound completely idiotic, but nothing came out. She went with a smile, while her brain scrambled for something to say. She took a deep breath. "I need to get the water inside the house tested. Today. Celia said they're talking about releasing Glory."

He dismounted and hopped up onto the porch, leaned in to look at the system. "Looks pretty standard; nothing appears to be corroded or leaking."

Eve leaned into the doorway beside him, glad suddenly of the denim and boots she was wearing, especially when he let his gaze roam over her outfit before coming back to rest on her face. He grinned, and Eve was reminded why all the girls in high school, herself included, had followed him around like lovesick puppies.

"You look good, Evie. We'll make a country girl out of you yet."

Eve grinned back, feeling like she was that high school girl again. Then she looked up at the shelves above the system and sucked in a breath. Cole followed her gaze to the gallon-size commercial fertilizer jugs sitting on the shelf.

He lifted each one. "All look to be full."

Eve turned back and went down the steps to what had once been a vegetable garden a short distance away. An empty jug lay on its side among the weeds. Eve studied the jar, tried to keep her thoughts from running away with her. Could this be the source of the contamination? Commercial fertilizers were full of nitrates. Had some gotten into the chlorination system?

The silence was broken by a sound she knew too well.

"You've got ten seconds to turn around and tell me what you're doing on my land. Hands in the air while you do it."

Eve and Cole exchanged glances as they raised their hands and turned to face Leon Daughtry, who had his shotgun aimed at their midsections.

"Well, dang, Cole. What are you doing trespassing on my land?"

Eve chanced a glance at Cole, who didn't look the least bit worried, despite the weapon pointed at them. "Meant no disrespect, Leon. We heard that Glory might be released from the hospital today and wanted to see if we can't get this water tested, make sure she doesn't get sick again."

"They already tested the well. There's not a thing wrong with it."

"That's true. But we thought it best to check the system, too."

"That's not necessary. I'll thank you to move along."

"Now, Leon, we just—" Cole began, but Eve interrupted.

"You can't seriously just let that baby come home and risk her getting sick again, maybe dying?"

At the last, Leon blanched, but he didn't lower the gun.

Eve went on in a rush, desperate to convince him. "If we know for sure the water is fine, that would be a relief, wouldn't it?"

"It'd be a relief to see you two get off my land."

"I heard tell that big-box store is interested in buying the property," Cole said, and Eve watched Leon closely, looking for a reaction.

"All due respect, Cole, this here is none of your concern."

"Except your niece almost dying," Eve shot back. What was wrong with this man?

"We don't know why she got sick. Nobody does. Now get off my land."

Suddenly Leon turned as an aging Oldsmobile pulled into the drive. He lowered the shotgun, and his urgency became a palpable thing. "Get on out of here, right now. I won't tell you again."

Eve climbed into her car and took the long way back to the ranch. She didn't want to get stuck again. She passed IdaMae's car, and the woman did not look happy. Cole got back on his horse and took a shortcut across the fields back to his place.

What was that all about?

She wasn't sure, but she smiled when she saw the cooler sitting on the passenger seat. All she had to do was get these samples to the lab within twenty-four hours.

Chapter 18

By the time Eve pulled up in front of the house at Sutton Ranch, Cole was waiting for her. He'd unsaddled his horse, and Hector was leading it into the barn.

"So what do you make of all that?" Eve asked the minute she got out of the car.

"Hard to say. It could be as simple as wanting to protect their privacy."

"How well do you know Leon?"

"Not much better than I did when you and I were young. He keeps to himself, even when he's here."

"Doesn't seem overly close to his niece or his grandniece. I've only seen him at the hospital once."

"Don't be too quick to judge. Not everyone can deal with hospitals."

Eve planted her hands on her hips, instantly in his face. "Nobody likes hospitals that I know of. But when your people are there, you show up. It's that simple."

Cole sent her a half smile. "It's that simple for you. Not for everyone."

Eve wondered if he was talking about himself, but she didn't have a chance to ask.

"Did you get any samples from the house?"

"I did. One from the kitchen and another from the bathroom. Do you know a local lab to take them to? Otherwise I need to overnight them to Jacksonville."

"I think I can sweet-talk someone. But before I do, I want to take a sample from my pond, which I forgot about when I had the wells tested." He shook his head and gestured toward the barn. "Want to come? We can ride over."

Eve narrowed her eyes. "You know I don't ride."

Cole's eyes were serious. "I know, and with good reason. But we can replace those bad memories with some good ones."

He waited and Eve was tempted. Oh, she was tempted. To spend time with Cole. To lose the fear.

But in the end, her heart wouldn't stop racing, and her palms were sweating just thinking about climbing onto the back of one of those animals.

"I can't. I'm sorry."

"No problem, Evie. We can walk over."

Everything inside her jumped at the chance, but they had to get that water to the lab. "Will we have enough time if we walk?"

"You have the right shoes this time, so yes, we'll have enough time."

He took her hand, and Eve walked beside him along the edges of the pasture, past the blueberries. Eve merely raised a brow when he offered her some. "I've had my share, thanks."

Within a few minutes, they reached the pond, shaded by a huge hundred-year-old live oak tree that stood nearby. Spanish moss dripped from it, and the whole thing looked like a postcard. A few head of cattle roamed nearby, cropping grass, while one of the cows stood belly deep in the water, cooling off. Eve laughed.

But before she said anything, Cole started muttering and stomping around.

She hurried over. "What's wrong?"

He stopped, blew out a breath, and pointed to some withered plants lying at the edge of the pond. Several more floated in the water, near the cow. He waded in and fished them out, showed them to Eve. "This is poison hemlock. Any cow eats that in the early gestation period, and you get calves like the ones my cows have been birthing."

Eve leaned closer to study it. Then she looked around, but didn't see where it came from. "Does it grow around here?"

"It can, but we check for it on a regular basis. Actually, we just checked a few days ago. This wasn't planted. Someone brought it here."

Eve heard what he wasn't saying. It was probably someone he knew well, one of the men who worked for him, most likely.

"You think someone deliberately fed it to your cattle."

He nodded once, scanned the area, his jaw clenched.

"Is that cow pregnant?" Eve pointed to the bather.

"She is."

"What will you do now?"

Cole studied the nearby tree. "I'm thinking a motion-activated wildlife camera is the first step. That way, it will record if someone else comes out here. I'll call Nick, too. But right now let's get this water sample and get out of here." He pulled out the jar they'd brought along and scooped some of the water into it. He also put some of the hemlock in another jar and capped that, too. "I'll get this to Pure Water, Inc., this afternoon, have their lab test it."

"I'd like to come along, if you don't mind. They sure didn't want to deal with me, but I have some questions they might be able to answer."

"They better talk to you. We have to figure out who's doing this." Eve heard the anger in his voice and saw the way he wrestled it under control. He paused. "I didn't have time to eat lunch. Do you want to grab food afterward?"

Eve raised an eyebrow. "You sure you want to be seen around town with the environmental wacko?"

Cole gave her that lopsided grin that always went straight to her belly. "I think I can handle it. And I think we could both use a break from all that's been happening."

When they got back to the ranch, Cole held the door of his truck open for her, and they drove straight to the lab about twenty miles away.

When Cole gave the woman at the reception desk both their names, Eve wanted to kick him. The woman's wide-eyed glance said she'd recognized Eve's name, but she made no other comment. She had them fill out paperwork, processed their payment, and assured them they'd have results as soon as possible. When Eve pushed for specifics, the woman merely repeated what she'd said. But as they turned to leave, the woman glanced over her shoulder before leaning closer to Eve. "My sister waits tables at the Blue Dolphin with Celia Daughtry. I'm glad you're trying to find out what made Glory sick. I'll do what I can to rush this."

Dumbfounded, Eve smiled and whispered, "Thank you so much."

Eve looked at Cole once they were back in the truck. "Wow. That was a nice change."

"Let's hope she can get that rush on it." Cole massaged the back of his neck as they headed toward the highway, shaking his head. Finally he asked, "Want to check out the new barbecue place that just opened?"

"Hm. That's where they serve dead animals, right?"

Cole laughed. "Right. Of course you're a vegetarian. How could I not have thought of that? OK, where else would you like to go?"

"The new place is fine. I'll just order a salad. They have that, right?"

"I'm pretty sure they do, even in this little hick backwater."

The unexpected edge to his voice surprised Eve. "That was a joke, albeit a lame one."

"Sorry. Just me. I forget sometimes that you're a big-city gal, used to all the finer things."

"I grew up here, just like you did."

"But you didn't stay, did you?"

"No, but neither did you." She held up a hand when he started to protest. "No offense intended. I know you were kicked out. True, I never felt part of the town, but I didn't exactly try to fit in. I was too busy trying to right wrongs."

"Like the 'calf caper'?"

Eve chanced a glance at his face, relieved to see a teasing grin. "Among other things."

His expression turned serious. "I heard people gave you a hard time because of the color of your skin, too."

"Call me naive, but I think that part would have resolved itself eventually if I hadn't caused quite so many, um, inadvertent disasters."

"Would you ever consider moving back?" he asked as he pulled into the gravel parking lot. The building had the rustic look of an old barn, though with a sheen of newness they hadn't tried to hide. Country music blared from a set of speakers into a parking lot containing mostly pickup trucks, along with several sedans and jeeps and a few convertibles.

Eve wasn't sure how to answer. He came around and opened her door, offered a hand down. "Would you?"

"Stay?" She looked around, shook her head. "I love my family, but my life and my work are in DC."

Cole met her gaze, and a flash of something that looked like disappointment slid through his eyes before he looked away and took her elbow as they entered the building.

The young gal at the hostess station smiled warmly at Cole. "Hi, how many today?"

Eve didn't like the possessive feeling that swept over her when the young woman gave Cole a once-over that lasted far too long, in her opinion. She almost wrapped her hand around his arm in a show of ownership, but caught herself just in time. She mentally rolled her eyes at her own behavior as they followed the girl to their table.

"Thanks," Cole said when she seated them in a booth, still completely ignoring Eve.

"If you need anything at all, you just let me know," Eve purred when the hostess had left.

Cole looked up and frowned. "What?"

"Seems the Sutton charm hasn't diminished since high school."

He looked confused for a moment, then glanced at the hostess, who gave a little finger wave from her spot behind the podium. "I was just being friendly."

"I know. She wanted to get a lot more friendly."

"Not my problem." He looked uncomfortable. "Can we talk about something else?"

"OK. Do you have any more theories about what made Glory sick?"

He studied her a moment, then folded his arms on the table and leaned toward her. "How about if we don't talk about anything like that right now. Let's just pretend we're a couple out for a bite, getting to know each other."

The temptation to pretend things were normal, just for a little while, proved irresistible. She smiled and nodded. "OK, then. I heard you were in Montana. Tell me what you liked best about it."

Cole started talking, and before Eve knew what happened, they'd been moving from topic to topic, laughing. A waitress took their order, and they laughed at Eve's water and salad and Cole's pitcher of sweet tea and platter of ribs.

They were almost finished when three guys walked past their table, ranchers from the way they were dressed in Western shirts, jeans, and boots that had seen their share of work. The first one, who looked to be in his midthirties, stopped at their table, looked from Eve to Cole and back again. Eve thought they might be guys she'd known in high school, but she couldn't be sure.

"Thought you had better taste than that, Sutton," he said, "hanging out with her kind. Didn't she cause you enough trouble in high school?"

Cole was on his feet so fast, the other man backed up a step. "Keep walking, Bo. I don't want any trouble."

"Still backing down from doing the right thing, ain't you? You always were a coward."

Cole's fist lashed out so quickly, Bo didn't have a chance to respond. One second he was in Cole's face, and the next he was lying on the floor by their table. A woman nearby yelped, and the restaurant went deathly quiet. Cole eyed Bo's two friends as they started toward him. "You don't want to do that. Take your friend and go."

He didn't wait for them to respond, just turned to Eve and dropped some cash on the table. "You ready?"

Eve nodded and slid out of the bench, and they walked out to the truck in silence. Eve moved fast, hoping to get far away from there before Bo and his friends came out, but Cole put a hand on her arm. "Slow down, Eve. It's fine. They won't come after us."

"How do you know?"

"Because I know Bo. He likes the attention. His buddies generally don't want any trouble." He helped her into the truck, then came around and slid in. He looked her way as he started the truck. "Sorry about all that."

"It certainly was unexpected. Thanks for defending me." She wasn't an advocate of violence, of course, but she couldn't deny the warm fuzzies his quick defense sent to the region of her heart.

He grinned and tipped his hat. "My pleasure, ma'am."

Eve sent him a quick grin, then rubbed her neck. It hadn't hurt before, but now it was starting to ache.

"You OK?" Cole asked.

She debated whether to tell him. "Someone tried to run me off the road. My neck is a little stiff."

Cole swerved, then pulled back into his lane as he shouted, "Why am I just hearing about this now?"

She should never have said anything. "I was unaware I had to check in with you."

He muttered under his breath as he stared her down. "Don't make this something it's not, Eve. Tell me what happened."

She sighed and gave him the rundown, including the chief's official shrug and warning to stop causing trouble.

Cole scowled the rest of the way to the ranch. But when he helped her out of the truck, he met her eyes, pulled her to him, and whispered, "Don't keep things from me, Eve. It makes me crazy."

Eve stepped back, completely thrown by the caring in his eyes. She looked away, then nodded once as he walked her to her car.

The look in his eyes haunted her for the rest of the day and through another sleepless night.

———

Nick Stanton arrived just after Blaze had left for school and Eve had finished the breakfast dishes. He knocked on the front door, and Eve hurried to open it. Only folks who knew them well ventured onto the screen porch before knocking.

"Morning, Nick." She motioned him into the kitchen. "Coffee?"

He removed his hat, stood there twirling it in his hands. "Sure. Thanks."

His anxiety created some in Eve, as well. "What's wrong? Mama is OK, right?"

"She is. That's not why I'm here." He sat, and when she placed the mug in front of him, he just turned it round and round by the handle.

Finally he looked up. "It's about Captain Demetri. They found his body in the jail this morning."

Eve plopped down in a chair, stunned. "What happened? Did he commit suicide?"

Everyone knew he'd been awaiting trial at the county jail, but Eve had heard he was handling it OK.

"Somebody shanked him."

Eve gasped and covered her mouth with her hand. She knew such things happened in prisons, of course, but here? To Captain Demetri?

"Do they know what happened?"

"Not yet. And they might not ever figure it out." Nick took a sip of his coffee, then met her gaze. "He was scheduled to give a deposition this morning in the case. I find that a little too coincidental."

The implications had Eve's eyes widening. "Oh my. What does the chief say?"

Nick scowled. "The usual: How sad. We'll look into it."

Eve studied his expression. "You think he's involved somehow?" It seemed impossible. But then again, knowing two of the local captains had been involved in drug smuggling for years and years blew her mind, too.

"I'm not sure what to think. But he seems a little too quick to shove things under the rug to let me sleep nights."

"If what you're saying is even a little bit true, or that he knows the people involved, you need to be really careful, Nick. He could come after you."

Nick flashed her a quick grin. "He's already told me if I wanted to keep my position, I needed to do my job and not question things."

"He really said that? Told a cop not to question things?" Eve shook her head. Unbelievable.

"I just thought your family would want to know. Will you let Mr. Martinelli know? I know they were friends a long time."

"I will. Of course."

"By the way, I haven't had any luck figuring out who left you that stuffed cat or the Barbie. They sell them at the local discount store, so there's no telling who bought it. I know Jesse was threatened when he first got here, too. I'm trying to see if there's a connection."

"A connection? But all that was solved when they arrested Captain Demetri, wasn't it?"

Nick looked as though he was debating how much to say. "I don't think those two captains were the masterminds behind the smuggling. I think they were the delivery guys, the ones who took all the risks while someone higher up the low-life food chain actually called the shots."

Eve's mind spun as she tried to process what he was saying. "You think whoever that is will try to get the network going again, somehow."

"They might have moved it elsewhere. But if whoever is behind this is local, they'd bide their time and start again."

"You know this all sounds crazy and far fetched, right?"

Nick sighed, rubbed the back of his neck before he glanced back at her. "I know. And I'm asking you not to mention it to anyone outside the, uh, family."

Eve shivered as she remembered the Tropicana race, when Sasha had almost been killed. She would have died if not for Jesse's quick thinking. The ramifications of all that, coupled with what Nick was saying now, made goose bumps pop up on her arms. "Be careful, Nick," she repeated. "We just found you. We don't want to lose you."

He responded with an awkward smile. "Thanks. Just be careful, OK? Maybe I'm way off base here, but I don't think so."

Eve walked him out to his SUV and sighed as she watched him go. She wondered if he'd ever get to the point where he could call the Martinellis Pop and Mama. But knowing the people who'd raised you had actually kidnapped you from your birth parents? That wasn't something you got over. And since the people he'd thought were his parents were dead, he couldn't ever get their side of the story, either.

Eve went back inside, her mind spinning. She hadn't even considered what would happen to the drug network after Captain Roy's death and Captain Demetri's imprisonment. Would whoever was in charge of the operation try to recruit other smugglers?

She'd have to start paying attention, certainly warn Sasha and Jesse and put them on alert, too.

But the bigger question in her mind was whether or not any of that was in any way connected to what was happening at Cole's farm. Because something dangerous was simmering just below the surface. She could feel it.

She just didn't know what to do about it.

Chapter 19

Eve drove out to Sutton Ranch and parked in front of the ranch house, but no one answered her knock. A quick peek around back showed that Alice's car was missing, as well as Cole's truck. Of course, he could be anywhere on the ranch.

She walked over to the barn with the office at one end, but it, too, was empty. She heard voices and a tractor starting and walked over to where Hector and Buzz were talking to Leon, who had his head in the bowels of the tractor's engine.

"Good morning, gentlemen."

All three men turned to look at her, and their expressions varied greatly. Buzz looked like he'd eaten something rotten; Leon merely looked annoyed at the interruption and went back to work. Hector's face split into a wide grin.

"Good morning, senorita," he said, bowing slightly and making Eve laugh, which earned her another scowl from Buzz. "What brings you here this morning?"

"She's dogging Cole's heels, that's what," Buzz muttered, then looked her square in the eye. "The boy has enough to worry about without you following him around."

Surprised at his seeming defense of Cole, Eve asked, "I'm wondering why my being here bothers you, sir. You don't know me at all."

"I know plenty, mostly that you stir up trouble wherever you go. We have enough of that here without you causing Cole any more."

Eve decided to sidestep the accusation. "Is he here?" she asked Hector.

"No, ma'am. He went to town, said he had a meeting with the bank." Hector shook his head, obviously worried. "I'm not sure when he'll be back." He muttered something in Spanish before he turned and headed for the barn.

"So what do you think, Leon, can this old thing be saved?" Buzz stepped over next to the tractor, effectively dismissing her.

Part of her wanted to stay and keep asking questions, just to annoy the man, but she decided against it. The fact that he'd defended Cole surprised her, but made her glad, too, for Cole's sake. He needed all the help he could get if things were as bleak as she'd heard.

As she turned to go back to her car, she hesitated. Why not have a quick look around while she was here? She was convinced that Cole had nothing to do with what was going on at the ranch, but she was equally convinced that someone was behind it. She looked over toward the tractor again, deep in thought.

"Help you, ma'am?" a voice asked. Eve spun around, startled, before the man continued, "Sorry about that, Eve."

She recognized Duane, dressed in the typical Florida cowboy uniform of jeans, Stetson, and T-shirt, but he also came with the smell of liquor, the kind that seems to seep out of the skin of a heavy drinker. "Hi, Duane. I came by to see Cole, but I heard he isn't here right now."

At the mention of Cole's name, the man's demeanor changed; his expression hardened. "That one is as stubborn as his daddy, God rest his soul."

"Were you and Cole's father close?"

The man chuckled, but there was more bitterness than humor in his words. "We were, before he married my sister and stole my land."

"Stole your land?" The words popped out before she could think of a better way to ask the question.

"This ranch has been in my family for a good long while. My daddy had no business selling it to Hank."

Before Eve could ask any one of the dozens of questions crowding her tongue, Duane spun on his heel and stalked off. Alrighty, then.

Eve looked around some more and decided to check out several of the outbuildings near the fields. It was a long shot, but she figured, since the problem with the fertigation system had happened in the fields, maybe there were some answers in the nearby sheds.

She wandered over to one building and found an assortment of both well-used and long-neglected equipment, piled on the floor and hanging from hooks along three walls of the shed. She didn't see anything there that helped in any way, so she walked over to the next building. This one had a padlock on the outside, but it hung open, so she undid the hasp and pulled the door open.

This place looked far more promising. For one thing, it was larger than the other shed, and instead of tools, it held shelves and shelves of fertilizers, as well as pesticides. A tingle of excitement ran over her skin. Could one of these products be the cause of the contamination at Celia's cottage? She ran a finger over the labels, possibilities growing with every can, sprayer, and bag. Any number of these things could have caused the problem. She pulled out her cell phone and started snapping pictures. Depending on what the water testing of Celia's house showed, it would be easy enough to identify if any of these chemical compounds matched it.

This could be the clue she'd been looking for.

Hands trembling in her haste to get the evidence and get out before someone caught her snooping, she snapped picture after picture, getting more excited by the second.

Slam!

The door banged shut and Eve spun around in the sudden darkness, her phone flying from her grip. What was going on? She didn't remember any wind this morning. She dropped to the floor and felt around for her phone, but couldn't find it. Frustrated, she stumbled over to the door in the pitch blackness, hands stretched out in front of her.

When she reached the door, she pushed, trying to open it back up. It wouldn't budge. Had it swelled from the heat? She snorted at her own wishful thinking. More likely someone had locked her in. She leaned her shoulder against it and pushed with all her might, but nothing happened.

She pushed, again and again, trying to ignore the suffocating heat and the trapped feeling of being all alone in the dark.

Defeated, she leaned against the wall, panting, trying to hold the fear at bay. She had to think. Phone. If she found her phone, she could call for help.

Bzzz.

Eve froze, every nerve on high alert. It was a bee. Was he inside or outside?

She listened, and heard a second bee. Then a third.

Her heart pounded like a freight train, and sweat broke out on her skin as she heard more bees start to buzz.

They were in the shed. With her.

Her EpiPen was in her purse. In her car.

Dear Jesus, no. Please, please make them go away. Make them stop.

There was no sudden silence, no quick rescue. Instead, she felt something crawl on the skin of her arm, and she held perfectly still, even though every single protective instinct she possessed urged her to swat it away.

But she knew what would happen if she did. She couldn't risk it.

She also couldn't move, or call for help, or do anything that might make it sting her.

Because if she did, and the bee got agitated and stung her, she could be dead before help arrived.

Sweat dripped down her forehead as she felt more bees walking along her exposed skin. She could feel at least three on one arm, five on the other.

Her heart thumped so hard it hurt, so she practiced the relaxation exercises she'd learned while taking photography classes, of all things. If you controlled your breathing while holding the camera, you could hold it much steadier. And right now she couldn't shake, couldn't wipe away the sweat, and most of all, couldn't hide from her fear.

One of the bees starting buzzing around her face, and Eve knew she was near her breaking point. She couldn't hold still much longer.

Now that her eyes had adjusted to the darkness, the dark shape dancing so close to her face made staying motionless even harder.

She had to distract herself. Think of something else—anything else—but that bee. She swallowed and tried not to think about the sweat slowly rolling down the side of her face and how badly she wanted to wipe it away. She thought her jaw would crack from the pressure she put on it. Her muscles quivered with the effort and she closed her eyes, but no. That made her sway, and she couldn't risk losing her balance. Her eyes popped open, and she came face-to-face with that bee again.

Oh, God. Please help me. Please don't let me move.

How had the bees gotten in? Dumb question. It was a shed. People came in and out all the time, opening and closing the door. The how was easy.

The hard part was thinking about who had closed the door. Had it simply swung shut by itself? She wanted to believe that, but the suspicious investigator in her wasn't buying it. She'd been threatened, so someone clearly wasn't happy with her.

But if someone had done this on purpose, it had to be someone right here on the ranch.

She thought about that as she felt more bees walking along her arms. She swallowed hard. Maybe the person knew about her allergy. Or maybe the culprit just wanted to scare her. But in either case, someone knew she was in here.

Whatever the reason, Eve knew with sickening clarity that she would die if she got stung and didn't get her EpiPen.

Spots started dancing before her eyes, and Eve knew she was hyperventilating despite her best effort to stay calm. She focused on her breathing. In. Hold for five seconds. Out. In for five seconds. Out.

Just when she thought she had this under control, she suddenly lost her balance. She stepped back to catch herself, but she tripped over something and crashed against the wall of the shed.

The bees let out an angry buzz, and without thinking, Eve batted a hand in front of her face.

Instantly she felt three stings. Two on her face and one on her arm.

Her knees gave out, and she slid to the floor with her back against the wall. She covered her face with her arms and felt another sting. The tears started then, pouring down her cheeks as she battled back panic like she'd never felt before.

Oh, God. Please don't let me die like this. Please. Send Cole. Send someone to help me.

She felt the swelling start on her face, the heat and tightness. It would be only a matter of minutes before her throat closed up.

Her heart galloped in her chest, and she tried to stay calm, to somehow slow her heart rate, even though she knew it wouldn't do any good.

Her throat began to close, and she started gasping for air.

Help me. Please.

Her world went dark.

Chapter 20

Cole drove down the gravel road to the ranch, hands tight on the wheel, frustration gripping him like a coiled snake. He'd tried to get an extension on one of the loans his father had taken out and gotten nothing but a bored "I'll see what I can do" from the bank president. The indifference on the man's face had not boded well, and Cole had been tempted to grab the man by his collar and tell him that people's livelihoods were at stake while he was busy in his pristine environment gazing at neat and tidy spreadsheets.

He blew out a breath. He'd figure something out.

He spotted Eve's car parked by the ranch house, and the familiar mix of emotions whenever she crossed his mind rolled through him, which happened all too often lately. First came the kick of pleasure at the thought of seeing her, the fire in her eyes, and the way she challenged life head-on, followed by a fair amount of dread, wondering what trouble she'd brought along with her this time.

In the end, though, pleasure won out. He pulled in beside her and bounded up the steps and into the house.

"Eve?" He walked into the kitchen, surprised to find it empty. His mother's car wasn't there, either, but he remembered something about a quilting meeting in town.

He retraced his steps, poking his head into all the rooms, but she wasn't there. He went back out onto the porch and looked around. So where was she?

He headed for the barn and went straight to the office in the back. When he walked in, his uncle Duane was seated at the desk, going through drawers.

"What are you doing, Duane?"

His uncle slammed the drawer shut and sprang to his feet, clearly insulted. "Don't take that tone with me, boy. Buzz asked me to find the receipt for the last set of tires we put on that old tractor. See how long it's been."

Cole ignored that for now. He might have been doing exactly that, but his uncle's guilty expression said he'd also been snooping. For what, Cole wasn't sure. Yet. "Where's Eve?"

"How would I know?" Duane shot back.

"Her car is in front of the house. Have you seen her?"

"Saw her earlier, looking for you. I thought she'd gone to the house. Isn't she there?"

"She's not." Cole waited for his uncle to leave the office before he followed him out. He headed outside to where Leon and Buzz were working on the old John Deere tractor. "How's it going, boys?"

Leon looked up and grimaced, their earlier encounter apparently forgotten. "I'm doing what I can to keep this old gal running, Cole, but you're going to have to invest some serious money not far down the road, preferably in a new one."

Cole clapped him on the back. "Appreciate your keeping her going, Leon." He looked from one man to the other. "Where's Hector?"

Both men shrugged, and he noticed Buzz wouldn't meet his eyes. He'd have to find out what was up with that later, but right now he had other priorities. "Have you seen Eve? Her car's at the house, but I haven't seen her."

Buzz frowned. "She came by here a while ago, looking for you. Thought she'd found you."

"I just got back." Cole turned, and worry started churning in his gut. Where had she gone? He decided to start searching, in case she'd fallen somewhere and was hurt. But then he dismissed that last part. Knowing Eve, she'd more likely gone snooping and lost track of time.

He looked around. So where would she have gone?

A quick scan of the fields didn't turn up the shape of anyone walking—or lying—there. His eyes landed on the group of storage sheds, and he started in that direction.

"Eve? Where are you?" He picked up his pace when he didn't get an answer. Something wasn't right.

"Eve! Let me know where you are."

Still nothing. He reached the first shed and flung the door open. There was nothing there but the usual assortment of tools and equipment.

The second shed was kept padlocked because of the chemicals they stored in there, so he dismissed it. "Eve?"

He paused. Waited. There. Was that a whimper?

"Eve? If you can hear me, answer me, or make noise. Something."

He heard a dull thud and realized it was coming from inside the padlocked shed. He raced over and saw that the lock hung open, but the hasp was in place. How was that possible? He ripped the door open and ducked just before a swarm of bees flew out.

Bees. Eve was deathly allergic to bees.

Hector shouted his name, and Cole looked back to see the man running toward him, Buzz and Leon on his heels, Duane not far behind. Cole ducked into the shed, and his heart skidded to a stop for one panicked second.

Eve was lying on the floor, eyes closed, hands wrapped around her throat. Her face was swollen and turning a deadly shade of blue. Bee stings. Anaphylactic shock. *Oh, dear God.* He felt for a pulse and found it, weak but thready, then realized checking was a waste of time since she was gasping for every breath.

Every second mattered, and it terrified him to think how long she'd been like this. "I've got you, Eve. Hang on."

He leaned back out of the shed. "Call nine-one-one, now!" Then he reached in and scooped her into his arms. He knew she carried an EpiPen, and he was betting her life she had it in her purse, which she'd probably left in her car.

He tightened his grip on her and ran for the ranch, running like he'd never run in his life, knowing her life depended on it.

When he reached her car, he set her down in a little patch of grass next to the driveway and dove for the car. He yanked open the door and snatched her purse out, pawing through the contents. *Come on, come on.* There! *Thank you, Jesus!*

He grabbed her EpiPen and took a second to read the instructions on the canister. It'd been a while since his last CPR/first aid class, and he didn't want to make a mistake. He placed the canister against her thigh and plunged the needle into her leg. She barely responded to the jab, and that sent another stab of terror through him.

He brushed the hair from her face. "I've got the meds in you, Eve. Try to relax. It's going to be OK."

Several seconds passed before he heard her take something even close to a regular breath. *Oh, thank you, God.* That was a good sign. It meant she was coming around. He took her hand and rubbed it, murmuring something or other as the gasps gradually lessened and her breathing became less and less labored. He couldn't have said what he told her; he just wanted her to know she wasn't alone.

Buzz and the rest of the guys arrived, huffing and puffing. "EMS is on the way," Buzz gasped.

"Is she going to be OK?" Hector asked. "What happened? She get the heatstroke?"

Cole looked at all of them, these men he'd known all his life, before he spoke. "She got stung by bees, more than one from the looks of it."

Leon leaned closer to Eve's face, then looked back at Cole. "Didn't you say she was real allergic to bee stings?"

"Yes." He motioned to the EpiPen lying on the ground. "She carries one of these, thank God, or she might have—" Cole stopped, unable, suddenly, to say the words aloud. She might have died. Just that fast, before anyone got to her.

"Well, why'd she go in that shed to begin with? All them outbuildings have bees in them."

"Probably snooping again," Buzz muttered.

Cole shot him a look, and Buzz raised his hands, palms up. "Just saying. She wouldn't have had a good reason to be in there, 'less she was poking her nose where it didn't belong."

"The door was shut when I got there."

"That doesn't make sense, boss," Hector said. "It's very hot today. Why would anyone close the door?"

"Unless she didn't want anyone to see that she went in there," Duane answered.

Cole wanted to tell them all they were way off base, but he held back. Because he couldn't discount that the scenario they proposed was entirely plausible. It was exactly the kind of thing Eve would do.

But what if she hadn't? What if she had wandered in and someone closed the door?

In the distance, he finally heard sirens. He huffed out a relieved breath when Eve's eyes finally fluttered open and she blinked at him.

Sweet Jesus, she'd almost died.

Chapter 21

Eve fought the panic threatening to overtake her. *You can breathe. Stay calm.* Not much, not yet, but it was getting just a bit better. She no longer felt the vice grip around her throat or the pressure building up in her chest until she thought she'd explode. The EpiPen was doing its job. Cole had said so.

Cole. Where was he? It was a struggle, but she forced her eyes open. Everything looked blurry for a moment, but then his face came into view, worry in every line and crease.

"You're awake." He let out a breath as though he'd been holding his right along with her. "Good, that's good." Eve didn't hear his words, so much as see them on his lips. Everything around her still felt like it was wrapped in a fog, murky and unclear.

Suddenly Cole was nudged out of the way as a pair of uniformed paramedics moved into her line of vision. She watched their mouths move and guessed they were asking questions, but she couldn't make out the words, couldn't hear them, and couldn't seem to respond.

A wave of weakness rolled over her, and she felt her eyes slide closed. Something pricked her arm and she tried to jerk away, but strong hands held her still.

Soon her heart started pounding like crazy, and she felt like she'd had too much caffeine. They must have given her more epinephrine.

But they must have given her something else, too, because she felt really tired and totally wired, all at the same time.

She figured she'd dozed for a while, because when she woke, she looked around and realized she was lying on a hospital bed. Cole sat in a chair next to the bed, a curtain separating them from the noisy room beyond. This must be the emergency room.

The minute he noticed she was awake, he leaned closer. "Welcome back, sleepyhead."

"How long was I out?"

"You slept for about three hours." He paused. "Do you remember what happened before that?"

Eve searched her mind, and slowly it all came back. She shuddered. "Bees. Everywhere. Tried not to move."

"What were you doing in the shed, Eve?"

Eve tried to remember. "Chemicals. Wanted to see if would match Celia's house."

Cole's jaw tightened. "The door was closed when I got there. Did you close it behind you?"

Eve thought a moment, then shook her head. "No. I wouldn't have. Too hot. Left it open. Bees there after it closed."

"How did it close?"

Eve struggled to figure out what he was getting at. She shrugged. "It just did."

"Did you hear anyone outside?"

At this, some of the brain fog cleared, and she focused on his face. "You think someone closed me in on purpose."

"It's the only thing that makes sense, though I can't for the life of me figure out who would do that."

Eve forced herself to a sitting position. When Cole started to protest, she held up a hand to stop him. "The meds wear me out, but I'll be fine. I'm feeling better by the minute."

"You just don't quit," he muttered.

Her eyes met Cole's, and everything stopped as they stared at each other. In his expression, she saw the last vestiges of panic mixed with worry, but there was something else, too, some unnamed emotion that looked a lot like caring, that felt like caring. But that was ridiculous.

He moved closer, sat on the side of the bed. His hand, when he brushed it over her cheek, trembled slightly. "You could have died today, Eve."

She wanted to brush it off, make light of it, but found she couldn't. "I know. Thank you for saving me."

Before she knew what happened, she found herself wrapped in his strong arms, his lips on hers in a kiss like nothing she'd ever experienced. There was caring and worry and underneath it all, a wanting that called to her and brought out the loneliness in her own heart.

Eve wrapped her arms around his neck, loving the feel of his hair as she ran her fingers through it. His tongue met hers, at first in shy invitation, but then he took control, letting her know all the things she didn't think he'd ever say. In that kiss, she felt the kind of soul-deep connection she'd never felt before in her life. For those few moments, she couldn't have said where she ended and he began. There was only the two of them, fused together, hearts and bodies, struggling to get ever closer, until they reached the other's very soul.

The kiss went on and on until Cole slowly pulled away and rested his forehead against hers, both of them breathing heavily. "What am I going to do with you, Evie? You are making me crazy," he muttered.

He tucked her head against his shoulder, and Eve swallowed whatever protest she might have made and simply enjoyed being held in his strong arms. She heard his heart pounding in her ear, and she'd be dead not to notice that rock-hard chest, but it was the gentle way he stroked her hair that made her throat choke with unexpected tears. Had anyone ever held her like this in her life? Like she was made of spun glass and needed to be handled with exquisite care? Of course, Pop and Mama had hugged her, even her mother so long ago, but this . . . this was completely different.

Which scared her so badly she pulled back with a jerk, smacking her head against his jaw.

Cole pulled back and met her eyes, and in his, she saw the same surprise, same level of confusion, which somehow made everything better. He opened his mouth to speak, but Eve couldn't bear it if he apologized, so she laid back down and pulled the blanket to her chin. "I think I'll sleep a bit."

He opened his mouth again, then, apparently, thought better of it. Finally he asked, "Are you going to call the police?"

Eve wasn't sure if he wanted her to, or was afraid she might. "And tell them what? That I locked myself in a shed and got stung by bees? Chief Monroe will love that."

"Nick would take you seriously."

"He probably would, but there's no way to tell if that door closed accidentally, or if someone else closed it." That last raised goose bumps along her skin, so she rubbed her arms.

"You should still call him."

She needed time to think, to go over everything that happened now that her mind was becoming clear again. She leaned up and kissed his cheek. "Thanks again for coming to my rescue. My knight in shining armor."

He chuckled at that, and a flush climbed his cheeks. "I'll check back with you later."

Eve watched him walk away and felt suddenly bereft.

In the silence that followed, a chill passed over her skin. Had someone just tried to kill her?

Chapter 22

Eve tried to sneak into the house like nothing had happened, but she should have known better. The minute she walked in, Blaze skidded to a stop, eyes wide. "What happened to your face?"

Eve felt around and realized she must still look a sight, what with the lingering swelling from the bites. It would go down, but it would take time. She tried for a casual approach. "I got stung by a bee." She went to the freezer and grabbed a bag of peas and sat down.

Blaze came over and studied her face, then squinted at her arms. "That's more than one bee sting." She looked up. "And aren't you, like, deathly allergic to bee stings?"

Eve smiled and felt the pull of her tight cheeks. "I am. That's why I carry an EpiPen."

Just then Sasha marched through the door. "I just got a call from—" She broke off when she saw Eve sitting there with the peas. "What are you doing here? You should be in the hospital."

"I was, but they let me go." After Cole left, she'd felt an overwhelming need to get to the marina, to her family. She hadn't felt safe in the hospital alone. The doctor had wanted to keep her overnight, but Eve told him she was leaving, with or without his permission. He'd signed the release papers, albeit reluctantly.

"I heard you were out at Cole's, and the bees were in a shed and you almost died," Sasha said.

Out of the corner of her eye, she saw the color drain from Blaze's face and shot Sasha a look. "Without my EpiPen, it would have been much worse. I'm fine."

"I still think you should—"

The old-fashioned wall phone rang, and Eve grabbed it like a lifeline. "Martinellis'. Who's calling, please? Yes, just a moment."

Her eyes met Sasha's. "It's your aunt again. She wants to talk to you."

Sasha paled, and her hand shook slightly as she reached for the phone. "Hello." Eve sat back down with her bag of peas, and she and Blaze exchanged glances as they listened. "Today? I, ah, I don't know about today." Sasha rubbed her forehead as she paced. She looked down at Eve, who nodded encouragement. "Um, how about on ah, Thursday, two days from now." Sasha scribbled on a piece of paper and hung up. She plopped into a chair at the table and dropped her head into her hands. "What have I done?" When she looked up, Eve was shocked by the uncertainty there. Sasha was always the strong one, who forged ahead without looking back.

Eve reached over and took her hand. "This is a good thing, Sash. A connection to your family. You want to reconnect, don't you?"

"But what if I'm not—" She paused as though searching for the right words. "I don't know, enough. Good enough or whatever."

The comment struck all the way to Eve's heart. Amazing that her confident sister struggled, as she did, with feeling she wasn't quite enough. Maybe everyone felt that way, that they were always just shy of the mark, didn't quite measure up.

So she said what she hoped she'd be able to believe herself one day. "You are enough, Sasha, more than enough. You are awesome, and your aunt sounds like she's thrilled to have found you. Give her a chance to prove it."

Sasha nodded and then headed for the door. "I need to tell Jesse."

Blaze studied Eve. "Why did you stay where the bees were? Why didn't you leave the minute you realized they were there?"

Leave it to Blaze to see right through the smokescreen. Eve kept forgetting how quick the girl's brain worked. "Because the door to the shed swung shut behind me, and once the bees were on me, I couldn't move to get away."

Blaze visibly shuddered, then narrowed her eyes. Eve expected her to ask if someone locked her in, but she didn't. Instead, she said, "I'm glad you're OK."

"Thanks. Me, too." But after Blaze left, Eve pulled out her phone—which Cole had retrieved from the shed and brought to the hospital. With trembling fingers, she told Nick what had happened, just in case.

———

The next morning, Eve headed straight for the hospital. She wanted to be sure Celia didn't take Glory home before they got the water-test results.

She stopped by Mama's room first and learned she was being released later that day. Eve took a deep breath and felt a tension she hadn't realized she carried simply melt away. Mama was going to be OK. She'd beat this monster. She had to.

She made a quick call to let Sasha know, then headed down the hall to check in with Celia. But when she got to the corner just before Glory's room, she stopped short when she heard IdaMae and Leon in a heated discussion with Celia inside. She paused, trying to decide whether to come back, or barge in.

"Those people from DCF are making it sound like I did something to my baby. How can anyone think that?" Celia demanded. "But the worst part is that if they decide it's true, they'll try to take Glory from me." Her breath hitched. "I can't let that happen. Don't you get that?"

"Of course we do, child," IdaMae soothed. "We just don't want to go pointing fingers at good folks for no reason, causing trouble."

"We're not asking you to pretend anything," Leon added. "Just to keep it all quiet-like. I'll look into it some more. I'll find out what happened. But we don't need the likes of Eve Jackson on our property, poking her nose into our personal business."

That was her cue. Eve stalked into the room and gave Celia a quick hug and a wink. "Hello, IdaMae. Leon. How are things?"

IdaMae planted her fists on her ample hips, but before she could say anything, Leon stepped into Eve's personal space, glaring. She didn't back up.

"You need to stop meddling in other people's business, Eve. Haven't you learned your lesson on that yet?"

"What's really going on here?" Celia demanded, before Eve could ask the same question. "There is something more to this, and I expect you to tell me what that is."

"I don't know what you're talking about—" Leon started.

IdaMae broke in before he could finish. "Mr. Blackwell's been good to me. I don't want to go putting my job in jeopardy over this."

"But if he's innocent, why would he take offense if we ask questions?" Celia countered. "Wouldn't he want to know the truth? Especially if he wants to buy the property?"

A stunned silence followed, and Eve's mind whirled at this bit of information.

"Who told you Mr. Blackwell wanted the property?" IdaMae asked.

Celia rolled her eyes. "Seriously? You thought it was a secret? In this town?"

"Look, child, we just don't want—" Ida Mae began, but Celia interrupted.

"I need to get back to Glory. Thanks for stopping by." She walked to the door and held it open.

Leon jabbed a finger at Eve. "Stay out of our business." Then he stalked out of the room.

IdaMae hadn't moved. She studied Eve intently, and Eve stared right back. She knew she was being tested, she just didn't know for what, exactly.

"We take care of our own, Eve. I'd advise you to do the same." With that she hugged Celia, whispered something in her daughter's ear, and left.

Eve met Celia's eyes and shrugged. "Guess they still haven't warmed up to me, huh?"

Celia fought a smile. "Guess not." Then she sobered. "I heard what happened yesterday at Cole's ranch. Are you OK?"

"Right as rain. I bounce back quick." Eve kept her tone light, trying to take the focus off herself. "How's that sweet little one today?"

Celia smiled. "Come see."

Eve followed her farther into the room and breathed out a relieved sigh when she saw the little girl, sleeping peacefully, her color back to normal. Glory slept on her back, arms flung out to the sides, and Eve stroked a finger down her arm as she swallowed the lump in her throat. This is why she fought so hard. Little people like this, who needed a champion. She still didn't know what happened to Celia's water, but right then and there, Eve renewed her vow to keep looking until she found out.

"Glory is lucky to have a mama like you, Celia. Always tell her you love her." She met Celia's eyes. "We're waiting on lab results for inside your house, so if they release Glory, let me know, of course, but make sure neither of you drink any water in the house until we're sure it's safe, OK?"

Celia's eyes widened, but she nodded. Eve hugged her, then headed back to her car. She had to get to Cole's ranch. They needed the results of those tests.

When Eve pulled up at the ranch, she took the EpiPen she'd just picked up at the pharmacy from her purse and tucked it into her back pocket, just in case. Then she slipped her feet out of her heeled sandals and into the boots Cole had given her. She still didn't wear them around town, but she found she really liked them. They were comfortable, and just sliding them on made her feel more connected to the land. And, OK, to Cole. There, she'd admitted it. She didn't know what to do with it, but there it was. Somehow, the man was getting under her skin in all sorts of unnerving ways, making her want things she'd stopped wishing for years ago.

She noticed the vet's truck as she got closer to the barn. She quickened her pace and walked down to the far end of the barn where Cole stood with Buzz, Hector, and the vet.

When she walked up, Cole's glance immediately went to her face, checking for swelling, no doubt, and then he sent her a slow grin she felt all the way to the soles of her cowboy boots. But his eyes were troubled.

"What's wrong?"

"You sure whoever called you didn't have a wrong number, Mo?" Buzz asked.

"No, sir. He asked for me by name, gave an address I wasn't familiar with, but said it was urgent." The veterinarian shook his head. "By the time I found the place, there was no one there. I called my office to see if maybe they'd brought the sick animal to my clinic, but they hadn't. And the place was clearly empty. Almost looked abandoned."

"You didn't go to the wrong place somehow, did you?" Cole asked. "No offense."

The vet was clearly troubled. "I don't think so, though I suppose it's possible. But if that were the case, I'm guessing whoever called me would have called back when I didn't show." He heaved out a sigh. "Again, I'm sorry, Cole."

"Not your fault. There are no guarantees you could have saved the calf regardless."

At this, Eve's eyes flew to Cole, and she suddenly understood the frustration and anger vibrating in the air. Cole had lost another calf. "Was this one deformed, too?"

"Yes. Just like the other three. But it was born with the cord around its neck and didn't make it. We didn't get to her in time," Mo said.

Cole held out his hand. "Thanks for getting here as quickly as you could. This isn't your fault."

"You still haven't found anything suspicious the cows could have gotten into? Like hemlock?"

"Hector and I have been over every square inch of this place, and we can't find any growing here." Cole's jaw clenched. "But Eve and I found some floating in the pond the other day."

The vet seemed to hesitate. He glanced down at the ground, then back up at Cole. "I hate to even say such a thing, but it's no secret around town that the ranch is in some financial trouble and that you've been turning down offers to buy you out right and left. I'm sure you've considered that someone might have given it to your animals on purpose."

Eve watched Cole's expression. Except for the anger in his eyes, he showed no outward reaction. The vet must have realized it, too. "You've already considered it."

"I have. One of many things that keep me up nights." He glanced at Eve, and she felt a flush creep over her face. "I ordered some wildlife cameras to install around the property, but they haven't come in yet."

The vet glanced at all of them and grabbed his bag. "I'll keep an ear to the ground and will let you know if I hear anything."

Cole nodded. "Thanks again for coming."

The vet tipped his hat to Eve. "Ma'am. Take care, y'all."

Buzz pulled off his Stetson and slapped it against his leg before he clapped it back on his head and went into the stall to check on the mother.

Cole turned and started walking away, and Eve hurried to keep up. Once they were outside the barn, in the shadow of the building and away from prying eyes, Eve put a hand on his arm to stop him. "Are you OK?"

Cole leaned back against the building, his expression bleak. "The look on that cow's face when all her licking wouldn't rouse her calf . . ." He didn't finish the sentence, just shook his head and closed his eyes. Eve stepped closer, unsure what to do, how to offer comfort.

Without warning, his hand reached out for hers, and she found herself pulled up against his hard chest, both arms around her, her head buried in the crook of his neck. He didn't say anything, just held her. Eve didn't know what to say, so she stayed quiet, offered what comfort she could just by holding tight.

Several minutes went by before he slowly set her away from him. His eyes were less bleak, though still sad. He looked up. "I'm glad you came by."

The thought that this big, tough rancher had needed her formed another crack in the hard, protective shell Eve had always kept around her heart. If she wasn't careful, he'd sneak past all her defenses, and then where would she be? She took a step back, physically and emotionally.

"What brings you out this way?" he asked.

"I just came from the hospital. Mama Rosa is being released today. Sasha said she wanted to go pick her up. Little Glory might get to go home, too. Any word yet from the lab?"

"Not yet. But we can give them a call, get an update." Cole studied her, then cocked his head. "What else is wrong? Why are you chewing on your bottom lip?"

"What? I don't do that."

"You chew your bottom lip when you're worried or debating something."

"I was thinking about what you were talking about when I arrived."

"The vet got called out on what appears to be a wild-goose chase, and in the meantime, my cow had a calf with the cord wrapped around its neck that died before he could get here to help us save the calf."

"He said the calf was deformed, too?"

"Yes. He's thinking poison. I don't disagree. Those poison hemlock leaves we found came from somewhere."

Eve caught herself chewing her lip again and forced herself to stop. "You do know that it could be someone here on the ranch, right?"

"I'd like to argue that no one here would do that, but I have to face facts. These are people I've known my whole life. It would have to have been done months ago, during the early gestation period, for the deformed calves to be born now. That means it was done while Hank was still alive." His jaw worked. "But those leaves we found in the pond mean it's possible someone fed them to more of my cows in the last few days."

Eve studied his bleak expression. "It could be someone not connected to the ranch."

"I appreciate the optimism. It could, but it's not likely."

"No, it's not."

Just then, Hector's pickup pulled up outside the bunkhouse, but he didn't immediately exit the vehicle.

"Hector!" Cole called his name, but the other man didn't respond.

They started walking toward the truck, and Eve had to jog to keep pace with Cole. Just as they reached the truck, the driver's door opened and Hector all but fell out. He caught himself on the door as he stumbled, just barely righting himself.

Cole ran the last few yards. "Are you OK?"

Eve raced up behind Cole and gasped when she saw Hector's face. He'd been beaten. Badly.

Chapter 23

Cole immediately hooked Hector's arm over his shoulder and pointed them in the direction of the bunkhouse. Eve raced ahead to open the door Cole indicated.

They exchanged worried glances as they helped Hector inside and into a recliner in his small apartment. Cole crouched down in front of him while Eve went to the small kitchen and retrieved a bag of frozen corn and handed it to him for his swollen eyes.

"Who did this to you?"

One of Hector's eyes was swollen shut, the other almost as bad. Blood covered his face, and his clothes were muddy and torn. He gave one quick shake of his head. "I don't know."

"What do you mean, you don't know?"

"Wore mask."

Cole studied him a long moment, then pulled out his cell phone. "Let me call Doc Hamilton, see if he still makes house calls."

"No. Let it go." The words came out barely a whisper.

"You could have broken ribs and a punctured lung."

"I will be fine. Please."

Cole narrowed his eyes. "Who are you protecting, Hector?"

There was a long pause. "He said would get worse if I told anyone." He winced, struggled to get the words out. "Don't want anyone else hurt."

"We'll protect you. You know that."

Hector closed his eyes. "Just leave me be."

By the look on his face, Cole was furious, but he nodded, then glanced at Eve. "See if you can find some ibuprofen or something."

While she went into the small bathroom, she heard Cole talking to Hector, but she couldn't make out what they said. Why would someone beat him up? He didn't seem the type to start trouble. In fact, he struck Eve as the kind of man who lived in the background, who never tried to draw attention to himself. The only thing that made sense was that it had something to do with the ranch. Of course, it could be over something as absurd as his Mexican heritage. Sadly, more ridiculous things had happened in Safe Harbor over the years.

She opened the medicine cabinet and reached for the ibuprofen bottle, truly intending to look only at that one. But really, she was an investigator. Who could resist taking a peek at the other things in there, especially the prescription bottles? She found several with drug names that she wasn't familiar with, so she pulled out her phone and snapped a picture before she talked herself out of it.

She didn't know why she'd need that information, except maybe so Cole would know what Hector was dealing with. She ignored the little voice in her head that said none of this was any of her or Cole's business. She was trying to help. Period.

She tucked her phone back in her pocket and returned to the kitchen, grabbed a glass of water, and approached Hector, who was leaning back in the recliner with his eyes closed, taking shallow breaths.

"Here's something for the pain," Eve said quietly. When he opened one eye, she handed him the pills and water. "Are you sure we can't take you to the emergency room? Or at least to see a doctor?"

"Thank you. No." He swallowed the pills she held out, drank a bit of the water, and then slowly eased back into the chair and closed his eyes. "Please. Leave me alone. I will be fine." He opened his one eye again. "I'll be back to work tomorrow, boss. Sorry about today."

Cole scowled. "If I see you out of this room in the next three days, I'll beat you up myself. You rest, and I'll stop by later to check on you. I'll make sure you get some food, too."

"No, please. It will be—"

"If you don't stop, I'll send my mother out here, and you and I both know she'll either haul your butt to the hospital or set up camp in here to keep an eye on you. Your choice."

Eve hid a smile at Hector's grimace. Alice Sutton might look like a gracious southern lady, but like most of her breed, she had a will of iron behind her pleasant drawl.

Cole nodded. "That's what I thought. Do you have your cell phone?"

Hector whispered, "Truck," and Eve went out to get it. She brought it back in and set it on the end table next to the recliner.

"Call me if you need anything or if you start feeling worse."

"I'll be fine," Hector muttered, chin jutted at a stubborn angle.

"You're family, Hector. Don't act like some stranger off the street. You need me, you call me. Got it?"

He nodded, eyes still closed, and Cole motioned Eve out the door ahead of him. Once outside, they walked far enough away to make sure they weren't overheard.

"Any ideas on who did this?" Eve asked.

Cole raised a brow. "Ideas, sure. Proof? Not a thing." He paced, looking like he wanted to punch something. Or someone. "This is insane. It's like the entire world has gone nuts. And for what? I don't get it."

"You know people want the ranch."

Cole looked at her like she was dumber than a rock. "I know, but it's a piece of land, and it doesn't sit on oil or a diamond mine or anything else that would explain this kind of craziness." He paced some more, shaking his head. "Somebody has an agenda that goes deeper than just this chunk of land—important though it is to me—and I can't for the life of me figure out what it is. But I will."

Eve's phone buzzed before she could respond. "Hey, Sasha, were you able to bring Mama home?"

"We did. Just got her settled. Where are you? Mama kept asking for you, so I told her you had some errands to run and would check in with her later. Seeing those stings on your face this morning upset her more than she let on, I think."

"Sorry about that. I debated on stopping by or not, but figured if I didn't, what she imagined from hearing people talk would be worse than the reality."

"You did the right thing. So where are you?"

"I'm out at Sutton Ranch." She started to tell her about Hector, but then changed her mind. Sasha had enough to worry about with Mama right now.

"Why am I not surprised?" Sasha teased; then she sobered. "Look, Eve, I just got the creepiest phone call here at the house. The caller sounded like a man, wouldn't give a name, but asked for you. When I said you weren't here, he said to ask you how Mama liked the scarf." She paused. "And then he said to ask you how important your mother is to you."

Eve sucked in a breath as red-hot fury raced over her skin, burning up the bone-deep chill that froze her heart. The scumbag had been in Mama's hospital room. And now he was involving Sasha? No. That Eve would protect Mama with her dying breath went without saying. But scaring her family went too far. "I'll take care of this, Sasha. I can't believe some slimeball threatened her," she muttered, mind racing.

"Whatever is going on, whatever hornet's nest you've stirred up this time, somebody just brought the fight to the marina's front door." Sasha's voice rose with every word. "Mama and Pop have been through enough. They can't deal with this, too, Eve. You need to stop whatever it is you're doing and make this go away."

It took every ounce of Eve's self-control to keep the fury out of her voice. "I didn't ask for it to begin with, Sash. Come on, give me a little credit here. Do you think I would deliberately put them in the line of fire?" Just the idea made her angry enough to wonder if there was steam coming out of her ears. She glanced up and saw Cole watching her, concerned, so she turned her back and kept walking.

"I don't think you intended to, no. But you did. So what are you going to do about it?"

Eve didn't care for the bossy tone any more than she had as a teen. "If I remember right, you brought plenty of it to their doorstep when you first came to town. I don't recall us blaming you for that."

There was silence. "Touché, sis. Look, I'm worried. You need to make it go away before whoever this crazy person is decides to try to hurt Mama in some way."

Eve felt like she was in the shed again, with the air being squeezed from her lungs. That wasn't going to happen. She'd never let something bad happen to Mama Rosa, something that was her fault. She'd never be able to live with herself. "I'll figure something out. I'll be in touch."

She hung up and started pacing, arms wrapped around her middle. *Not Mama. Please, God, don't let anything happen to Mama.* But how to stop it? Especially when she didn't know what it was about. But by threatening Mama, whoever was behind this had just lit up every single warrior instinct Eve possessed.

On her next pass by Cole, he stepped up behind her and pulled her back into his arms, stopping her momentum. She felt antsy and twitchy and tried to jerk out of his embrace to keep pacing, but he simply tightened his hold. "Easy, easy. Slow down and take a breath."

He murmured quietly in her ear, and Eve figured he used that same soothing tone on his horses and cows. But she wasn't an animal to be placated. "Let me go."

He pretended he hadn't heard her as his calm voice tickled her ear. "Talk to me, Eve. Tell me what's happening."

She pulled away, and this time, he let her go. She paced some more, trying to gather her thoughts, to think past the panic that made her want to run to try to escape it. *Mama Rosa. Dear God, Mama Rosa.* She had to protect her.

Cole stepped in front of her, but didn't try to touch her again. His eyes bored into hers, and the worry there, coupled with his obvious concern, made her stop. She took a deep breath. "Someone just called the marina and threatened Mama, if I didn't stop doing whatever it is I'm doing."

"You mean investigating the problem with Celia's water."

"That's what I'm guessing. They didn't say. They just asked how important my mother is to me." *Oh, dear God, no.* Just saying the words brought a fresh wave of terror, and she stepped around him and kept walking, trying to calm down enough to think, to process. How dare someone threaten Mama? No. No way would she let anything happen to her.

"Stay here at the ranch."

Eve stopped, spun around at his words. "What? No. I need to be with Mama, keep her safe."

"How will you protect her while you're trying to figure out what's going on? How will you keep looking for answers while you're at the marina?"

Eve felt like she was being ripped in two. She had to keep digging, had to figure out who was behind everything that was happening. But if she did, and left Mama alone and something happened to her . . . no. She couldn't risk that. "Sasha and Jesse will help protect Mama while I look for answers."

"Of course. I have no doubt. But Jesse has a marina to run, Sasha is pregnant, and Sal . . . he's not as young as he once was."

Eve swallowed hard. "You're assuming whoever is doing this would actually hurt her."

"Are you willing to gamble Mama's life that he won't?"

She wrapped her arms around her middle, chilled to her very soul. "Of course not." There had to be a way to do both. "Nick." She pulled out her cell phone and called him, told him about the threat. He was silent for a few moments, then said, "I don't suppose I can convince you to stay with Mama while I try to figure out what's going on?"

"You know I can't."

"Yeah, I know." He sighed. "Where are you now?"

"Sutton Ranch."

"Stay there. You and Cole keep digging from your end. I'll work from my end and spend nights at the marina with Mama. The rest of the family will circle around her during the day. If this person is working alone, they can't be in two places at once, and that way we'll keep you both protected."

He'd basically said the same thing as Cole. She still didn't like it, but it made sense. She couldn't just sit and watch over Mama. She needed the freedom to be able to figure this out, because Mama wouldn't be safe until they did. "Let me get back to you, OK?"

When she hung up, she turned back to Cole. "He offered to spend his nights at the marina, and he'd do what he could from his end. He thought my staying here was a good idea, so we could get to the bottom of whatever is going on."

"It makes sense. Nick and Jesse will keep an eye on things at the marina, keep your mama safe."

"And Sasha." Her sister was no slouch in the taking-care-of-people-she-cared-about department.

"Of course. Goes without saying."

Eve bristled. "No, actually, it doesn't." She and Sasha had been verbally patted on the head too many times to count by self-proclaimed macho men.

He pinched the bridge of his nose like she was giving him a colossal headache. "Look, I meant no offense. You and Sasha are some of the toughest, smartest women I've ever met, no lie, but I also know that in this world, and especially in a town like Safe Harbor, a strong man is more of a deterrent than a woman. Doesn't make it right. It just is."

Eve couldn't argue with that because it was true, doggone it. Even though it chaffed like starched panties.

"I think what happened to Celia's water and what's going on here at the ranch are definitely connected."

He met her eyes, his own troubled. "I agree. And I think you're the connection. Or maybe the catalyst. Either way, you've made someone very, very nervous."

His cell phone rang. "Sutton. Hi, Doc. What? Say that again." He listened for several minutes, his face getting darker by the second. When he hung up, he turned to Eve. "The vet says his office was broken into while his office tech was at lunch. File cabinets were ransacked. But when they put everything back, only one file was missing: the one with all the records from the Sutton Ranch herd."

Eve snapped her jaw shut, absorbing this latest news. Someone clearly had an agenda. But who? Did it really just come down to someone wanting Cole's ranch? She opened her mouth, closed it again.

Cole didn't say anything, either, just stared off into the distance. Eve could see him thinking through the possibilities, just like she was. He finally looked at her. "I'll follow you back to the marina to get your stuff, then get you settled here."

That got her back up. Even though she'd already decided to stay, she didn't like him thinking she'd meekly fall in line. "I didn't say I was staying."

He met her gaze, eyes hard. "You're not stupid, Eve. Don't play games. Whoever this is, they're escalating."

Eve lifted her chin and waited for him to continue.

"I don't want anything to happen to you."

Eve wasn't sure what she'd expected him to say, but this blunt admission of his feelings shocked her all the way to her toes. This was Cole, high school football hero and the guy most likely to have girls throw themselves at his feet. But now, he was worried about her, the girl most likely to get arrested for protesting something.

She cleared her throat, but still had no idea what to say, so she simply nodded and got into her car.

Chapter 24

Eve couldn't deny the relief on Sasha's face when she'd said she would be staying out at the ranch and Nick would be spending nights at the marina until they figured out what was going on. Back at the ranch, Eve stood on the porch and felt some of the tension leave her shoulders. She'd made the right decision.

Alice could not have been more welcoming, and even Buzz hadn't looked like he hated the idea. After supper, he and Cole had talked about taking shifts to keep watch, but Alice briskly dismissed the idea as ludicrous. She'd keep her shotgun by the bed, as always, and suggested they do the same.

Eve wasn't sure what to think of that. At first glance, Alice appeared to be a stereotypical southern mama who loved to cook and feed her family, though she turned fierce when it came to protecting the people she loved. But for all that, from what Eve had picked up on, she hadn't stood up to her husband. Had the shotgun by her bed been Alice's way to keep Hank in line? Eve shook her head. Alice was a complex woman, though clearly a kindhearted one. And her quilts were works of art.

Eve looked up and saw a cloud of dust heading down the lane. Gradually she could make out Duane's dusty black pickup barreling toward the ranch, and, as if on cue, Cole walked out onto the porch and stood beside her. The sight of him here, so completely at home, tugged on her heart in ways she was afraid to examine too closely.

Duane skidded to a stop and lurched out of his truck. He stomped up the stairs and poked Cole in the chest, the smell of alcohol thick in the air. "What happened to Hector? Who beat him up?"

Cole stepped out of the other man's reach, eyes hard. "I don't know. Hector won't say."

Duane focused in on Eve and stabbed a finger in her direction. "I bet she had something to do with it. Whenever there's trouble, she doesn't seem to be far behind."

"Did you stop by for a particular reason, Duane?"

"I came by to check on Hector. Someone has to look out for this ranch, since you're doing a dang poor job of it."

Cole moved faster than Eve would have thought possible. Before the other man could blink, Cole had him by the shirtfront, pushed up against one of the porch's support posts. "I am doing my level best to take good care of this ranch and everyone on it. You are entitled to your opinion, but I'll thank you not to voice it in my presence."

He let him go, and Duane swayed for a moment before he found his balance.

"Go ahead and check on Hector," Cole said. "I was just heading that way myself. Then I'll drive you home."

Duane glared at him. "If I need to go anywhere, I'll drive myself."

"Not when you've been drinking."

The two men stared each other down. Duane looked away first. With a disgusted wave of his hand, he stormed off toward the bunkhouse. Cole followed, and Eve brought up the rear.

She tried to give them a bit of privacy and couldn't quite hear what was being said, but somehow, Cole had his uncle laughing before they made it halfway across road. Amazing, his way with people.

As she followed them, Eve passed by Duane's truck and saw some kind of leaves caught between the door and the frame. A quick glance confirmed that Cole and Duane weren't paying her any mind, so she stepped over and opened the door. A clump of wilted leaves was jammed in the doorframe.

But as she pulled them out, she realized these weren't just any leaves. She peered closer and stiffened in surprise. Her brain kicked into overdrive. She was looking at a wilted clump of hemlock. Just like the leaves they'd found floating in the pond. Eve whipped out her phone and snapped a quick picture before she quietly closed the door again.

Cole heard the sound and sent a questioning look over his shoulder, but fortunately, Duane didn't seem to notice. Eve made a little "come here" motion with one finger, and Cole raised an eyebrow but didn't say anything. He and Duane walked into the bunkhouse, and a minute later Cole came out alone and hurried over.

"What's going on?"

Eve thrust the clump in his direction. "You know what this is, right?"

Cole looked at the leaves and bit back a curse. "Where did you get this?"

Eve nodded toward Duane's pickup. "It was caught in the doorframe of his truck."

Cole rubbed the back of his neck. "Doesn't mean he's responsible for the calves."

"Doesn't mean he isn't, either."

Eve spun toward the bunkhouse. "I want some answers."

Cole caught up to her and took hold of her elbow to stop her momentum. She swung back toward him. "Don't you dare try to stop me with some lame-brained family loyalty garbage. I was there, remember?"

"I'm not trying to stop you. But I need you to let me take the lead on this."

"Give me one good reason why I should."

"My property. My problem."

They stared each other down. Finally Eve looked away. She didn't like it, but he had a point. "Fine." She waved a hand in that direction. "After you."

Without warning, he leaned over and planted a quick kiss on her lips. "If you aren't cuter than a June bug when you're mad."

Eve stiffened at the condescending words, but then she caught his grin and realized he was teasing. Maybe. Since the look he shot her was hot enough to melt paint, she decided he meant it as a compliment.

By the time she gathered her wits about her, Cole had his hand on the doorknob, waiting for her. As soon as she caught up, he strode through the door and into the living room, earning a startled glance from Hector, whose face was turning more colors with every passing minute.

Cole walked past him and stopped in front of his uncle, who slouched in a recliner, beer in hand. He thrust the leaves under his nose. "You want to explain this?"

His uncle sat up in surprise, sloshing beer over the front of his T-shirt. "What are you accusing me of now, boy?" His eyes focused on the leaves, and Eve watched him visibly pale.

Gotcha, old man, she thought. *Now, here comes the part where he tries to explain it away.*

Cole wouldn't let him look away. "You know what this is."

"'Course I do. It's hemlock. Found some down by my pond and been clearing it out, so no animals get hold of it. Or the neighbor kids, always cutting through my property."

"If a cow gets hold of it in early gestation, she can birth a deformed calf."

Eve watched Duane's face, saw the flicker of fear before he exploded out of the chair, clutching the beer can in one hand, pointing with the other. "Are you accusing me of feeding it to your cows, boy? Are you crazy?" He hitched a thumb in Eve's direction. "Or you just listening to this busybody tree hugger's nonsense and turning on your own kin?

I told you she was trouble from the day she showed up in Safe Harbor." He stalked toward the door. "I don't have to listen to this."

Eve couldn't believe Cole just let him walk out the door. She waited until it closed behind Duane before she said, "Seriously? That's it?"

His voice was clipped. "If you know of a way to prove it was Duane, I'm all ears. Otherwise, all we have are speculation and circumstantial evidence."

"And the look on his face when he saw the hemlock."

"I saw it. But it doesn't prove a thing. Maybe he did it—although I can't for the life of me think why he would—or maybe he knows who did."

"He wants the ranch pretty bad, boss," Hector said.

Eve had forgotten about him, all her frustration focused on Cole.

"And he has been telling everyone around town that he plans to get it, too, and turn it back into the place it used to be."

"It used to be on the brink of foreclosure," Cole snapped.

Eve felt the puzzle pieces swirling around in her head and tried to fit them together just right to make the whole picture clear, but so far, it was still a random jumble of disconnected information that may or may not matter at all.

Cole looked Hector over. "You holler if it gets worse."

"Sure thing, boss," Hector said, but Eve suspected he'd writhe in pain before he asked Cole for help. By the look on Cole's face, she figured he thought the same.

By the time they left the bunkhouse, Duane's truck was gone, and so were any remaining hemlock leaves.

Chapter 25

The sound of boots pounding down the hallway roused Eve from a fitful sleep. She glanced at her phone and realized two things: it was three o'clock in the morning, and the boots and muttering came from Cole. When she heard him ratchet a shell into his shotgun, she flew out of bed and into the hallway, not surprised to see his mother there as well, pulling on a robe, shotgun in hand.

"What's going on?" Eve asked. Her heart rate kicked into overdrive, not just from the jolt out of sleep, but from the rock-hard expression on Cole's face.

"Not sure yet. Might be rustlers. Go back to bed. Both of you."

Rustlers? Here? In Safe Harbor? This wasn't exactly the Wild West.

"I'm going with you." No way would she let him face this alone.

Cole stopped, sent her a look that could freeze ice. "Stay here. I have enough to worry about without you underfoot, too."

Eve reared back as though he'd slapped her face. "I can help."

"You know how to fire a gun?"

"Um, no. But—"

"I don't have time to argue with you. You want to help, then you stay here so nobody accidentally shoots you in the dark."

He slammed out the door before Eve could voice any other objections. Part of her knew he was right, but she didn't like being told she would be a hindrance instead of a help. And she liked the idea of Cole facing armed men in the dark even less. There had to be a way to help.

Eve stopped pacing and met Alice's eyes. She saw the worry in the older woman's expression, and her focus changed, just for a moment. "Would you like me to make some coffee? I don't think I'll be able to sleep anymore tonight."

Alice nodded. "Sure, thanks." But her eyes kept going back to the windows and the commotion outside.

Sweet Jesus, were those gunshots? Eve hurried to the kitchen and peered out the window over the sink, but couldn't see a thing from this angle, especially with the lights on inside. What was going on? Was Cole OK?

She tapped her fingers on the edge of the sink while the coffee brewed, then poured it into mugs and handed one to Alice, who sat at the table, shotgun propped beside her. Eve sipped her coffee, but she couldn't sit still, not while Cole could be in who knew what kind of trouble out there.

"He'll be fine," Alice finally said.

Eve nodded. "I'm sure he will be. He's tough." She wondered whom they were trying to convince.

Alice studied her over the rim of her mug. "I'm glad you're here, Eve. You're good for Cole. He needs a woman like you in his life."

Whoa. Not only did the words make everything inside her freak out a bit, but there was no way she would talk about her jumbled feelings for Cole while there were gunshots outside. "Um, while I greatly admire your son, I'm not staying in Safe Harbor. My life and my work are in DC."

"Seems to me we have enough environmental issues right here to keep you plenty busy."

Eve didn't know what to say, how to respond, so she simply smiled and sipped her coffee. Outside, she heard several trucks drive by and then the sound of more gunfire. She hopped up and reached for the phone on the kitchen wall. "We need to call the police."

Alice shook her head. "No. We'd better let Cole decide that. He doesn't trust the chief."

Eve didn't, either, but this was Cole. She picked up the receiver as Alice said, "Let Cole handle this."

Eve set the receiver back in its cradle. "What if he can't call, because he's too busy trying to stay alive?" Her voice rose at the end, and she saw Alice flinch.

"It will be OK, Eve. Cole will be OK. We have to trust him. And God."

Nothing in Eve's nature made her willing to sit idly by and let others handle things, not if she could help. And therein lay her dilemma. How could she help? Cole was right that she didn't know guns. She shuddered. They scared her, though she saw their value. Like right now, when someone showed up on your property with evil in mind. She believed God looked out for people; but she believed people were expected to do their part, too.

She looked over at Alice, whose expression hadn't changed, though the fine tremor in her hands made Eve believe she wasn't quite as calm as she pretended to be.

"I think I'll go back to bed," Alice said, and rinsed her mug in the sink. "You should do the same."

Eve watched the other woman pick up the shotgun and head down the hall. She didn't believe for one second that Alice actually planned to sleep, not with Cole in danger, but she didn't press for an explanation. She waited until she heard her bedroom door click shut before she rushed back to her own room and grabbed her cell phone. Alice didn't want her calling the police? Fine, she'd call her brother, Nick, instead.

"Eve? What's wrong?" He sounded wide awake.

"Nick? I need your help. I'm here at Sutton Ranch, and Cole just ran outside saying something about rustlers."

Nick muttered something Eve couldn't hear, then said, "Sit tight; I'm on my way."

He hung up before Eve could ask him not to call Chief Monroe. She tossed the phone on the bed while she threw on jeans and a dark-colored top and grabbed her cowboy boots. She tucked her cell phone in her back pocked and eased the bedroom door open. No light showed under Alice's door, so she hoped that meant the other woman had gone back to bed.

She tiptoed down the hall, boots in hand, and slipped out onto the porch before she slid her feet into the boots. Eve stood for a moment and waited for her eyes to adjust. What to do? How to help?

Outside, it was darker than dark, with very little moonlight. There were the occasional pools of light from the security lights in front of the barn and larger outbuildings, but that didn't help much, as nobody was standing under them for her to get a read on the situation.

She heard the sound of vehicles in the distance and spun around, trying to figure out where they were and what they were. Wait. Those were ATVs. She finally spotted them and realized there were two of them, and even with the headlights off, she could finally see that whoever was driving them was using them to herd the cattle toward the opposite end of the pasture. There had to be a truck waiting there to load them into.

She heard another gunshot and focused back in on the buildings closer to her. Where was Cole?

She wouldn't figure it out sitting safely on the porch, that was for sure. What if he needed her help? Eve hopped off the porch and hurried over to Cole's truck, frustrated to find he hadn't left the keys inside.

She headed off to the bunkhouse, staying low, hoping Hector had left the keys in his truck. Sure enough, there they were. Eve hopped in and closed the door as quietly as possible, then started the engine, which sounded much too loud. But hopefully, hidden behind the bunkhouse on the opposite side of the lowing cattle, no one would hear her.

She eased the truck in the direction of the cattle, no lights on, trying to spot Cole or one of the other ranch hands in the dark.

She hadn't gone more than fifty yards when a shot rang out, and the truck's back windshield shattered. Eve swallowed a scream and gripped the wheel tighter. Dear Jesus, someone was shooting at her.

Well, what did she expect, coming out here in the middle of a gunfight? For a moment, she wondered if she'd made a terrible mistake, then dismissed the idea. No. She hunched over the steering wheel and kept going, determined to be there if Cole needed her. Come on, come on, where was he?

Off in the distance she heard the distinct rumble of a diesel truck engine firing up. That must be what the rustlers were using to move the cattle. But seriously? Did they not think anyone would hear them? Although, given how far away they were from the ranch, the idea made sense.

Eve kept going, slowly—scanning, always scanning the shadows as she went. Where had everyone gone? It seemed like when she'd first climbed into the truck, there was activity everywhere. Now, she felt like the only person on the planet.

Where are you, Cole?

She squinted through the front windshield at a flash of movement. Another ATV was racing through the pasture, also without lights.

A dog barked, and Eve's worry climbed higher. "Don't be a hero, puppy," she whispered, hoping it wasn't Coco, Cole's sheepdog. Not long ago, Bella, Sasha's yellow Lab, had almost gotten herself killed protecting Sasha. She didn't want the same thing happening to Coco, but she knew the pooch would protect Cole.

And probably lead the way right to him. Good doggy.

Eve turned the truck in what she hoped was the direction of the barking dog and the big truck. She hit a pothole and almost smacked her head on the ceiling of the cab as the truck bounced along.

Her fingers ached from gripping the wheel, but she forged ahead, the sense that she had to get to Cole, and get there fast, making her drive faster than she ever would have in the dark, without lights.

With the windows rolled down so she could better hear what was happening, Eve leaned her head partway out the window. She still wasn't sure she was heading in the right direction. Where were they? Come on.

Another shot rang out, and Eve felt the breeze as it whizzed by her head. She jerked her head back into the cab, breath wheezing in her chest as she realized how close that bullet had come to hitting her.

"Stop!" Cole's voice came from somewhere nearby, so close she stomped on the brake, rocking the truck.

He pulled open the passenger door and heaved Coco up onto the bench seat, then climbed in behind him. "Turn around right here and go back to the house."

Eve felt the fury rolling off him in waves, heard it in the clipped tones.

"I specifically told you to stay in the house, so what in the blue blazes are you doing out here?"

"I was trying to help."

"Me watching people take shots at you is not helping."

As if to prove his point, another shot hit the bed of the truck and made it shudder. Eve tightened her grip as she stomped the accelerator.

"I said to head for the house, Eve."

"If we do that, by the time you finish lecturing me, they'll be long gone with your cattle."

Before he could respond, another shot rang out, then another, and Eve knew one of the tires had been hit. The wheel jerked out of her hands as she fought for control, and suddenly they slammed into a fence post. The truck didn't have air bags, and when Eve slammed into the steering wheel, she wished she'd taken time to put on her seat belt. Cole had grabbed Coco and tried to protect him from the impact, but both man and dog yelped.

The truck came to a rocking stop. Eve shook her head to clear it, then immediately slammed the truck into reverse, but it didn't go. The tires simply spun.

Cole checked Coco and set him back on the seat, then let out a sigh. "Stop. Eve. Let it go."

"But they'll get away."

He huffed out a breath. "They've already gotten away."

Coco sensed the tension and whined, then came over and licked Eve's face. She rubbed him behind the ear and then buried her face in his fur.

Silence settled over the truck, and remorse crashed over her in waves. She'd tried to help, she really had. And it had made things worse, not better. A tear sneaked down her cheek, and she turned her face away to swipe at it without Cole seeing. "I'm sorry. I was trying to help."

He opened his door and Coco jumped out. Before Eve realized what he was doing, he yanked open her door and pulled her out of the truck and into his arms in one smooth motion.

"You could have been killed, you reckless woman." And then his mouth was on hers, and she tasted frustration and relief and several other emotions she couldn't name on his tongue. He wrapped his arms tighter until Eve couldn't have said where he started and she began. His heart thundered in his chest, and hers pounded in rhythm as she realized he was alive. Relief flowed through her veins. They were both alive. *Thank you, God.*

The kiss started out hard and desperate, but slowly, slowly it gentled into something else, something Eve wasn't expecting. Cole cradled her head with his big, strong hands and feathered kisses along her jaw and her neck.

"Don't ever scare me like that again, Eve," he growled.

Eve smiled. "Right back at you, cowboy," she murmured.

His head snapped back. Wrong thing to say. "I know how to protect myself, and I know how to handle a gun. Can you say the same?"

Eve opened her mouth, closed it. She had no argument because he was right, doggone the stubborn man.

He didn't give her time to formulate an argument, simply tugged her close for another drugging kiss. This kiss carried apology and need and a protectiveness she had never experienced before. She was always the champion, the defender, the protector. She wasn't quite sure how to be on the receiving end of all that. She didn't know how to let someone look out for her.

But as she wrapped her arms around his neck and sank into the kiss, she realized she liked it. Liked it a lot. She could get used to someone else carrying at least part of the load. Protecting her.

She froze. No she couldn't. She would be leaving in a little while. She couldn't get too comfortable here.

Cole felt her stiffen and slowly eased back. Eve figured the dazed expression on his face probably mirrored her own.

"We should, ah—"

A police siren broke the silence. He speared her with his eyes. "You called Monroe?"

"No. I called my brother. That should be Nick. Though I didn't expect lights and sirens."

Cole held out his hand, and together they walked back to the ranch house and met Nick. He eyed their joined hands, then asked what was going on.

After a succinct rundown from Cole, he asked, "Neither one of you got a good look at that big rig? No license plate?"

"No, sorry," Eve said.

"I'll call you later, Cole," Nick tossed out as he hopped back into his SUV and raced off in the direction the trailer had gone.

Cole's mother came out of the shadows of the porch as soon as he left, still cradling her shotgun. "He's not going to be able to catch them, is he?"

Eve heard the defeat in her voice and shook her head, exhausted suddenly.

Cole sounded equally tired. "Doesn't look good, Ma, but he'll try. The boys and I will take inventory at first light, see how many they got away with."

"Nick's a good boy." She nodded toward Eve. "I'm glad you all found each other again." Then she looked them over. "Are you both OK?"

"We're fine." Cole leaned over and kissed his mother on the cheek. "Go on back to bed. I need to check in with Buzz, make sure Hector is OK."

"I'll go with you," Eve said, and fell into step behind him before he could voice a protest.

He didn't so much as glance her way, just stalked off toward the bunkhouse, all his focus on his men. She couldn't blame him. Hector hadn't been in good shape to begin with.

Cole picked up the pace when they got close to the bunkhouse and found the door halfway open. "Hector!" Cole burst through the door, Eve right behind him.

They found him facedown on the floor, and Eve's heart jumped into her throat. Cole crouched down beside him and checked for a pulse. "Hector, can you hear me?"

Hector groaned and tried to roll over. Cole helped him and put an arm around his shoulders as he struggled to a sitting position.

"Sorry, boss. I tried to get out there and stop them, but it didn't do any good."

"You should have stayed here."

Hector shot him an incredulous look. "And done nothing while they stole our cattle?"

Cole nodded. "I know. Thank you for trying. This is not your fault, man."

"Can we trace the brand? Find them when they try to sell them?"

"That's one of the things I'm sure Nick will be looking into."

Cole helped Hector to his feet and back into the recliner, where the other man sank down with a sigh. "Somebody is very determined to destroy the ranch, Cole. We have to stop them."

Eve understood Hector's use of the word *we*. For her, the ranch had become hers to protect, as well. She couldn't imagine what Hector was feeling after so many years here.

"And we will. But not tonight. Get some rest. I'll check in with you tomorrow."

Cole eased the door shut behind Hector, and they walked out to the paddock and leaned on the fence. Cole looked around and shook his head.

They both turned at the sound of hoofbeats and saw Buzz riding toward them on Morgan. He slid off the horse and stomped over to them. "The dirty, rotten thieves got most of the herd."

"Any idea who it was?"

"No. This was well organized, Cole. They knew exactly where they were herding the cattle and had the trailer ready, and the minute they got them inside, they took off, riding those ATVs and disappearing into the woods. And they made sure the loading area was far enough away that we couldn't get there in time to stop them."

Cole clapped him on the back. "I appreciate you trying to stop them. Nick will do what he can to track them down, but I'm not holding out much hope."

Eve looked from one to the other, heard the dejection. "There has to be a way. A tractor-trailer like that doesn't just vanish with no one noticing."

Nick pulled up in his SUV. At Cole's unspoken questions, he shook his head. "That tractor is long gone, but I've already called our dispatcher to have someone stationed by the main roads. We'll get the word out locally and to sheriffs' departments around the state, plus FDLE, the Florida Department of Law Enforcement. They'll all keep an eye out, too, but if the thieves are as organized as they sound, they've already changed out the license plate on the trailer, changed the numbers and markings on it, and will do everything they can to hide it in plain sight. I'll get a cast of the tire tracks in the morning, too, but I don't know how much good it will do." He grimaced. "Sorry."

Eve couldn't believe what she was hearing. "So that's it? We all shrug and move on?"

Cole planted his hands on his hips at her tone. "For tonight, yes. But if you know something we don't, I'm all ears."

She wanted to snap that she didn't like his tone, but he was right. She didn't have a better idea. She didn't have any idea. They were all frustrated and angry and exhausted, and all any of them really knew what that someone wanted to destroy the ranch who was willing to go to great lengths to do it.

The thing she couldn't figure out—and she knew all of them were thinking it, too—was who would do this?

She eyed Buzz. Could he have helped them, then showed up to offer support to Cole? He had the know-how. But why? He seemed to love the ranch, even if he didn't have much use for Cole's newfangled ways, as he called them.

Eve shook her head. "I'm just frustrated."

Cole shook his head and sighed. "We all are." He turned to Nick. "Thanks for coming out here, Nick."

"I'll keep looking, follow up with any contacts I can find. This is not over, not by a long shot. I'm just getting started."

"I appreciate it," Cole said, voice heavy.

Nick climbed back in his SUV and drove away. Eve scanned the ranch as they walked back to the house, trying to focus on the thieves, the sabotage, anything but how right her hand felt in Cole's much larger one, and how much this place was beginning to feel like home. Actually, it felt more like home than anyplace she'd ever been. Which was enough to send her running for the airport. She had to fight that feeling, that pull, with everything she had. Her place was in DC, championing those who needed her help, who couldn't fight for themselves. She couldn't atone for her mother's death if she stopped fighting.

Cole suddenly tugged her to him, and she realized they were on the porch of the ranch house. He put his hands on her shoulders and kissed her forehead. "Stop thinking and get some sleep. We'll deal with this again in a couple of hours."

Eve nodded, her emotions too tangled to utter a single word. He turned her and led her to the door like she was a child, then held the door while she went inside. The adrenaline drained out of her, and she stumbled down the hall and fell onto the bed without even climbing under the covers.

As she fell into sleep, her last thought was, *home*.

Chapter 26

Cole didn't get much sleep. Every time he dozed off he saw Eve in Hector's truck again, bullets whizzing by her head. He'd wake with a jolt, heart pounding and temper flaring. Several times he hopped out of bed, ready to blast into her room and shake her until her teeth rattled. Or wrap her in his arms and never let go. Neither of which would help a thing. Dang fool woman was going to get herself killed in her efforts to save people.

At 6:00 a.m., he gave up on sleep and made coffee, then grabbed a flashlight and paced every inch of the ranch, scanning high and low for any possible clues the rustlers might have left behind. He knew the chances were slim, but he'd take what he could get right now. Once the sun came up, he could start taking inventory, get an idea of just how many head of his cattle they stole.

Rustlers. He still couldn't believe it. Somebody wanted to destroy the ranch, that much was patently clear, but he couldn't figure out who. Blackwell wanted the place, no question, but he was a businessman. The things happening here at the ranch seemed personal. He knew Duane was desperate, but he didn't think his uncle had the smarts to pull off something this organized. Not with the way he was drinking lately.

So who was left? He rubbed a hand over his face. He had no idea.

He climbed onto the porch and plopped into one of the rockers, more tired than he could remember being. He leaned his head back, thinking he'd rest a few minutes, then get back out there as soon as the sun camp up.

———

"Cole. Time to wake up."

He started at the quiet voice, then sat up abruptly, blinking the sunlight out of his eyes. When he finally focused, he realized Eve stood there, wearing a T-shirt and jeans, her hair held back in a colorful band and a smile on her face. He wanted to wake up with her smiling at him just like that every day, he decided. Wait, what? She drove him crazy. He shook his head to clear it, then reached for the mug of coffee she held out to him. "What time is it?" His voice came out a croak.

"Almost nine." She held out a piece of paper. "The lab called the house and asked you to call them. I asked for the results, but they wouldn't give them to me." She grimaced.

He grinned at that. "Bet you tried, though."

She sniffed. "Of course, but they said they could only release them to you."

"This could be a good thing, Eve. If you'd put your name on the request, sure as shooting somebody would have accused you of trying to skew the results."

She rolled her eyes, but nodded. "Just because you're right doesn't mean I have to like it."

Since her impatience matched his own, he walked back inside and called the lab.

"Hi, this is Cole Sutton, returning your call."

"Hi, Mr. Sutton. We have the results of the three samples you turned in to us. So, for the two from inside the home, labeled *kitchen* and *bathroom*, the nitrate levels showed forty parts per million, which is far above the allowable ten parts per million here in Florida. That is definitely something you should investigate further. Right now that water is not safe to drink, especially not for infants or anyone with a compromised digestive system. The other sample, marked *pond*, contains nine parts per million of nitrates, which is well within the established guidelines. Would you like me to mail you a copy of the report?"

"Can you email it to me?"

"Certainly. I just need your email address."

Cole rattled it off, thanked the woman, and turned to Eve. "The nitrate levels in the samples from Celia's cottage are way high. Forty parts per million."

Eve gasped. "No wonder that baby got sick. Ten parts per million is the maximum considered safe."

"I know, that—"

"Wait. Sorry to interrupt. The health department said her well tested within acceptable margins."

Cole immediately understood. "That means the problem isn't coming up from the aquifer through the well. Someone tampered with the water *after* it reached the house."

"The chlorination system. It has to be." Eve started pacing. "But I still can't imagine Celia doing such a thing. Even with hormones sometimes messing with a mother's mind, I've seen nothing, not a single hint that would indicate anything like that is happening with Celia."

"Which means someone else contaminated it."

Eve squeezed her eyes shut and shook her head in frustration. "Which still leaves us where we were before. Trying to figure out who. And why." She stopped, grabbed her cell phone. "I need to call Celia. Make sure she's not using water in the house."

She dialed and put the phone to her ear. "Celia, are you and Glory home? Oh, that's good news. You're not using any of the water in the house to drink or make formula, right? We just heard from the lab. The nitrates are way too high, and Glory will get sick again if she ingests the water."

She paused, and Cole saw the tension drain out of her. "Good. You are one smart mama, Celia. Glory is lucky to have you. Yes, I would definitely use the canned formula, or bottled water to mix it up from powder for the foreseeable future. I'll stop by later, OK? Take care of that baby."

Cole opened his mouth to tell her he'd come with her, when her cell phone rang.

"Hey, Sash, is Mama OK?" She paced to the end of the porch and back. "For lunch? Of course I'll come, but wouldn't you rather have Jesse there? OK, I'll be right there." Eve disconnected and turned to face him. "Sasha's long-lost aunt wants to meet her for lunch today, and she wants me to come along. Jesse is manning the bait shop while Pop is with Mama." She paused. "I don't want to leave you alone dealing with all this." She waved a hand to indicate the ranch.

Cole smiled. "You need to go. Be there for Sasha. The only thing we'll be doing here is calculating how many cows we actually lost."

They both looked up as a Safe Harbor police SUV started down the drive. "That should be Nick," Cole said.

Eve still looked torn, but then she nodded. "OK. I'll call you when I'm done, and we can head over to Celia's place. Tell Nick if he needs anything from me to call me later."

She turned to go, but Cole stopped her. He put a finger under her chin to tilt it up. "Be careful, Eve. No heroics."

She flashed him the saucy grin that got him every time. "It's lunch at the Blue Dolphin. How dangerous can it be?"

He shook his head. With Eve, you never knew, and that's what worried him.

Chapter 27

By early afternoon, Eve felt totally unnecessary, an unfamiliar and uncomfortable sensation. Though she'd been quizzed on the rustlers by the lunch crowd at the Blue Dolphin and then gotten all teary-eyed at Sasha's emotional reunion with her late mother's sister, they didn't need her there.

As she drove Sasha back to the marina—after Sasha and Sophia promised to get together again in a few weeks—she smiled at Sasha, who sat in the passenger seat looking dumbstruck. "You OK, Sash?"

Sasha looked at her, eyes bright. "I'm overwhelmed, I guess. I never, ever expected to feel such a connection to someone I've never met. It's so unexpected, but so . . ." She lapsed into silence, and Eve didn't respond, just kept her eyes on the road. Watching Sasha and Sophia had created a jealous tug in Eve's heart she wasn't sure what to do with. For the first time, she longed to be a mother, to create her own family ties. Cole's face appeared in her mind, and she shoved it away.

As soon as they reached the marina, Sasha headed directly to the bait shop to find Jesse. Unsettled by her thoughts, Eve went into the house to check on Mama, who kindly but firmly told Eve she wanted to rest and told her to leave her in peace.

Eve got back in her car and called Cole to let him know she was headed back so they could stop by Celia's, maybe get some answers there, but his phone went right to voice mail.

She pulled up to the ranch house, completely at loose ends. She didn't see his pickup, but that didn't mean anything. He could be anywhere on the ranch. She got out and then drummed her fingers on the roof of her car. She had to think, to figure out what was going on, once and for all. Growing anxiety simmered just below her skin and made her antsy, desperate to keep her hands busy so her brain could process. Maybe she could cook dinner, let Alice have a night off. She kept offering, but Alice always said she had it taken care of. Maybe today she could convince her otherwise.

She didn't see Alice's car, though, so she was probably at a church meeting or something. Which was the perfect opportunity.

Eve headed into the kitchen and went right to the big pantry to take inventory. Between that and the freezer, she found everything she needed to make a nice baked ziti, a la Rosa Martinelli. Perfect. She'd have a big pan ready to go into the oven by the time Alice returned.

Feeling better now that she had a plan, Eve set to work, browning ground beef on the stove and boiling water for the pasta. She rummaged around in the fridge and found salad fixings, so she made that, too. Meanwhile she mentally reviewed every piece of information they had while her hands kept busy.

The list of those who wanted Cole's ranch wasn't long. Richard Blackwell wanted to expand his agribusiness. That was no secret.

Did Buzz want the place? He didn't seem to, but he also didn't seem impressed with how Cole was running things. Then there was Duane, who had a chip on his shoulder that got bigger when he drank, which, sadly, was too often. But if he wanted to buy the place, why try to sabotage it?

Eve stirred the meat as she tried to sort everything out. There was something here she was missing, that they were all missing. Some clue or . . . something.

She stepped over to the sink to wash a tomato and glanced out the window. What she saw stopped her heart.

The hay field was on fire.

No! She had to tell Cole. She grabbed her cell phone from the table and raced out the back door, dialing with one hand as she ran full-out toward the barn.

It rang three times and then his voice mail came on. "This is Cole Sutton. Leave a message."

"The hay field is on fire! Hurry!"

She shoved the phone in her pocket and kept running in the direction of the flames. Halfway there she slowed, realized she had nothing to fight the fire with. But it was spreading, and fast. She grabbed her phone again and dialed 911, knowing it would take time—time they didn't have—before the volunteer Safe Harbor Fire Department could get organized and get here, but she had to try. She couldn't just watch it spread.

"The hay field at Sutton Ranch is on fire, and it's spreading fast. Hurry!" She ignored the dispatcher's questions, hung up, and kept running.

She raced through the big open doors of the barn. "Cole! Buzz! Hector! The hay field is on fire!" She raced down the center aisle, calling their names over and over, but nobody answered.

When she got to the other end, she ran out the door and scanned the area, trying to spot them. If they were off in the back pastures, she knew she wouldn't be able to see them from here. Inside the barn, she heard the horses shifting, getting restless, several kicking at their stalls. What if the fire came this way?

OK, one thing at a time. But what should she do first?

Shovels. She ran back outside to the tool shed, made sure she propped the door open behind her, and ducked in, eyes out for bees. She grabbed several shovels and a pair of gloves, ran back outside, and hopped onto an ATV parked nearby. She'd never driven one before, but how hard could it be?

Someone had left the key in the ignition, so she fired it up and goosed the throttle just a little too hard and almost went flying off the back. She overcompensated when she hit the brake and stopped so suddenly, she almost flew over the handlebars. Heart racing, she forced herself to take a deep breath and focus. She eased it into gear and sped up as she raced toward the fire's edge.

Once she got there, she took a moment to see which way the wind was blowing the flames and made sure she parked the ATV well out of the fire line. She hoped.

She tugged on the gloves, grabbed a shovel, and got to work, scooping sand onto the flames, trying to keep them from advancing. She had no idea if it would work, but she'd seen it on TV once, and she didn't know what else to do. But if there was one thing Florida had plenty of, it was sandy soil.

It didn't take long to realize this was seriously hard work. And it was hot. The flames emitted enough heat it felt like she was standing in an oven. Her clothes stuck to her skin and sweat ran down her face and neck, but she didn't slow. She couldn't.

She bent and scooped, tossed. Bent and scooped, tossed. But before long, the toss started to get shorter and the amount of sand on the shovel, smaller. She was running out of strength.

Where was Cole? She eyed the angry flames and kept going. *Please God, don't let it all burn. Please don't let it all burn.*

Eve lost all track of time as she focused on the next scoop and then the next.

Suddenly a hand reached out and grabbed her arm, spinning her around. She jumped in surprise, then looked up and thought her heart would stop.

She was surrounded by flames. How had she not realized what was happening? Cole scooped her into his arms and took off running, muttering the whole way. He ran over to the ATV, plopped her on the back, climbed on, and took off, away from the fire.

Eve grabbed his waist so she wouldn't slide off the back. He didn't go far, just far enough that Eve didn't feel her face was melting off. He stopped, pulled her off, and studied her from head to foot. "Are you OK? Did you get burned anywhere?"

Puzzled by his panic, Eve glanced down at herself, surprised to see several burn marks on her jeans. "No. I'm fine. Really. But we have to get back." She turned to look and saw the fire moving farther and farther into the field.

"The fire was all around you, Eve. Had you not seen it?"

"No, I'm sorry. I hadn't. I was so focused on trying to smother it or create some kind of barrier, I wasn't watching. I just kept shoveling."

His grin melted her from the inside out. "You are one of the toughest cowboys I've ever met, Eve Jackson." Then his smile disappeared as he looked in the direction of the flames. "I don't think we'll be able to stop it. It's moving too fast."

"I called the fire department."

"I appreciate it, but I'm not sure there will be anything left to save by the time they get here." He turned back to the ATV, grabbed a bottle of water he had in the back, and tossed it to her. She caught it and hurried over to him, hopped on the back, and wrapped her arms around his middle.

He looked at her over his shoulder. "You sure you have any fight left?"

"I'm sure." Though her shaky knees might argue otherwise. She wouldn't give up. Not while she could make a difference.

He dropped a quick kiss on her lips. "Warrior." Then he hit the throttle.

Eve held tight as he raced around to the far side of the field. Hector and Buzz were there, doing the same thing she'd been doing. Buzz was shoveling sand, and Hector had the water tanker going, wetting down the sand perimeter.

And still, the flames greedily consumed more hay, almost laughing as they danced along.

"Where's Duane?" Buzz asked. "Did you find him?"

"No. I found Eve instead." Cole turned to her. "Duane's pickup is out by the barn, but we can't find him. Did you see him?"

Dread coiled in Eve's gut. "No. I ran through the barn calling for all of you, but nobody answered. The horses were getting restless—nervous about the fire, I think."

"I'm sure they are. Ma is standing by to lead them out if the flames head that way."

"I'll go look for him while you guys work."

"I don't want you getting too close to the flames again."

"I'll pay closer attention. I promise."

Cole nodded and grabbed his shovel. Eve hopped on the ATV and set off toward the barn. She called Duane's name as she went, thinking that if he'd fallen or something, he might hear her—though with the sound of the engine, she had to stop regularly so she could hear him if he responded.

She got all the way back to the barn and hopped off to run inside. "Alice! Have you seen Duane?"

Cole's mother was standing by one of the stalls, murmuring and stroking the forehead of one of the horses. At Eve's question, the color drained from her cheeks. "You didn't find him?"

"No. But Cole hadn't had much time to look for him before he found me. So I'll keep looking while they work on the fire."

She looked her over. "Are you OK?"

Eve wondered just how bad she must look, since everyone kept asking her that. "I'm fine. Just sooty, I think."

Alice nodded. "Check the sheds. He may have gone into one to, ah—"

The word *drink* hovered in the air, but neither woman said it out loud. Eve nodded and ran back out to the ATV. She took off in that direction, her worry hitching up as she saw how much the fire had spread in the past few minutes. Off in the distance, she could see Cole, Buzz, and Hector hard at work. Where was the fire department?

She skidded to a halt by the sheds and ran into the one she'd gotten shovels from, but Duane wasn't there. He wasn't in any of the other two, either.

She hopped back on the ATV and drove all the way around the barn, then over past the berry fields. She stopped every so often and stood on the seat to get a better vantage point in case he'd fallen somewhere, but still nothing. Where could he have gone?

Could he have circled back to the house? She checked there next, grateful when she remembered the stove and saw someone had turned it off. Then she drove around the paddock and back to the barn from the opposite direction, calling Duane's name as she went.

Sirens finally sounded in the distance, and Eve breathed a sigh of relief. But as she looked at the flames, she wondered if it was too little, too late, as Cole feared. There was so much blackened earth where the hay had been.

Eve saw the big pumper truck, followed by four pickups that must belong to the firefighters, make the turn onto the ranch. She took off around the paddock, figuring they could find their way easily enough. But she had to find Duane.

She raced back toward where the fire had started. Her heart clenched at all the blackened earth, but she couldn't think about that or she'd cry. That would come later. She stood on the ATV again and scanned the field. "Duane! Where are you?"

Wait. Was that a groan? "Duane? Are you here?"

She waited. There it was again. She climbed back on the seat and slowly headed in the direction she thought the sound was coming from. "Duane? Let me know where you are."

"Here." The sound was so faint, she almost missed it.

Eve stopped the ATV and stood up on it again, scanning the area. There! She jumped off and almost stumbled in her haste. Just on the edge of the burned-out field, in a slight depression, lay Duane. Facedown.

Eve skidded to a stop and crouched down beside him. She bit back her horror at the burns on his back. Had he been completely caught in the fire? "Easy, Duane. I'm here. I'll get help, OK? Don't move."

She reached for her cell phone, but couldn't find it. It must have fallen out of her pocket at some point as she raced around. She turned back to Duane. "I'm going for help. I'll be right back. Stay put. Please."

He didn't respond, and Eve's panic climbed higher. She hopped back on the ATV and raced over to the fire truck, which was just getting to work. It seemed to take forever to get there. But as soon as she did, she ran to where Cole and the firefighters were working.

"I found Duane, but he's badly burned."

"Show me," one of the firemen said, and she recognized Chad Everson, Nick's friend and the high school football coach. "Let me grab my truck and some gear."

Cole turned toward the trucks. "I'm coming with you."

Chad grabbed his arm. "You'll be more help here. We'll take care of him."

Cole looked torn, but then someone called his name to help. He closed his eyes and then mouthed "Thank you" in Eve's direction before he ran over and grabbed hold of one of the fire hoses.

Chad ran back to the fire truck and pulled out a medical bag while one of the other firefighters put a backboard into the bed of a pickup truck and got behind the wheel.

"Lead the way," Chad called as he hopped into the passenger seat of the pickup. Eve turned the ATV around and led them back the way she'd come.

For a volunteer fire department, their skill and competence impressed Eve. She crouched down beside Duane in case they needed help, but she couldn't look at his burns for fear she'd start sobbing. She prayed silently and watched as they quickly checked his airway and gave him oxygen, then started IVs, urgently talking into their radios in codes and numbers she didn't understand.

Chad glanced her way. "I called for a medevac to take him to the burn center in Gainesville. This is more than our little hospital can handle. He needs specialized care."

Just then there were more sirens, and Eve turned to see Chief Monroe pulling up, followed by Nick in his official SUV.

Nick was the first to reach her. "Are you OK?"

She stood and walked a slight distance away. "I'm fine. But Duane . . . it's bad."

Nick glanced over. "What happened to him?"

"I found him facedown at the edge of the fire. His burns . . . they're really bad."

Nick scanned the area. "Do you know how the fire started?"

Eve stopped. Stared. In all the chaos and panic, she hadn't given it a single thought, and she said so. "We were all focused on trying to put it out."

"As you should have been."

"We didn't know where Duane was. His truck was here, but we couldn't find him."

Eve heard Duane moan and sent up another silent prayer. She couldn't say she liked him much, but no one should have to suffer like this. The EMTs were working like crazy, but it was obvious that Duane's injuries needed immediate care.

It seemed like hours before Eve heard the helicopter approaching. Alice came running over from the barn. She took one look at her brother and tried to reach for him. Eve grabbed her from behind and stopped her. "Easy, Alice. Let them do their thing."

"Duane, oh, dear God, Duane. Oh, you poor, dear man. Oh, Jesus . . ." The words tumbled out amid a torrent of tears as she struggled to reach her brother. Eve didn't know what to do, so she simply turned the other woman in her arms and held her while she sobbed.

The helicopter landed quite a ways away, so as not to make the fire worse. The second EMT turned to Eve. "We're going to drive him to the chopper in my truck."

"I'm going with you," Alice cried.

The man's eyes were kind, but his tone firm. "I'm sorry, ma'am, but there isn't enough room in the chopper."

Eve looked Alice directly in the eyes, tried to reach past her panic. "They're taking him to Gainesville. I'll drive you, OK?" When Alice nodded, Eve turned to the EMT. "We'll meet you there."

Eve turned Alice back toward the house and away from the sight of her brother's burns. They hadn't gone far when Buzz stalked up to them and cut off their progress.

"We'll find who did this, Alice. Don't you worry."

Her smile didn't reach her eyes, but she tried. "Thank you, Buzz. I appreciate all you're doing. All you've done."

He reached out as if to touch her, then drew his hands back and shoved them into his pockets. The two of them exchanged a long look Eve couldn't decipher before he turned back. Alice looked over her shoulder and watched him go.

Eve helped Alice into the car, and they set off, Eve praying all the while. She might not care much for Duane but he was Alice's brother, and from what she'd heard, a good man when he wasn't drinking. She asked God to spare his life, but also to bring healing.

As she drove, Eve also thought about the field and wondered what Duane had been doing out there. Had he accidentally lit the fire?

Or worse, had he set it deliberately?

The thought sent goose bumps over her skin. It was no secret Duane wanted the ranch. Would he have done such a thing to try to get it? Eve wasn't sure, hated to even think such a thing, but she knew if it had crossed her mind, it was on Cole's and Nick's and everyone else's, too.

Where would it end?

Chapter 28

Cole watched as the medevac helicopter lifted off and Eve drove off with his mother. He couldn't remember the last time he'd been this exhausted, but they weren't done yet. He turned and headed back to the burned-out field with the fire chief, Chief Monroe, and Nick Stanton.

"No idea how the fire started, Cole?" Chief Monroe asked.

He shook his head. "Seems like it started in an instant and turned into an inferno in ten seconds flat."

The fire chief suddenly quickened his pace, bent down, and picked something up. "I think we know what started it."

Cole's heart sank at the gas can the man held. They weren't standing far from where they'd found Duane, and from the looks on everyone's faces, they were all thinking the same thing. Would his uncle really have stooped that low to get the ranch?

"This doesn't necessarily mean Duane started the fire," Nick was quick to point out. "Duane might have seen someone else set the fire and have gone out to try to stop them or figure out what was going on."

"We won't know for sure until Duane can answer a few questions," Chief Monroe added. The EMTs had said the hospital would put him into a drug-induced coma for a few days. Still, the fact that he had a bump on his head could indicate someone had knocked him out.

———

Three mornings later, Cole scrubbed a hand over his stubbled jaw and tried to clear his head as he walked down the hall in the ranch house. After a two-day vigil at the hospital, Cole had finally convinced his mother to come home last night to rest and get cleaned up. They all needed sleep in the worst way.

He walked into the kitchen to find Eve at the stove. He stepped over and put his arms around her from behind, needing nothing more in that moment than to absorb the feel of her in his arms. He breathed in the citrus-and-coconut scent that floated from her skin and hair, a stark contrast to the smoke that still seemed to ooze from his every pore. "That smells great. You smell great."

She smiled at him over her shoulder, but her eyes were worried. "Did you get some sleep, finally?"

He leaned his head on her shoulder. "Some. You?"

"The same. Grab some coffee. I'll have breakfast ready in a second."

He didn't move. It felt too good just to hold her like this, to see her in the ranch kitchen, cooking. Something inside him shifted, and he realized he wanted to do this every morning. Not that he expected her to cook breakfast every day, but he wanted Eve here, on the ranch, so he could hold her just like this every day. The thought had slipped through his mind before, but he'd shoved it away.

This time the thought took root, even though every instinct said to pull away. But he forced himself to stay where he was, to absorb this feeling, see how it fit.

Once he eased his mind past the panic, he found he liked it. He liked it a lot. Being with Eve felt like coming home. Her, the ranch, all rolled together in his mind, and he saw his future—their future—spread out before him. He pictured a few kids running around the yard, chasing another dog or two, and he and Eve sitting on the porch, watching them.

The vision was so clear, he started when she spoke.

"If you don't let go, cowboy, the eggs will burn." The tone was stern, but he heard the smile in it.

He placed a quick kiss on her neck and smiled as he poured coffee. "You didn't have to cook, but man it smells good."

"My pleasure," she said as she slid the eggs onto a plate and added bacon and toast.

"Sit down and join me," he said when she turned back to the sink to start washing up. "And I'll do the dishes."

Her eyebrows shot up. "You do dishes?"

"Smarty-pants. Yes, I do dishes. Whoever cooks shouldn't have to clean up, as well."

She grinned as she scooped eggs onto a plate, grabbed bacon and toast, and sat down across from him. "I like the way you think, cowboy."

"I'm hoping that's not the only thing you like about me, Evie the Crusader," he quipped, then watched her eyes. They darted around the room, and he could sense the panic humming just beneath her skin. He reached across the table and took one of her hands in his, surprised to feel her trembling. He didn't think Eve was afraid of anything. But from what he'd seen, feelings scared her.

Which he understood, because the feelings racing around inside him right now made him want to head for the hills, too, as it were. Instead, he took her other hand, as well, and held tight when she would have pulled away. Then he waited for her eyes to quit darting around the room and look at him.

"Look, Eve, I—"

His mother walked into the room, fully dressed for the day, looking like a woman on a mission. Which surprised him, since she'd been dead on her feet last night.

Eve tugged her hands away and studied her food, her obvious relief making him wonder what she'd been afraid he was going to say. Especially since he wasn't entirely sure himself. But it had something to do with—

"I need to talk to you, Cole," Alice said, tone brisk as she poured herself a cup of coffee.

Her tone put him on alert, but he kept his voice casual. "Sure. What's up, Ma?"

"I've saved up a little money from my quilts, and I'm using it to put a down payment on a little cottage just off Main Street. I've also been hired to work at the new quilt-and-yarn shop Junie Ryder is opening in Safe Harbor."

If his mother had said she were running for president of the United States, he would have been less surprised. He tried to process what he'd just heard, but came up blank. "You're buying investment property?" It was the only thing that made sense, but given the ranch finances, actually, it didn't.

"No, not as an investment. To live in."

"But you live here. You've always lived here." Cole knew he sounded like an idiot, but he couldn't seem to stop. "I don't understand."

His mother slid into the chair beside him and took one of his hands, much like he'd taken Eve's, only this time, he felt like he was five years old again, and the look in her eyes said he wasn't going to like what he heard.

"I've been thinking, for a while, actually, that it's time for me to make a change. I think I'd like to live in town."

"But you've always lived on the ranch."

She smiled. "I have, my whole life. So it's time for a change, don't you think?"

"What about the ranch?"

"I'm signing it over to you. I want you to have it. I've always wanted that. I think your father did, too."

Cole snorted at that last bit. "What about Duane?"

"I love my brother, and honestly, coming so close to losing him reminded me how fragile and how short life can be. He can't run this place, much as he says he wants to. I won't sell it to him, in any case." She paused, waited until he met her eyes. "This place was your father's dream, not mine."

When Cole started to protest, she held up a hand. "Let me finish. You are not your father. You are a different kind of man entirely, one who will love and care for this ranch and the animals and people who call it home. I think this place has always been your dream, too, whether you realized it or not. I'm signing it over to you."

"I can protect you, if you stay."

"Of course you can. It isn't about protection. It's about me moving on with my life. And you moving on with yours. You need to be the boss of Sutton Ranch, not my ranch manager. I'm giving it over to you, lock, stock, and barrel. It's not worth much right now, especially with that loan, but if anyone can make this place profitable again, it's you."

Cole let the words roll around in his brain while he tried to process. "You don't want the ranch."

"It isn't that I don't want it so much as that I want you to have it. To make it your own, run it however you want, free from the past."

"Why didn't you ever say any of this?"

She shrugged, the shadows in her eyes telling him without words that it was because of his father, out of some misguided loyalty to him. "You never asked."

He had no idea what to say. Until he screwed everything up when he was still in his teens, he'd been planning to take over the ranch one day. His father had said as much, over and over, and Cole had believed him. Until the day Hank kicked him out and told him to never come back. Which he hadn't, until now.

She wanted him to have the ranch.

Cole stood, hugged his mother once, hard, and walked out of the kitchen, grabbing his Stetson from the peg by the back door on his way out. He had to think, to process, and he couldn't do that with her watching him, with Eve watching him.

Is this what he wanted? At eighteen, absolutely, it had been. Even after he left, the need to come home, to come back, had always been there, surprising him with its intensity at odd moments.

But now? Was that still what he wanted? He'd come back for Ma, to help her. And he'd been glad to do it, never mind the emotional quagmire that had been. The place wasn't just a chunk of dirt, and she knew it, too. Sutton Ranch held memories that were as much a part of the place as the fence posts and outbuildings. Everywhere he turned were memories. Some good. Some not, but they were there.

Did he want to stay?

The question circled round and round as he went out to the barn, saddled Morgan, and headed out. The best way to clear his head was still a gallop on his favorite horse.

He hadn't gotten past the paddock when he heard Eve call his name. He almost kept going, pretending he hadn't heard her, but he wasn't that big a coward. He slowed, turned, and dismounted when she came running up to him.

She stopped safely out of Morgan's reach. "Are you OK?"

He nodded. "I just need some time to think."

"Want some company?"

"Are you offering to come riding with me?"

She paled. "Um, no, not really."

"Then I guess I'll see you later."

He tried to ignore the hurt in her eyes as he swung up into the saddle and turned the horse away from the ranch. The fact that she so obviously didn't belong in his world struck him like a blow. She might be wearing cowboy boots, jeans, and T-shirts these days, but Eve wasn't a ranch girl. She was a city girl, and he couldn't think with her around.

He'd have to apologize later for being a jerk. Right now he needed a quick gallop to clear the cobwebs and help him turn his world back right side up, after his mother had spun everything out of control.

———

Eve watched him ride away and almost sank down into the dirt. But she wouldn't cave, wouldn't let anyone see how much he'd hurt her. Sheer force of will kept her spine stiff as he rode farther and farther away. Would he look back? She didn't think so, but her foolish heart hoped he would anyway.

He had almost disappeared from view when her cell phone rang. She checked the caller ID before she answered. "Hello, Mr. Braddock."

"Eve, we have a situation here." He launched directly into a lengthy description of another tip on suspected illegal dumping of chemicals, without so much as saying hello or asking how things were going. Which was how he'd always spoken to her, but somehow, now, it grated. How hard was it to take a minute and ask about her mother, how Eve was doing?

When he finally paused for breath, Eve said, "My mother seems to be improving, so we're thankful for that."

The silence lengthened; then he cleared his throat. "Good, good. Glad to hear it. I also read about your little investigation in Safe Harbor. Sounds like you're doing a bang-up job, but we have bigger fish to fry than a single well in a small town. The amount of chemicals these criminals are dumping . . . well, I need you on the next plane back to DC. I need my best investigator on this, and you're it."

Eve had known, as soon as he'd started talking, that this was the reason he'd called. But hearing him dismiss her investigation here so casually left her with a hollow feeling she hadn't expected. She couldn't just abandon Celia. Or Cole. Not before she figured out who was behind it all.

At the sound of hoofbeats, she turned to see Cole galloping back toward her with an urgency that made her stomach clench. Had something else happened?

"I need to go. Thanks for calling, Mr. Braddock. I'll have to let you know."

"It wasn't a suggestion, Eve," he ground out, but she didn't hear whatever else he said because all her attention was focused on Cole.

He pulled up and slid from the horse, then pulled her into his arms with enough force that she landed against his chest with a whoosh. Before she could form a single coherent thought, his lips were on hers and those powerful arms had her wrapped so tight she could barely breathe. His heart thundered against hers, and she tasted panic, and desperation, mixed with a hefty dose of confusion in his kiss.

Which perfectly mirrored her own stormy feelings. She responded with all the churning emotions spinning in her own heart and mind in what became a mind-numbing kiss.

Cole cupped her cheeks, and the kiss changed from stormy to calm, welcoming.

Eventually Cole eased her back a bit and brushed the clouds of hair back from her face. He ran the back of one finger down her cheek. "You have the softest skin," he murmured.

She smiled, but the intensity in his eyes unnerved her.

"Stay with me, Eve. Here on the ranch."

Her heart pounded, and panic made her hands shake. "I-I, ah, I don't know what to say." She couldn't live on a ranch in this tiny Florida town. How could she make a difference from here? If she quit her job, more water would be contaminated, more children would get sick and die. She had work to do. Work that mattered. Her work stopped criminals and saved lives.

Cole seemed to sense her hesitation, and she saw a protective shield come down over his eyes a split second before he slid his hands away and took a step back. "You're leaving."

Eve rubbed her arms as the chill in his voice washed over her. It wasn't a question, but she answered anyway. "My boss wants me on the next plane. But I'll hold him off until we figure out what's going on here." She paused. "I never planned on staying."

"Plans can change."

"Sometimes. My work matters. Can you understand that?"

He nodded, eyes sad. "I can. And it does."

Without another word, he swung back into the saddle and left again. Eve stared after him, the tears she'd held back pouring down her face.

Here was a terrific guy, promising her a good life, and she couldn't accept. Because she was afraid that he would see through her, see the fraud she was. She fought so hard for others, but all those years ago when her own mother had desperately needed Eve to be her advocate, her champion, Eve had hidden in the alley as her mother had asked, scared to death while the woman she was trying to protect died, alone. Never mind that her mother had ordered her to hide. Eve shouldn't have listened. But she'd followed the rules, while others hadn't, and her mother had died because of it.

That's why she didn't always do what she was supposed to, not when lives were at stake. She'd vowed to be a champion for others, to protect them from unsafe water and chemicals that could cause illness or death. In a small corner of her heart she hoped that someday, if she won enough battles, eventually the guilt that still wanted to suffocate her would ease enough so there was room for something—or someone—else in her life. But it wasn't that day yet. And until it was, she had work to do. Alone.

Eve shook off the dark thoughts as Hector came up beside her and gave her a thorough perusal, his dark eyes missing nothing. "Cole is a good man. Very different than his father."

"Different how?" Eve swiped at her tears. She'd heard bits and pieces. Maybe Hector would finally give her the whole story.

He shook his head. "I don't like to speak ill of the dead."

"I need to know, Hector."

Hector studied her intently for a few moments, then nodded. "Hank was a hard man. He thought that being tough was the way to make a man out of Cole. He beat him with his belt—too much. He never had a kind word, never tried to encourage Cole in any way, even though Cole has always been wonderful with the horses."

Eve's heart clenched at an image of a young Cole being subjected to a belt.

The unfairness of it all made her appreciate the man Cole had become even more. It would have been easy to succumb to bitterness, after a childhood like that. But she'd seen no evidence of that in Cole.

"What about Alice?" Her blood ran cold at the idea that Hank beat his wife, as well.

He wouldn't meet her eyes, and the silence lengthened as she watched him debate how much to say. "She tried to protect Cole when she could. She made sure Cole never saw, never knew."

She heard what he wasn't saying. "Hank beat her, too."

"*Sí*. Especially if he was angry with Cole, or things at the ranch did not go well."

"Which happened a lot."

Another shrug, averted eyes. "*Sí*. Too often. I tried to stop him, but he said if I interfered again, he would throw me off the ranch."

"You stayed to protect Cole. And then, Alice."

There was steel in his voice. "She is a strong lady and should be treated with respect."

Eve wondered if maybe Hector had feelings for Cole's mother. "I'm sure it means the world to Cole that you were there when he couldn't be."

Alarm flashed in Hector's eyes. "No, senorita. You must not tell him. I just did my job."

Eve hurried to reassure him. "This is not my story to tell, Hector. Please do not worry. But I think it explains why Alice might be ready to live elsewhere."

He stiffened. "She is leaving the ranch?"

Oh dear. What had she just finished saying about telling other people's stories? "I think she's considering a change. But you should discuss that directly with her, I think."

He nodded, clearly troubled by the prospect. Then he looked out toward where Cole had disappeared into some trees. "Cole is a good man. He should be the boss of the ranch." He eyed her sideways. "You are good for him, senorita."

Eve tried to smile as his words brought a lump to her throat. "He is more than a good man. He's the best, and he deserves the best. I am not that person." She kept her tone light. "I'm a crusader, always off on a mission to right wrongs, save the world."

"Perhaps the wrong you are trying so hard to right is something that happened long ago, and can't be fixed. It can only be forgiven."

The words froze Eve's smile and hit like an unexpected blast. How could he know what happened in her past? But when she looked into his brown eyes, she saw understanding, and recognized a kindred spirit, someone who had seen too much, perhaps, but had still found a way to move forward, to look for the positive. She envied him that, wanted that for herself, but didn't think she deserved it.

"Grace is what we get when we let go of the burden we are struggling to carry. When we hand it over to el Señor, God himself, he carries it for us and gives us a new start, another chance. But we have to stop carrying the burden first, and lay it down."

The words were spoken quietly, but with great conviction. Looking into Hector's bruised face she realized she didn't need to know the details to know he spoke from experience. She wanted what he was talking about. But after so many years, she didn't know where to begin.

All she knew was how to fix things, to try to make amends.

On impulse, she reached up and hugged the older man, and she could swear the tips of his ears turned red. "Thank you, Hector. You are a good man." She stepped back. "And I'm sorry—again—about the damage to your truck. The mechanic said he'll have it ready for you in a couple of days."

She ignored Hector's protest about the cost as she turned back to the house. Right now she still had battles to fight on Cole's behalf.

And maybe, just maybe, somewhere in the middle of it all, she'd figure out what to do about Cole.

Chapter 29

Cole galloped away from Eve a second time, calling himself eight kinds of fool. She'd never said she was staying, never let him believe, for even a second, that living out in the middle of nowhere on a struggling ranch with an ornery cuss like him was something she might want to do. What had he been thinking?

He'd been thinking about what he wanted. About how right she felt in his arms. About how he hadn't realized how lonely he was until Eve showed up in his world with all her fire and passion and zest for life. She shook him out of his detachment and made him long for connection, something he had deliberately stopped wanting when he was a teenager. If you didn't get involved, you couldn't get hurt. But Eve had changed all that. She'd made him want to open his heart, more fool him.

She, however, had been thinking about the same thing she'd been obsessed with since she was a teen: her latest crusade. He admired her need to help people, he really did. It was a big part of what made Eve, Eve. But couldn't she save the water supply and save the planet from the ranch?

He sighed. She probably could, if she wanted to. But therein lay the problem. It didn't appear she wanted to. So, now what?

Did he want to stay on the ranch without her?

He looked up as Leon drove by in his pickup truck, heading for the back field, near where the rustlers had loaded the cattle.

What was he doing way out here? Cole turned and headed in that direction, watching as Leon got out of the truck, picked something off the ground, and got back in.

He met him as he was heading back. "Hey, Leon? What brings you out this way?"

"Thought I dropped something last time I checked that ramp."

Cole thought the other man seemed uncomfortable, which surprised him. "Didn't realize we'd had a problem with the ramp."

"No equipment to fix, that's a fact, but I was helping Hector check the fence after those rotten thieves done stole part of your herd, and lost one of my tools." He held up a pry bar. "Gotta have this baby to get things done."

Cole smiled. "Glad you found it, then." He tipped his hat and backed away as Leon drove over to the barn. The conversation bothered him at a level he learned long ago not to ignore. Something was up with Leon. But was it personal stuff—everyone knew his wife had left him recently—or something to do with the sabotage on the ranch?

He headed back to the barn to talk to the hands. He knew he wouldn't figure it out standing here.

———

Eve went looking for Buzz. He was seated in the office, booted feet propped on the desk while he checked over a list of some kind. When she walked in, his feet hit the floor and he stood up and said, "Cole's not here."

Eve kept a pleasant expression on her face. "I know. Any word on Duane today?"

"Heard they took out the breathing tube, which is good." He shrugged. "Haven't heard any more. Still can't figure out what he was doing out in that field with the fire."

Eve had a few theories she wanted to discuss with Nick about that. For now, she shrugged. "It's hard to know, but I'm glad there is some improvement. This has been really hard on Alice."

"It has, though I don't know why she cares so much about the stubborn drunk." He stopped, shook his head. "I get that he's her brother, but he's done nothing but make the people who care about him miserable for too long. Alice doesn't deserve that."

"Agreed. Seems she's had hardship coming faster than she can keep up with." Eve paused, tried to decide how to phrase her next question.

Buzz studied her, then folded his arms over his chest. "Spill it, whatever it is you came to say."

Eve's chin came up at his tone. "I came to ask if you'd consider helping Cole get through this rough patch, financially."

He didn't say anything for a moment, just studied her from narrowed eyes. "Cole—or his mama—don't cotton to charity."

"I didn't figure they did. But a helping hand from a friend isn't the same thing, now, is it?"

When he didn't say anything, Eve added, "You and I both know Cole is doing all he can, but someone is sabotaging him at every turn."

"Don't see you coughing up your hard-earned money, missy."

An embarrassed flush crept over Eve's cheeks. "Fighting the good fight has never paid well," she shot back, then sobered. "If I had any to give, you can bet I would have already done it."

"You think I have pots of cash sitting around?"

"I think that fancy car you drive didn't come from Walmart. You may not be rich, but I'm betting you could help if you wanted to."

"And what makes you think I'd want to?"

She studied his harsh expression. "Alice. You may not care that much for Cole, but Alice is a different story." She held up a hand when he started to protest. "And don't try to pretend differently. I've seen it. So, will you help?"

"I'll think about it."

"Fair enough."

"And while I'm thinking, you might want to take another look at Richard Blackwell's place. I've seen quite a bit of activity there at night that might bear looking into."

She remembered what Celia had said about seeing Buzz ride by late at night. "Where?"

He sketched a quick map of the area he was talking about.

Unsure what else to say, Eve thanked him and left.

As soon as it got dark, she would go check it out.

———

Restless and edgy as Cole's words, combined with Hector's, played over and over in her mind, Eve stopped by the marina. She had only planned to stay a few minutes, just to see how Mama Rosa was doing, make sure all was as it should be. But the minute she pulled up and saw Mama in her rocker on the porch, she knew she'd be here a while. The trick was to not let her guard down and tell Mama everything—no matter how tempting that could be—because Mama had enough to worry about right now without adding Eve's romantic issues to the list.

"How is my Eve? Come give me a kiss," she commanded when Eve climbed the steps to the porch.

Eve smiled and leaned over to kiss the familiar cheek, shocked anew at how much weight she'd lost. Mama had always been apple-round and soft; now her skin hung on her frame. The scarves she wore around her bald head always made panic flare in Eve's chest. Especially now, with the threat to Mama still surrounding them.

Eve pulled another rocker up close and sat down, gently taking Mama's hand in her own. "How are you, Mama?"

Mama smiled, some of the familiar twinkle back in her sunken eyes. "It is good to be home, my Eve. There is nothing like sleeping in your own bed, even though Sal snores loud enough to wake the dead. Even that, I missed. Though the family's hovering is making me crazy."

Eve smiled, as she'd been meant to do. And they'd keep hovering, as long as they needed to. "I'm glad you are home."

"Tell me how little Glory is doing."

Eve assured her the little girl was back home and improving steadily. Instead of a smile at that update, Eve saw sadness. "Mama? What's wrong? I thought that would be good news."

"It is. The best." She paused and bit her lip. "But it means you will be heading back to DC soon, no?"

Eve hesitated, tried to gentle her tone. "Eventually, yes. But not until we know what happened to make Glory sick. You knew I wasn't staying forever, right?"

Mama's brave smile felt like a knife to Eve's heart. She wanted to say, *No, don't cry. I'll stay forever.* But she didn't. Couldn't. Because it was almost time to leave.

"Cole asked me to stay." The words were out before she could call them back.

A quick flash of joy appeared in Mama's eyes, but then she sobered. "You told him no."

Eve shrugged, looked away, then back. "My work is in DC. I have a job to do. I make a difference there."

"You could make a difference here, too. With all those computers they have today, you could work from anywhere, no?"

Eve couldn't meet her eyes.

"Look at me, my Evie."

Eve turned at the command. Mama squeezed her hand, and her voice was firm. "Your work matters, Eve. There is no question. You help protect the drinking water, protect families and little children like Glory. Keep people—keep children—from getting sick and dying. And that is commendable and good. But no matter how many things you make right, you will never make up for your mother's death. Because. It. Wasn't. Your. Fault. You didn't poison that water, Eve."

Mama had said this to her before, many years ago. She couldn't accept the words then. She still couldn't. Could she?

"You were a child, and you obeyed what your mother asked. There is no fault in that. If you hadn't hid like she told you, that terrible man would have taken you away. You know this. And I fear to think what your life would have been like."

Mama reached out and cupped Eve's cheeks. "It is time to set down that burden. You can never bring your mother back, but it is time to let go of the guilt. It's false. You are taking on the responsibility for keeping your mother alive, and that job belongs to God alone."

Tears she hadn't been aware of streamed down Eve's cheeks, and she swiped them away with angry hands. "He didn't do a very good job that day."

"We will never understand why some live long lives and others don't. But I know that there is always a bigger picture, and that included God sending you to us. I have no doubt He sent you here, Eve. Else how would a city girl like you have found herself in a little town like Safe Harbor? We needed you in our family, Evie. We still do."

Mama paused, sat back as some of the energy appeared to drain out of her. "If you need to go back to DC, then you must go. But be sure you are going for the right reasons and not simply running away. Or because of misplaced guilt. Cole is a good man. He's steady and dependable. A nice balance for your fire."

Eve thought of the way he'd kissed her and realized he had his own fire; it was just more carefully banked. "I need to go, Mama. I love you. Get some rest, despite Pop's snoring."

Mama kissed her cheek. "Follow your heart, Evie. It will not lead you wrong this time."

Eve kissed her back and headed to her car. It still wasn't dark, so she drove into town and bought a new camera. Not as fancy as her other one, but it would do. Then she walked the short length of Main Street and back, trying to picture living here forever. Beatrice stepped out of the salon and asked about Glory. Someone waved and she waved back.

She wandered through Annie's Attic and browsed the jumble of old and new that was gathered here. She exchanged pleasantries with the elderly part-time clerk, who said she appreciated Eve's gumption in trying to help little Glory. It was just a simple day in a small town.

And yet, someone from this town had poisoned Glory and threatened Mama. Eve glanced around, feeling both settled and anxious at once. She got back into her car and headed toward the Blackwell place, hoping she'd finally find the answers she needed.

Chapter 30

Eve drove out past Blackwell Farms, one eye on the sketch Buzz had drawn for her. She found the dirt road partially hidden behind overgrown bushes, just like he'd said, and turned down it. The old lean-to he'd mentioned was also right there, so she drove into it and parked the car. This road didn't look well traveled, and even if people did come by this way, they wouldn't be able to see her car.

Darkness wouldn't be for a while yet, so Eve rolled down the windows and pulled out her phone, glad Hector had found it near the barn. She grabbed a notepad from her purse and started yet another list. When things weren't clear, nothing helped like some freewriting: simply jotting down all the random thoughts and puzzle pieces rattling around in her mind. Once she had it all on paper, she started looking at what she had, trying to make connections, looking for patterns.

But as the darkness deepened and she couldn't see her notes anymore, Eve's frustration grew. She was still missing something. Something important, but she had no idea what it was.

She mentally shifted gears, hoping that would let her subconscious keep working on patterns while she did something else. She scrolled through her photos and pulled up the ones she'd taken at the library.

She grinned at her nerdy younger self and at how much everyone else had changed. Even Leon, whose face had lots more lines than before.

When no clue jumped out, she leaned her head back and let her mind drift. She had learned patience over the years, mainly when she was on a stakeout. She sat and listened to the night sounds outside the window, the whiff of earth and manure that drifted by on the breeze.

By nine thirty, she figured she'd waited long enough. She turned the ringer off on her cell phone and put it into her back pocket, then tucked her hair under a ball cap and grabbed her camera. She took her time, slowly easing her way over behind the sheds that Buzz had mentioned. Once there, she peeked out around the corner, but didn't see anyone.

Which she'd learned didn't necessarily mean a thing.

She leaned against the side of the building and watched. And waited. And waited some more.

As she did, Mama Rosa's words circled round and round in her head. Especially the part about keeping her mother alive not being Eve's job, but God's. She'd never thought about it quite that way and instantly rebelled at the idea, because wasn't it our job to protect and care for those we loved? Wasn't that why she was here? To help take care of Mama?

And yet, she knew—though she hated the reality with every fiber of her being—that no matter how hard she tried, she would never be able to cure Mama's cancer. Only God could do that.

So was it possible that the same thinking could apply to her mother's long-ago death?

Eve wasn't sure, but suddenly, the idea held an appeal that drew her like a magnet. Was it possible it really wasn't her fault?

Before she could fully wrap her mind around the idea, she heard an approaching vehicle. A white pickup with the Blackwell Farms logo on the side pulled up near one of the sheds, and two men got out.

Excitement shimmered over Eve's skin as she saw the barrels lining the truck bed. The men lowered the tailgate, removed a handcart, and started unloading the barrels. She eased her camera into position, made sure the flash was turned off, and began taking photos.

They put each barrel on the handcart and took it to a spot just out of her line of sight, then came back and got another one.

If they were merely storing the barrels in a shed, they weren't doing anything wrong and this had been a colossal waste of time. But if they were burying the barrels . . . that was, as Pop would say, another kettle of fish entirely.

Eve eased back around the side of the shed and worked her way over to another one, which gave her the perfect vantage point to see what they were doing.

And hot diggity, they were burying the barrels, all right. *That lousy liar,* Eve thought, snapping pictures. Getting Avery Ames to take pictures of his eco-friendly practices for the *Gazette*—and now here he was, burying . . . something.

She zoomed in as far as she could, but she still couldn't make out the labels on the sides of the barrels. She had to get closer.

Just as she stepped forward, something hit her from behind.

The world went black.

Chapter 31

Eve came to in a total panic as water closed over her head. Heart pounding, she remembered to quickly close her mouth, but when she tried to use her arms, she realized they were tied behind her back. She opened her eyes, but couldn't see much in the murky water.

She felt herself sinking and tried to kick with her feet, but they were tied, too.

Oh, dear Jesus. Don't let me drown.

First, hands. She pulled her legs up to her chest and managed to get her hands around and up in front of her. When she tugged on the bindings, they came loose, so whoever had done this hadn't expected her to wake up.

She reached for the rope tying her feet, and the same thing happened. It didn't take much effort at all to free her feet. She touched the murky bottom and sank down into it up to her ankles. With it that spongy, it wouldn't provide much help, but she had to try. She pushed off with all the energy she could muster, and using her arms and legs, she finally burst to the surface, gasping for air.

Thank you, God.

She spun in a circle, trying to figure out where she was. Too small to be a lake, so a pond. But where?

The night sky was clear, the moon bright. Once her eyes adjusted, she knew she was on a farm, based on the shape of what appeared to be a barn in the distance.

Splash.

From the corner of her eye she saw something dark slip into the water, and her earlier panic seemed like nothing compared to the terror that pounded through her like a freight train.

Alligator!

Eve lunged for the banks, scrambling to get a foothold in the soft mud. She grabbed handfuls of grass, desperate to pull herself up, but she still kept slipping and sliding, not making any headway.

Please, please, please, God.

Water dripped in her eyes as she struggled to find purchase. She glanced over her shoulder and saw the gator preparing to lunge up out of the water, mouth open, rows of teeth clearly visible.

She heaved herself up once more, and this time—*Thank you, God*—her feet found grass instead of mud, and she landed on her stomach several feet away. She lurched to her feet and took off running, even as a voice in her head reminded her that alligators could run faster than humans on land.

She looked around as she sprinted away, trying to find a tree, truck, anything she could climb up on to escape the huge animal. He was big, and on her tail, and if she didn't get off the ground quick, she was facing a death much worse than a mere drowning.

She glanced off to her right and almost stumbled in her relief. There. A huge live oak loomed not too far away, the strands of Spanish moss that draped its branches glistening like beacons in the moonlight. She could climb up into the branches.

She veered sharply in that direction and risked a glance back at the gator. He hadn't skipped a beat and was still right on her tail.

Dear Jesus, help me. Please.

Eve reached the tree, panting and desperate, searching for a way to climb. But her heart sank as she looked up. The tree was huge, its lowest branches much farther off the ground than they had looked from a distance. Eve ran around the tree, the alligator right behind her, desperate tears mixing with sweat and water running down her face.

Renewed terror gripped her as she realized there was nowhere to go. She couldn't get up into the tree. There was nothing anywhere out here she could climb into or hide in. The sheds were probably all locked, and she didn't have the strength to run all the way back that way, even if they were open.

At that moment, Eve almost gave up. Her lungs burned as she gasped for air, and despair slapped her, hard. She was going to die. Right here. Right now. With this crazed alligator looking for his next meal.

I'm sorry, Mama. Be happy, Cole.

Just as the thoughts slipped through her mind, Eve rejected them. No! This was not how this was going to end. She wasn't giving up without a fight. There had to be a way, and she wouldn't give up until she found it.

She made another circle around the tree, wider this time, and as she glanced back to check the gator's position, she tripped over something and went sprawling on the ground.

She rolled and leaped back up onto her feet, then checked to see what had tripped her. A branch! Yes!

She spun around, and her heart leaped when she realized it had fallen from the tree and broken into several pieces. She grabbed one, but it fell apart in her hands. Rotted through. She grabbed another branch; this one still had leaves, so she knew it wasn't dead.

She yanked the leaves off, then turned and faced the gator, holding the branch like a club. *Jesus, help me!*

The things she'd learned years ago popped back into her head, and she smacked the gator with the branch. When he turned his head away, annoyed, she moved in closer and pounded the end of the branch on the top of his head.

He whipped his head away and lunged again. Eve prayed her timing was right, and just as he came at her again, mouth open, she shoved the branch in his jaw, straight up, using it like a wedge and hoping it was enough to keep that jaw from closing.

Did it work? He whipped his head from side to side, trying to dislodge the branch, but it held.

Eve didn't know how long it would, though, and she wasn't hanging around to find out, so she took off running again, back toward the sheds and hopefully all the way to her car.

Her only thought was to get away.

But as she kept running, she felt the adrenaline that had propelled her start to slip away. No, she had to keep going. But telling herself that and doing it proved to be two different things. Her steps slowed, and her breathing got more and more labored. Her lungs burned with every desperate breath, and the pain in the back of her head suddenly started pounding like a jackhammer.

Almost afraid to look, she risked a glance over her shoulder, but thankfully there was no sign of the gator.

Her steps slowed to a jog, then she stumbled to a walk, and finally she stopped moving altogether. She swayed on her feet, trying to steady herself. She had to get out of here. Whoever tied her up and smacked her in the head could still be around, watching.

She took several more steps, but she had nothing left. Her strength had all been drained out of her, and her reserves were empty. With tears of frustration streaming down her cheeks, she slid to the ground.

She lay there a minute, gasping for air, gathering her strength to get up. She tried, but fell back down. She wasn't giving up, doggone it. She rolled onto her stomach and pushed herself up onto all fours. She could do this. She had to.

"You really don't give up, do you?" a male voice asked.

Eve looked over her shoulder and froze when she saw Leon standing there. At first she thought he'd come to help, but then his words sank in, and all those puzzle pieces fell into place. All but one. "Why?" she croaked.

"You'll find out soon enough." His voice was angry, but sad, too.

Before she realized what he planned, his arm came around her neck, and Eve felt the blackness steal over her again.

Cole.

Chapter 32

Cole dialed Eve's cell phone for the sixth—or was it seventh?—time. "Come on, Eve. Pick up." He'd been a jerk, and he knew it. She deserved better than the way he'd treated her, and he intended to tell her so. To grovel if necessary. If she wanted to leave, he couldn't stop her, but he could sure as shootin' be a gentleman about it.

When her recorded voice instructed him yet again to leave a message, he said, "Eve. Call me. Please. If nothing else, just let me know you're OK." He paused. "I'm sorry."

Then he hung up and wandered out to the paddock. He pulled his harmonica out of his shirt pocket and started playing "Amazing Grace," since it reminded him of the night he'd played it for her.

After riding for several hours, he'd finally admitted that this was home. His home. Every pasture and paddock no longer reminded him of his father, but of the future. It was a good place, with good people on it. People like Hector, who'd been more of a father to him than Hank had ever been.

He still didn't completely understand his mother's need to leave the ranch, but then again, maybe he did. This place had defined her whole life, and much of that had been with Hank. He could understand needing to make a fresh start.

He'd thought his was in Montana, but now he knew it was here. He'd have to call his Realtor and put the place back on the market.

He heard footsteps behind him and looked around to see Buzz approaching. The older man strode toward him like a man on a mission, and Cole braced for whatever lecture he wanted to deliver this time.

"Evening," he said.

Buzz nodded and leaned on the railing beside him. "Nice night."

Cole waited, knowing he'd come out here to discuss more than just the weather.

Finally Buzz said, "Eve came to see me."

That was a surprise. "What did she want?"

"She said I should get off my high horse and help you out here, instead of working against you."

Cole hid a smile, picturing that conversation. "She does speak her mind."

Buzz looked away, rubbed a hand over the back of his neck, then looked directly at Cole. "She was right." When Cole started to protest, he held up a hand. "Let me finish. Hank was my friend, but I wasn't blind to his faults. I've always felt he was too hard on you, and he didn't treat your mother the way he should have."

"Did you ever tell him that?" Would it have made a difference if he had?

"I did. Once. The day he kicked you out. I told him he was making the biggest mistake of his life and he'd live to regret it." He sighed. "I think he realized that, too, but by then you'd joined the military, and it was too late."

"Not to make things right with Ma."

"Hank was a prideful man, Cole. I'm not sure he knew how to behave any other way."

"He was a stubborn, mean son of a gun who didn't treat his family right."

"I won't argue that. But I know, in his own way, he loved you and your mother. He just didn't know how to show it."

Cole thought of all the times his father had shown what he thought of him with his fists or his belt. Finally Cole looked over at Buzz and said, "You may be right."

"He always hoped you'd come back," Buzz admitted.

Shock rippled through Cole, then the familiar anger, but it wasn't like it had been before. He took a deep breath and realized that somehow, since he'd come back . . . he'd stopped being angry. Or more accurately, since he'd met Eve and seen her courage and determination to keep trying, keep fighting the good fight, keep moving forward, he'd gradually begun letting the past go. His father was gone, and he'd never tell Cole he loved him or that he was proud of him. And for the first time, Cole realized he didn't need that anymore.

He supposed Hank had had his own regrets, just like Cole. He'd never be able to apologize to Candy for his callous dismissal when she'd told him she was pregnant. Since she knew he hadn't been the father, she'd clearly been protecting someone. He hadn't known who, and he surely hadn't taken the time to figure out why. He'd just said he wouldn't marry her, not without proof. She'd driven off in tears and crashed her car, then Hank kicked him out, and he'd never found out the truth.

Buzz cleared his throat. "You've made some good changes here, Cole. Brought the place into the future, instead of leaving it in the past the way Hank wanted it. I resented that at first—loyalty to him, I guess—but you're doing the right thing. I wanted you to know that."

If the man had suddenly sprouted a ballerina tutu and done a pirouette, Cole would have been less shocked. "I appreciate that."

"I also wanted to say that I've got a little put by I'd be happy to lend while you get this place back on its feet."

Cole couldn't believe what he was hearing. Buzz wanted to help him? "I, ah, don't know what to say."

"Just accept it. Don't let pride ruin your life, too."

Well, that was putting it bluntly, wasn't it? His pride did have him wanting to turn it down, but instead, he smiled. "Then I'll say thank you. I hope it won't come to that, but if it does, I will take you up on it."

"Fair enough." Buzz leaned back on the railing, but his hands were fidgeting, and Cole figured he still had something else on his mind, though he couldn't imagine what.

"I heard your mother is moving to town."

"That's what she said."

"She's a strong, lovely woman, your mother. I'm glad to see her doing something for herself for a change."

Cole raised an eyebrow. Interesting. Buzz fidgeted some more, and suddenly, Cole knew. "You interested in my mother, Buzz?"

The man's head whipped around, wariness in his eyes. "She's a fine woman any man would be proud to know."

"And are you one of those men?"

Buzz straightened and met his gaze head-on. "I realize I don't need your permission, and I haven't mentioned it to her yet, but I'd like to court your mother. I'd rather you were on board with it, but it won't make a difference either way."

Cole grinned. This was the Buzz he knew. He thought about it and realized they'd be good for each other. He clapped the other man on the shoulder. "If she'll have an ornery old cuss like you, then more power to you. I just want her to be happy."

Buzz nodded and turned back toward the bunkhouse. Cole stayed out there for another hour, letting the sounds of his harmonica drift over the paddock, bringing a few minutes of peace.

But it disappeared when he called Eve's cell phone again, and still got her voice mail.

He finally went into the house and paced, too worried to sleep. He debated calling Sasha, but didn't want to worry all the Martinellis.

Eve was probably just ticked off at him and wasn't answering.

But he couldn't shake the feeling it was more than that. He climbed in his truck and drove into town, then out to the Martinellis' marina and back to the ranch, just in case she'd had car trouble somewhere along the way, but there was no sign of her. Unsure what else to do, he sat on the porch the rest of the night and prayed she was all right.

———

Blaze was in the kitchen at the marina attempting to scramble eggs for Pop and Mama when the house phone rang. Surprised at a call at seven forty-five in the morning, she grabbed the phone and tucked it between her ear and shoulder while she kept stirring the eggs.

Thinking it had to be a telemarketer, she barked, "Martinellis', who is this?"

"Good morning. May I speak to Rosa Martinelli, please?" The voice was deep and male and vaguely familiar, but she couldn't place it.

"Who's calling?"

"A friend. Mrs. Martinelli, please. It's about her daughter."

All the blood in Blaze's veins turned to ice. "Which daughter?"

A long-suffering sigh came from the other end. "Please get Mrs. Martinelli."

Mama shuffled into the room, using the cane Sasha had bought her. Just until she was steadier on her feet, they said, but the sight of it worried Blaze. Made her wonder if things were worse than they were saying, if they were trying to keep stuff from her again, like she were some little kid.

Mama kissed her cheek, then motioned for her to hand over the phone. "This is Rosa Martinelli. Who is calling, please?"

Blaze moved closer, trying to listen, but she couldn't hear what was being said. However, watching what little color Mama had in her cheeks drain away had Blaze reaching out to support her. She guided Mama to a chair at the table and eased her into it.

Mama listened for several more minutes, then said, "Thank you for letting me know. We will be right there."

She just sat there holding the receiver, so Blaze eased it from her limp fingers and put it back in its cradle on the wall. "What's wrong?"

Mama shoved to her feet, her shock giving way to a determination Blaze knew well. "We need to get to Sutton Ranch, right away. He said Eve is in trouble."

Blaze stiffened. "What kind of trouble?"

"He didn't say. He just said I should come right away."

"Who said? Cole?"

"No. I don't think so. I'm not sure." She grabbed Blaze's hands, her grip tighter than Blaze would have thought her capable of. "We have to go. Now."

"Let me get Pop. He's down at the bait shop."

"No. Leave him be. I don't want to worry him. Get Sasha."

Blaze shook her head. "Can't. She and Jesse had to go to Tampa today, remember?"

Mama nodded. "Then you will drive me. Let's go."

Blaze started to remind her that she didn't have a license yet, but decided now was not the time. Something about this whole thing didn't feel right. "Give me just a minute, OK?"

She turned off the burner, then ducked into her room and called Eve's cell phone. It went right to voice mail. She didn't have Cole's cell number, so she dialed the ranch, but the phone just rang and rang.

Heart pounding, trying to figure out the right thing to do, she dialed Nick Stanton. Surely their cop brother could offer some help. Instead of reaching him, though, the robotic voice said, "We're sorry, the number you have dialed is currently unavailable."

Which Blaze had learned meant that the caller was out of cell range. She would have to try again in a while.

She pulled on her tennis shoes and, at the last second, reached into the back of her underwear drawer and pulled out the knife she hadn't needed since she arrived at the marina. But she wasn't taking any chances with her family.

She hurried back into the kitchen and tried to curb her impatience as she helped Mama slowly shuffle down the steps and finally get settled in the front seat of her big barge of a Buick. Blaze climbed into the driver's seat, inserted the key, and prayed like she hadn't prayed in a very long time.

Please let Eve be OK. Please.

Chapter 33

Eve came awake slowly, unsure where she was. Her head pounded like someone was beating it with a big stick, and the sunlight piercing her eyes made her slam her lids closed again.

It must be morning. But where was she? How did she get here?

The throbbing in her head brought it all back in terrifying color. She'd been at Blackwell Farms and had gotten hit from behind—hence the pounding head. Then she'd been tied up and tossed into a pond, along with a gator, of all things.

Eve felt a moment's pride at the way she'd escaped the huge creature—*Thank you, God*—but it was short-lived. What happened after that? How had she gotten here?

Everything in her head felt fuzzy, and she couldn't sort it out, couldn't make sense of the simplest things.

But two things were abundantly clear: she had to get out of here, and she had to do it quick.

———

Cole walked out of the barn and into the morning sunlight as he checked his phone again. Still nothing from Eve. His anxiety crept higher with every minute. He tried to call again, and it went right to voice mail.

"Look, Eve. Just let me know you're OK." That came out harsher than he meant it to, so he added, "Please."

Something wasn't right. He dialed Sasha's number, but it, too, went right to voice mail. He decided to drive out to the marina. Maybe she just wanted some space to think and he was acting like a crazy man, but every instinct screamed there was more to it. So he'd go, confirm with his own eyes that she was in fact fine, and then he could get on with his day.

And his life.

He turned and almost ran smack into Leon. "Morning, Leon. When did you get here? I thought you had that tractor running like a clock when you left yesterday."

Leon nodded. "I did. She runs good as new, but I had a bit of unfinished business to attend to."

Puzzled, Cole studied the other man, the rigid way he held himself, the set of his jaw. "You know I'll make good on the money, Leon. I won't leave you hanging."

"You always make good on what you owe, Cole?" he asked.

Cole narrowed his eyes at the question. "Of course. You know that."

"I don't think I do. I think you've always done exactly what suited you and left others to clean up the mess."

Completely floored, Cole regarded Leon carefully. "I have no idea what you're talking about."

"I'm sure you don't. But you will. And you'll finally get what's coming to you."

"What? Look, Leon—"

"No more talking. Get in the truck."

And with that, he pulled out a gun and aimed it right at Cole's heart.

———

Blaze couldn't remember the last time she'd been so scared. Not only was she not that great at the whole driving thing yet, but Mama Rosa's fear hovered in the air like a fog, making it hard to breathe and even harder to focus on where she was going.

She almost missed the turn to Sutton Ranch and swung the wheel too fast, making the car skid on the gravel road. She straightened the wheel and overcorrected again, narrowly missing a fence post. "Sorry, sorry," she muttered, clenching the wheel even tighter than she had been. Her hands were cramping, but she was afraid to take even one from the wheel for a second, for fear she would crash Mama's huge car.

"You are doing fine, Bethany. Just keep your eyes on what you are doing."

"Did they say what's wrong with Eve?"

"No. Only that we should come right away."

"Who called you?" she asked again.

"I'm not sure. He only said he was from the ranch."

"It wasn't Cole." Why hadn't he called them?

Mama shook her head, her face even paler than usual under the colorful scarf she wore. "No, I don't think it was Cole. But I'm sure he asked one of the men on the ranch to call us."

"Why didn't Eve call us herself?"

There was a long pause, during which all sorts of terrifying possibilities raced around in Blaze's head.

"I am not sure. But we will soon find out. He said to park over near the barn and meet him there."

Blaze turned the big boat of a Buick and tried to line it up next to two other pickup trucks, but it went in at an angle, so she backed up and tried again. Better. At least now there was enough room for Mama to get out of the passenger seat. But once she turned off the ignition, she looked around, and the instincts that had kept her alive while she lived on the road jumped back to life. Something was seriously wrong with this picture. She couldn't say what, but she'd learned to trust her gut.

She glanced over at Mama and saw her scanning the area around the buildings, a worried look on her face, so Blaze figured she felt it, too.

"This doesn't feel right."

Mama nodded, her hand on the door handle. "We will be careful. But Eve needs us."

Blaze grabbed her cell phone. "Let me try Nick again."

"Yes, Tony—I mean Nick—can help. He is a good policeman."

Blaze was already dialing, but he didn't pick up. The good news, though, was that she didn't get the out-of-area recording this time. When his voice instructed her to leave a message, she said, "This is Blaze Martinelli. We're at Cole's. We think Eve is in trouble."

Then Blaze hurried around the car and helped Mama climb out, one hand at her elbow.

———

After she managed to rub her cheek against the dirt floor with enough force to loosen the gag, Eve frantically scanned the shed for something, anything, to cut the tape around her wrists and ankles, but she couldn't spot anything, anywhere. She rolled over and managed to get up onto her knees. Wait. There. Would that work? But before she could inch her way across the shed to investigate the rusty tool, the door to the shed burst open and Leon barged in, a body draped over his shoulder.

"Move, or I'll drop him on top of you."

She rolled out of the way, and he dropped Cole down beside her with a thump that made her cry out. "What is the matter with you?"

Leon's dark eyes narrowed, and he reached over and retied the gag, tighter than before. Then he cocked his head to listen. "Stay put. I think the rest of our guests have arrived."

The minute the door closed behind him, Eve worked her way over to Cole, panic galloping through her at his stillness. She bumped him, but he didn't respond. She tried again, but still nothing. Blood welled from a gash on his head, but he didn't appear to be hurt anywhere else. Eve squirmed around far enough to put her ear to his chest and almost cried with relief. He was alive. *Thank you, Jesus.*

While she tried to figure out a plan, Eve kept her head on his chest, listening to the beat of his heart and praying for whoever these other "guests" were.

Although the terror sliding around in her belly told her she already knew.

Leon was going after Mama Rosa and the rest of Eve's family.

———

Blaze and Mama made their way slowly toward the barn, and once they reached the big open door, Blaze stopped them and waited for their eyes to adjust. "Hello? Eve? Cole?"

They waited, but all they heard was the shuffling of hooves and creak of harnesses. Blaze thought she heard a whisper of movement behind them, but when she spun around, there was no one there. Another shiver of apprehension slid down Blaze's spine. Something was really, really wrong. "We should head back to the car and wait for Nick. Or Cole."

Mama shook her head, though her eyes reflected the same unease as Blaze's. "Evie! Where are you?"

There was no answer, but as Blaze tried to turn them back toward the car, a shadow suddenly loomed in front of them. Startled, she gasped and stepped back, almost knocking Mama down. "Sorry, Mama," she said, trying to help them both regain their balance.

Mama squinted against the sunlight streaming into the building. "Who are you? Where is my Evie?"

"Now, now. Don't go getting all worked up," a male voice soothed.

Blaze tried to place the voice, but before she could, Mama held a hand up above her eyes. "Leon Daughtry? Is that you?"

"Yes, ma'am, Mrs. Martinelli."

"Where is my daughter? Are you the one who called me? What's happening?"

"Easy now. We'll get to all that. Come on down to the office where we can talk."

He tried to take Mama's arm, but she pulled it out of his grip. "Not until you tell me where my daughter is."

"All in due time. Now let's go." He gripped her arm so hard she yelped.

"Hey! You're hurting her," Blaze shouted, but he ignored her as he marched Mama down the big aisle in the center of the barn. Blaze went around to Mama's other side and gripped her hand. Blaze was scared. By the look on Mama's face, she was, too.

Leon forced them down the aisle until they reached a small door to what must be the office. He shoved it open with one hand and propelled Mama through with the other. The minute she crossed the threshold, he grabbed Blaze's arm and shoved her in, too.

"Hey!" she cried as she stumbled into Mama. She righted them both and turned around to see Leon standing in front of the closed door wearing a huge grin, but his eyes were hard. And mean. She'd met men like him before. All warm and friendly on the outside, but scary crazy on the inside.

She eyed the door and tried to think of a way to get them out of here.

He just grinned wider and shook his head as he aimed a gun right at Mama's head. "You do anything dumb, and Mrs. Martinelli's brains are going to make one heck of a mess."

Blaze froze, heart pounding, her eyes on the crazy man. She'd heard Mama's yelp, but wouldn't risk a glance in that direction. It took major effort to keep her voice calm. "What are you doing, scaring an old lady like that? What's going on? Where's Eve? If you'll just tell us where she is, we'll get out of your hair."

He laughed, long and loud, and Blaze's foreboding grew.

"Oh, you'll get out of my hair, all right." He paused. "But not just yet." He reached into a drawer, pulled out a roll of duct tape and some rope, and motioned with the gun. "This way."

Blaze edged up beside Mama and gripped her hand. It trembled, just like her own, but Blaze would not let her down. She'd stay strong and try to think of a way out of this. If only Nick would get here.

As they walked down the barn's center aisle, Blaze's horror grew when she saw a pair of booted feet sticking out from one of the stalls. Had he killed one of the ranch hands? Why? What was going on? Blaze released a breath she hadn't realized she was holding when the man moaned, but quietly, like he was trying not to make any noise. Good, that meant he was still alive. Maybe he would be able to help them. To cover any other sounds, Blaze used her most childlike voice. "I don't understand what's happening. Why are you doing this?"

Leon prodded her in the back with his gun. "Stop talking and keep moving."

Out of the corner of her eye, Blaze caught a glimpse of another man lying in one of the other stalls. He wasn't moving at all, or making any noise. *Please don't let him be dead.*

This whole thing felt like they'd landed in some crazy alternate universe, but she had to stay sharp, keep her mind focused on trying to escape. No, not escape. She had to get his gun. Because if they didn't do that, as soon as they tried to leave, he'd shoot them in the back. The man was seriously unhinged, but he seemed to have an agenda. If Blaze could figure out what he wanted, maybe they could talk him off the ledge.

Once they walked out the other end of the barn, Leon prodded them toward a group of sheds a short distance away. What little strength Mama had was fading fast, and she leaned more and more heavily on Blaze's arm as they plodded over uneven ground. She stumbled, and Blaze wrapped both arms around her and tucked her more firmly against her side. She shot Leon a malevolent look over her shoulder. "Please, she's just a sick old lady. Let her go."

Leon narrowed her eyes at her tone, and Blaze regretted the outburst. "That sick old lady has been nothing but trouble. She should have kept her nose out of my business."

Beside her, Mama gasped. "Did you poison the water that made little Glory sick?"

Leon stiffened as though he'd been slapped, and a dangerous glint came into his eyes.

"Shh," Blaze whispered. "Keep walking."

"No." Mama stopped and turned on the man, hands on her hips, indignation shooting from every pore. She straightened to her full height, and even with her head scarf, she looked like a warrior going into battle. Blaze was both proud and terrified.

"Why would you do something like that to your own kin?" Mama demanded. "What is the matter with you, Leon? Your mama would turn over in her grave to see you behaving in such a shameful way."

Leon grabbed Mama's arm hard enough to make her cry out and all but shoved her through the door into one of the larger sheds. "If you hadn't sent your bulldog of a daughter to go snooping around, none of this would be happening. It's all your fault."

Blaze saw Mama open her mouth to fire back, but then she spotted Eve lying on the dirt floor, bound and gagged. Fury flashed from Eve's eyes, but it was Cole, lying on the ground beside her, that worried Blaze. Blood ran down the side of his face, like he'd been hit hard, and he wasn't moving. Was he breathing? She couldn't tell. *Please let him be alive. Please.*

Chapter 34

Nick Stanton shook his head, annoyed. How many more times would Chief Monroe send him out to check on Mrs. Hinkley before her no-good family finally stepped up to take care of her? The ornery old lady's dementia was getting worse, but none of her three adult children wanted to take charge of her. From what he'd heard, she'd been a mean one when she was younger, and now old age and dementia had made it much worse. He couldn't really blame her family for avoiding her, but he was getting tired of them calling to say she wasn't answering her phone and him having to go out there and find her and coax her back into her little cottage out in the woods. She needed someone to take care of her. A caregiver, not a police officer.

He sighed, knowing his frustration had less to do with that whole sad situation than with his frustration over his own life. He didn't know how to become a real member of the Martinelli family, wasn't even sure he wanted to. He felt like he was getting to know Sasha and Jesse, Eve, and even Blaze. They'd all gone out of their way to make him feel a part of the family, and he did. Sort of. He didn't share their family history, but then, when he thought about it, he realized their whole history was as much a hodgepodge as his own life. It was easy to forget that none of the Martinelli sisters were actually related by blood. But they were certainly a family. He longed for that sense of connection. As an only child, he'd never been part of that.

Even Mama Rosa had made him feel welcome, but he felt awkward around her overwhelming love. He knew she wanted him to return all that emotion, but all he felt right now was . . . sad. The anger toward the people who'd raised him was slowly fading, but he wasn't sure what should take its place. His anger toward Sal Martinelli was something unexpected and frustrating. The man had suspected who'd taken him all those years ago and had kept quiet. Nick could sort of understand Sal's need to protect Mama.

Actually, no. He couldn't. You didn't just shrug when your child disappeared and claim silence was better. Safer. If he'd been in that situation, he'd have moved heaven and earth to find his child, figure out what happened.

He sighed. No matter how many times he thought about it, this was where he always ended up. Frustrated and tired and unsure what to do next, how to behave.

He drove past some imaginary boundary that put him back in cell range, so his phone started beeping with incoming texts and voice mail notifications. He glanced down the list, surprised to see a voice mail from Blaze. Dread hit him hard.

Mama Rosa. That had to be it.

He listened to the voice mail. "This is Blaze Martinelli. We're at—" The message stopped. What? He played it again, and the same thing happened. He stepped on the gas as he called Blaze back, tapping his fingers on the steering wheel as he waited through several rings. When it went to voice mail, he swallowed his frustration. "Blaze, it's Nick. Call me."

He turned on his lights and siren and flew down the road toward the marina.

Please don't let it be Mama Rosa.

Eve growled low in her throat when Leon shoved Mama and Blaze into the shed. Mama almost fell, but Blaze grabbed her just in time. *Good girl.* She met Blaze's eyes, and they exchanged a long look. If there was a chance to escape, Blaze would help her find it.

At the same time, Eve was terrified for Cole. She knew he was breathing, but she didn't know how badly he was hurt. Blood still welled from his wound and ran down the side of his face. Leon had carried him in over his shoulder and dumped him on the floor like a sack of feed, which had probably made his injuries worse.

Eve nodded toward Cole, and Blaze took a quick look and then shrugged. *Please God, we need him.*

Leon grabbed the roll of duct tape he'd set on a shelf and tied Blaze's hands behind her. "Sit so I can tie your feet."

Blaze's chin came up. "No."

Faster than Eve thought possible, he tossed her onto the floor amid shouted protests from Mama. He scowled in her direction while he wrapped the tape around Blaze's ankles. "Be still or I'll gag you, too," he warned.

Mama quieted, but her eyes promised retribution. Eve tried to catch her eye, but Mama wouldn't look at her. She had to make Mama stop. She'd only make things worse. Of course, how much worse could they get? As soon as the thought crossed her mind, she shoved it away. It could get much, much worse, and that made her break out in a cold sweat. Why was Leon doing this? What was this all about? The ranch?

Leon finished tying Blaze's feet, slapped a piece of tape over her mouth, and turned to Mama, whose chin came up exactly the way Blaze's had. Eve again tried to catch her eye, but couldn't. Stubborn was good, but sometimes, stubborn could get you killed.

"I do not know why you are doing this, Leon, but I know Althea's heart is breaking to see it. She did not raise you to be this kind of man."

"Sometimes, a man's gotta do what a man's gotta do. The guilty have to pay."

"They do, but the good Lord says vengeance belongs to Him."

"And sometimes, He needs a little bit of help." He grabbed Mama's arm and yanked it behind her, then grabbed the other one and tied them with the tape.

"No good will come of this, Leon. There is still time to change your mind."

Leon pulled off a length of duct tape. "Last chance. Either shut up or I gag you."

Mama pursed her lips and stared daggers at him. He waited a moment, then shoved an overturned bucket in her direction and forced Mama backward to sit on it. At least he didn't toss her on the floor like the rest of them.

Behind her, Cole let out a low moan. Eve hoped Leon hadn't heard it, but her hope was short-lived.

"Good, he's coming around. Then we can get this over with."

Trying to figure out what that meant had dread roiling in Eve's gut. She watched as he went to the workbench against one wall and grabbed several bottles. Her eyes widened after she squinted to read the labels. They were all insecticides, and all had the skull-and-crossbones symbol for poison stamped on them.

He reached for two plastic glasses, which he filled partway with water from a jug on the workbench. Then he added several ounces from each of the bottles to each glass.

When he turned with a grin, Eve looked directly into his eyes and realized that somewhere along the way, he'd lost his sanity. The friendly son of her Sunday school teacher had turned into someone Miss Althea wouldn't recognize. The grin turned to fury as he walked over to Cole and slapped him, hard.

"What in the—" Cole came to with a jolt and sat up. He looked around the shed, and Eve could tell the moment everything he was seeing registered. His jaw hardened and he stilled, a plan of some kind already taking shape. When his eyes met Eve's, they narrowed, and she read his determination to get them out of here.

Like he had all the time in the world, he rubbed a hand on the side of his face and carefully examined the blood, which he wiped on his jeans. Then he met Leon's eyes.

"What are you doing, man? Let these ladies go. Whatever beef you have is between you and me. They have nothing to do with this."

"A few weeks ago, I might have agreed with you." He pointed a finger at Eve. "But then she came along and stirred everything up, made a mess of things."

Eve wanted to protest, but with the gag, she didn't have many options.

"Fine, then at least let Mrs. Martinelli and Blaze go. They don't have any part in this."

Leon's grin came back, and he giggled. The sound was terrifying. "They might not have before, but they are an important part of your punishment now."

Eve watched the color leach out of Cole's face and realized they were both thinking the same thing. Leon was going to hurt them to make Cole pay for some wrong, real or imagined.

Cole leaned back against the wall like they were just having a friendly get-together. "Tell me what's going on, Leon. If you tell me what's wrong, I'm sure we can figure out a way to fix it."

"It's too late to fix it. Years too late."

"I don't understand."

"Of course you don't. You were always too cocky, too arrogant to think about anyone but yourself. You took what you wanted and never gave a single thought to the rest of us. The heir apparent of Sutton Ranch who could do no wrong."

Leon started pacing, waving the gun around, and the knot in Eve's gut grew. He was getting more and more agitated, more out of control.

He stopped, stuck the gun under Cole's chin. "Except you did wrong, the worst wrong a man can do. Your family has always called yourself Christians, holier than thou, looking down your rich noses at everyone. But you went too far."

He jabbed the gun harder and forced Cole's head back against the wall. "Too far! You took the only good and beautiful thing in my life and you used her, and then you threw her away like she was manure under your feet."

Eve was watching Cole's face, and she saw the moment he realized what Leon was talking about. The words clicked in her own mind several seconds later, and she felt the color drain from her face, just as it had from Cole's.

Candy Blackwell. All those years ago. Had to be.

Cole's body language showed no anxiety as he studied Leon's face. "You were in love with Candy."

Tears suddenly rolled down Leon's dark cheeks, a stark contrast to the gun he held against Cole's throat. "She was the best thing that ever happened to me. She was good and kind, and we were going to get married." His eyes narrowed, and he cocked the hammer on the gun. Eve vibrated with the need to jump up and stop him, to get that gun away from him, but she was as helpless as everyone else in the shed. "And then you stole her from me: you talked your way into her bed, and then you abandoned her when she needed you most.

"You killed her." The last words came out as a choked whisper.

Cole didn't speak until Leon looked at him again. "I didn't sleep with her, Leon. Not ever. If she was pregnant, it wasn't by me."

Eve's breath caught as she watched Leon absorb this news.

"You're lying!" The roar sounded like it came from a wounded animal.

"No. I wasn't then and I'm not now. But I was an arrogant fool, as you said. There had to be a reason she lied about it, but I never stopped to find out who she was protecting or why. I was too busy trying to protect my own future." He paused. "Was it your baby?"

Leon reacted to that news as though he'd been slapped. He jumped to his feet and began pacing, running his hands over his head, muttering and waving the gun around. Eve glanced over at Cole, saw the remorse in his expression. He blamed himself, for all of it. Then and now.

Eve shook her head, trying to make him see it wasn't his fault. How could it be?

Leon whipped back around and took aim at Cole. "This is all your fault. If you hadn't turned your back on her, if you'd been man enough to step up, she wouldn't have been driving too fast, wouldn't have, wouldn't . . ." He broke down, sobbing.

Eve glanced at Mama's shocked face and then at Blaze, who was tugging at the tape binding her hands behind her back. She gave a quick tilt of her head, like she was pointing behind her. Had she found something sharp back there to tear the tape?

"I can't believe you poisoned my cattle, Leon. You have a problem with me, that's one thing. But to do that to my animals?" Cole shook his head in astonishment.

Leon's sobbing stopped as abruptly as it started. "What are you talking about? I didn't poison your cattle. I'd never do such a thing."

But apparently, threatening people was something else, Eve thought. "Then who did?"

"No idea. But it wasn't me."

"But you messed with the fertigation system, didn't you?"

Leon shrugged and kept pacing, kept muttering.

Cole cocked his head. "Who did you get to help you steal my cattle? That wasn't a one-man operation."

Leon stopped, laughed. "You think I'm the only one who hates the Martinellis?"

Chills raced down Eve's spine at his words. Were there more people involved in this?

"I'm done talking to you," Leon said. Then he stopped, grabbed the duct tape, and trussed Cole up just like he had the rest of them.

Chapter 35

The man had obviously gone loco. But he hadn't gagged him yet, so Cole planned to keep him talking long enough that hopefully Hector or Buzz would come looking for him. His hands and feet were tied so tight he was losing all feeling in them, so there was no way he could protect everyone. Worse yet, this was his fault, just as Leon had said. He could pay for his own arrogance, but there was no way he'd let Eve, Mrs. Martinelli, and Blaze suffer for his own long-ago selfishness.

"Did you lock Eve in the shed, too?" The minute the words popped out, he wanted to call them back. He didn't want the focus on Eve.

Sure enough, Leon swung the gun around and pointed it at Eve, who said nothing, simply narrowed her eyes at him. "She's been nothing but trouble since she got here. No, since before she got here." He changed direction and aimed at Mrs. Martinelli. Instead of cowering, the older woman hitched up her chin.

"Althea was a good friend to me, Leon. She would not like knowing you were treating my family this way."

"You started this, all of it, getting your nosy Nellie of a daughter down here, sticking her nose into things that were none of her business."

Mrs. Martinelli's eyebrows rose almost to the scarf she wore, and her voice was filled with horror. "Are you saying you did poison the water at Celia's cottage? You made little Glory so sick?"

"I never meant to hurt anyone! She wasn't supposed to drink the water. I thought Celia was nursing her. How was I supposed to know she'd made formula from that water?"

"Why did it matter, Leon?" Cole asked quietly. Sure enough, Leon's attention and the gun swung back to him.

"Because I didn't want our property going to that big-box store. I wanted it."

"And if the water wasn't good, they wouldn't buy it," Cole guessed. He waited a beat, then added, "But you didn't poison the well."

"'Course not. You can't ever get nitrates out once they're in your well. Dang kid from the water-testing company was supposed to take the sample from the house so the big-box store would drop their offer when it showed all those nitrates. Instead, he skipped town with his girlfriend." He leaned closer, put the gun right in Cole's face. "That property should have been mine. After I flushed the chlorination system, the water would be fine and I could sell it for enough to force you out, take away what mattered to you. Same as you did to me."

"So you're the one behind most of the sabotage." Cole would have to think about who helped Leon pull off the cattle heist. But right now he had to stay focused, look for an opportunity to disarm him.

Leon puffed up with pride. "That's right. Didn't none of you all know it was me, neither."

"No, we sure didn't. Mainly because I couldn't imagine you ever doing such things, Leon. Duane could die. Hector almost did."

"They started poking around, asking questions. They got what they deserved."

"Let the rest of them go, Leon. This is still between you and me."

"Oh, it is, all right, but they are part of it. Just shooting you quick-like is too easy. You're going to watch them suffer first." He strode over to the workbench and grabbed one of the cups of poison. He held it out to Mrs. Martinelli and said, "Drink it."

———

Nick Stanton pulled into the marina with a spray of gravel. He was out of his official SUV and running up the porch steps almost before the vehicle slid to a complete stop. "Blaze! Eve! What's going on?"

He crossed the porch and pounded on the door to the house, but there was no answer. He turned back to see Sal Martinelli hurrying up from the dock.

"Nick. What's wrong? Why are you here?"

"Where's Blaze? She called me but now she won't answer her phone."

Sal looked around. "Rosa's Buick is gone. But she's not strong enough to drive these days."

"So Blaze is driving." She didn't have a license, but that was the least of their worries. "She knows how?"

Sal nodded. "We need to find them. Something must be wrong with Rosa. We should go to the hospital." He headed toward his ancient pickup truck.

Nick debated for less than three seconds. "Hop in and I'll drive you."

Sal looked surprised, then nodded and hurried to the SUV.

When they raced back to the main road, Nick dialed the hospital. "This is Nick Stanton with the Safe Harbor police. Has Rosa Martinelli been brought in today?"

"Hey Nick, this is Crystal. We met at church, remember? I've been at the desk here all morning, and she hasn't been brought in. She's so sweet; everyone loves her. I would have known if she were here."

"Thanks, Crystal. If that changes, call me, OK?"

"Sure. Is she all right?"

Connie Mann

"I think so. Just covering all the bases."

"Um, OK. So, do you think you might want to, ah, have lunch or—"

Nick cut her off. "Thanks, Crystal. Gotta go." He turned to Sal. "I'll drop you off in town."

"No. Wherever you're going, I'm coming with you." Determination lit his eyes, and he looked prepared to force Nick to physically eject him from the SUV. "You're going to Sutton Ranch."

"Yes, but you're not a cop. I can't put you in danger."

"I won't let my family down a second time," Sal said. "Give me a chance to make things right."

Nick couldn't argue with that. It went against every protocol, but he spun into a quick U-turn that had Sal grabbing the door handle for support, then hit the accelerator as they raced out of town. "Do not get in the way when we get there."

"You think this is about the sabotage."

The worry gnawing at Nick's gut grew teeth. "Yes. If Eve is in trouble, Mrs. Mart—Mama Rosa and Blaze would go try to help."

Sal's hand trembled as he rubbed it over his face. "All the women in my life are too stubborn for their own good."

"But they're tough, too, every one."

"That's what I'm counting on." Sal made the sign of the cross, and Nick saw his lips move in prayer. The old man—he still couldn't quite think of him as his father—had a lot to atone for. He just didn't want him paying with his life.

———

When Leon shoved the cup of poison in Mama's face, Eve shouted, "No!" through her gag the same second Blaze did. Eve tried to lunge to her feet, but she tripped over her bindings and landed face first, still yelling for him to stop.

Leon turned, studied her writhing on the ground, and a speculative light came into his eyes that chilled Cole to his bones.

"Fine. We'll do it your way." He hauled Eve to her feet and turned her around. He stuck his gun in his waistband and pulled a wicked-looking knife from a sheath at his waist and sliced through the tape. Before she could do more than give her wrists a quick rub, he thrust the cup into her hands. "You give it to her. That will be just perfect."

Eve paled and froze, and for a moment Cole thought she'd buckle under the horror, but she was tough, tougher than Leon realized. At least, that's what Cole was counting on. He quietly eased his bound legs into position and got ready. She glanced at him, and he nodded once.

Before Leon could react, Eve tossed the poison in his face. As he stumbled backward, screaming and rubbing his eyes, Cole kicked out, hard, sending Leon sprawling to the floor, then tried to scramble over and help. Eve followed Leon to the floor and wrestled him for the knife, but even blinded by the poison, the former football lineman was bigger and heavier than she was. He tossed her off him, and she landed with a groan that made Cole's blood boil.

Leon staggered upright, knife raised, while still cursing and swiping at the poison. "You blinded me. You'll pay for that, girly. You'll pay dearly."

He shook his head to clear it, and Cole figured if he just took one more step in his direction, he could take Leon down again, tape or no tape. *Come on, come on.*

Behind Leon, Eve struggled to her knees, then set about undoing the tape around her ankles. Blaze started to ease closer to her, and Leon spun around. "Don't you move. Stay right where you are."

"I believe that's my line," Nick Stanton said, gun aimed at Leon's back.

Chapter 36

Leon spun around, drawing his gun as he went. Cole launched himself at him and felt, rather than saw, Leon raise the gun and fire off a round before he hit the floor.

Another gunshot exploded in the small space, and through the chaos, Cole heard Mrs. Martinelli scream, "Sal!"

Nick loomed over them, gun at the ready, as they lay panting on the ground. "You OK, Cole?"

"Think so."

Nick reached over and checked Leon's pulse. He met Cole's eyes and shook his head. He holstered his gun, then pulled out his own utility knife and cut Cole's bindings.

"Sal, oh, Sal, no!"

Both men spun around to see Mrs. Martinelli sobbing her husband's name. Sal lay at her feet, bleeding from a chest wound. Nick immediately got on the radio to dispatch, explained the situation in curt sentences, and asked for an ambulance, stat.

While Nick grabbed his handkerchief to put pressure on the wound, Cole cut Blaze and Mrs. Martinelli's bindings off, and he and Eve helped Blaze to her feet.

It seemed to take forever before they heard sirens and longer still before they got Sal loaded into the ambulance, with Eve following in the Buick with Mama Rosa and Blaze.

He wanted nothing more than to hold her and never let go, but he never got the chance.

———

Chief Monroe had Nick off to one side, getting his statement, and Cole watched while they loaded Leon's body into the coroner's van. Hector and Buzz waited outside the shed, where Nick had told them to stay.

Cole sagged against the wall, exhausted beyond words as the adrenaline seeped out of him. How on earth had his arrogance so long ago caused so much heartache?

"Cole! Let me in. I need to see my son!"

He walked to the door of the shed where his mother was trying to shove past a young police officer. "I'm OK. I'll be out in a little while."

She covered her mouth with her hand, and tears started pouring down her face. Cole couldn't stand it, so he walked out the door and gathered her in his arms and held her while she cried.

"I thought it was you. I thought I lost you."

"I'm OK, Ma. It's finally over."

She raised a tearstained face to his. "They said it was Leon."

Cole nodded. "He was the one who got Candy pregnant all those years ago. But she never told him. And when I wouldn't marry her and she died, he blamed me."

She sighed. "So much tragedy." Then she studied his face. "But this was not your fault."

"I should have handled things differently back then."

"Maybe. But that in no way makes you responsible for all that happened here. Leon made choices. Deliberate choices. Sadly, he paid a high price for them."

Chief Monroe stepped out the door of the shed. "I need to speak with Cole, ma'am," he said.

Alice stepped back with Hector and Buzz, who immediately formed a protective circle around her, while Cole turned to the chief.

"I need you to go over what happened here, Cole, from the beginning. And then we need to talk about everything else that's been going on here and how it all ties together."

———

By the time Cole finally walked into the hospital waiting room, Eve felt like they'd both aged several days. Pop was still in surgery, and all the nurses would say was that these things take time. Mama's color was terrible as she leaned against Blaze, whose eyes held more worry and sorrow than any teenager should have to deal with. Sasha sat beside Blaze, rubbing the girl's back in a gentle motion while Jesse paced the room.

Eve eased away from Mama's other side and walked right into Cole's arms. Until she felt his heart beating next to hers, she hadn't quite believed he was alive. But as soon as those strong arms closed around her, the tears she'd been holding at bay rolled down her cheeks. She burrowed closer as he stroked her hair and murmured soothing words she couldn't understand in her ear.

After a few minutes, he eased her back and brushed the tears from her cheeks. "You holding up OK?"

She nodded. "Pop is still in surgery."

"He's one ornery old fisherman. He's tough."

"That's what I keep telling myself. How's Nick?"

"He'll be fine," Nick said from behind them.

Eve pulled out of Cole's arms and flew into Nick's, hugging him hard before she pulled back to study his face. "You saved our lives today. Thank you."

He shrugged. "It's my job." Then he looked at Blaze. "If not for this one trying to call me, I might not have gotten there in time."

Mama suddenly sat up straight, and angry color flooded her face. "Why you bring my Sal into the middle of that? He should not have been there."

Nick crouched down in front of her. "No, he shouldn't have. But he insisted on coming along, and I knew if I didn't bring him myself, he'd find another way to get there." He paused, cleared his throat. "He said he had to be there. Had to make sure he didn't let his family down again."

Mama studied him a moment. "You shot Leon to protect Sal, to protect all of us."

He shrugged again, looked away. "It's my job."

"You serve and protect. And today, you did that for your family." She reached out and pulled him toward her, hugged him hard. "Thank you, my Tony."

"You're welcome . . . Mama."

Chapter 37

Like most small towns, the news traveled fast and gossip ran rampant, but folks came together. They showed up at the hospital and stayed with Mama Rosa until the day they finally moved Sal from the ICU to a regular room. Then they bullied her into going home to sleep for a bit, while they sat vigil.

Meals showed up at the marina, flowers were delivered to the hospital, and folks also gathered around Celia and IdaMae as they mourned Leon. The community church was packed the day of his funeral.

Sal had been released from the hospital, and after much consideration, he and Mama Rosa went to the service, for IdaMae and Celia's sake. They left right after, but everyone understood. Nick stopped by later on to say he'd tracked down the young man from the water-testing company. Nick had arrested him after he'd admitted to poisoning Cole's cattle, though he'd refused to say who hired him.

The day after that, Eve packed to head back to DC, saying she'd put her career on hold long enough. She'd put her emotions on hold, too, stuffing them down deep where they couldn't shred her heart anymore. She had to go. It was safer this way.

Blaze, Mama, and Pop were waiting in the kitchen when she came down with her bag. She'd been hoping she could just sneak out since she hated good-byes with a burning passion, but she knew that would never work. Still, it would be so much easier just to go.

Mama beckoned her over from her place at the table. She insisted she was fine, but Eve saw her added frailty, the way she sat whenever possible. "Thank you for coming, my Evie. And thank you for fighting for little Glory. You are my fighter." She hugged Eve hard and kissed both her cheeks. "I am proud of you."

Eve swiped at her tears as she turned to Pop. He struggled to his feet, so thin and gaunt Eve thought a strong wind could blow him over. Their relationship still wasn't quite what she'd hoped for, but they were making progress, and Eve figured that was more than anyone could ask for. Hadn't he taken a bullet to protect Mama? It made up for a lot.

"Be safe, my girl. And come back to us when you can." He kissed her cheek and then turned and left the room.

Blaze leaned against the counter, her belligerence worn like a shield today. Eve pulled her into a hug and whispered, "Thank you for taking care of them. But don't forget to take care of you, too, OK?"

Blaze nodded, and Eve wiped more tears away, grabbed her bag, and headed outside. "I'll call you when I get there." If she didn't get out of there quick, she might never leave.

Sasha stood beside Eve's rental, Jesse behind her. Just the sight of them made Eve cry harder, but this time they were happy tears. They were so good together.

"You know you're being an idiot, right?" Sasha asked. "Cole loves you. And I think you love him."

She couldn't think about that right now. "I need to get back." She quickly hugged them both, then got into the car and headed out to the main road.

But even as she did, part of her was sure she was making the biggest mistake of her life.

Cole knew Eve was leaving for DC this morning, and he'd spent most of the night debating whether to beg her to stay. But what did he have to offer her? A ranch that was still teetering on the brink of bankruptcy. When he'd asked her before, she'd said she'd stay until they figured out what was going on. Well, they'd done that, in spades.

He heard a car coming down the drive, and he whipped around, thinking she'd changed her mind, but it wasn't her prissy little Prius. It was a shiny pickup truck with the Blackwell Farms logo on the side.

Cole swallowed his disappointment as none other than Richard Blackwell himself stepped down from the cab.

The man walked over with the kind of swagger only those who think they're untouchable seemed to have. He extended a hand. "Cole. Heard your troubles seem to be at an end, finally."

"What brings you by this way?"

"I wanted to see if you'd changed your mind about selling the place. My offer stands."

"I'm staying, but thanks for the offer. You should be getting my check for the loan you made Hank within the week." He'd hated borrowing the money from Buzz, but he'd rather owe him than Blackwell. Sutton Ranch was home. Would always be home. And he wouldn't give it up without a fight.

"I figured that's what you'd decided, but can't blame a man for trying." He shrugged, then looked around. "You'll do well with this place. I hear you have a way with animals and people that's been missing here for a while."

The older man looked off into the distance, and Cole waited for him to mention his daughter. He didn't have to wait long.

"I judged you harshly, Cole, and didn't stop to get all the facts. If I had . . . my baby girl might still be here."

"I should have done the same, asked Candy why she claimed I was the father."

Blackwell studied him a moment. "I think there's been enough blame to go around for too long." He looked like he wanted to say more, but then he extended his hand again. "Good luck. If I can help, let me know." And with that, he climbed back into his truck and left in a cloud of dust.

Chapter 38

"Right, Ms. Jackson?"

Eve's head snapped up as she realized everyone in the conference room was looking at her, and she had no idea what her boss had just said.

"I—ah—" She looked around at her coworkers, but no one offered more than an averted stare or shrug. She blew out a breath. "Of course, sir."

Eve heard several sighs and one snicker and wondered what, exactly, she'd just agreed to. But as everyone filed out of the conference room several minutes later, she realized she didn't care. Not really.

Since she got back from Safe Harbor last week, she couldn't seem to focus on work. What before had seemed so all consuming now seemed like just so much paperwork. It wasn't that she cared any less—she still did. It just didn't hold her attention.

She spent her lunch hour and every evening poring over the *Safe Harbor Gazette* and trolling social media looking for mentions of her hometown. When she wasn't doing that, she was calling Sasha and Blaze for updates, often enough that Blaze had told her this morning to stop calling or come home already.

She spent her sleepless nights replaying her conversations with Mama Rosa and Hector. Was it truly possible to lay down the guilt of her mother's death and build a new life? Inch by inch, the possibility started to settle into her heart.

"Ms. Jackson, a word, please."

Eve jumped. She hadn't heard her boss come up behind her. "Yes, sir. I'd like to talk to you about my future with Braddock Environmental."

He raised an eyebrow, and she smiled as she followed him to his office, her mind suddenly clear and focused for the first time in a week.

———

Cole stepped out of the taxi and stood on the sidewalk for a moment to get his bearings. Braddock Environmental's offices were housed in a stately old building in an equally stately neighborhood. He ran a finger under the collar of his starched white shirt, wondering for the hundredth time if he were crazy as a June bug to even be here. Eve had never given an indication that she'd be willing to live in Florida. That was simply wishful thinking on his part.

But when he remembered that day in the shed, the way she handled herself, and how her family all tried to protect each other, he knew beyond any doubt he wanted a family like that, and he wanted to build it with her. The kind of partnership where they both looked out for each other. Where they laughed and loved and forgave each other when they messed up.

Cole tightened his grip on the bouquet of gerbera daisies he carried and walked into the lobby.

The receptionist took one look at his tuxedo and black Stetson and murmured, "Oh my. What can I get for you, handsome?"

"Not what—who. I'm looking for Eve Jackson."

Her eyes ran up and down the length of him again. "Well, that lucky girl. She didn't say a word."

"Is she here?"

"Let me get her for you, handsome. You just caught her. She said she was heading out. Sit right over there so I can look at you while you wait." She picked up the phone. "Eve, honey, you got a special delivery out here. Those boxes can wait, but I wouldn't leave him alone for too long." She hung up. "She'll be right out."

Cole kept his eyes trained on the door at the end of the hallway behind the receptionist's desk. He saw Eve walk through, wearing a tidy pantsuit and another pair of those crazy-high heels. She almost stumbled when she saw him standing there.

He grinned and held out the flowers. "Hello, Evie."

"Wha-what are you doing here?" She took the flowers and grinned. "My favorite."

He grinned back. "I know." He looked over her shoulder at the receptionist, who wasn't even pretending not to listen to every word. "Why don't we walk outside?"

At her nod, he took her elbow and led her through the double doors.

Once they were outside, his carefully rehearsed speech vanished, and he pulled her close and kissed her like he was a starving man and she a banquet. After a moment of shock, she kissed him back as though she felt the same way. Which Cole took as a positive sign.

He could stand out here and kiss her forever—and hoped to be able to do exactly that—but first . . . he eased her back and cradled her cheeks in his hands. "I was a complete idiot to ever let you leave Safe Harbor. Come home, Eve."

"Why?" she asked, but there was a twinkle in her eye.

"Because I miss you. I want you with me."

She narrowed her eyes and waited.

He huffed out a breath. "You're going to make me say it, aren't you?"

"Oh yes. Absolutely."

With that he fell to one knee and took her hand, holding fast when she looked around at the curious passersby and tried to step back. "Eve Jackson, I love you. I love your determination to make the world a better place; I love your devotion to your family. And I'm hoping that you love me, too. Will you marry me and live on the ranch with me?"

Eve's eyes filled, but she cocked her head and pretended to consider the matter. "That depends. Can we build an eco-friendly house?"

His eyes widened. "You mean like a sod hut?"

"Something like that."

"I'll live in a tent, if that's what it takes. Marry me."

She pulled him to his feet and wrapped her arms around his neck. "What took you so long to get here, cowboy?"

After another long kiss, he pulled back and met her smiling eyes. "Is that a yes?"

"Yes, yes, yes."

"Then I suppose I should give you this." He pulled out a platinum band with a square-cut emerald and slipped it on her finger. "The emerald is lab created, of course."

She grinned. "Of course." She angled her hand to look at it. "It's perfect. And so are you."

"You haven't said it." He raised his eyebrows, made an out-with-it motion with his hands.

Eve cupped his cheeks and said, "I love you, Cole."

There wasn't an ounce of hesitation in her eyes, and his last worry vanished. "See, that wasn't so hard." He pulled her close for another kiss before he said, "The receptionist said you were heading out. Am I keeping you from something?"

She tipped her head and shot him that saucy grin he loved. "Only my riding lesson. Want to come?"

Cole threw back his head and laughed before he pulled her into his arms and swung her around. Life with Evie would never be dull.

"Oh, and I have some boxes in my office I need to get, but I can explain about those later."

He flagged a cab, and they headed for a riding stable not far out of town while Eve filled him in on her conversation with Mr. Braddock.

She talked a mile a minute the whole way, but all Cole remembered was that she'd said she loved him. And she was coming home.

Epilogue

The wedding was held at Sutton Ranch in a smaller barn that had been cleaned out and converted for the event. Sasha, Jesse, and Blaze, together with Hector, Buzz, and Alice, had transformed the place with hundreds of fairy lights that were strung from the rafters. There were hay bales arranged as seating and long tables with wooden benches; mason jars with candles inside dotted the tabletops.

Inside the ranch house, Eve paced the back bedroom. "Is it time yet?" she asked Sasha.

"Relax, sis. You've still got another thirty minutes."

"That can't be right. I've been waiting forever."

"It just seems like forever. It'll be here before you know it."

Blaze poked her head in the room. "Mama Rosa and Pop are here."

Eve turned as Mama came into the room and gasped at the sight of her. "Oh, my Evie, you are beautiful." Tears rolled down her cheeks, and Eve started fanning her face.

"Don't you make me cry or I will have to redo my makeup."

Pop stepped around Mama, took her hands, and held them out at her sides. "You are a picture, Eve. So beautiful." He leaned over and carefully kissed her cheek. She leaned into him, smelling his familiar aftershave, and suddenly the last of the anger over what happened to

Nick finally drifted away. Family did the best they could. Sometimes it wasn't enough, but in this case, it would have to be.

Several minutes later, Blaze poked her head in again. "Cat is here."

Eve and Sasha exchanged a glance. It had taken quite a bit of doing on Eve's part to get their sister to agree to come to the wedding, and even more persuasion to get her to bring her violin and agree to play for both ceremony and reception.

Cat walked in and Eve's eyes filled, but she resolutely blinked the tears away. Today was not the day for tears. Cat looked beautiful in her flowing green dress, but she was still too thin, and her eyes looked haunted. Her straight black hair accented her pale skin, making it almost translucent.

Eve gathered her in a careful hug, afraid Cat would break if she squeezed too hard. "I've missed you, Cat. Thank you for coming."

Cat glanced at Sasha, then back to Eve. "Nobody twists arms like you do."

Sasha, who never wore a fancy dress if she could help it, grinned and indicated the gauzy blue dress she wore with a snort. "No argument there."

Eve squeezed Cat's hands. "I can't wait to catch up with you. After the reception, OK?"

Cat's eyes darted around the room before coming back to Eve's. "I'll stay as long as I can. No promises, though, OK?"

Eve's radar twitched. "Cat? What's wrong?"

Cat shook her head. "It's complicated. Just enjoy your day, and we'll catch up when we can." She brushed a kiss over Eve's cheek and slipped back out the door.

She and Sasha looked at each other.

"There's still something bad wrong in her life," Sasha said.

Eve nodded, wringing her hands. "I know. I need to find out what it is."

But before she could follow her, Blaze poked her head in again. "Nick is here."

Sasha checked the clock. "It's showtime. Send him in."

He walked in looking a bit uncomfortable but extremely handsome in his new suit. "You look beautiful, Eve." He glanced around. "You, too, Sasha. And Blaze."

"You clean up pretty good for a cop," Blaze responded. High praise indeed.

Eve linked her arm with his, and then they walked out into the hallway and she linked her other arm with Pop's. She would walk down the aisle with both of them. Her past and her future, all together. It seemed only right.

As soon as Eve walked through the door of the barn and laid eyes on Cole, everything else faded away. She still couldn't believe this amazing man loved her. Cat played beautifully, the preacher spoke, and she and Cole exchanged vows, but it all slipped past Eve as though it were a beautiful dream. Between one heartbeat and the next, the ceremony was over and she was dancing to a slow song with her new husband.

Her heart full, she looked around and saw Mama Rosa and Pop, her head on his shoulder as they shuffled in place. Her eyes widened as she caught sight of Blaze, held in the arms of the young man who regularly picked her up for school. She locked eyes with Sasha, who noticed and raised her eyebrows as she and Jesse slowly swayed to the music of Cat's violin. Even Sasha's aunt was there, smiling from her table.

Eve watched Cat, amazed again that her sister had agreed to come after her long silence, but she was here, and that was all that mattered. Eve caught her eye and Cat winked, then kept playing.

Eve swallowed back more tears and smiled as Cole lifted her chin. "I love you, Mrs. Sutton."

"I love you, Mr. Sutton."

"What do you say we get out of here and get our own party started?" He raised his eyebrows, and Eve grinned, then gave a little yelp of surprise as he swooped her into his arms, just like her first day back in town.

She glanced down at the cowboy boots peeking out from under her gown and grinned. This time, she had the proper footwear for whatever came next.

ACKNOWLEDGMENTS

My heartfelt thanks to these wonderful folks who helped bring this story from idea to book.

For Amanda Leuck, my fabulous agent, who worked so hard on my behalf.

For Sheryl Zajechowski and the whole Waterfall team. You all are such a pleasure to work with.

For Leslie Santamaria, who makes this crazy writing journey such fun—and always knows what I meant to say.

For my lovely FCRW chapter mates. Your support and encouragement mean the world.

For Lisa Saupp, who lent her extensive water expertise and answered myriad water questions. Jim Carty let me pick his brain on all things ranch related, and Maria Klopfenstein helped me think through all my medical scenarios. Any mistakes are totally my own.

My thanks, always, to the Great Creator who gives us the gift of story, and to my family, who cheer me on and graciously accept the wacky world of a writer.

And last, but never least, thank you, dear readers, for reading my stories and inviting me into your lives. I am so very blessed.

ABOUT THE AUTHOR

Connie Mann is a licensed boat captain and the author of the romantic suspense novels *Tangled Lies*, *Angel Falls*, and *Trapped!* as well as various works of shorter fiction. She has lived in seven different states but has happily called warm, sunny Florida home for more than twenty years. When she's not dreaming up plotlines, you'll find "Captain Connie" on Central Florida's waterways, introducing boats full of schoolchildren to their first alligator. She is also passionate about helping women and children in developing countries follow their dreams and break the poverty cycle. In addition to boating, she and her husband enjoy spending time with their grown children and extended family and planning their next travel adventures. You can visit Connie online at www.conniemann.com.

81178377R00202

Made in the USA
Lexington, KY
12 February 2018